A MILITARY FANTASY ADVENTURE

# SGT. THOR

## THE CUNNING BK.02

D1059761

## JASON **ANSPACH**
## NICK **COLE**

# WARGATE

An imprint of Galaxy's Edge Press

PO BOX 534

Puyallup, Washington 98371

Paperback ISBN: 979-8-88922-040-4

www.wargatebooks.com

# CHAPTER ONE

TALES OF THE DEEDS OF THE WARRIOR KNOWN AS Sergeant Thor spread across the sands of the desert and the yellowed maps of the lands called the Ruin. Storytellers spoke of a blond-haired, sharp-eyed giant with a strange anti-materiel rifle in hand, the word *Mjölnir* scratched along its deadly length, a thief, a slayer, a brawler with terrible rages in combat against the worst of odds, and a quiet dark humor in the blackest of situations. Legends grew as the man called Thor traveled deeper and deeper into the lands of the Ruin... seeking its keenest razor's edge by which to test himself.

He trod lost places under his worn combat boots, acquiring skills, armor, weapons, and of course enemies... and hoard. His grim visage set on some far horizon, his killer's mind working the problem of survival, of hack-and-slash in heated combats, of pulling the trigger on any who stood between him and where he would go as a free man of his own wills and his titanic temperaments. Leaving behind only a trail of corpses and cautious tales told of mythic deeds done, defying expectation, his road-eating stride devouring the miles between him and the destiny he sought out there along the edge where magic blurs reality and monsters are quite real.

In time, his story began to match the stories of the places he passed through, each having its own collection of mythic deeds, fables, and dark whispers. The warrior became part of that tapestry and those songs that record such deeds before the sands of time devour, as they must, all things. Even heroes.

Now this is the story of the Ranger's time in the City of Thieves, where he became one of them and learned their stealthy way, acquiring their enemies as his own, and others all his making, along the way out to the edge where little is known, for no one returns from such places. So say the sages and tale-singers.

And it must be said here... it is also the story of the city itself. For such strange places have stories all their own, just as interesting as the legends of great warriors and perhaps even mighty wizards, and yes even the piles of silent watching skulls of great forgotten battles on the plains that lie beyond the Cities of Men.

If you are to hear his tale, then you must hear it as it is told when the night winds come to whisper, and the sands are driven across the sleeping camels and the pegged tents. When the camp women come out, eyes made up and silks to delight. When the meat smokes and the drink is passed about, for all days are hard and pleasures and tales must come and comfort between the times of work and battle that are life.

And so it would begin this way, an old man muttering in a singsong voice, yet another tale of legend. Another tale of Sergeant Thor.

"Such was the City of Thieves and hither came the Ranger," the tell-sayer croons in the night within some tavern or inn when the desert winds come to add their say to the last of the day, turning from their acid hissing whispers to their keening mournful howls out there beyond the firelight and the watch. Comely wenches come to fill your cup and pick your pocket, too, while roasting beasts drip succulent fats into the fire that is the only light other than the few precious candles among the deep shadows near the teller of legends of heroes and diabolical wizards.

*Hither came the Ranger...*

In the City of Thieves it is another bloody and decadent day of theft, murder, mayhem, and of course pleasure, a day the same as all the merciless others that have come before it, and will surely come after this one too, a day that now dies a hard death under the merciless glare of the big red sun sinking into the west of the Ruin. Shining on other lands known to but a few, or perhaps falling off the edge of the world as some swear.

Who can say?

Merchants are robbed. Enemies put to the knife and left to die among the garbage and shadows that can be found on the streets of the city by which the thieves are called.

Fortunes stolen.

Wrongs settled.

And night comes on then...

Cool shadows lengthen along wide sandstone streets where everything is agreed upon by the various powerful factions, for there is no law in that lawless city, that City of Thieves, other than the unrestricted power exercised by the powerful through their agents of organized violence and sorcery.

Here in the cool of the early night, fine ladies are carried atop palanquins behind drifting silks, nibbling candied dates and casting veiled eyes upon whom they wished. Warriors of renown, armor polished, weapons sharp as a razor's edge, preen and present themselves for lust or work.

Hustling clutches of the *sorcerati*, that caste of workers of magics and dabblers in the forbidden arcane, hustle between the spell-warded citadels and heavily defended fortresses of one and another of the powerful named wizards, intent on some night's quest for more power and knowledge and wickedness, and of course the debaucheries that are certain, for this is a city where such things were common.

The quiet, lotus-scented and candle-lit gardens that wait behind the walls of the wizardly mansions reek of floral scents and exotic perfumes. Music lingers in the air like a pleasant yet unobtrusive guest who is always there at just the right time with a chord or a string, or even a song in strange chants not known in the northern lands along the Great Inner Sea. Poets in other common places give verse outside inns in the broadways, verses that are often clever insults contrived to spark a duel with some rival for some beautiful lady carried aloft behind gossamer fine silks, or even perhaps for some legendary and renowned whore in one of the fabled pleasure dens along the Street of Sighs and Pleasures.

And it is here, in the broadways of the City of Thieves, that fine families of new wealth made via the merchant trade come out in their best, protected by grim-faced and hard men with large weapons, making the scene in the cooler twilight beneath lanterns and among the gardens, walking these broadways to be seen at this moment of earliest night, and to see also, in what the City of Thieves called the Social Hour.

Later, when it is darker, and the fat moon rides low and

SGT. THOR: THE CUNNING

swollen like some corpulent leering mischievous gent, then the gates will be locked, torches lit, and revelries attended to within these secure places, for the city is dark and rivalries are settled in the streets where bodies cool and leave their pools of blood for the dogs to come and lick at.

Deals done.

Murders arranged.

Wealth acquired.

Such... is the City of Thieves at all hours.

Opportunity and catastrophic loss like the intertwined snakes of the Dark Cultists who now quietly make their way into the eastern districts of the city and the vast necropolis there along the edge, creeping upon the waste that was once some ancient battlefield no one much beyond a doddering sage or two remembers anymore.

In these later hours the *mandarini*, the eunuchs who serve at the behest of the named wizards, doing the work of organizing and administering like endless ants, the city protected, the taxes collected, and the treasuries of the poor thoroughly looted, these worthies behind elite bodies of finely draped guards of dark blue-cloaked sellswords, each a man of war who has seen combat from Skeletos to far Kungaloor itself, make their way to their masked balls and obscene feasts, murmuring and *pooh-pooh*ing to one another about the poors and wretches and the states of affairs across the city they are solely responsible for and the annoyance of it all. Their faces made up like women, their dainty hands uncalloused, their bodies perfumed with fine oils and powdered with narcotic dusts.

Secret plots are made too.

Dangers marginalized as best can be mitigated.

And tragedy... definitely capitalized on. Of course.

But these are the broadways within the high walls of the City of Thieves. And there are only two major broadways, one running east-west and the other north-south, and four minors, bisecting the majors as though designed by some lost, long-ago organizational intent of the Accadions who once ruled this hot steaming mess of a city of men at almost the farthest southern reach of the known lands of the Ruin. To bring some kind of loose order to what could not be ordered, and law to what by its very nature was... lawless.

The City of Thieves is chaos itself and anyone who tried to make it anything else lies rotting in the sandy wastes of graves spreading east into the haunted hills and dry runs.

Grand, and very low at the same time, such is the place. Endless wealth, and soul-crushing poverty in the next street over. Palaces and gardens that those in rags just on the other side of the wall would have found unbelievable had they been allowed entrance. Lives traded like coins for everything and anything, from all of it... to none of it.

The City of Thieves does not care. It just is. So say the murmuring sages who have tried to define it, distill it, capture it.

In vain.

Grand minarets high and proud, thick cyclopean walls as solid as a giant's fist. Thieves and cutthroats at all levels in partnership from the picking of the meanest pocket to the ruining of the most fabled of empires.

The City of Thieves is all of these things at once, and woe to those who come to it expecting less.

But these clutches of mincing eunuchs and finely adorned sellswords, mixing with the great families, both upcoming and ossified, old money and new, for there is always new money to be had in the City of Thieves, are along the broadways and not in the numberless, countless, twisting streets and rude little alleys that comprise most of the mud-brick, sunbaked, blood-soaked city within the strong giant's-fist walls.

Here in neighborhoods all their own, each with its individual character and flavor, are the merchants, from makers of maps, both true and bogus, to crafters of weapons of war and dark magics. They close their shops if they are reputable and known, the families or slaves that run them bending to a meager meal and perhaps some liquor or smoke to wait behind the thin walls at the back of each shop and mean dwelling for tomorrow and a chance to change their fate. This is the hour that is known as the Retreat. The beginning of the wait for the new day and the chance to cheat, rob, steal, and take advantage, again, hoping the night merchants, the thieves, or even the shadow servants of the named wizards themselves, will not make trade of them in the waiting hours of darkness when they must wait behind the walls and listen for a clicking lockpick or padded step.

Above that, the corpulent wretch of a moon comes down to cast its naked bone-light where it will shine as it will, and into darknesses deeper where it will not.

And then... there is still yet more... there are the other further districts, and these are meaner, darker, more simply desperate than what has been noted in the beginning of the story of this place and the legends that have tried to survive it and failed. Here there are no torches near massive gates. Just quiet great darkness and serpentine alleys that twist like the secret serpents the Dark Cultists worship. Twisting and ending as suddenly as do those who dare try them for whatever they thought worth it to come out to these further districts. Death and endings of more brutal and fateful natures lurk ever in the shadows here, whether in the necropolis, the death houses, the caravan stables, the tanners with their honest smells of death, or the cheap whorehouses where disease is warm and foul just like the drink the dreamers who never want to wake cast themselves into both day and all through the night.

Suspiciously open graves. Vast fields of sand-blasted sinking monuments and falling markers and the occasional forgotten monument no one knows the *who* or *why* about... even the sages. Here the dead aren't collected until morning. Here no one disappears, because few know to note their absence, and words of meaning are seldom exchanged.

Just furtive glances and superstitions signs.

Those who know... know that the mysteries are deepest here. But... that is not commonly known.

Who can know the City of Thieves? Its black heart is deceptively wicked.

Even the armies of the feuding yet allied wizards do not venture here, for sometimes even these fine sellswords, hard and veteran, do not return from these outer districts. Nor do the eunuchs, though they may send some sly and capable agent, but not an army, for they value their defense above all, though they cannot and would never defend themselves, but yes they would send a skilled and very dangerous man to lay their bets on the many games of chance that take place out here each night in the mean streets where such games of chance, games of life and death, take place.

Will Surronto the Crooked be murdered before last bell?

Will Lady Trieste take Carsu the Hero of Al-Sarim, or

perhaps Hamondides the Caravanner who travels the Wyrm Wastes to her fabled perfumed bed of delights this night?

Bets are laid.

And...

Who will survive the Pit this night and be the one to reach his blood-soaked hand into the Prize Chest to take what one can pull forth, having bested all comers this night in a contest of violence, skill, and of course... luck within the Pit where the challengers are challenged under the watchful eye of the High Priests of the Game.

At those wizardly councils of the *sorcerati* and the decadent and debauched feasts of the *mandarini*... news is breathlessly awaited of the contest within the Pit this night.

Fortunes ride...

Dirty urchins are given coppers to take the messages as the developments appear, and it is not uncommon for dangerous men to have at least twenty of these dirty, unwashed, and unwanted children ready to run the most dangerous gauntlet of the meanest streets, enter the broadways, and present themselves to the stern-faced guards at the wizards' citadels to relay the news of what has gone down within the Pit. Some even appear at the gates of the citadels from which the corpulent and soft *mandarini* rule, presenting themselves to the finely adorned guards of the eunuch palaces where every dainty and all the delicacies are served as news comes in throughout the night. News of who has died, murdered and bleeding out in the streets with his throat slit, or who has conquered which lady of lust and renown, or other minor things made major important. And of course, who is dead next in the Pit as the contest weaves its way to conclusion under the stern gaze of the High Priests.

The Pit is the most important news. Murders are common in the City of Thieves. Fabled whores and their conquests a little less so.

But the Pit...

Now *there* is the bet that the city, all of it, breath held, waits for news of, from the going down of the sun until the midnight bell, for often by then all contestants are dead within her shadowy halls and dark falls.

But sometimes not...

Occasionally these forgotten urchins are waylaid by bands of toughs or reckless drunken adventurers who have come out just after the sounding of the dread Doom Bell from deep within the city, stopping these ragged messengers with a clenched fist, a growled threat, a strong hold on the tattered shift or shirt and then demanding what news they possess be handed over and listened to.

News bought and paid for by someone else, intercepted.

Thieves nearby and unseen in the shadows listening... like thieves.

But news nonetheless exchanged.

And though this news be given to these brutes and bullies, locals who did a trade or labor in the heat of the day, all that will likely be paid to the messenger urchin is a severe ringing blow, or occasionally a nick with a little razor as though that was needed.

Never a murder. Never that. Because of course some named dangerous man, silent, cloaked, and waiting near the center of the action, will come to find out who interfered with his message to his employer. And dangerous men are dangerous for a reason, so best not have that trouble to add to all the troubles.

The best outcome for the little barefoot dirty-faced messenger, an unwanted boy or an extra girl for some family with never enough, waylaid by the bands of reckless adventurers who linger in the taverns and waste the days waiting for tales of deeds needing done out there somewhere, or even lost tombs recently discovered with promises of lost idols or artifacts of power, spending their diminishing wealth by gambling on outcomes of the Pit, or that fabled whore, or the murders between *so and so* and *such and such*, is that perhaps a coin, not a precious one, though all coins are precious to those who lack them, a coin stamped with a long-lost Accadion emperor might be given out and the youth hustled along, no harm no foul in the exchange.

Better the loss of a thin coin than to fall under the gaze of the locals who live at the razor's edge between great failure and final ruin.

Better that than those.

This hot night in the City of Thieves, as the urchins run across the breadth and length of the city, as one tiny wretched youth runs by an inn where a band of reckless adventures stands, drinking under the torchlight, music and loud talk murmuring out into the street like a mumbling drunk never being quiet, harsher, more threatening voices ask what news he bears.

"News of Babella," croons the little one. "She has made eyes at Carsu. The caravanner has gone off to talk with the Black Hand on the Street of Lies and Smoke at arranging matters, sir." The passing unwanted boy yells this out as he runs, his tiny legs and dirty feet carrying him off into the night to meet a dangerous man who would give him coin for news, not rough scowls and rougher slaps.

Tall warriors and bandy-legged lockbreakers murmur one to the other in the soft light outside the inns along the meaner streets. Hedge wizards and fallen holy men attached to some band sip their wine and nod knowingly to one another as they listen.

Wenches remember their bets and hope they'll pay off tonight, for perhaps that might mean a chance at something... else... tomorrow.

But these bits of news of whores and settlings between rivals are not much to chew on for these listeners or any other, for this night all ears wait on what news there is from within the Pit.

Who lives.

Who died.

It was the Pit that held the most talk of the day that had been. Making it like some unmarked Day of Celebration and Feasting. For it was this night, this hot and torrid night of murder and intrigue even still going on despite the contest, unremarked upon and unwatched, that the one called Thor said he would try his hand at the Pit.

And much, *much* wealth and hoard had been staked on the outcome in the city that was the City of Thieves.

Into this maelstrom... hither came the one called Sergeant Thor.

Finding an edge against which to test himself.

# CHAPTER TWO

"YOU UNDERSTAND THE PLAN, WARRIOR?" ASKED SATO once again as he secured the breastplate Thor would wear into the Pit this night. The heat was rising, and the cool winds were not coming off the desert as they had at dusk. In the shadows all around, the thieves came and went, all busy about their tasks and the plan that had been hatched to do what they intended to do this night.

"I do," rumbled the giant warrior, stretching his muscles and getting ready for the fights that lay ahead within the darkness out there.

Each piece of armor and gear he put on was tested for its fit, and for its silence. It was mean and not ornate by the standards of the sellswords. But it was the best their money could buy, and it would do what was asked of it for that was all that could be expected by the thieves of the lot into which he had fallen.

"Your part is simple," said Sato, studying and adjusting

the armor. Watching his friend. "Just stay alive, Warrior."

The Ranger chuckled to himself.

*Sure*, thought the Ranger. *Going into a dark haunted house of a decrepit keep that was once both prison and madhouse and contained a* were-demon *or so the sages said, a dangerous and uncertain one at that, and entering into what was basically a winner-take-all game of death, him against twenty other deadly* killers *with nothing but a gladius, his personal knives, a shield, and armor. That was... apparently, to the thief Sato... the easy part.*

"I said simple, Warrior. I did not say *easy*."

Sergeant Thor didn't realize he'd said what he'd been thinking aloud. He pulled on his assault gloves, checking the stitching. They were starting to break down, falling apart.

The ancient nano-plague that had changed the world that he and the other U.S. Army Rangers had come from was still doing its work. Breaking down everything, over time, and there seemed to be no rhyme nor reason to it.

"It is straightforward," continued Sato, "to think and do only fighting, Warrior. It is the rest of the guild this night that must do the craft and the cunning to get us near the Prize Chest while you distract them with slaughter and bloodshed. But no, what you do will not be easy. Yes, Warrior, even this old thief understands the challenge in the part you must play, for memories say he once played the goat himself. As all thieves do."

Thor said nothing and took up the shield he had chosen for the mission he had planned. He'd spent the last three days combing the bazaar for it. It was steel. Not bronze. Well-forged, circular, and medium-sized with a small crescent cut into it at eye level when raised. Perfect for what he needed and the tools he still had to work with.

"Ahhhh... Warrior," said the singsong-voiced little man who'd sold it to him over a long three-hour negotiation tea in which the man had shown him every weapon the Ranger didn't want. "You have a fine eye for such armor. This was Karthian-made. Their long-lost Spartans used the crescent to interlock their shields and create an effective combat wall against which none could stand. Great warriors all of them until they perished, to the last man, at Hellstrom. Or so the legends say. This piece was traded to me for three comely slaves, young girls from Kungaloor, soft of skin and skilled in healing and love, for its owning. I could part with it for nothing less than one hundred gold in coin, Warrior. A fabled sum I doubt one such as you would possess this deep into the city. Though I presume much, I am an honest merchant in a city of lies, who foolishly prides himself on that honesty. Call it... a *weakness*, oh master swordsman."

Thor had held the shield and studied it, turning it over and over in his great thick calloused hands. The strap needed repairing. But the surface was almost undamaged. He popped his Contego knife and delicately ran it along the surface.

The diminutive weapons merchant with the soft high voice did not make a move or give a cry that his merchandise was being damaged. For it was not. Even as Thor ran his sharpest blade along its surface, it remained unmarred.

"*Seeeeeee...*" crooned the merchant. "No damage." He smiled like a man holding all the cards. "Perhaps it is fabled? No?"

The Ranger said nothing and watched its surface and judged its weight. He would place his life behind it. It needed to be infallible under the heaviest of assaults.

"They say," continued the merchant, "that the Spartans of Karth could not be defeated in ordinary battle. I do not know if that is true. But the shield is unmarred by damage of any kind. And, as all know... it was the treachery of Kaz the Foul that slew them all. Their arms failed not. So say the fables and talk of scribes who know such things, master warrior. I can send you to my friend Barani the Wise, for he has studied such matters and is ranking in the Sage's Guild. He will tell you this is so. Whether it is magic, or just finely made beyond the craftsmanship of our times or forges, he does not know. But see..."

The spindly little man bent close in the shop as they sat

on his intricate rug, the tea near at hand in a bronze urn finely made and stamped with many designs.

"No damage."

A slip of a young woman, veiled, large deep dark eyes watching everything, entered with a beaten copper tray laden with coffee now, and baked honey sweets also, to refresh as the next round of bargaining began without marker or suggestion.

In the shadows near the door, keeping an ear on the street for the day was growing late, Sato waited and cleared his throat softly.

"Ah... my beautiful daughter, my greatest treasure, brings hot sand coffee and powdered date maamouls. Put down the Karthian piece and let us select you a great shield from Skeletos to protect your impressive frame in places most dangerous. Do you seek adventure in the necropolis east of the city, or even the wastes beyond? Then I dare you not. Men of your kind, the Dire Tribes of the North, they always go that way, Warrior. They are lured by tales of wealth and war that lay beyond the known of our city. Like sailors to sirens they go to their destructions and are never seen again."

The Ranger ignored these genteel murmurings, the coffee, even the seductive gaze behind the veil of the merchant's prized daughter that indicated she was not as "good" as her father might think.

The defense of the shield was good. But the Ranger had other plans for the rear of the shield. And the piece would serve his plan.

"I'll take it," he rumbled, his voice like a boom within the small quiet low-ceilinged place.

The merchant made a face, a small, stunned *O* of a look as he lifted the delicate scroll-worked cup of steaming black coffee to his thin wrinkled lips and smiled that such fortune had come his way at such profit.

What cared he how the northern barbarian died tomorrow? Everyone in the City of Thieves who is not of the City of Thieves dies.

*So it is said. So it is so*, as they say.

Sato stepped forward and produced a small, full sack from within the folds of his shirt. Then he began to count out the coin, for the thieves' guild bears all cost of the heists for the thieves who serve the guild, and... the Queen of Thieves.

And Sergeant Thor, of the Rangers, was soon to be one of them. This was his test. This was his plan.

# CHAPTER THREE

"YOU UNDERSTAND THE PLAN, WARRIOR?" ASKED SATO once again, one more time before everything went live and it was for keeps... winner take all. Losers die in their own warm blood.

The master thief, wizened and ancient beyond his middle-aged years, squinted his narrow, weathered eyes, studying some bit of kit on the Ranger's impressive frame, jacked, swole, tatted and scarred... all this as Sergeant Thor secured the shield he would wear into the Pit this night in a game of death like nothing ever known ten thousand years ago in the Before.

The world that was...

"You understand the plan, Warrior," muttered Sato a little louder in the quiet busy silence of the thieves' den near the heist along a dark and shadowy alley with easy access to the scene of the crime.

Thor was somewhere else. All over his plan and every

detail in it, checking for flaws and failures and developing contingencies as everything updated with thieves and urchins coming into the dark space to whisper updates on what they'd been charged to observe and report on.

"I do," rumbled the giant jacked Ranger who stood at six foot four strapped in some piecemeal armor, the shield, blades, and a gladius. Looking every inch the killing machine he really was.

"As I have said... your part is simple. Stay alive, Warrior. That is all. Our part... this we will do and see the morning sun to laugh over. Nothing more, nothing less, Warrior. Tonight you are the goat for we thieves. Tomorrow... you will be one of us. In full. *Sune.*"

"You're repeating yourself, Thief," rumbled Thor, taking a deep breath, a final breath he'd been holding for too long as he studied every unseen detail on the sand table in his mind. Letting it all go. Now he would do his part and fight to survive in a dark crumbling pit filled with enemies both martial and sorcerous. Some teamed up, others singletons who didn't need a wingman or allies because they were deadly, all too deadly all by themselves.

"*That's all, Ranger,*" muttered the old sergeant major in his mind, just as the mentor, or tormentor, was wont to do at these times when the minutes seemed too small and the air too thick with go-time enough to cut it with the shank on his thigh.

Thor studied the Glock he'd holstered behind the shield one last time. Good to go. And his last two grenades. The frag. And the flashbang. Also good to go.

Day by day, the last of the gear he'd brought from the Ranger detachment's Forge was being used up or breaking down along the way.

The OD-green Timex had finally given up the ghost. The Glock wasn't long for the Ruin as the fading effects of the nano-plague continued, relentlessly, even ten thousand years later, to break everything down that had come from the Before so long ago.

"I am no warrior," whispered Sato, stepping back, assessing the Ranger in armor one last time. "What we intend this night is no easy task. What we attempt, what you have led us to plan for your final test... no one has ever done this. Audacity... does not begin to describe what we do. And even if we succeed... we invite the Hells down on us all. Not just a hand into a wizard's chest of curiosities, or some warlord's war chest, but the chest that no one ever dared plunder. For these priests of the game were smart, betting that if *some* could be taken from it as a prize, then that would make it immune to *all* of it being spirited away on the night winds by some clever master thief. None of the three guilds has ever accomplished such a feat of renown as now we play for,

Warrior. You understand this..."

Thor studied his choice of how to get to the weapons on his person as fast as he could. That was where his mind was. He'd pulled and drawn, landing the front sights on a straw man set up for just such a purpose back in the guild's watched streets and private dens few in the City of Thieves knew about or had ever been into.

It was called Shadowrun, for the buildings that protected its ungoverned and twisting length were tall and kept the sun in latest morning and earliest afternoon. It was a cool and pleasant place, Shadowrun was, for the Little Guild into which Thor had fallen, led there by Sato after the events in the Sea of Riddles, were professionals and not just murderous thugs and bullies of the type that filled many other guilds and cabals. They prided themselves on their work and provided valuable and sometimes life-saving services. Ask any fighter or wizard trapped in a tomb, the ancient locks sprung, if some thief had saved their life from such ambushes, or poisoned chests, or traps along the walls, floors, doors, and sometimes... even the whole place.

The Saur had planted many false tombs that were little more than traps to take care of tomb robbers. Seeding these near the true great tombs where vast amounts of wealth and magic lay for the taking if one was bold and clever.

Thor listened to the master thief as the fatal and final

stakes were laid out. Failure ominously not touched on except to acknowledge that it would be final. For all of them.

The Ranger's mind was on his weapons, the ones strapped tight to his body and ready for use in every possible situation so that he might kill forward one step more at a time. That was his part now. That was all. Combat and killing. That was the only way forward through this plan. And the plan to steal it all, the greatest unimagined prize in a city filled with those who thought constantly of little beyond the stealing of other possessions not just as a job, but a way of life... once the killing was done, the plan, the real plan of the greatest unimagined heist in the City of Thieves ever... would begin.

With the gladius razor-sharp in its sheath sunk and attached to his battle belt, there was no room for the Glock there. Now where the sidearm would normally be skinned lay the weathered old leather sheath the blade had come with. A day at the forge of Mahkmadi the Blademaster, friend of the guild for a deed done in darkness some time ago, and the fine work on the deadly killing blade the Ranger would wield in the Pit had been accomplished.

Favors were called in.

Threats made.

Markers offered.

Deeds promised.

Much coin spent.

The Little Guild as it was sometimes known, for the two others were larger and had more far-ranging interests and were definitely in with the power brokers of the *sorcerati* and the *mandarini*, had bet big on this play not just for the glory and the bragging rights. Knives were out and many wanted the Little Guild and their leader, the mysterious Queen of Thieves, out of the way going forward. This heist would change things. Definitely.

And, as Sato had said truly, *"Invite the Hells down on them all."*

The breastplate the Ranger wore, an ancient and unremarkable piece, was found and purchased at no small price. It barely fit the jacked and swole frame of the hulking Ranger sniper.

Armor for the likes of him would have to be crafted at great cost and over several months. So the ancient battered breastplate was a real prize.

The combat inside the Pit, in the close darkness, would be little more than a hack-and-slash contest in which each battler knew there were no second prizes. But Thor had never made the mistake in any of the wars, battles, conflicts, and brawls he'd found himself in of thinking there were. He would go into the ancient pile that was known in the City of Thieves as the Pit with a breastplate over his naked, scarred, occasionally burned, and tattooed torso.

His fading Crye Precisions and the shredded kneepads protecting his legs.

Combat boots that were working still but looking more and more worn and ready to blow out by the day.

The Ranger shank on his opposite thigh, behind and protected by the shield.

The Contego blade on the carrier he'd barely gotten across the armor. The yoroi-doshi punch knife on his back inside the belt. A final last chance to peel anyone too close off the armor if that's how far they wanted to take it. Pull and punch straight up through their jaw.

The sharpened gladius in its supple yet worn leather sheath on his right hip.

The Glock behind the shield along with the two remaining grenades.

One of them a flashbang. He'd pop that on multiples if he ran into a group that had allied within the Pit in order to get as close as they could to the fabled Prize Chest.

The frag for something worse down there deeper in the basements, or so the rumors of the sages who specialized in the Pit had said. There were monsters and the demon down there. Mostly they waited for the slaughter of the game to end and then they'd go take for feasting what was left behind, dragging it down into their dark dens, warrens, and oblivion black holes from which none ever returned.

Sergeant Thor practiced the draw of the gladius a few times once more. Many were the nights he'd spent doing only that. Now it made barely a sound as it cleared leather, ready to draw quick blood first. And finally, an assault-gloved hand to the shield to draw the Glock and fire behind the crescent nick that had been cut in the shield where long-dead Karthian Spartans had once locked shields and fought forward as some long-lost legendary fighting unit in the tales and myths of the Ruin.

The sidearm was cheating but none involved here ten thousand years later after the last firearm was manufactured and the world that had died out in nano-plague darkness knew what a firearm was. So was it really?

Besides...

Magic was a thing here in the Ruin. And many of those going into the Pit this night were what the locals called *Twilight Bastards*. Wielders of sword and some kind of trickster war magic they'd picked up along the way. Occupiers of neither camp, warrior or wizard.

These, as Sato told Thor, were reckless bands of adventurers who would either die out there in the Eastern Wastes beyond the dead and dusty necropolis of dry hills and silent valleys at the edge of the city, or would sell their services to great expeditions financed by the wizards who would try their luck beyond the Sea of Riddles and the River of Night back in the Lands of Black Sleep down in the tombs of the Saur.

Hoping to find there, wealth beyond imagining. Power beyond reckoning. And, of course, death and suffering unimaginable.

All those things the tombs of the Saur promised, and the Ranger knew that well, for he and his kind had gone deep into that land and fought a battle against impossible odds.

More often than not, those well-financed and heavily armed expeditions consisting of mercenaries, great warriors, thieves, ambitious young wizards and even seasoned sorcerers, wayward priests, and blue-eyed holy warriors... and of course a gaggle of Twilight Bastards ready to do the weird they did deep down there in the tombs, and with them all the porters, cooks, guards, apothecaries and alchemists, stable boys and mule skinners, beast handlers and scouts, sages and scribes, slaves and washing wenches, and always the harlots, thieves, and assassins that followed such great outlays of coin... often all of them were never heard from again once they crossed beyond the River of Night.

So a sidearm and a couple of grenades weren't cheating, and so what if they were?

*You ain't cheatin', you ain't tryin'.* So sayeth the Book of Joe.

The thieves around Thor, seeing to their last-minute tasks, were gathered in the burned-out remains of what had once been a tanner's warehouse in this wretched, horrid, and much-forgotten district of the city.

Sato, Quickmar, and Shindar were here. Thieves of what was known as the Little Guild. The least of the three guilds of thieves who plied the City of Thieves and not really a guild if the other two had anything to say about it.

An upstart.

A mistake.

A problem to be dealt with. Soon enough.

It was into this guild, having survived the Sea of Riddles and all the dangers in it, that Thor had been indoctrinated and trained in the ways of a thief.

Lockpicking. Shadowing. Traps. And yes... picking pockets. The thieves were excellent at what they did, and the Ranger admired them for how intently they studied and kept up their craft.

There were some who specialized in certain aspects of thievery that were small but important. Counterfeiters. Vault-breakers. Gem snatchers and magic disarmers. Roof walkers and tightrope acrobats were especially handy for the heavily guarded wizards' towers.

"You will be a thief tonight," said Sato proudly, smiling in the candlelit darkness. Quietly. His warm rich growl of a voice the only sound in the district it seemed at this hour, for it was quiet on the Street of Death and Ruin where at its long twisting end the old pile called the Pit lay. "But for now, you look like a warrior, Warrior."

Thor, armored in bronze, shielded in steel, a razor on his side, looked like a finely carved and cut statue of one of those lost Karthian Spartans perished long ago in a battle of impossible odds remembered only in song and lay. He picked up the ancient helm they'd acquired for him, placing it over his great bearded head.

Now, in the darkness between himself and the three thieves he'd sworn brotherhood to, his blue eyes glittered like a killer within the shadows of the helm, for to them, most of them possessing the brown eyes of the south, such was said of blue eyes here in this part of the Ruin.

*The eyes of a killer.*

The darkness of the helm concealed his face and features within.

But that mattered not, for much coin had been spent making sure the named wizards, their *sorcerati*, the eunuch power brokers and their *mandarini*, and every wealthy merchant and mean trader, even laborers, whores, and slaves, knew that the great blond brute who'd come from the sea to the west, a Ranger, whatever that was, a survivor of treacheries and dangers in the Lands of Night or so it was rumored, was wont to try his hand at the Pit this very night.

And so much gold had been spilled into the Prize Chest and along the rough wood tables of many a gambling den in hopes that he would die, or perhaps live, and that their lives would be somehow changed by the outcome they'd wagered on.

Perhaps...

Thor the thief left them through the ragged gap in the burnt-out old hulk that was the tanner's warehouse, and once he was gone Quickmar and Shindar faded into the shadows and were also gone, leaving Thor alone with only silence and the sounds of the life of the city in the distance.

# CHAPTER FOUR

THOR RAN GARRO THE SLASHER THROUGH JUST INISDE THE old wreck of the prison that had once been called the Pit.

The Doom Bell rang out five ominous times as a signal to all who would dare that the Pit was open for those to enter. Cloaked warriors made their way from the surrounding ruin of this unkempt and burnt-out district, choosing their entrances into the contest via rents, cracks, and holes in the ancient outer walls of the old prison, asylum, temple, keep, and everything else it had once ever been before being forgotten long ago. Some used ancient doors, an old drawbridge that was almost what it was in name, or climbed the high and shattered remains of the many small towers along the wall. Fights broke out and contestants were assassinated by arrow fire from compatriots who'd remained in the shadows, hoping to give their chosen man the best shot.

The cloaked man called Garro the Slasher, murderer and

taker of thirty-one souls, had sprung at the Ranger from a dark corner near the rent in the wall Thor had decided to thread, and died for the attempt. Dying amazed that he'd received a sudden lightning bolt 'Z' of slashes so quick from one so large, even as he himself had been ready to slash with both of his beaten-steel blackened hatchets by which he had come to earn his title of Slasher. He died there in the pile of the Pit he'd been hoping to conquer, died within seconds and not minutes. His guts spilling out and the artery in his neck pulsing blood in spurts onto the dry rotting wreckage of the old place that had once been something other than the haunted lair it had become.

Another few shadowy corridors in, moonlight spilling through the ruined roof and the tall looming towers above, three killers who'd made a quick alliance desperately fast in the moments as the game in the Pit began, each nevertheless intent on killing the others if they got within sight of the chest, were the next to die as the hulking Ranger crept stalker-quiet through the ruined dark looking for tangos as Rangers have always done.

He was in his element now, the night, and as it is said, Rangers own the night. The planning, preparation, organization, and walkthroughs were past. All things were live now, all pieces in motion.

Just as he was. A killer without remorse, threading a

battlefield, unquestioned and ready to slay.

For a man like Sergeant Thor, there was a purity in this. No questions. No bargains. Only outcomes.

What more can a Ranger ask of the world?

Nothing.

Nothing but the chance to survive.

Thor thrust his sword through a Caspian leading the way for the three who'd thrown in together. The man was covered in black greasepaint across his narrow torso as a kind of night-fighting camouflage. He wore only black pants and soft supple leather boots of good quality as he led the trio of killers forward on an unknowing intercept with the Grim Reaper made Ranger. This one also had two small dark axes out and forward, held akimbo as though that was his fighting style. Leading the men behind, each a killer and looking to take all the prizes this night.

There was no battle yell in this move by the Ranger. Not even a grunt or some sound warriors make to get over the hump of the first moment of action. The Ranger had merely pushed the blade forward like some pneumatic killing machine and run the man through, his breath neither held nor increasing. Steady and ready for the PT session of real live close-quarters combat with Bronze Age weapons that would surely come next.

The struck man gasped. Whites of his eyes wide in the

thick darkness. Then he struck, unable to muster breath for his own cry of alarm or battle. Thor easily deflected the blows then slammed the heavy steel shield downward to punch the wounded man's gut again. Now the rogue screamed fresh pain, his wounded voice ringing out as he bent over double whether he liked it or not because pain and reality were taking over, presenting a perfectly exposed long neck. Thor swiped the gladius, breaking hyoid bone and spine as he savagely cut through bone, muscle, and tissue.

That one was out and no longer screaming in the twilight shadows as the combat with the other two became the next step in one-step-at-a-time survival.

Drawing in a smooth, easy, slow breath, Thor made ready to deal with the other two, reminding himself that *slow is smooth and smooth is fast.*

The other two were already starting to hyperventilate, one roaring suddenly as he pushed over his dead recent ally, trampling him with heavy boots to get at his first kill. Unaware he'd just gotten more than he'd ever bargained for. Ahead of the other, both men reacting quickly from their spots on the wedge they'd been using to move through the shadowy darkness of this section of the old structure that was the Pit, the first came in roaring and swinging.

Pivoting into a crouch to receive the new leader, Thor, gladius held back in the classic Spartan fighting position, rammed the shield edge onto the top of this new enemy's foot. The shadowy man in the dark bent, and Thor reached up, took hold of the man's helmet, and slammed the man's neck onto the top of the shield he held in front of him, his huge biceps working like some heavy forge of doom to destroy the man in an instant against the unforgivable edge of the shield he'd taken from the bazaar at the cost of the guild's stolen coins.

Two down in less than fifteen seconds. Screams and gasps, and yet no sounds from the Ranger but one titanic grunt as he pulped the second man to attack him against the edge of his heavy round Spartan's shield.

The man behind the shield-crushed man now presented the singular silhouette of a drawing archer in the dark. Then a sudden heavy *twang*, a hush of half a whistle, and Thor jerked the shield up, catching an arrow to the shield with little room to spare. The missile fired by the third and last man in the trio, and fired at extremely close range in the desperate dark, shattered against his huge shield in the tight body-littered corridor, and the Ranger lunged forward unexpectedly fast as the man pulled and attempted to nock another arrow for the draw and fire. Thor thrust the razor-sharp gladius right into this last enemy's neck and listened to the darkness all around them for more attackers as the man softly gurgled, hissing some other tongued final curse in the dark, still hanging from the blade that had run him through at the end of the powerful warrior's tree-trunk-sized arm.

Thor didn't move. He let the man die on his blade until he was still like a statue in the dark.

Others would hear. They'd come like carrion vultures hoping for someone wounded or busy looting to pick off.

SLLS.

*Stop.*

*Look.*

*Listen.*

*Smell.*

Thor waited for others, but it was clear there were none close at hand in this section of the decrepit old ruin that was the Pit.

Rats scurried among the shadows, excited and ready that the night's feast was laid out in the dead that Thor had slain.

He lowered the weapon and the dead man slid from it, crumpling in an unceremonious heap with the other two and the hundreds of years of trash and sorrow that had accumulated along the lost and forgotten passages of an old structure no one remembered much about or spoke much of other than to sign and mutter prayers to their uncaring gods that they never become so lost, or so poor, as to try their luck in the haunted corridors of the old eyesore.

Passing beyond the shadows and flotsam-ruin of

smashed furniture and crumbling interior that was the outer cloisters of an old temple on the periphery of the crumbling ruin of the Pit, Thor passed through two looming ruined doors, the wood rotten and the smell even fouler from what came from within the room they guarded as he treaded carefully and quietly forward, deeper and deeper into the maze of piecemeal construction that was the thousand-year-old place.

Beyond and within was the old temple, dedicated to some forgotten god or gods no one remembered. Old smashed statuary and smoke-burnt frescoes hinted at past observances long uncelebrated, and yet... here candles almost burnt out and down to waxy drools forming globs that were almost demonic in shape fluttered and flickered indolently, and by their firelight Sergeant Thor could see small shrines of fresh bones and dead flowers arranged in gruesome piles to some new horror that had come to take the dead god's place. Blood-scrawled runes adorned every surface, and the writing was unknown and seemed to the Ranger, who cared little to understand such pedantic lunacy, some mathematical in nature, though the symbols were also obscene at times, bizarre and arcane.

It was quiet, and for a long moment Thor waited and listened to distant halls and the interior of the places that joined to this corrupt temple, and slowly he heard the crunch of heavy steps coming his way carefully through the ruin. Destroying and disturbing, but surefooted where they were not deft and silent.

A new enemy approached.

A warrior, armored heavily and carrying a pretty hefty blade out in front of him came through the dark recess of the inner sanctum beyond the desecrated temple Thor had lingered in. The new threat immediately went into a combat stance and advanced against the Ranger, rear boot following leading boot, shuffling close to get to Thor and strike out with his longer two-handed blade that seemed both solid and well-made.

Ancient runes along its runnel glowed dimly in the twilight gloom of the old, smashed ruin.

The Ranger, working the circular shield and the gladius, readied and held both in a boxer's stance. The armored warrior got close enough, quick enough, and struck out hard with the heavier blade meaning to crush and disable. Thor took the solid hit on the shield, the blow beating him down with a weight he had not expected but handled easily enough due to his powerful frame and taut muscles. He pulled his weapon elbow down and back, whipping the gladius at the other guy's exposed neck as the armored warrior leaned in to follow the tremendous blow of his two-handed blade like some cobra suddenly striking hard and looming in to see what damage it had done to its poisoned prey. Things happened too fast next to know if the Ranger's blow was fatal, what with the heavy armor his opponent was wearing, and so, using the shield, he pulled the man's heavy two-handed blade down and out of the way. Then began to jackhammer the razor-gladius in his assault-gloved hand into the exposed neck, throat, and finally the armpit where the warrior's armor didn't protect in the least.

The armored warrior grunted with each blow, struggling to get his unwieldy and large blade up into play against the looming battle-demon stabbing him over and over again in the darkness of the old ruined and desecrated place of worship. The dying man emitted a sharp breath, almost a sigh as though accepting that he had erred greatly in daring to confront the Ranger in battle. He tried to stumble away, holding up one armored glove and collapsing into a kneel as his boots went out from under him. He died slowly, falling first to his butt, then onto his back where he lay bleeding out, rasping in the silence now that combat had ended.

But by then Thor had turned away and was already stalking forward through the darkness toward the inner sanctum from which the man had come, looking for a way deeper into the decrepit pile that was the Pit.

The old prison as the sages say... this was the area beyond the forgotten temple.

The vast spreading ruin of the inner sanctum was quiet, and high above, the once-ornate dome that had towered over the holy place had crumbled and been hauled away. All that remained were the fractured remains of a large and grotesque statue the priests once paid obeisance to.

There was a way leading back out to the dark streets where the man he'd just dispatched had probably come through, seeking, like his intended prey, a way deeper into the old wreck of the place for the final battle down in the Pit. Instead finding the Ranger and death in a wrong turn.

A quick and silent search by the stealthy Ranger, the soft tread of his boots the only sound in the ruined old place, revealed a passage beyond the shredded thick curtains, stairs leading down to a small crypt where thick sarcophagi had long since been smashed open and the bodies turned out in search of burial trinkets and treasures on the skeletons with names no one remembered a long time ago.

Whatever valuables had been here had long since changed many hands many times in the bazaars of the City of Thieves long ago to be sure.

Thor left the dusty old crypt by the way he'd come and followed a secret side passage that had been badly concealed, through a small dead garden that hadn't been tended in years. He'd first checked the secret door he'd found just as Sato and Mingo, a guild specialist in traps specifically on and designed around secret doors, had shown him. Beyond the garden lay the massive outer wall of the keep, and a solid old guard tower was the way through the temple grounds and into the old prison beyond. The opening was like a gaping wound and Thor treaded carefully toward it, expecting a trap or an ambush. He stopped as a dozen bats, small with beady red eyes, suddenly hurricaned outward and flew off into the night, screeching and seeking small prey to feast on.

The smell of death came on a cold and unexpected breeze.

Then a low rising whine-growl of some jaguar in the night came from high and above across the cracked and broken walls and the upper reaches of shattered towers that comprised the old prison.

He entered the gap and made his way into the yard that lay before the gray and dirty walls.

He had no idea how many, at first, he slaughtered here. It was an ambush by some of them, that was clear. But then another group came into the developing fray and were done to death as everyone hacked and slaughtered all at hand, uncertain who was friend or foe. Deciding in the end everyone was an enemy and that the only way out was to be the last man standing.

After it was done...

Thor. Bloodied and cut, huge chest heaving as he calmed

his breath, willing himself to stillness as he counted the bodies on the other side of the ambush and found eight total.

The gladius dripped with the blood on the dusty forgotten ground of the yard before the high walls he would need to get beyond.

It had been nothing but chaos and slaughter for several minutes. No quarter was asked, and none was given.

Perhaps others had gotten away when they realized they'd have to fight a cornered wildcat to win their way out of there. Perhaps they'd decided to flee the Pit realizing fortune and the gods were not on their side this night. Or they'd take their chances later with arrows or bolts fired from concealment at a warrior pushing through slaughter after slaughter and getting tired and wounded. Or even a hasty trap to finish the killer Dire Man psychopath they thought surely he was. A well-placed poison. A needle in the rubble. A toxic jelly on some surface he must brush against.

The Ranger could hear them moving away from him. Some further in, toward the prize. Others racing pell-mell for the exits and the burnt district and quiet ruin where thieves and assassins waited out there for who would win, and... who could be picked off.

The City of Thieves is hard on all. There's no denying that. And even in such a dishonest place, we must be honest about this. Or so say those who are counted wise and live longer than most.

Beyond the ragged gap in the guardhouse wall was a deep darkness, and here Thor had gotten the first one to ambush him quick. The rogue sprang the trap by trying to run him through with a long thick spear that was more a pole with a jagged blade at the tip. The skinny man shouted, "Heeeyyyyyahhh!" and thrust for the Ranger's armored midsection. Thor turned his body, the competent footwork learned through extensive study of Jeet Kune Do, and allowed the jagged blade of the spear to pass by with room to spare. Barely. Then he savagely counterstruck into the enemy's face as the man realized his miss yet couldn't stop his momentum into the Ranger's circle of fatality that was constantly about him.

The rogue screamed in the darkness, and the fight was on with a huge gash in the man's scalp. But there were others...

The next to die in the hasty ambush got a savage kick to the shin to off-balance the man swinging a scimitar out of the dim that gleamed suddenly in the dark all of its own accord, throwing a green light over them all. This one was dressed like a desert warrior. Cloak and turban. A veil that covered his face. Dark eyes alight and greedy by the venomous glow coming off his wide curved blade. The sharp and savage shin kick from the Ranger at close quarters caused the turbaned warrior with the magic scimitar to step back suddenly, reeling in fresh pain from the unexpected blow. The Ranger took advantage of this break in momentum and struck again with another kick of his combat boots. He smashed the front of the man's knee, putting all his weight into it, making a brutal bone-breaker push against the mechanics of the human body. The man screamed, and fell, and Thor stomped his boot on the man's throat in the next instant and heard the savage crunch of bone.

*So much for a magic sword*, thought the Ranger grimly in the bare seconds he had before the next assault came at him out of the shadows where they'd decided to ambush him as he made his way relentlessly forward.

He had seconds to run another fast-moving shadow through that came at him from another quarter. The man stumbled and fell, screaming, then a new attacker swept a blade at the Ranger and Thor ducked beneath it. Then returned the favor with a Muay Thai shin kick to the back of that one's thighs, aiming for the knees. He missed, but still swept the attacker from his feet. Sergeant Thor, weapon ready for anyone else, shifted his feet with a hop, then football-kicked, toes squeezed tight because there were no steel inserts like in the jungle boots the Rangers back in the day wore. The man was down as he tried to get up and slash again, now on his face as Thor delivered another terrific stomp from his powerful tree-trunk legs into the back of that one's neck to break the spine good and solid.

The man went unceremoniously limp in the gloom on the floor of the decrepit place.

The Ranger's boots, feet, and legs had done much of the work, keeping his hands free for whatever he needed to react to fast. The shield wasn't heavy, but it wasn't light. And the blade was precious and not the kind to get involved in an exchange of blows like in some space-fantasy movie from ten thousand years ago.

When there were such things in the Before.

The gladius was little more than a long razor-sharp dagger. He'd keep it back to stick and move as the next round of warriors came in to trade blows with him. Or he'd just get them onto the ground and quickly finish a downed opponent.

The work was fast and desperate, and he moved like a cat stalking prey, practically hunting those who came for him, then suddenly becoming like some powerful grizzly in the savage blows he beat them to death with. The gladius serving as a kind of unforgiving deadly claw that punctuated the utter brutality of his ferocious strikes in that quick little desperate battle they'd wagered their lives on.

In the dark at the end of it he side-kicked the final compatriot of the initial ambush, or at least the assaulters' section of it, with just the heel of his boot into the front of the man's knee. The fat oaf, carrying an axe, his job to deliver a knockout blow from an unconsidered quarter when the first two had the target occupied, but they were dead now, fell back and down to one knee, using the axe as an impromptu crutch all of a sudden to stabilize his clearly uncertain position. The man raised his hand as though asking for a breather, or a break, or a bit of mercy, and opened his mouth to say something, but the Ranger was in motion already and neither mercy nor a break were anywhere in his mind as he moved to finish the man and be ready for whatever bad guys might have hesitated and failed to join the assault against him. Thor finished with a hop-skipping stomp-kick to the side of the oaf's head. It was a brutal swing of his heavy boot, and it caved the fat oaf's skull in with a solid crunch.

He gained his feet, breathing heavy in the dark, and was rewarded with confirmation of his expectations as more men whooped and ululated, springing the second assault from a large low corridor that ran off into the darkness at another angle from the one he'd intended to follow. They came screaming like demons, weapons raised, out of the misty darkness down there.

Thor turned, crouched behind his shield, ready to meet them and decide who was walking away from this one.

# CHAPTER FIVE

THE SECOND AMBUSH CAME RIGHT ON THE HEELS OF the first—or perhaps these just happened into the fight that had suddenly gone wrong for the first ambushers and decided to exploit any opportunities or survivors.

Thor didn't care. They'd die too.

He was in it to win it.

Like Rangers do.

Battle and odds don't matter. Only victory.

"*Here's that edge, son,*" hissed the ghost of the smaj.

Thor roared and lunged to meet them, swinging and chopping to get in and among them all at once and break their attack.

The first round of traded blows rewarded him with no deaths, and they backed away, spreading out to deal with him.

He was fine with this too. It showed they were cowards of a sort. They'd see who could wear him out, or who would die doing so, updating their odds for survival. That would give him time to take them one, or a few, at a time.

His warrior's mind, a killer's instinct, did this fatal math of battle even as he parried blows and deflected attacks with the Spartan shield.

These men were lightly armored and smart. Or so they thought. They spread out quick and one of them, the first of the Twilight Bastards he would meet, wielders of both blade and magic, raised one hand into the air and threw a flashbang of magical light across the room.

The Ranger was not expecting this treacherous sorcery, and suddenly for just a moment he was blind, seeing nothing but white stars and shifting shadow images.

Some hot draconian wind seemed to come from nowhere, searing his skin. Whether it was some flaming magical attack cast like the Magic Meteors Ranger Wizard PFC Kennedy could make, or an effect of the dancing lights and hypnotically shifting colors trying to blind him, Sergeant Thor didn't know.

Blind fighting wasn't strange to him. He'd had an NCO in the Ranger Batts that had had a fondness for blindfolds and pits and training daggers and had forced the Rangers to get it done with the senses they had to work with instead of what they'd been robbed of by a flashbang or some trick of the light and NODs suddenly going dark.

Those were bloody and hard days.

Thor stabbed out at the first one to come for him, hearing the scramble and shift of boots against the rubble and ruin of the floor. He missed and swept his blade after the trails the shadow who'd tried to stick him had left in his wake.

Someone screamed when he landed his gladius in them, sweeping after smelling their ripe scents closer rather than farther away. The screamer pulled and dragged Thor's blade away from his powerful grip.

Someone shouted with glee, though there was a pained whine at the end of the exclamation. The blade had been taken at some cost, and that was good.

A quick smile crossed the Ranger's face as shadows became blurs. His vision was just seconds away from coming back.

They thought he was defenseless without his sight and without his blade. He'd make them pay for that mistake.

In the next instant he took a solid shot from some weapon off his breastplate. It was hard and heavy, but it didn't knock the wind out of him. He pushed himself backward, boots shuffling rearwards and feeling like a boxer giving ground he could easily retake when he was ready with a series of strikes from both jackhammer fists.

*Nothing to cry about*, he thought. *Just play the hand*

*you're dealt for the next few seconds.* That was something Sergeant Joe would have said, but he couldn't remember if the mentor NCO ever had.

He pulled the shank, popped the Contego blade off his carrier, and moved each into a reverse grip with surprising deftness as he crouched and studied all the coalescing shadows around him dancing this way and that, shifting for an easy kill that wouldn't cost them much.

Or so they thought.

This wasn't his first rodeo fighting this way. He'd done it once in a bar he never should have been in down in South Am getting a fellow Ranger out of trouble there in an argument over some local beauty who wanted to follow him back to the Land of the Big PX and all that.

The details weren't important now.

Neither was the fact that it was a *Muertos Eighty-Eight* drinking establishment. That was the local cartel the Rangers had come down there to slash and burn and dome the cartel leaders and mid-level managers of at range, out in the jungle.

The only thing that mattered was the fellow Ranger wanted his new girl, a real dark beauty with those big eyes they all had, and he was taking her. He needed a wingman. So his team sergeant went and...

... in the end it never happened.

Officially.

Too many dead Eighty-Eights in a town where it wasn't legal for there to be dead cartel guys. Out in the jungle, well, that was another thing.

Now Sergeant Thor had two knives and if they thought they had the advantage then they were about to find out how gravely mistaken they truly were about that failure.

It wasn't fancy what he did to them next. Reverse-grip boxing with sharp and pointy boxing extenders. He was breathing heavy now. Working. Inhaling as much oxygen as he could get because it was about to get real busy and contrary to fantasies, boxing rounds are a real long minute long with highly trained professionals who train their whole lives and are young and full of violence and rage because that's all they've got in 'em to sit there and slug it out for that minute, and usually they're all done halfway through that.

They came at him as one and he landed a hook punch, a heavy impact from the knife in his assault glove, and gave out a trailing slash for the guy's troubles.

That one wasn't dead, but he danced away wiping his blood and hoping it wasn't bad, though his bell felt rung from the savage blow the surrounded Ranger giant had dealt out.

Keeping an eye on that one, Thor went after the next one because there was no time for anything else but to keep whittling them down before they could get their act together. Front hand out for thrusting, he jabbed this guy a few times with the Contego then slashed with the secondary shank. That guy deftly, or luckily, danced out of the way, throwing his arms wide to avoid getting cut as the giant war demon that was the Ranger came in slashing and working both knives. Which was exactly what the Ranger wanted. The guy off-balance. Like a cannon firing a round, he shot forward and thrust his shank toward the guy's face. The guy was good, and he batted that attack away, his eyes wild and fierce as Thor caught his wrist, then used the Contego to stab in under the ribs and right into the guy's heart where it matters most.

Lights out instantly.

The guy just died on his quick little feet and fell over and Thor reacted to the first one who had gotten away from him. His lead knife saber, in his off hand, ice-picked this one, stabbing at the weapon hand holding the short little blade the guy was coming at him with. The Ranger savaged the back of the guy's hand with quick slashes and the guy dropped his blade and turned to run.

Thor *murked* him straight through the back, driving the shank right down through and out the front of the guy's chest.

Then he ripped the heavy chunk of steel dripping blood out of the man's body as the guy fell down into the shadowy dark, groaning pitifully as he failed to breathe ever again.

Panting, the Ranger was breathing hard through his nose now. But his mouth was closed, and he listened to the darkness beyond the ruined and wrecked old guardhouse they'd fought inside, waiting for what would come for him next.

The last pair of mercenaries seemed to have realized they were in over their heads. They had fled, exercising the prudence of living to fight another day, with the realization that sometimes you can just leave a bad situation and the only thing keeping you there is ego.

And the price often when ego makes that decision... is sometimes your life.

Thor watched the shadowy corridors, lined with prison cells, filled with the bones of skeletons that seemed to watch and do nothing more.

Off in the distant gloom, nothing moved.

# CHAPTER SIX

THE RANGER WENT DEEPER INTO THE PILE OF RUIN AND wreckage that was the sprawling shadowy ramshackle destruction called the Pit. Hours and desperate short fights interrupted leaving only the last breaths of the dead to mark their passing in the thick ghostly silence that enshrouded every passage, corridor, and uncertain stair. Passing through the rest of the guardhouse, the barracks, then into the solitary prison that was the aged keep surrounding and protecting that primordial hole that had first drawn the long-ago nomads to become dwellers of whatever this part of the coast had been before the City of Thieves had come to take its place on the maps, few that there were, of the Lands of the Ruin.

Deep in a shadowy cluster of rusted cells where ancient skeletons turning to mummy dust lay still chained to the moldy walls, their sightless sockets seeming to watch him as he passed, deep in this lonely and forgotten place, the Ranger fought a dwarven warrior whose bearing was dark, his eyes soulless like a shark's. The fiendish little warrior was quick and came at him with a hammer saying not a word, no battle cry given as the titanic struggle between the two began.

Even though Sergeant Thor towered over the stout little warrior, the dwarf rushed to meet him in combat, hammer upraised over one shoulder. Eyes somewhere only cold murder knew.

Even the Ranger was amazed at this.

And out of respect, he gave the dark dwarven warrior no quarter. And that was a good thing...

The Ranger's fine circular shield low, the dwarf swung mighty blows against it, battering the Ranger who thrust with the razor gladius, missing only by inches as the fighter he faced shifted face and swung relentlessly with the timing of a stopwatch. Tireless and without break he hammered at Thor's shield in the first two minutes of combat, each seeking some advantage to deliver a blow that would shift the balance and see the other dead in the next instant.

There was a darkness about this one, thought Thor as he worked shield and blade. The little warrior, eyes emotionless, sneering mouth hissing silent whispers that seemed to trail in the wake of his relentless hammer strikes against the sturdy shield Thor wielded, breathed through his nose like some bull bellowing and snorting, heaving more and more in the dark, dank quiet of the lower torture chambers of the Pit.

The Ranger was not one to judge for size. Some of the toughest soldiers he'd ever known back in the regiment had been smaller than the rest of the Rangers who trended rangy, long-legged, and taller than average. If the smaller Rangers were well trained and knew what they were doing, they could cut a big man up easy.

And often, they'd been fighting their whole lives, larger bullies mistaking them for easy prey, learning the hard way they were anything but.

Or as Tanner had remarked about Sergeant Kang, the EOD NCO with the detachment who was smaller than most and built like the Tasmanian devil, "It's like giving a raccoon a gun, Sar'nt. Still a wild animal that can cut you up good and you'll be sorry, but now the little trash panda has a gun. And in Sar'nt Kang's case... a ruck full of daisy-chained claymores just so you don't live to ever forget what he did to you."

Generally, as most everyone had learned over time and trips to the medics, the combatives pit with Sergeant Kang was gonna be one of the bad days you'd learn a lot from.

Crouching in that boxer's stance, leading with the shield and keeping the gladius back behind his shoulder—he'd recovered it from the mess of bodies back in the guardhouse —Thor waited for his opening and handed out check slashes against the relentless dwarven warrior to keep the grim and hearty battler who spoke not a word but the obscene hisses, moving and never resting.

He'd wear him out. And then... strike.

But the dark dwarven warrior seemed not to tire in the least as their battle raged on and on through the cells and torture chambers, missed blows disintegrating rotten instruments of diabolical suffering. The outcome remained in doubt until the hissing dwarf heaved yet another blow with the terrific hammer, fracturing Thor's forearm as he did so, each hearing and knowing the damage, then fell away from Thor's trembling shield breathing heavily and muttering dark curses in the language of the dwarves of the Ruin.

Sergeant Thor had heard the dwarves in the detachment use this same language, but the one being spoken now was a variant on what he remembered. Different. Hissing and slurring. More Middle Eastern than the almost Cyrillic sound it had been before among the dwarves of Wulfhard who had joined the Rangers on their quest.

But that was a background thought in the Ranger's mind, below the screaming cold shock of pain that was his fractured forearm.

Thor gritted his teeth, said not a word, and felt a cold sweat break out across his head and back. It ran down through his armor, and he knew he was fighting the chasm of shock trying to take him and suck him down into its fatal depths.

He took three quick breaths, held the last, then breathed out, letting the pain go. Ordering it to the bottom of the list of things to be concerned about right now.

It was for later, when the murderous, hissing, little dwarf was dead.

The pain became distant because of this, and because of the fatigue. Somewhere other than right where it wanted to be at the front of his mind.

Not important. Not important right now because of the murderous little dwarf in front of him.

The hissing, muttering, grumbling little dwarf in the shadowy corner of the room they'd come to had rebounded off his shield after delivering that terrific blow. It had cost Thor something and he wasn't sure he had any more credit in the ferocity bank to finish the job. Black candles guttered in waxy blobs lit by who knew and how long ago. Half-burnt smoky torches flickered as though some unseen ghost had passed by and found this contest for life and death uninteresting compared to the sorrows of the afterlife, and even the wronged grievances of the life it had once possessed.

The dwarf gasped, inhaled, and tried to draw breath that would make the little beast angrier. The dark soulless eyes were cast down. And then the Ranger saw the opening he'd been waiting for...

Simply and briefly he gave his response, and it was a sudden and unexpected charge that quickly changed to a savage lunge for all the marbles despite a broken forearm and all that fatigue in place of strength and awareness after such an adrenaline-sucking battle without honor or humility. It was the end of the brawl right there in those ancient cells where eyeless skeletons, prisoners of bone and torture, seemed to be mildly interested in the last of the contest.

At the end of the desperate lunge, Thor delivered a brutal thrust to the belly of the dwarf with the sharp razor of a blade in his huge fist, then leaned in with the hip, ignoring the banshee's scream in his broken forearm, to simply twist and rip the tip of the sword free of the dwarf's midsection once it was full in all the way.

Gutted in an instant, the little man backed away, his guts slithering out onto the dank dark dungeon floor, muttering absently his dwarvish curses until he was gone and his soul-dead eyes joined the watching of the blind skeletons along the moldy and ruined walls.

Thor bent to the dungeon floor on one knee, laying the gladius down where he could get to it.

The pain was coming...

Leaving the arm strapped to the shield, he studied it,

swearing under his breath at the abnormal damage he saw there. He could move it. Some. But there was savage screaming pain, and each blow going forward would light up all the pain centers good and long.

He reached into his cargo pocket for the last tin of dip.

Refilled at a tobacconist in the city.

Not the Ranger's preferred Skoal.

But it would do for now.

He pinched some out and put it between his cheek and gum. Swore as he closed the can of dip and spit, letting the hatred for the dead little dwarf replace the pain that tried to come and stay.

"That's what you get," he swore at the corpse on the floor beneath him. Its blood and guts drooling out into the hungry stone.

Then he grasped the leather strap that kept his arm to the shield, unfastened it, took a deep breath, and then pulled the strap as hard as he could, grunting as the white-hot blinding pain came. For a moment he saw nothing but raw red murder.

He fought the darkness.

Told the pain what it could do with itself.

Then, fingers shaking and trembling, he raised the shield higher, seeing how far he could go, how much his arm could bear the movement of the lift.

He spit a stream of dip and swore silently.

There was no other sound in all the world down there. That's what it felt like.

He grabbed the gladius off the floor, stood, and waited for a second to see if he would just fall over from all he'd done to himself. Then he sheathed the razor-bladed gladius.

He'd do it this way now. Useless arm and all, he'd get it done.

And once more, he was off into the deeper darknesses of the old place, getting closer and closer to the prize he'd come for.

Sergeant Thor would have it no other way.

# CHAPTER SEVEN

BEYOND THE TORTURE CELLS LAYMORE GRUESOME rooms that probably hadn't been used in years. Bones stacked. Prisoners walled up. Pits where bones lay shattered and mangled and the torches the Ranger borrowed from the wall didn't even shine their light to the bottoms of these drops. As though there was no end to them. As though whoever had been tossed in to die, had instead fallen forever and ever.

This thought, when it came, bothered Thor, and he stood near one pit, near its edge, considering what lay down there...

He kicked a stone and waited, for a long time hearing nothing, and then finally, maybe, the collision strike with some distant unseen bottom echoing back up as though it wasn't even there and just perhaps his mind filling in the gaps so reality and sanity could go on as they had.

The floors were thick with dust, and the bones dry and

brittle crunched and shattered easily, almost soundlessly they were so old, beneath the heels of his combat boots.

No one had been here for a very long time...

Decades even. It smelled like death to the Ranger anyway and now he moved quiet as a ghost through these abandoned underground districts, on the stalk and reminding himself he'd get to the end of this by getting it done quick, and preferably by surprise.

The sages the thieves' guild had consulted had said this was the fastest and safest way to the Pit itself. That there were other wide avenues through the fortress, the prison, the temple, and the whole labyrinthine ancient place that would arrive at the endgame. But that those ways would be the ways most would take.

And there would be much fighting.

On the other side of the vast ossuaries, bone rooms, and seemingly bottomless dark pits, there were more torture cells. This area was an almost unending variety of ways to cause pain, humiliation, and death, the shattered and broken bones of many left everywhere. Between the empty darknesses, small areas were illuminated by lone guttering candles left by someone unseen and perhaps watching though it was impossible to be certain.

In time the Ranger found the lower catacombs that the sages had said would lead him to his destination.

Descending ancient rotting wooden stairs, the stone platforms like towers, bloodstained and crumbling, he followed the few guttering candles like distant light posts through this area where the webs of giant unseen spiders swayed and drifted in the drafts coming up from the deep caverns that lay below. Taking alternate passages beyond the stairs continuing deeper down, he waited for his eyes to reveal in the darkness who else might be down there with him. Then he moved cautiously, keeping the few candles leading toward the Pit down here like a treasure map, within sight but never getting close to them.

He shadowed their path suspecting traps, ambushes, and assassins in the dark. But for a long time it was quiet and the Ranger wondered if perhaps none had made it down here... or they had and they were that good.

"Best to assume..." he began to himself softly, watching the dark shadows near a distant black guttering candle.

And then he heard them.

Others. Down here. Another group that had decided to work together to get this far, this deep, into the pile and nearer the final prize. He couldn't tell what they were saying out there in the dark, but he could hear they were arguing, insulting, by the sounds of it, one another.

There was clearly a leader, asserting power. And some who didn't like it one bit. You could practically hear the murder and revenge in the responses to the orders and organization being dealt out.

These were desperate, low, and dangerous men. And that and the fact they'd made it this far... made them killers.

Thor crept along a nearby passage, carefully threading ancient wreckage along the dark floor, moving without a sound, one step at a time, until he was close enough to see them gathered around a corpse on the floor.

Someone they'd done to death.

They were rifling pockets and holding up newfound weapons, exploring them by the light of the candle lantern one held aloft for all to see by.

Six of them.

Easy decision.

When in doubt, frag out.

The grenade would get it done.

But... that was the last of the powerful grenades that could ruin a heavier foe like a war ogre he might meet down here. Or destroy an advancing shield wall. Or even clear a room through overpressure if it was a room he had to take with not enough gunfire and the time to do it right through violence of action was well-staged and well-planned.

The Ranger way.

Six was too many even with a good arm instead of the broken one being held together by his shield. He had to ignore the pain otherwise it would come, uninvited, and stay. Six while in his condition was a great way to receive a solid beatdown. Especially if they knew what they were doing.

He was certain they did.

Down low and crouching in a passage just a few feet away from them as they argued over the dead man's things, Thor rehearsed his movements.

Then...

They began to struggle over some fine thing the dead man had once possessed, and the Ranger changed his plans because he could hold the grenade back and get it done with the flashbang and some gunfire now that they were drawing weapons, swinging at each other, and generally preoccupied. He popped the flashbang and rolled it toward them, because the path was clear by the thin candle lantern waging a losing battle against the dark down here. He covered behind the wall of the wet stone corridor he'd come down, pressing one ear against it to block that ear and covering the other with his free hand wrapped in the shredded assault glove.

When it detonated, he was on his boots an instant later, pulling the Glock from its holster where he'd mounted it on the inside of his shield.

Then he advanced behind the shield, using the cut corner to aim, steady, and cover behind.

He shot the leader first, the one he'd seen towering over the others and handing out slaps and quick barking strings of their language to get done what he wanted done already and not later. Thor shot that guy right in the head taking his time to get it done as the man staggered away from him. Fat spitting lips working soundlessly now as he reached for his head where Thor had put the kill pill from the Glock at fourteen hundred feet per second.

Thinking, *There's Ruin magic. And then there's Kraut Space Glock magic.*

The round went through the guy's mouth and tore out the back of his neck and spine. Then he went backward and died beyond the wan candle lantern light in the gloom down here and some part of Thor's mind, already busy on the fatal killing math of wiping out everyone in the room, whispered, *Good luck with all your problems... over there.*

Sergeant Thor had a passionate hatred for bad leaders. Even the enemies.

Done. That guy wasn't anyone's problem anymore. Now he'd do the rest.

Thor pivoted and started punching tickets with the Glock as they staggered away from him still reeling from the effects of the flashbang down here under the fortress of the Pit. He caught brief snapshots of each man's terror after the flashbang and incremental muzzle flashes in the dark highlighting Sergeant Thor as he smoked them, then faded into the dark toward his next target.

The cacophonic thunder of gunfire roared across the dark and empty districts of the old forgotten place, drifting and echoing away to unseen horrors that made this their hunting grounds and home.

It wasn't even hard.

They had no idea what was happening to them as he did it to them.

The last guy to get it was some kind of wizard or something. He called out in a high-pitched voice some last-second doomsday spell as lethal fiery snakes started to crawl across his arms and hands in the shadowy clutching darkness that had enshrouded them as the candle and lantern fell to the floor, smashing and going out.

Thor had no doubt this was some kind of Magic Meteor spell the wizard would try and rock him with. By this time most of the mag had been used getting it done and his grip and aim were all gone to hell from the fatigue of the past fights and the screaming pain in his arm. So he just emptied the rest of the rounds into the conjuring wizard and the man went down, the fire snakes leaving his body, slithering off into the rest of the charnel house that was this hellhole place, hissing like dying sparklers as they went. Their hellish light fading off into other darknesses out there where no one ever went, and those who did... never returned.

They were all dead now and only the fading hiss of the spell-wrought fire snakes lingered in the soundscape and distances.

Thor stood above them as even the thunder of his savage yet accurate gunfire faded off into deep vaults and the vast cavern system below all this that the sages knew only rumors of, and made signs of warding at this dire knowledge as though rejecting unseen evils.

Now there was only the smell of burnt cordite and the hearing of nothing beyond the ringing in his ears.

And the dead at his feet.

Again, he moved off into the darkness.

# CHAPTER EIGHT

THE SOUND OF THE BIG CAT, A JAGUAR, GROWLED AND cried out, low, menacing, and pure evil itself as the Ranger closed with the Pit and the final moments of the edge he'd set himself against this night.

He was closer now...

The Pit sat at the center of the second-oldest district in the vast spreading metropolis that was the sprawling den of iniquity of the port City of Thieves along the Coast of Robbers on the eastern edge of the Sea of Riddles. Most assumed that the decrepit structure that surrounded the Pit, the old fortress-prison-asylum-temple, not to mention the catacombs and other deep and deeper darknesses beneath, had been constructed by the Accadion Legion during their occupation of the city back in the glory days of a fading empire, their fantastic builders and conquerors making the best concerted attempt to rebuild human civilization into the pale shadow it had once been.

But it was older than that.

The old fort was built by a lost race consumed by the dark rites and the thing they'd evoked from the bottom of the pit and the horrible beyond it gave access to. A race of dog-men who'd swept out of the steppes beyond the Eastern Wastes, conquering many of the near Bronze Age tribes of humans and demi-humans just trying to survive the Long Dark Age after the nano-plague had destroyed the Before.

The Saur had not yet awakened from their long slumber in their tombs and vaults beneath the desert floor to the west in the Lands of the Black Sleep. Not even the Grand Pyramid of Sût the Undying had yet been built. Foul Sût had yet to issue forth and conquer most of the known world in and around the Great Inner Sea. He was still crossing the destruction and dark ages of the Ruin, collecting the dark rituals and spells that would give him all the time in the world to acquire lichdom and everlasting death in defiance of the foe itself.

The Pit was an ancient place even by the standards of ancient places in the ten-thousand-year history of the Ruin.

And...

It was a fetid place. An evil place. Foul and corrupt. It drew the evil and vice and those who hungered for power, or even just the lies of it, to its depths. The Accadion Legion's most wicked and tactically brilliant general, Kalveras Canus, the Dog of War himself as he was called in those glorious and bloody days, had made the old fort his command center for the glorious campaign against the tribes of the Red Desert and the Pirates of the Scarlet Brotherhood in the southern waters beyond the Sea of Riddles. This was before he would return as imperator to the golden streets of Fair Accadios, murder the then-current emperor with his own bloody fists, and almost destroy Accadios itself in an astonishing orgy of bloodshed, lust, violence, and black magic, before the royal line was restored.

But it is said... that before the usurpation, it was the Pit where the Dog of War made his home during those fabled campaigns against the South. In the blackest depths of the old forgotten place, that is where he became who he would be. Where he lost his mind, and his humanity, and became a beast. It is said, for when the coin flows, of course the old wizened sages in their singsong soft trembling voices have much to say, that this is where he went from being a brilliant light cavalry officer of many daring deeds and adventures in the face of overwhelming odds, a hero in shining armor atop a brilliant white horse, to what he would become, a relentless murdering conqueror who showed no mercy... and before him none could stand, for he was more than a man. He was darkness and terror itself. And as he grew colder, more corrupt, wrapped in darkest armor the dwarves could be convinced to craft at great price, draped in a cursed gray ragged cloak that was said to be the grave shroud of a powerful sorcerer from the very heart of the Dark Ages after the fall of the Before and the beginning of the Ruin, what few traces of humanity he still possessed faded as he became fully the ravening beast that cursed his blood.

It is said... that somewhere deep in the Pit, he met this corruption that led him to become who he would go down in the scrolls and ancient writings as.

And it is further said... this corruption still waits there to claim its next conqueror, whispering lies of glory and hoard and the price of blood, and humanity.

So say the sages, uneasily, their eyes casting about in the bloated shadows as though hungry spirits there lurk to feed on their tales. So they say when plied with sufficient coin, or drink.

The center of the Pit is now a fallen pile, falling inward, collapsed perhaps by the great evils that have been done here. Human sacrifice, deals with devils, vows to the Outer Dark of what can be offered in exchange for powers of might and magic. Open to the burning skies above at brightest noon, and to full-blooded moonlit nights when the alabaster light of the cold moon makes the ruin appear as the bones of strange giants never known. When the contest for the Prize Chest is not ongoing, the Dark Cult, who have begun once again to flourish of late, are said to form parties of seduced adventurers to discover what lies in the levels below the Pit, within the Pit, for it is said the dog-men never stopped tunneling downward toward the lost civilizations of the deeps, intent on the thrones of the hells themselves as a destination from which the pack might serve a dark master who hates the Ruin and the Cities of Men.

Numbers, numbers, and numbers are whispered of by the frailest of sages who make their living trading hard-won and long-researched info for what dangers the Pit contains here at its very black heart, a pestilent wound of crumbled ruin and dark oblivion. Numbers like eighty-eight, or nineteen, or even six hundred and sixty-six.

Perhaps nine hundred ninety-nine are the levels the dog-men made it down to the throne rooms of hells where the fire giants and their dragons guard those great thrones of the damned.

*Perhaps*, whisper sages, running crooked fingers along ancient texts inked in blood. *Perhaps...*

There are deeper levels than these, other worlds the ancient texts whisper of in their mad and bloody scrawls by the heretic and the insane.

And not a few sages have lost their minds reading these forbidden writings. Wandering off into the desert to become mad hermits, seeking lost oases that never were far from the

City of Thieves, or from the Pit inside the old fortress.

The desert takes.

The desert disappears.

So whisper the sages. So it is said.

It is the center of the Pit where bloody and wounded Sergeant Thor found his way through the last of the crumbling walls of the lower torture rooms of the remains of the old fort that—when one studied the grand defenses, the cyclopean walls shattered in great rents and ruins, the grim-visaged gods and heroes looking on from the stonework—weren't actually defenses to keep out an enemy, but more, perhaps... to keep *in*... an enemy. Thor, stumbling every other step, spitting bloody dip onto ancient stone, passing the long-dry drowning pools where the sacrifice to ancient horrors was done, arrived at last at the center of the ruin.

The Pit itself.

He came out into a bloodless bone-white moonlight and stood there for a long moment studying the collapsed wide circle of destruction. It was as though some great meteor had come down and struck at a great fortress built long ago, leaving little more than jagged and torn hints of what once was, and a great depression from which lifelessness and death itself oozed, at its center.

The Pit.

Around the sides of that gaping black pit at the center of

the wide destroyed ruin that lay before the Ranger, the maze of haunts and horrors and mean battles of life and death behind him, was an amphitheater of destruction. To the Ranger from ten thousand years ago it looked almost like an open-air football stadium, vast, silent, and waiting to be entertained by unseen, or seen, ghosts.

It was said certain hidden stones within the Pit could be used as a kind of stair leading down into the dark.

And all the "other" below.

Except... there were also treacherous stones along the way. Stones that would cause a seeker, a delver, to fall into the endless levels below, cartwheeling until they shattered every bone on some distant unseen level no one ever returned from. And it was further said, whispered really by these thin, trembling, ghostly-paper sages who sat on rich carpets inside their quiet studies, illuminating what they knew to those who would pay the coin to their palm, that these treacherous stones were replaced by some unknown denizens of the lower levels, so that they might again and again cause seekers to stumble and fall to their dooms far below.

In other words... death was everywhere here at the center of the Pit.

But it was here, in the wide ruined football stadium of piled rubble surrounding the black and bleak center, rubble that had once been the gray collapsed towers of war, rubble that was now the faded crushed remains of fabled gates once called the Manticore's Gate, or Basilisk Gate, or the Dragon's Gate...

Ancient drawings hinted at how fantastic these grand structures must have once been when the Accadions remade everything great and glorious, writ large in marble, bronze, and gold, everything seeming so permanent and indestructible, but which now lay in great dusty piles of shattered stone like some end of the world that had all been carefully managed to happen in just one place and all at once...

... It was here that Thor stood, among the skeletal remains of towers, the corpses of gates, the bodies of the palaces that had once been here at the center, gazing in vanity upon themselves, now lying in shattered piles around the Pit.

The Pit.

The Pit that had been here long before. And would still be here... long after.

That jaguar demon called out in the late night. Unseen and nearby.

From his entrance high up on the sides of the pile, Thor could see what moved down there. It was quiet as a graveyard and he wondered for a minute if the other two contestants he'd just dispatched to get through the last of the crushed corridor he'd followed to get here, if the gunshots had echoed out across this vast space and announced his coming presence.

He leaned against a shattered pillar, blending with the statues, gaining what rest he could.

Coming through that dark passage, he'd seen the tracks of the other two contestants in the dust and ruin like the good scout he was. He'd followed them, stalked them, and come upon them in the near dark, little shafts of bone-white moonlight poking down through the rubble in the passage roof like skeletal fingers looking for something in the sweet dark below. The shafts of light making the darkness darker.

They must have known he was on their trail. They'd clung to the shadows in a small room that must have once been some kind of minor audience chamber for those lost Accadion conquerors in which to hear petitions of aid, mercy, and revenge. One on each side in the darknesses that waited there. They came at him together, as one, each dressed in black cloth armor, like ancient practitioners of ninjutsu. One had a staff. The other grasped two forked knives that gleamed in the moonlight like forks of lightning.

They were good.

Thor skinned the Glock and muzzle-thumped the first guy in the face because it all happened that fast and they were close all at once, moving swiftly and silent, their feet making no sound, only the rustle of cloth at the last as they came for him. Thor face-thumped the first guy with the Glock, causing that one to back up. Then drilled him with three in the chest to make sure it got done.

That was the guy with the lightning forks.

The other was already pressing him with the whirling staff. The guy charged, staff high and on the downswing ready to thump the Ranger's skull good and hard. Lights out in the connection. Thor casually put one into the belly, dropping the gun close in and pulling the trigger at the last because the guy was fast and he could have brought the staff down on the arm, or hand, holding the Glock. The guy got it in the belly, went right, and leaned against the wall, reaching for where the hot burning poison had just torn him straight through. Then the Ranger gave him one in the face when the enemy reacted to the first shot right in the gut, the man's falling body crossing through a shaft of moonlight reaching down and into the darkness of the floor below.

That gunfire had sounded like thunder inside the old place, and now, standing there surveying the Pit and the black hole at its center, Thor wondered who else, unseen out there, had heard it.

Perhaps no one, he thought, as immobile as all that piled and cracked rock around him. Waiting to see who would move out there in the rubble.

Perhaps he was the only one who'd made it this far.

The Prize Chest was down there. A lone dark square block, waiting near that gaping and mysterious hole that, if the sages were to be believed, was a portal to the Hells themselves.

And then, out there in the quiet dusty ruin, low and guttural, he heard that big unseen jaguar's growl and low clicking moan.

And Thor knew... someone else had made it too.

# CHAPTER NINE

THOR BACKED AWAY FROM THE DEAD WERE-JAGUAR. Half man, a warrior of some sort with emerald-green eyes now glazed over in death. The other half the spotted deadly jungle hunting cat. The Ranger dripped with his own blood from the savage rake marks the thing had left along his arms and back with its claws when it had jumped him on his way toward the treasure chest near the Pit's edge, coming out of the last of the moonlight and darkness to attack with speed and surprise.

"There you are," hissed Thor as the attack came. He'd smelled the animal on the bare night's desert breeze. He'd also felt the electric danger in the air. And in the end, he'd known that thing growling out there in the darkness, a hunter, a real-life contestant for the apex hunter of all time, would only come if he moved on the chest that was the endgame of the whole affair.

And the half-jaguar warrior had come.

And they'd fought. To the death in fact.

Now, dead, it was turning back into the man it had once been. What or whoever he'd been before the curse of the Ruin Revealing had fallen on him.

The Ranger's arms were shredded and bloody and he couldn't tell where the injuries stopped. What was his own running blood drooling and coursing down over his bruised and battered skin, and what was the blood of the beast he'd traded blows, claw and fist, sword and tooth, against to win. Finally resorting to his last most deadly weapons to blow the side of the thing's face off and pepper it in a dozen places with a frag.

He'd stuck it with everything he had. The razor gladius was now shattered and lying in the bloody dust nearby. Near the dark square of the Prize Chest beside the gaping dark hole that was the Pit, the gaping dark hole that he'd kicked the beast into after he'd popped the spoon on the grenade, arming it, and stuck the grenade in the tattered remains of the armor his opponent wore, grasping the flailing, screaming, growling thing as it clawed and snapped at him, then kicking and flinging the were-jaguar with all he had, even as his fractured arm screamed, into the Pit and the dark down there.

It didn't go so easily. It clawed the edge, scrambled back up out of the Pit just as the grenade detonated, blowing chunks of it away.

Stunned, its jaws and sharp fangs working silently, its cat's eyes wide and murderous, it nevertheless continued to crawl back up onto the cracked and broken pave, millennia old, to die at last panting horribly with large parts of its humanoid cat body missing.

Then it began to change...

The blood spray, the Ranger's and the beast's, all around and across their battlefield, now looked like black ink under the last of the cold white moonlight the night would see.

Thor bent and pulled the Ranger shank out from the thing's heart where he'd left it as the thing tore away from him in the second-to-last pass, leaving only the grenade seated behind the battered and claw-raked shield as an option to make one last play for survival.

The shank should have done it, *had* done it, but the thing was going to try to kill him one last time anyway because it was more mindless wounded animal than the man it had taken over. Who knew how? It wasn't magic. The last mag he'd brought with him for the Glock hadn't been enough even though the Ranger had put several rounds into the were-beast as it swiped, scrambled, and charged, doing everything it could like any animal predator... to get on his back and sink its fangs into his neck and spine for the kill. Then drag him off for the feeding.

Or would the man inside the beast take over, growling and gaining control? Licking the blood from its fur and lips as it strode toward the Prize Chest, the victor.

"Ain't gonna find out now..." mumbled Thor as he stood there listening to his own blood drip onto the ancient stone. Silent and immobile like the statue of some forgotten gladiator by which all men who fought in the arena of life and death that is combat are measured by.

If there was a Bad Guy Number Two, he'd come now.

"*What then, Ranger?*" whispered the ghost of the smaj.

Thor chuckled, controlling his body as it tried to shake.

"Be... meaner... than... it..." He took a deep breath. Nothing rasped. No lung punctures. No tension pneumothorax in progress. "... Sergeant Major."

But it was the shank and not the Contego or the punch knife that had done the thing to a death it wasn't ready to accept. Neither of the other blades had killed the beast though he was sure he'd gotten the were-man in an artery with the Contego and put the punch knife right in its eye when he'd had to peel the thing off his armor after it had gotten past his shield.

Neither had killed like the shank had when Thor drove the big chunk of steel, roaring and battle-mad in the hottest most desperate moment of the second-to-last pass, crafted by some long-ago Ranger that made them, right into the were-beast's beating heart.

And then left it there because *die already.*

The Ranger grunted. His mind AARing even as he tried to move his feet off the death ground he'd been rooted to in the last driving of the shank in, watching it go, then deploying the grenade and playing toss-the-were-beast-feral-killer-in-the-Pit.

He heard Tanner's laugh from some memory of Rangers tossing orc bodies off the objective of a great slaughter. Seeing who could get the prize for the farthest toss.

*Rangers, Sar'nt,* Tanner had laughed. *We different. That's for sure, Big Sarge.*

From the rubble and ruin of the fallen palaces and temples that had once ringed the old black pit of despair and mystery that served as the backdrop, and simply drop, for the final battle for the Prize Chest, a nearby large stone, an ordinary stone that had once been part of some grand structure here, one that would have been easily mistaken for yet more flotsam and wreckage of the great pile of antique ruin that was the Pit, a place of lost towers, wrecked gates, and a fabled collapsed palace that had taken thirty years and the best craftsmen from across the Ruin to build, moved aside on a slow, soft, relentless grind in the deep silences of the night.

The High Priests of the Game, as the whole contest was

known, the contest to kill one's way to the Prize Chest, now emerged in a torchlit procession.

They were silent and hooded, their grim faces hidden in the shadows of their large cowls.

Who knew why they did this? Hosted this game of death? No one knew who they were or whether they were elite members of the city itself, having a pit-of-death sport to keep their lives interesting, or strange priests come up from the lower levels of the Pit seeking some savior, conducting some rite.

Rumors abounded. The truth remained hidden.

But they maintained the Game anyway and the city waited with bated breath for the nights it would occur. Warriors of renown came from far and near to try their hand. And it was Sergeant Thor who'd spent weeks playing the role of such a one so that the deception that came next, the heist, would misdirect and send many off on red-herring trails in attempt to gain the greatest prize of all.

Whether the treasure and hoard that waited inside the large and ornate bound chest came from the deeps of the Pit and the ancient tombs, lairs, and lost civilizations that were hidden there, or from the wealth of the city, was the secret of the Priests themselves.

But whoever died within the Pit at the center of the district of the old fortress... was theirs. The Priests'. The body that remained, and all the possessions.

Never to be seen again.

Nevermore a name that would be uttered out of fears and superstitions that ranged wide across the spreading City of Thieves.

And so the Game grew richer in the playing. And strange and fantastic treasures, or wealth beyond imagining, lay within the hold of the chest for the one who could slaughter their way to the edge of the Pit.

So warriors and adventurers, killers and assassins, came... and tried.

Most died.

The leader of the High Priests of the Game, taller than the rest, arms folded within his hooded robe, studied for a moment the wild bloody scene their procession had come upon. The desperate fight between were-beast and man. A man of renown the city had been abuzz with. Strange tales of the man. Rumors that he was even of... the Before.

A thought that was impossible to believe for most.

The were-beast had been theirs, the High Priests', unknown to most, though suspected by a few sages and silent wizards who tended to their research and had no interest in the folly of gambling over life and death.

*Life and death... bah*, those bent and cruel wizards muttered as they turned to their blasphemies and obscene rituals to pursue lichdom that would free them from such petty concerns.

Krom the Curst. That was his name. The were-jaguar warrior. A brawler, a reaver, a mercenary, a warlord, and even a king a time or two. Some even said a pirate on distant seas where the world ended, and a thief of tombs lost in the ancient west, beyond the Atlantean Mountains and the Great Ocean that never ends. A man who some mistook for a god in strange and foreign lands most thought were only myth and made up as tales for children. He'd fought in great battles and stacked mountains of skulls, sang the songs.

Most of those forgotten twenty years or more now.

Then he'd come, hearing of the Pit and the Game. He'd gone deep into the Pit on his own after winning the Game many times. Seen dark things.

And come back with the curse of the beast upon himself.

Becoming a murderer who prowled the streets of the City of Thieves and was responsible for many of the bodies cleaned up the next day.

The Priests gave him sanctuary during the day. And held the door open for his night feedings. More beast than great warrior now.

They didn't play the cursed warrior's card for most games they held. But for this one, for the renowned Thor who would tempt the gauntlet this night, they'd set him loose. They'd had their own reasons for this. But really it was the wizards who'd been to the oracles, prophets, necromancers, and witchy-women fortune tellers even in the meanest districts and lowest hovels, who'd demanded it. The spirit world and even the gods themselves were said to croon that this one must die. This one called "the Ranger." Called "Sergeant Thor."

*They sing for his death* moaned the oracles, whispered the prophets, rattle-hissed the bones dice of the necromancers.

"The Ranger must die, my love," murmured the seductive and hoary old fortune-tellers with each snap-turn of their old cards in the hour of death when the *sorcerati* were sent out for their answers to the questions the wizards had asked.

So they, the High Priests, had been asked to, and then did, set the cursed and tormented legend, Krom the Curst, to slay, to dispose of some foe the wizards were concerned about. This... *Ranger.*

But the High Priests had had their own reasons for complying known to none but themselves for they were so secretive, and secrets of the Game and the Pit were best kept, so many said and made signs to ward ill luck away at such mentionings.

Now the hooded figure of the High Priest himself studied bloody Thor, amazed that the massive warrior they'd heard so much about was still on his feet even though he was covered in blood and his gear and armor were shredded by the fierce battle that had taken place between the Ranger and Krom the Curst.

The Ranger wiped the bloody shank off on his thigh and stuck it back in its sheath. The sound was final.

Then he reached for more dip.

The hooded leader nodded, and now the business of the Prize Chest was attended to swiftly, for despite the wants of wizards and gods... the rules of the Game would be kept and seen to. Other furtive priests moved quickly to disarm its traps, magical and mechanical. Keys and chants were brought forth upon the Prize Chest, unknown prayers muttered, and at last, as one, the hooded and silent coterie of the High Priests of the Game backed away and their leader, tall and gaunt, wordlessly bade the Prize Chest be opened now and the last rite of the Game observed.

The moon hung low and lecherous over the western rim of the spreading ruin of that district and the heart of the City of Thieves. The night was more than half gone and soon it would be blackest.

The contest was over.

The Game won.

Brightest gold, highly polished and seemingly minted just, dazzled the dark into obscurity as the lid of the chest was opened and all the fantastic within was revealed.

This was the kind of gold coins few have ever seen. As though the coins themselves were what regular gold dreams of being some better day than the one it has been cast and minted into. Each disc rich and shining, lustrous from its low inner light even though the torches of the priests and the fading light of the moon felt thin and wan near the thick radiating dark of the ignored Pit that defied existence.

As though it was more an absence, than a thing.

The gold coins were shining and fantastic, numerous in number.

But all that gold paled in comparison to the fat and generously cut diamonds that lay within the pile of beautiful gold coins inside the chest. Each alive with the fire of some tiny otherworldly elfin dancer of light and magic.

Large.

Each a fortune beyond imagining.

There were other, and the word here is poorly used, but... *lesser* stones. Emeralds, rubies, sapphires. Only lesser in that they were not the fantastic and beautifully cut diamonds. These were alive and seductive with magic and intrigue, a mere one of them worth an orc khan's throne and all the vast lands he raided and pillaged in.

Some of these enigmatic and stunning stones shimmered as though they were not just gems but possessors of magic and fables that would aid or protect or tell the stories of great lost empires and beautiful women over which armies had slaughtered themselves to the death over. And old magic of the Eld that granted strange powers to the possessors of such translucent living fire stones.

There were rings with gems set in them. And the gems were alive with the nature of the particular magics held within. One looked as though the waves of the sea rolled along its circumference. Another seemed woven of autumn leaves, red with the color of fire and seeming to have just fallen from the limbs of great oaks and the last of the best of fall. These and other rings were rings of great power, or so said the sages who coveted and made trade on such tales.

And of course, it was well known that the sword one gazed on in the chest, a wide-bladed longsword, possessed the soul of an *efreeti* warrior. The blade was called *Flametongue*, and sages said kingdoms not of the Ruin, kingdoms and lands of other realms, existences, and even times, could be conquered by the warrior who held it.

Again, the sages had told the thieves and Thor this was so, that he would see these treasures and other wonders here inside the chest at the edge of the Pit on the other side of all the slaughter to earn the *Rite of the One Draw*, as it was called.

Now the High Priest spoke, his voice stentorian and

ringing out in the night here at the center of the ruin for there were no other sounds one could hear.

"As victor of the Game you are permitted to reach in and draw out once all you can with one hand. No more, no less. This is the Rite of the One Draw. But beware, victor... powerful curses still lie over the chest. Should you reach in with both hands, or seek to slay us now so that you might take all that is within, for it is clear"—here the priest nodded at the inert body of the once-man were-beast, pale and bloodless in the last of the light of the moon—"that you are more than capable... Should you do this... you will age a thousand years in one night and be dead by morning. Know this... and heed, victor."

Many of the sages had indicated they believed this curse was merely show and not true at all. Still, no one had dared it... for who would?

Thor spat some dip and waited, watching the hooded priests, unconcerned with the wealth inside the chest, standing like silent sentinels in the darkening night.

The moon was gone now. That darkness beyond their torches and the brilliant illumination of light and gold and gems and magic within the chest seeming to smother everything else.

It would be a very dark night.

A thief's night, some say.

And a night for murder, or so say others.

The High Priest watched Thor for a long moment, then nodded once.

"You may take your prize now, victor. You have beaten... the Game."

Thor walked forward, shrugged off his assault pack, ignoring the pain and his own blood, set it down, and opened the mouth of it. Unceremoniously he stuck his shredded-assault-gloved fist deep into the chest and pulled out a large handful of shimmering gold and one of the fantastic diamonds all in one unbelievable grasp of his massive bloody paw.

He dropped the pile into the open mouth of his assault pack, cinched it, grabbed it with the one arm he had that didn't scream in pain, and left without a word, walking back the way he'd come, disappearing into the dark cavern of the passage he'd found that led to this place. Passing the dead he'd made.

By morning's light, shocking and incredible news spread fast across the City of Thieves that the chest had been looted to the last coin sometime in the night.

All jaws worked as fast as they could to spread the unbelievable story that somehow this warrior had pulled a trick and taken it all. Magic, thievery, something not known, had to explain how the incredible heist had been done by the bloody Ranger.

Ears were open wide.

And every thief, every guard, every wizard's mercenary, every hired killer and desperate cutthroat, was soon on the hunt for the strange northern barbarian who had most likely taken the haul of the entirety of the Prize Chest.

Or had some idea how it had been done...

Every dive, every inn, every hideout was tossed as all hunted the Ranger Thor, sure he was somehow the key to finding all that years-accumulated wonderful loot that had taunted and tantalized all in the City of Thieves for so long.

The High Priests of the Game had even issued a reward by secret means and secret sources. Or so it was said.

There was talk of a bloody running battle through the streets having occurred after the Game in the dead of night beyond the moon's last light. Many from all the guilds and cabals were dead or missing, leaving no tale of who had done their murder. But somehow it was all connected to the heist and the strange warrior. It had to be.

The city seethed with rumor and heat by noon.

The wizards were meeting this night to discuss.

The eunuchs were silent but spies were everywhere, and it was clear they would know what happened, and perhaps... make use of it.

The business of the city that hot steaming day was the

business of what had happened the night before.

But Sergeant Thor...

... the Ranger was not to be found. Anywhere.

He had pulled the fade.

And the City of Thieves was in an uproar.

# CHAPTER TEN

*EXFIL OFF THE OBJECTIVE,* THOUGHT THE HULKING Ranger of that blood-and-body-littered mess as he faded from the Pit, *was the easy part.*

"Here's where the fun begins," he muttered as he kept picking up one boot after the other, one step at a time making his way out of the dark twisting corridors and wide halls strewn with the dead he and others had left behind. That there were predators out there in the night waiting beyond the Pit to take what he'd won... was a given. That had always been part of the Game.

"Rare that the one who makes the plan plays the goat, Warrior," Sato had muttered as he studied the warrior's plan back in the cool dark taverns that served Shadowrun.

The Plan.

Inside the Pit you were... protected... for want of a better word, Thor had reasoned. All you had to worry about were the killers inside the Game with you. And once they were dead you had a little room and time as you exited the Pit before you stepped out into the city dark where the jackals were waiting, looking for easy pickings when a victor made it to a healer, or a bar, or any dark alley or even wide lit boulevard where they could knife you in the back and take the prize.

Out there in the streets it was all of them against the winner. All their weapons, spells, traps, and whatever they could summon from the nether realms to get for them what you had taken from the Prize Chest.

To believe anything else was folly. This was the City of Thieves after all. The Game didn't stop after the bodies dropped.

It just moved to its next phase.

For now, however... as Thor stumbled through the last of the pile of the old ruins of temple, prison, and fortress surrounding the Pit... he was... safe. He did what first aid could be done, and ignored what could not be helped right here and right now.

Best to keep the fractured arm still bound by the shield and as immobile as possible. He'd taken to carrying it up now, higher than he normally would have used it for defensive purposes. Making his thick bicep do the work. It screamed less there in that position. He'd stopped once and loosened the straps a bit, letting some circulation in. Then re-strapped it harder, grunting as he did and the fresh pain came and mixed with the old, letting the darkness of unconsciousness that tried to take him pass, slowly, then spit dip off into the shadows and onto a smoking corpse some twilight bastard had lit on fire with malefic magic.

The spit dip hissed when it landed on the blackened corpse.

Back to the plan for what the Game was now...

Once the contestant, the winner, was beyond the last crumbling columns and cracked outer walls of the old fort all called the Pit, it was heads-up time.

The winner was now the prey for the dozens, and teams of dozens in fact, that cared not to try their luck at the game and instead waited to pick off the beaten, hacked, poisoned, or even seared winner who'd probably burned all his magic and luck just to survive and get to the One Draw.

Easier to fight one than many. Especially when that one was injured, depleted. Hurt.

Even if he was the victor.

Thor would make them pay for that mistake in their thinking. He was a Ranger. Odds like this were not new. Surrounded and outnumbered was standard operating procedure for Rangers. And he had allies now, though most didn't know it. The plan to pull the heist had that part covered. No one outside Shadowrun knew that the Ranger,

Sergeant Thor—or *the strange Dire Giant* as some whispered about him in the city—was also the second most junior member of the third-rated thieves' guild inside a city that basically the entire known world called... the City of Thieves.

The most junior member of the guild was a kid called Spritle. The crafty and likable chunky kid had recently worked his way up from the gangs of children, urchins, and orphans who worked for the guilds as watchers and low-level pickpockets. More often than not simply serving as messengers when a heist was going down or operations were underway in some part of the vast and spreading Bronze Age metropolis that was the city where information needed to travel for coordination of operations.

Spritle had a goblin that followed him everywhere. No one knew where it came from, just that the kid had always had it following him around and that it was good for limited tasks, much like a dog, and so no one minded it much, or killed it.

It was the guild's Jabba. Kurtz's gun team back with the detachment had picked up one, a goblin that is, and the gunner, Soprano, had trained it to act as a kind of assistant gunner and ammo belt bearer. Though everyone dumped all the gear on the wild monkey-like thing they could. It called itself "Jabba" and shrieked on and on about the Moon God Potion of the Rangers.

Also known as Coke.

The Forge could crank that out too, besides most weapons systems and explosives and a ton of other stuff. The goblin was nuts for the Moon God Potion.

The Rangers preferred Rip-It.

"I'd kill a SEAL for a Rip-it right now," muttered Thor as he made his way toward the edge of the old fort and spit more dip in disgust at his wounds, fatigue, and SEALs in general.

The kid's goblin's name was *Shim Shim*, maybe. If only because that was all it could say in what passed for pidgin-goblin-speak.

As Thor lumbered from the ruins under his heavy shield, weapons, and treasure-stuffed pack, gold is heavy, he felt himself fading, shaking, and trembling here and there. He'd slaughtered close to twenty in there. Mostly hand-to-hand including boot stomps and face kicks and the occasional hoist-twist-and-turn broken neck.

He'd been badly injured too. Cuts and slashes, yeah. Significant. Some deep. And the fractured shield arm. That... was not good for the plan going forward but... oh well. He'd known Rangers who'd busted legs on jumps and crawled or been wheelbarrowed through the rest of the mission. He'd keep the arm strapped to his shield, tight, if just to cut off the pain centers, and hope that one hard strike against the shield wouldn't make it go all floppy in the wrong direction.

He shucked the Glock and checked the load, counting his weapons and what he had to work with to make the long walk up the street and fade into a particular alley the plan had designated for the fade. Then make it down to the docks and the Temple of Poseidon on Fish Street. The Glock had failed to feed during the battle with the were-beast. Failed as he dumped a mag into the ferocious thing as it came for the Ranger snarling and sharp claws out.

And it wasn't a jam.

Thor had tapped, racked, and rolled it.

No joy.

Normally he would've thrown the malfunctioning sidearm at the guy coming for him, knives out next. But... this was the Ruin and firearms were hard to come by. So he'd skinned it back in its holster and swept his leg in a savage kick that caught the were-beast right in the thigh, the IT bands to be exact if the thing had such, and backed it off for a second, watching it limp and howling as it temporarily lost use of the fur-covered leg. Thor went after it with the shank then and stuck it right in its twisted black beating heart.

The close-quarters fight that happened then had cost him all the open wounds from the beast's raking claws across his chest. Shredding beaten plate like butter, drawing fresh blood underneath.

The chest rig across his huge torso was now tattered and ragged, but it still hung from his broad shoulders.

He inspected the sidearm as he held it here in the last shadows of the Pit that was all the safety he could expect before what happened next... happened. It wasn't a magazine spring failure. The damn slide had cracked, and the thing was done for.

The Ranger ejected the mag just for the remaining rounds.

He could use those to get at the gunpowder and perhaps make a small explosive for some emergency usage... later.

He shoved the magazine in his cargo pocket and tossed the Glock into the darkness. He wasn't angry, but it sounded like it as he breathed heavily and the gun clattered off into the past-midnight nepenthe of the shadows there, breaking down further as the nano-plague hardwired into everything now, every atom of reality, continued its work.

He wasn't mad.

He was dead inside. That's all.

This was the plan. He'd have to do without one of his two firearms going forward.

And *Mjölnir*...

It was hidden along with the Pearl of Fate and some other gear. He could get to it eventually. But for now, inside the City of Thieves... it was safer hidden.

Thief work wasn't sniper work. *Mjölnir* would ride pine for a while more.

Funny, he could almost feel the anti-materiel rifle out there in the night, lying stashed where he'd hidden it. Feel its sullenness at being kept out of the fight. Feel it talking to him... just like the intelligent sword that had wanted nothing to do with him after the strange island in the Sea of Riddles and the battle against the Dead Pirates.

Talking to him even though it didn't know how to use words.

Odd...

The Ranger pushed those thoughts away and wondered if he'd taken a blow to the head. The only modern weapons that talked were the two-forties when the gun teams began to alternate fire to devastate anyone who dared go up against them.

"And a Barrett don't talk..." grunted Thor. "It thunders, bruh."

He didn't laugh at his own joke. It hurt too much. But a grim smile did cross his features. Even that hurt a little though.

Now... the plan.

Support and cover would pick him up in the alley. The rest of the guild. A no-nothing guild that was little more than a gang of eccentric and hard-working thieves intent only on the perfection of certain heists. Pursuing some arcane goal beyond mere thievery and the acquisition of wealth.

Oh, and a mysterious leader no one ever saw called the Queen of Thieves. Thor himself had certainly never seen her, and he half doubted she even existed. More... a legend used for street cred.

This was the guild Sato had led him to.

There were two guilds in the City of Thieves that mattered.

The Brotherhood of Thieves.

And...

The Smugglers of Sand Street.

Those were the heavyweights. Always at odds, locked in a mutual struggle that was part uneasy alliance, part merciless cutthroat fight for total supremacy. A struggle that took place as much in the murky powerbroker back rooms of the *sorcerati* and the *mandarini* as on the streets where the petty and not-so-petty crimes and deceptions kept the engines of the city humming.

There were other guilds, too, many of them, but they were mostly specialists who managed a particular trade, or a certain vice, or a precise type of work. For instance, the Stranglers. A Kungaloorian cult that... well... strangled people.

Specialists like that.

And there were also some gangs that were little more than daring bandits and those didn't really count especially when the two bigger guilds got around to dealing with them. Then it was either join or go for a long swim in the sewers of the City of Thieves where the crocodiles and other darker things waited down there. Every day the city had dead in the sewers, canals, and out along the rocks of the sea that protected the port from the storms of the Sea of Riddles.

The Little Guild, as it was called, Sato's guild, and now Thor's, occupied a middle space. Big enough to be considered a player by the two bigger guilds, worthy of a certain grudging respect, yet small enough that neither larger guild felt threatened by them or even, on a good day, so much as had cause to remember they existed. A collection of lockpickers, second-story artists, burglars, tomb robbers, pickpockets, safecrackers... and one Ranger.

The Little Guild had been bigger once. Fortunes rise and ebb in the City of Thieves.

Ahead and on the move, the Ranger spotted in the well-beyond-midnight distance the next part of the plan.

The certain alley Thor needed to reach was about a block ahead when a lithe assassin approached out of the darkness from the far side of the street the Ranger was hustling up the best he could under his load and unaddressed wounds. Keeping away from the walls, dark ruined buildings, and shadowy outlets as he stumbled forward toward the next part of the plan.

He could still feel his own blood trickling into his boots. He needed either serious medical attention soon, or some time to stop and see what he could do for himself.

But now was neither the time nor place to do so. The dark figure smoothly approached the Ranger on the lonely street in a supposedly deserted district of the city, now no doubt crawling with hit teams looking for him as urchins and spies spread out to trade information for mean little coins.

"How be ya," said the lithe assassin in gaudy blue clothes, a wide hat, and a vicious-looking sword and dagger in his belt.

He was some kind of dandy, or perhaps a gambler looking for that quick score to settle up and perhaps have a little more to start over on the next round of owed debts. He needed money to probably pay some debts off to some very bad people, or change his luck at the table.

So he'd be this stupid, thought the Ranger and made ready to deal with the idiot.

Words were not an option.

The main language of the City of Thieves was an Arabic

version of Gray Speech with some Accadion and Portugonian mixed in. There were many other languages here, but that seemed to be the market *patois*, and most used it to get by, and get things done.

Sergeant Thor heard the hiss of both the dandy's blades pull free, and the lithe figure lunged forward. Thor, unsteady, the inside of his boots wet with his own blood, didn't hesitate.

The lunge wasn't unexpected. It had been sudden, yes. But Thor had his own lunge ready, and it was the only thing the Ranger had to deal with this guy fast and keep moving on the next phase of the operation. *Surprise, loser.*

The Ranger lunged forward at the drawing hiss of both deadly weapons. The man probably expected the opposite, and it showed because he paused just enough to make a fatal mistake and let his prey get too close. Thor slipped inside the man's drawn weapons, wide and held apart, both blades now made ineffective at this fatal-close range. The assassin tried to give ground on his hard riding boots, their clunky strikes against the pavement suddenly thumping out in a staccato beat as he attempted to get himself some distance between him and the murder giant Sergeant Thor with the impossible pack on his back and the scent of fresh blood close and acrid.

The Ranger wasn't going to give him the luxury of getting too far away and quickly moved to disabuse the man of any notions of dancing weapons or a continued heartbeat.

Sergeant Thor shot an assault-gloved rocket-powered jab right to the guy's face, rocking the assassin and snapping the man's pretty head back suddenly, revealing a wicked, white, livid, long-ago scar running down the man's hollow cheeks in what light there was on the dark streets. Some prized award from long ago in better duels not this one.

The city was silent here except for their brief struggle as Thor closed and moved fast to deal with the minor problem in the rapidly unfolding plan that had time hacks and objectives that needed to be hit and hit real soon if they were all going to see dawn.

The game had only just begun.

The brief exchange of solid and savage blows was so sudden that others, already now closing with poisoned crossbows or blackened knives in the night, coming up the alleys and through the old ruined warehouses, paused, saw the swift brutality, and stopped.

Some... even turned and left, understanding that whoever this mysterious northern blond bearded giant was, he was not to be trifled with.

Thor finished, punching to the throat and crushing the trachea, and the assassin instantly crumpled at what had seemed the very start of the fight.

The giant warrior's speed was impossible.

The man was dead and probably knew it. The Ranger left the assassin hitching in the street, down on all fours and trying to get air that would never come into his lungs again.

By the time Sergeant Thor made the dark alley that was the next part of the plan, the man was just a dark inert shadow lying on the street. Motionless.

A lot of bodies got left on the streets at night in the City of Thieves. Nothing new to see.

The City sleeps.

The City disappears.

In the morning they would be found, of course. Already cleaned of anything valuable in quick and furtive lootings as pockets and secret pouches were turned out and hasty rats shooed away. What was left, a body, would be taken away by those who served under the eunuchs for the appearance of taxes collected, services rendered.

Who knew where the bodies went?

That wasn't anyone's problem, or business, anymore.

Such is life in such a city.

If it sounds hard, that's because it is.

Measure twice, cut once.

The assassin had failed to measure properly and found the fate that had been headed at him all along the way.

Anyone could've told him that.

And soon his body would be someone else's business.

The City sleeps.
The City disappears.

# CHAPTER ELEVEN

The alley became half funhouse of horrors and half nightmare kill zone as every fast-to-get-there killer, or bands of killers, went for broke and tried to stop the Ranger's progress up the tight and narrow egress out of the district and off the $X$ where violence and ambush combined to see who won, and who died. Here, the thieves of the Little Guild, Thor's guild, had secured an exit up the twisting shadowy alley of ruined warehouses and old businesses long out of trade in order to get their own Sergeant Thor out of the district and avoid the walled watchtowers between districts and the gangs of sellswords that served the wizards and eunuchs who'd be on the hunt for the winner of the night's game.

The sages held that most winners of the game... died on their way back to their hideout. Or within three days of having won. The highest likelihood of survival had been with those who had acquired and reached a fast dhow heading off to foreign parts and other lands where they could not be found easily.

But that was not this night's plan. The Ranger's plan. In fact... the opposite was the plan because by morning much more than just a winner's One Draw was going to be what everyone sought.

And Thor... was going to lead them on a merry fade that would cost many of them their lives.

Now... he was truly the goat, as Sato would put it. They'd do a lot just to get him tonight thinking he had a fistful of gold and a diamond or two. Tomorrow, with the whole Prize Chest missing? They'd turn heaven and earth to find him and steal the greatest heist a city known for such had ever seen.

When he'd told them his plan, his fellow thieves had gone totally silent. And wide-eyed. Some whispered it would be the greatest they'd not just ever seen but heard tale of.

Where Thor came from, "goat" had two meanings. He would show them the other meaning if all went as planned. And that, to him, like a well-placed shot from *Mjölnir* at ranges even other snipers considered extreme, in high winds, and even under fire, was an edge he would try himself against.

But for this escape now, surrounded by his fellow thieves, working in teams of three, the exit off the *X* they'd secured was necessary not just to not get robbed or murdered, or both, for the haul he'd pulled from the Prize Chest, but also as part of the plan. Part of the fade.

It would be absolutely vital come morning, when the whole city caught fire and freaked with news that the impossible had happened, that he leave them a trail to follow... yet a trail they could *not* follow.

Sergeant Joe, wily Ranger Ruck Hobo that he was... would have had it no other way.

*Let 'em follow but make 'em pay. Always make 'em pay.*

That the Prize Chest had been looted down to its last coin all under the nose of the High Priests of the Game would set the city and everyone in it on fire. And the Ranger... he liked that. And for his guild... well then, things could happen.

But more about that later. If they survived this night of ambush and murder in a running street battle that would leave many dead. Strangled, shot from secret hides, set upon by ambushes and traps well-laid to disable, maim, and crush, which the Ranger would lead them through as he... "fled."

The strange northern barbarian who'd been in the city of late would be the only clue, the only scent when all the hounds released tomorrow morning. And that would make the running street battle Thor threaded all around him crucial as his guild sniped, strangled, and IED'd, or the

Bronze Age Ruin version of such, all the killers and ambushers who'd come out for a little night's work, hoping for big gains and easy prey.

If only there'd been someone to tell them Rangers are never easy prey. Even when you've got the numbers and the odds and it looks like victory. Go corner a badger and see how that works out for you. Except *these* badgers have explosives, guns, dip, and run on pure cold hatred against anyone that identifies themselves as an enemy. And if you're in a situation where you think you have them, Rangers, where you have advantage over them, and that this is turning out to be easier than you thought it would be...

... then you should think twice real fast. And real good and hard about it.

Because you're probably about to walk into a trap and die.

Measure twice. Cut once.

Flee and live. You face killers.

Tomorrow, and all the days that followed, would be some of the wildest the desperate and dark city of thievery had ever known as Thor played the Ranger's game of hit and fade and the epic treasure that had been stolen got farther and farther out of reach.

"Wanna play games," muttered Thor as Seringa the Shooter and her team of archers sent a fusillade of shadowy poisoned arrows from their little recurve bows, hidden in the burnt and blistered rooftops above the street, into a gang of bandits planning skullduggery just ahead of Sergeant Thor.

"Then let's play games."

The men were dead as Thor hobbled past under the weight of the plundered gold and gems, hearing Seringa's soft signal whistle that this section of the alley was clear forward and Harrad would pick him up at the next turn as her team shifted to cover the pursuit on the back trail.

Steps and seconds later, the sweating Ranger heard more hissing arrow fire as pursuers were shot down closer than even he had expected. It was getting hot and perhaps more jackals were about than expected.

Fine, the plan could handle it. The plan could hold. Hit and fade.

All involved in the plan knew: no one survived the pursuit. That was the plan. That had never been up for debate. Only the tale survived. The tale of the pursuit that had occurred. It would be the sweetness for rumormongers and aside-whisperers in morning's golden light as news of what had happened, and what went wrong, was traded like coin.

But the bodies would disappear and so would the real trail. Leaving another false one for the second round of ambitious treasure hunters to follow, giving the Ranger a small break to heal and reposition for the next part of the plan.

Now Sergeant Thor, peeling away the bloody scraps of the battered and destroyed armor he no longer needed, kneeling in a small square further up the alley where once there had been a fountain whose stones had long been hauled away for other building projects, shucking what no longer served, what was no longer needed, made his way through the darkness as the mephitic shadows of his guild brothers dealt with the incoming jackals all about in the night. These were brothers now, thieves he'd sworn his life to, and they to him. And they were shutting down the counterattacks coming through the lifeless warehouses long ago burned out, or the lotus dens where bleary-eyed dreamers, dreaming dreams of sleeping demons, barely raised their bony claws up from their drifting pipes to watch as a press of desperate killers threaded the shadowy dark of their dens while perhaps a meager candle guttered away and some deranged bard, fallen on hard times, lost in the lotus haze and long gone on his talent, murmured his way through half-remembered and mostly forgotten songs he once knew.

Walls collapsed, crushing bandits wrapped in black cloth and carrying blowguns to disable and paralyze the prey they'd thought the Ranger would be this night. Floors suddenly fell away beneath hard-bitten sellswords, hustled into action with the private funds of some wealthy eunuch who thought perhaps to redirect the taxes and more he looted from the city toward securing something that would give him some extra advantage over his fellow eunuchs in the morning light.

Warriors whose hard scarred bodies and deadly weapons lay twisted and broken or gored by the stakes they found at the end of these falls, were out of action. The junior members of the guild roped down into these new pits and finished the stunned and disabled mercenaries with quick and quiet cuts. Doing it right and clean just as they'd been taught by the professionals who handled such work in the Little Guild that was mainly just for the true work of thieving and not murder. But every guild needs men of this kind. The Waste Men, high-ranking journeymen in the guild given to few words and long lonely hours in outskirt taverns in high rooms, where they watch the shadows and shapes on the street and wait for the dark as the day fades. Waiting to be called to do... what they do.

These were the pipe hitters. And that's how Thor thought of them. They'd taught the less skilled in this art in the weeks leading up to the heist to do what was being done to the downed. But they were not in it here along the alley of death the plan had intended for the jackals of the City of Thieves.

They had other work.

Prime agents for sellswords were being taken out even as the blood spilling in the alley got underway in earnest all around the steadily moving wounded Ranger working his way up the alley. In the taverns and small dens, these agents interfaced between the wizards, eunuchs, and the mercenaries who could be sent out at an urchin's notice at the behest of the *sorcerati* and the *mandarini* to exploit some advantage with armed violence done by more-than-capable teams of hired mercenaries skilled in the art of death and warfare.

As Thor had pointed out, this terminated the lines of communication and hiring and shut down the deployment of forces that could be used against him in the alley.

Mingo had slapped his bald head with his nimble hand and started muttering about a dozen heists gone bad they could have used that technique on.

"Whatta trick we coulda played..."

Meanwhile, even with the guild out and handling the teams of jackals, more and more killers and opportunists threaded the lotus dens, closing in on the alley from several points. In one den, some crazed and bearded bard who'd once been the toast of the city, having even entertained in the eunuchs' courts and beneath the wizards' pavilions in the summer festivals of light and magic, mumbled out the ancient hymn all bards knew to sing, "The End," never really understanding how ancient the song truly was. He tapped out his rhythm and ornamentations on old wooden buckets, holed and useless, that were his only instruments now, having long ago traded his guitar for just a little bit more jade lotus on some desperate day when the string of bad things had only just begun to come to fruition. Killers lightly armored in leather with shields and small cutlasses, coming for the Ranger, passed the music being played, hands motioning to watch the corners and shadows, for it was clear there were other forces out working on this night.

These were killers who didn't mind the work. Any other day they probably would've been pirates just offshore, or mangrove haulers if the price of teak was right in the markets of Accadios or Caspia. Hard work. But this night they'd change their luck with the prize the northern barbarian carried through the dark alley just beyond this smoking den of lost souls where a bard murmured words he could no longer really remember, and tapped out that hypnotic devil's brew of a beat in a song going back to the Before as some songs in the Ruin did.

Chuckling like a dead zombie all to himself, hearing instruments they could not, seeing the magic they couldn't.

*The lotus provides*, say the dead.

Four of them threaded the hazy den in the candlelit dark.

Killers and murderers all. Same work, different day.

Sato strangled the first with a bit of cloth.

The urchins had alerted them this crew was staged and ready to take Thor just two streets over. In fact, that crew had hired the urchins to tell them which way the big barbarian would try to escape. And the urchins had indicated the route just as the guild had told them to.

Other children ran to and fro, dirty little feet beating the streets, to let Sato the master thief know of yet another band to try and thread the lotus dens as the deranged bard, drooling and smiling, beat out his hypnotic beat and made the magic that covered Sato and his crew's shadows and footsteps as they closed on their kills.

So Sato had arranged their deaths already, and he took the man at the rear, coming out of the shadows like an unseen ghost with a bit of strong silk grasped between both of his powerful hands.

The smiling wise thief was gone now. This was the Sato of many talents unknown to most.

And...

The warrior's friend, for Thor had rescued him from the rowing benches of a pirate galley deep in the Sea of Riddles.

The man was strangled quickly. Sato gently, almost motheringly, laid the man's lifeless body down in the rubble of the smoking den's shadowy compartments as the rest of the man's killing team moved on and ahead without him, sure that the dead man Sato had taken had their rear.

Lerdo took the point man from an old room where lotus dreamers lay in a stupor for not just days but weeks, giving the point killer a solid *crack* across the face with a stout wooden club, coming out of the dark ahead like nothing more than the blur of a notion that danger might be about to happen.

The bard's hypnotic beat and crazed mumbling gifted the magics of confusion and stealth to those all about.

The point man of the killing crew caught it right across the face and went down. Lights out.

The Little Guild were not killers. That must be said.

Especially when they didn't need to be.

But tonight was different and needs must. There needed to be no witnesses. And so Hitch and Well Well stuck quick little knives in the two that followed the one to get cracked across the face as soon as the clubbing blow came.

Hitch came out of an old closet that had once been the master brandy hideaway of a prosperous merchant and inserted his long fish knife, rather deftly, right into the man's ribs, placing one hand at the last second to feel the spacing and then pushing in and upward toward the ventral sac to switch the man off right then and there.

They are not killers in the Little Guild. But that does not

mean they don't know how to kill.

The man softly grunted as the blade went in so quiet, while the crazed, scraggy and unkempt bearded, lotus-addled bard's beat distracted the one ahead with a magic all its own. This one was the one for Well Well, who was named so because almost every sentence he began started with *Well Well*.

"Well well... I found myself a nice velvet pouch of fine coin in a lady's chamber who thought I was there for something else."

"Well well... it's a fine night to steal the wizard's finest eye... but what night, isn't I always say to myself."

Rumors abounded that he'd once been on the path of becoming a sage but had acquired a desperate passion for crooked games of chance along the way and that a thief in a guild was much better suited to that kind of work.

But he was fond still of sagely wisdom and would always listen to the plans and schemes of other thieves and counsel them that if they didn't heed wisdom, the Devil would drag them under. And that the Devil was always in the details.

Well Well muttered softly, "Well well... what do we have here, my little puppet..." as the club in the face got the first guy and the second guy got a fish knife between the ribs. Then Well Well pulled his gleaming straight razor across the third man's throat from the dark of a side room he'd just come through, shattered ceiling above no longer filled with cross-hatched moonlight because the hour was late and dark indeed.

Well Well's slashed man reached for his deftly ruined throat, instinctively, but the razor was gone in the dark and the slash was not painful but killing all the same.

Well Well, who had been groomed to be a Waste Man by the guild, stepped in front of the slashed man and did a little more work with the straight razor.

Just to make sure, mumbling to himself in the soft darkness under the bard's hypnotic beat, "The Devil will drag you under, my little puppet..."

Ignoring the man's eyes and smiling to himself at the process as it happened. Now Slashed Throat's belly and, more importantly, sternum and xiphoid process were exposed, and Well Well's other knife went in right there... like some surgeon surgeoning, some craftsman crafting.

The Devil will drag you under... some say that is the way once you get a taste for this kind of killing work the guilds occasionally have need of. See the Waste Men in the quiet taverns, staying to their high rooms and watching the streets for shadows and shapes.

The Thieves of the Little Guild didn't like killing. Wasn't smart. Wasn't posh. Wasn't good business.

But that didn't mean they didn't know how to do it.

And do it quite well.

The jackals were finding that out this night. And even in the morning, with all the alarm and tales aflame like a brushfire gone wild and out of control, there would be no love lost for these.

This was not their first jackal rodeo.

Whores with black eyes and no coin would weep not.

Merchants shaken down would say little prayers to the Hidden King, thanking him for the relief and eyeing their children who would take up their trade as safe for the moment.

Urchins with broken arms, twisted a bit too far to give up a bit of desperate info... would spit and chant.

"The Devil take 'em under..."

You don't live long in the City of Thieves in certain kinds of work unless you know what you're doing. And the Little Guild knew its business this night as the Ranger fought and hustled his way toward the next deadly turn in the alley.

And then again... most don't live long in the City of Thieves regardless.

Sato came out of the darkness after the killing work was done and the Devil had dragged the dead under. Speaking little more than a whisper of a haunted wind moving through cemetery trees late in the night when no one watches.

This was the Sato of many unknowns. Dangerous. Professional. Deadly.

Using cant, he told the others in his team what to do next.

Then...

"I move on to handle the next ambush and keep them off the warrior's back. Make sure these get to the carts and end up in the port waters by dawn. Then we meet at the Bloody Bucket... and we were there all night as agreed upon."

Thieves when they use *the cant* use a minimum of words and often sub in hand gestures or even just the odd sound to maintain the flow of quiet and arcane communication. In this case each thief, Lerdo, Well Well, and Hitch, merely clicked their teeth together softly, twice, making clear they'd heard their master thief's orders and would obey.

Then Sato was gone like a ghost in the dark to stop the next bunch of soon-to-be-dead jackals on this night that seemed it would never end.

# CHAPTER TWELVE

CAMBYSIS MAEDRAGONE WAS A SORCERER EXTRA-ordinaire and now he moved along over the blackened and burnt rooftops and through the ravaged remains of the district, following the chase as teams of cutthroat killers and smaller gangs—neither of the two bigger guilds yet involved in any coordinated manner because they'd had no idea this operation, the biggest the city would see in centuries, would be going down this night—pursued and closed in on and died at the hands of their prey in the streets below.

And the two bigger guilds had their own projects besides all the usual. A team of thieves from the Smugglers was lifting the Eye of Horum, a great and fantastical cut gem worth an armada of treasure ships, for one. The Eye was in the possession of a decrepit old wizard, the eldest of those who occupied the high tower and ran the High Table, a wizard who was dying badly this night as his decades-long research into lichdom and eternal life had failed badly with a spell-reading gone awry, perhaps due to the efforts of one who would gain the open High Table seat, and the old wizard was now being consumed from within by dark magical energies in the bad reading of the ancient spell that granted yet one more step toward permanent undeath.

Plus, there were those demons coming to collect on the pacts and bargains he'd made for the long-forbidden knowledge he'd so quested and thirsted for along the way to his mastery of magic and death.

The Smugglers were not responsible for this death. But they had, through their channels within and among the *sorcerati* whose machinations may or may not have led indirectly to the dark and deadly events taking place in the eldest wizard's tower this night... foreknowledge of it. So their team of men, cloaked and darkened, bags loaded with magic disarming dusts, powders, and even scrolls that could be read off by those little trained in the arcane arts, aimed merely to accept with grace and alacrity the opportunity that presented itself.

They were instead about to be dragged off to the Hell of Neverending Thirst by a clever gate trap the desiccated old mummy of a wizard had left to guard the fabulous prize he'd intended to be his new eye in the constant death-life he'd so sought. The very same gate the demons coming to collect were currently coming through.

Fun times for the Smugglers...

The wizard would die, the last of his magical energies unable to stem the tides of death inevitable. And so would the Smugglers' men.

But those were other guilds and other wizards and other heists. Cambysis Maedragone was an itinerant sorcerer without a tower. Yet.

He had worked as an adventurer, but his parties all kept coming up dead and unreturned victors from raids into the Lands of Night across the sea to plunder the tombs of the minor priests and warrior-kings of the Saur in some of the lesser shadow valleys that abutted the great and grand Valley of Kings and Priests where all the most fantastic tombs lay deep within the ancient rock of Sût's Plateau.

When no one would work with Cambysis Maedragone any longer he went deep into the Eastern Wastes, hiring himself out as one with knowledge to delve the lost cities of the Rift beyond the Cliffs of Madness and the Desert of No Return. There Cambysis collected enough wealth to return to the City of Thieves and secure the lower levels of a disreputable inn within the gravediggers' district out along the eastern edges of the city beyond the great wall that protected the city. The wall lay fractured there along this edge of the city, but that was fitting for a district that was ruined throughout to some lesser or greater extent due to the hard nature of life here, and what came in from the desert and death fields late in the night, seeking revenge or something even more diabolical. Much, much more diabolical.

Reality and time were strange in the gravediggers' district. Weird things happened both night and day, and most people shuttered themselves in at night, saying to all who would stay and listen that the ghosts of lost enemies and the murdered dead, unrequited and vengeful, had a tendency to wander the sandy lanes and buried streets after sundown nearest the vast necropolis that spread away in every direction to the east.

*The east is curst.*

Long had Cambysis Maedragone watched the game the High Priests staged, and he finally decided, deep in the dusty old cellar of the quiet inn known as *The Deep Hole Year Inn*, that this night was the night to begin new methods of income acquisition in order that he might one day have a tower of his own, becoming a wizard of note in the process.

Cambysis Maedragone stroked his Fu Manchu mustache and eyed the war scrolls he'd scribed to capture and take the great northern barbarian who'd try the Pit this night. Precious coin spent among the harlots and diviners had told him that the one called "Ranger" would win and dire things would come to pass for all the city if he did.

One whore had thrown herself down screaming that she might be delivered from the fire and flame she saw, writhing as though she were being burned alive. Cambysis snatched back his payment to her as her eyes rolled back in her head and the demon that had hold of her spirit tormented her.

He always paid... unless he didn't have to.

Later, over the war scrolls, he laughed evilly at how clever and well researched was his plan to snatch the Ranger. As everyone else got murdered, he would slip in like an unseen ghost.

Spells. Bargains. Pacts.

And perhaps... all these wizards watching the Game and wagering portions of their great accumulated fortunes would see how clever he was and promote him. And in time, he would become the greatest among them.

*Wouldn't that be nice?* thought Cambysis Maedragone as he bounced over the rooftops and the debris there on this late-night hunt, while teams of bandit-like jackals, come out to feed in the full night that marked the Eastern Wastes he'd barely survived, got done to death by the Little Guild all about and below him at times. His Boots of Bounding gave him great leaps, silent flights through the midnight black above them all, and then... soft landings as he tracked the great murderous idiot known as Sergeant Thor who'd managed to survive the Game and get away with a bit of loot from the Prize Chest.

Who knew how much?

Who knew, thought Cambysis as he prepared to fling a web spell at the great northern oaf as soon as he landed just behind the lumbering bloody giant overloaded by pack and weapons steadily and doggedly stumbling up the alley.

*Web* was one of his great spells, but not his greatest. He'd studied under the tutelage of Arach the Red Spider to learn it, and while some knew web spells, catchy webs that stuck and were sticky to all who dared touch them, Arach had taught Cambysis web spells that did all kinds of other diabolical things. Catch, yes. And also *crush, poison, pierce,* and *disappear.*

Cambysis Maedragone intended to make this as easy as possible for himself, and so he'd studied the right spell, *Catch and Disappear,* for almost sixteen hours in preparation for the night's skullduggery. Words and phrases, flung powders at just the right moment, and of course a small pouch of silk spun from deadly whisperdark spiders he now rubbed between his hands while hoping not to die from the inherent poisons if he erred in the slightest. If he did... there would be a moment in which he would feel as though he would die quickly, cold shock and burning itching setting in like he was being both boiled alive and turned to frozen dire ice at the same time. Not a pleasant death. But he'd prepared a little something for that too. And if all went well, then he could fling the web spell at the lucky warrior who'd managed to slaughter his way to a prize he had no brains for and take what could be taken all for his own.

He would put that loot toward the tower he had in mind, murdering the owner and refurbishing it for himself, repairing the cracks in the spell forces that protected it, cracks the current owner was unaware of due to the fact that he worked only in the forging of great weapons of magical power. Of binding dark spirits from other realms into weapons that would become renowned.

*The simpleton*, Cambysis Maedragone had hissed every time he passed the small yet ornate structure. *Soon, very soon...*

Some of the invisible stalkers and shadow lurkers Cambysis Maedragone spun out and sent into the Pit to apprise him of the doings of the contest had relayed in their whispering hisses that the great oaf had merely taken gold and a gem for the One Draw and was on his way toward an exit through an unremarkable alley that would be the site of much activity this night as messengers spread out and teams of bandits and thieves and armed killers prepared to intercept.

Well, thought Cambysis Maedragone, it wasn't an artifact of great renown the oaf had taken, and there were many of those rumored to be inside the chest, but it would be something he could pay to the stranglers to put to death the binder in the tower he wanted for his own if this was successful, and then perhaps he would do this more and have his Tower of the Maedragone, as he'd intended it to be called, soon enough.

Cambysis readied the web spell, *Catch and Disappear*, his second most powerful spell, and floated via his magical boots, descending softly after his last jump to just above and behind the barbarian who labored under a huge pack, limping up the alley silently, almost socially.

The wizard floated like a vampire coming for prey.

It was clear the oaf he intended his web for, this "Ranger," was badly wounded. Probably too stupid to know how much pain he was in, or how badly he was really hurt, thought the robber sorcerer just alighting to the stones of the alley behind Sergeant Thor.

And... how much danger he was in now.

Cambysis Maedragone would cast his web spell, the huge warrior would be engulfed in ghostly but all-too-real magical webs of holding, and the more he struggled the more he'd be dragged to another place, a place he would never escape from.

Cambysis had murdered blind old Arach for that spell.

It was both a web incantation and... *a teleportation spell*.

The victim would be taken, unwillingly, to a place Cambysis had prepared with charms and bargains. And oh how, how the sorcerer had prepared this bit just perfectly, for it was better not to work harder but much *smarter* than those you intended to stab in the back.

It would take a few days to retrieve the body and the goods. Deals would need to be made.

But... it would be worth it.

This "victor" of the Game, this brawny stud bull of a warrior, would shortly find himself inside an old and ancient well that had once been dug into the dusty cellars of an older and ancienter inn. Some past owner had intended a smuggling operation to take in artifacts coming from the great necropolis and the wastes to the east, for those expeditions that returned often went into those eastern streets of the city to lay low for a while and set up the deals and transactions they would finally conduct to fence the plunder they'd looted from lost tombs and dog-men-haunted cities crumbling out there on the distant plains.

The wizards who ruled the City of Thieves often sent their watching birds to find these expeditions and apprise themselves of what had been taken out of the ancient and historied necropolis where kings and dead gods lay buried.

Of course, many expeditions never returned from these trap- and curse-haunted vaults. So there was that to consider...

But if an expedition could lay low for a few days after escaping certain death and coming away with some fantastic relic and a bit of plunder, and avoid the intelligence gathering wizards' servants in the skies above them, bats by night, crows by day, then the party, or at least those who'd survived, could perhaps keep their acquired treasures.

And even sell them.

Perhaps...

Theft in the City of the Thieves wasn't just about thieving. It was also about thieving from the thieves. And even... thieving from the thieves who'd thieved from the thieves.

And so on, and so on, and so on...

The dusty ancient and forgotten cellar was offered to adventurers laying low in the quiet eastern district, biding their time until they could escape the watching crows and bats, and other darker things that flit and flutter and walk on two feet, and the well had been dug to supply them with water, for days and even at times weeks would pass before the skies and coast were clear.

The innkeeper was paid handsomely, or received a cut of the haul, cursed or not.

The well would now serve a different purpose. For a different haul.

Cambysis Maedragone floated down just behind Thor, landing quietly and proudly on both booted feet. Spell already coursing down his arm to his long, splayed fingers on which there were a few rings of minor protection, power, and spell storage...

The itinerant sorcerer doubted the stupid barbarian had heard him land, coming up behind him and ready to cast certain death, the man was heaving so heavily with his labored breath, muttering some marching song to himself under his ragged gasps.

Cambysis opened the pouch of the expensive webs he'd paid a party of reckless adventurers to acquire for him in the High Rock Tombs of the Spider Kings who once ruled beyond the mysterious Canyons of the Red Desert. Walking slowly now he spread the sickly webs across his splayed fingers, working them in and wordlessly mouthing the chants and incantations that would ignite the devastating spell.

Again, Cambysis Maedragone doubted that the doomed oaf, obviously stupid and only hungering for a pretty tavern girl who would make doe eyes at his swollen thews and powerful arms, and perhaps a joint of beef and cold beer... Cambysis doubted his prize knew the wizard was there, his tread was so soft and the words of his spell so silent as he shadowed Thor like a specter in the night.

In just seconds, the stupid Ranger would end up at the bottom of the well where the dark sorcerer had left many little paralyzing scorpions in the dark, little-fed and waiting along its now-sandy dry bottom. Irritated and ready to sting and feed.

And then... there were the grub worms.

And if they didn't do the job, he'd arranged a small hidden passage he could open and let loose a damnable quivering cube he'd trained to serve him. The thing would dissolve the body and leave the coins and gem if Cambysis could get to them in time.

Timing was everything.

It was all in the timing.

*Work smarter, not harder*, thought the cynical Cambysis Maedragone with a cruel sneer framing his lips as he prepared to cast his specialized web spell.

*He probably doesn't even hear me*, thought the arrogant spellcaster smugly at the last second.

In that, he was wrong.

Dead wrong.

Thor turned and flung the tomahawk he'd removed off the assault pack on his back. He'd been carrying it up the last length of the alley, uncertain of his fading strength to engage in close-quarters knife combat. With the hawk he could chop and crush. Hook a kidney and rip and it was all over for whoever had chosen badly to come upon him making his way off the *X*.

He always had two.

These were the ceremonial hawks he'd used back in the battalion to conduct his rituals. But they were also real tactical tomahawks, sharp as a junkie's edge. Balanced and well made. Expensive too.

Thor turned like a struck rattlesnake in an instant and hurled, overhand, the ancient savage weapon, burying it right in the wizard's chest just as the sorcerer's spell of webs and teleportation began to form and fire.

For Cambysis Maedragone at that moment, things began to go horribly wrong.

Tomahawk buried in his purple silk robes, Cambysis reached to pull the small axe from his chest only to gasp in horror as the spell fired and flung its sticky self all over him. The tomahawk had shattered his sternum, perhaps even punctured a lung. It had hit like a jackhammer though he had no idea what that was. Perhaps a bull's powerful kick was something he would have understood better.

But that wasn't the worst of his problems at the moment. No, not at all... In fact, things were about to get much, *much* worse.

As the webs splattered all over him and took him, the scene in the alley faded away, the ghostly teleportation effects of the spell taking over. Cambysis Maedragone screamed in terror, his voice fading from the alley even as he disappeared from before the heaving Ranger who watched his prized tomahawk disappear with the wraithly sorcerer who'd tried to ambush him, threading Sato's rolling handoff to get in a surprise attack.

Thor, senses on full alert, had felt the dark presence of the man coming down behind him in the dark twisting alley. Using his predator's peripheral vision, he'd seen the man on his six, and identified him as a magic user thanks to Ranger Wizard PFC Kennedy's classes on his strange little game of pens and paper and funny dice.

"These kinds of tangos are always priority targets," Kennedy had told them all, pushing his RPGs up his pale freckled nose as his half-Korean features stared uncertainly out at all the jacked and tatted Rangers, lifetakers and heartbreakers all of them, that he'd been assigned by the smaj to educate and inform regarding the Ruin and all the dangers they found themselves in currently.

"Bad guys, PFC," thundered some platoon sergeant tersely from the back of the training session. "We don't say *tangos* until they're down and not our concern, or anyone's anymore for that matter."

"Yes, Sar'nt," warbled the Ranger wizard who was only a private first class and had been, just the hour before being assigned by the sergeant major, digging yet another slit trench for a latrine for the detachment to avail themselves of.

The detachment linguist had asked about this later, when Kennedy had been returned to his Sisyphean task. "He's a valuable asset now, Sar'nt Major, now that he can do magic none of the rest of us can do," the linguist said. "Why make him dig piss pits?"

Weirdly, only the detachment linguist could question the smaj. It was like he didn't understand the seniormost NCO could make or break, or even disappear him into a shallow grave out beyond the wire, like every other Ranger NCO in the detachment understood, feared, and respected.

In this case the smaj didn't even look up from his Kindle and coffee and just muttered, "Keeps him humble, Talker. Go help him. Learn somethin'."

So, on the move and getting hit all across the rolling line of defense moving up the alley, the Ranger had expected someone, perhaps even a user of magic, to cast something and get himself close enough to do damage.

That's why he had the hawk out and ready. And also why he practiced not just hooking kidneys or chopping limbs with it but throwing the deadly thing like a thunderbolt right into trees.

In the fading look on Cambysis Maedragone's horrified face, the Ranger saw the sorcerer was all too aware of where he was going next.

Taking Thor's hawk with him.

Cambysis Maedragone knew exactly where he was going now that his spell had gone so horribly awry. He'd prepared that place. The small paralyzing scorpions he'd acquired that immobilized your central nervous system but kept you alive and awake for the whole fun show. The grubs that would come and eat his flesh, slowly, finally burrowing into his brain, his mind.

There was no escape.

As the teleportation effects took him to that dry bricked-up well deep in the cellars of the inn he'd murdered everyone in, the sorcerer resolved to spring the secret passage and let the cube do its mindless work on him. There would be no one to help him. No one to hear his screams...

Still, he screamed.

And in the inn beyond the fractured wall of the city, out near the vast spreading ancient necropolis, that night his scream was heard by none who stayed there, for there all were dead, or gravediggers, or marker carvers. The vivisectionists, perhaps, were up late in the night, haunted, sleep not coming to them, but even they barely heard anything that was unusual that night, for there were always such sounds out there along the edge of the city and the wastes beyond.

Screams in the night as though coming from deep below the earth. Somewhere out there in the dark.

Best not to go out in the night.

And then dismissed as nothing more than unquiet spirits from the great graveyard come in with the night to wander the edge.

And Cambysis Maedragone was never seen again.

# CHAPTER THIRTEEN

That tactical tomahawk was gone now.

Gone who knew where with the spectral mage sticky with webs that had faded right before the very eyes of Sergeant Thor. In the last seconds before the attack, the Ranger had only barely heard, recognized dimly through the screaming wounds and consuming fatigue, the sounds of something, someone, behind him. His adrenaline system had crashed after the battle in the Pit. He was running on fumes and most men would have quit by now. But most men weren't Rangers. A long line of ghostly NCOs only he saw, and all the Rangers that had humped rucks from World War 2 to the jungles of Vietnam and all the sandbox wars after that, paying the ultimate price in some cases, wouldn't let him quit.

And Thor had already met *the wizard*, as Sergeant Chris would say. The "wizard" is that limit each man thinks he possesses after which he can go no further. This far and no further. Thor, like every Ranger, had met the wizard and blown past it.

That was standard to pay rent in the batts.

Or as imminent barracks sage and two-DUI-two-stripper-ex-wives PFC Tanner would've put it, "Limits're what ya blow past on your crotch rocket after the first sergeant's weekend safety brief. Gotta add and subtract from the population, contrary to what Top says. That's where all the fun is, Sar'nt. Ain't gonna lie about that."

The wizard...

And if it wasn't the fatigue... it was the pain of his many injuries that competed to distract him as he pushed off once again up the dead alley subtracting his prized tomahawk from his list of assets.

He'd blown past. Killing the materializing, or dematerializing, sorcerer, who looked like a real smug fiend. And he was so tired and wounded, he felt like just hurling the tomahawk on pure bitter rage had exacted some withdrawal the bank of himself couldn't cash.

That was when the wizard of limits, fatigue, pain, and doubts whistled from the shadows telling the Ranger he'd never move again.

He stood there for half a second noting the weapon was gone.

All he'd done was recognize danger was close, and as a

Ranger the next step was easy.

Eliminate the threat.

And that's what he'd done. Like it was automatic. A bodily function.

After he'd dumped the broken Glock on the street, he'd pulled one of two tomahawks off his ruck. Telling himself he'd use that as a ranged weapon as he didn't think he was at his best right now with hand-to-hand combat what with the broken, or fractured, forearm and the blood running down his face and into his eyes.

The injuries were bad but there was no time to figure how bad... so he kept moving. Doing the ruck hobo shuffle and saying goodbye to the wizard to reach the next qualification station like he was back doing the expert infantry badge test, or at Ranger School, or just training in the regiment and paying rent on the scroll that day so you earned the chance to do it all again tomorrow. Run down the hills, hump up the hills. But whatever you do, keep moving and don't stop.

Don't ever stop.

He'd stopped, dully staring at the place where the spectral wizard who'd been just about to lay some magical hate on him had suddenly disappeared, encased in ghostly webs, Thor's tomahawk sticking out of his chest and split sternum.

If Thor had to guess... remembering everything from Kennedy's classes on magic, monsters, the Ruin, and *remember guys, things here IRL might not match my game*, then the bad guy who'd come up on him had been a magic user of some sort what with the almost magical silence and the floating, or flying, through the air. And no visible hand weapons, just fingers splayed and ready to do sorcery, no doubt.

*We know*, they'd shouted at the PFC Ranger wizard.

*We know*, chanted the young Rangers. *Now tell us how to kill it!*

That's all they wanted. They told the PFC Ranger wizard to get on with whatever it was that could kill them next, and more importantly... how they were going to kill it first with nothing but dip, hate, and *Ranger Smash*.

The spectral sorcerer was gone now and so was Thor's tomahawk. Tallied. Accepted. His body was too sore to reach for the other tomahawk. That was the bad side. The broken side. It screamed with fresh movements and to be honest... the blood was still running. How long before he lost too much?

He'd have to get the ruck off to find out and he didn't have time for that.

Had to keep moving... now.

He turned, drawing the Contego because that was all he could handle right now. He was at an edge.

"Been here before..." he grunted and got moving again.

Battles raged up and down the street as the Little Guild attacked incoming gangs of bandits and hard-bitten mercenaries hoping to knife the Ranger in the back from the nearby shadows and take his hard-won prizes of gold and a beautiful diamond. Loud groanings and dusty collapses told the Ranger sniper that traps were tripped and rickety old buildings' central or outer walls suddenly came sliding down on packs of thieves with iron bars and blowguns who'd thought to get close to him. Magic wards got tripped too, for some thieves specialized in magical traps, and suddenly fireballs lit up heavily armored fighters not on guard duty for the wizards and looking to pick up some extra plunder as they followed some opportunist who'd been sure they could take the big warrior who'd won the contest just hours before.

So far... everything was according to plan. And if it kept going that way, what was happening now, all the sudden death and short-lived duels to drive off any larger groups that managed to thread the wards and traps... would pale in comparison to tomorrow morning when all hell broke loose across the city with news of the total looting of the fabled Prize Chest.

"Ain't done yet," rumbled Thor and stumble-humped the burden of the gold-coin-overloaded ruck forward to the rendezvous with Sato just ahead.

# CHAPTER FOURTEEN

THE FINAL AMBUSH SHOULD HAVE NEVER HAPPENED. Not according to the plan. It was in fact, wholly unexpected by the Ranger and Sato.

The fact that three highly competent members of the Little Guild—Manadarc, Sura the Smooth, and Coins— would die at the hands of the sudden appearance of a group of Dark Cultist cutthroats exactly right where they never should have been would be much discussed in the hushed whisper of the guild cant and at taverns like the Bloody Bucket and the Green Cloth where the Little Guild could speak freely of such things and raise their tankards to lost brothers.

The other thieves' guilds would speak of it too, though they would know not the precise details or location, for it was yet one more concerning event in which the problematic cult had once more reared its ugly, seemingly many-tentacled head, again, to disrupt plans and intentions within the City of Thieves.

The Dark Cult was becoming a problem for all. A new player had entered the game that was the city somewhere in the dark when no one was watching.

This time the Dark Cultists appeared after Thor. The blood had stopped flowing from his various wounds for the moment and his strength and mental acuity were returning as the adrenaline spike, and subsequent drop, normalized and he got down to the serious business of survival post the operation on the $X$ and the fade that followed.

He was almost free. Now he'd fade into the city and leave a cold and empty trail. For the night, at least.

Out there beyond the last hideout at the end of the twisting alley of death's length, screams and whistling arrows still penetrated the night as the final bands of usurpers and marauders were done to death by the teams of the Little Guild.

The irony that the fight outside the Pit, here in the late night, seemed more desperate than the winner-take-all battle royale inside the Pit and the Game that had dominated the evening, wasn't lost on Thor.

Out there in other districts beyond this ruined and burnt one of old wounds and forgotten darknesses that lay at the ancient heart of the City of Thieves, fortunes bet had been won and lost.

All of that would pale in comparison when morning came, and the news began to spread of what had really happened.

That was what Sergeant Thor thought as he watched the shadows of the burnt-out old inn with no name from just down the alley, just before linking up with Sato and the other thieves. Sura, Coins, and Manadarc.

It was not uncommon to find bars, markets, or whole hidden and inviolable neighborhoods down some dank, twisting, unremarkable alley just like this one out there across the vast dark sprawl of the City of Thieves. But since this district had fallen to fire and ruin by the total lawlessness that reigned near the Pit, the secret tavern they'd set for the final aspect of the fade had long been burned down in some forgotten firefight between sorcerers and deadly assassins resorting to fire arrows to burn their way free of the trap they'd found themselves in, or so Morfido the Sorcerer who served the guild had intimated had happened some twenty years ago.

Thor stuck more dip in his mouth, worked it, switched the Contego from his off hand to his primary, then pulled the shank and wiped the blood on it off on the thigh of his torn Crye Precisions.

One last push through the late-night, almost early-morning dark and he'd make it to the inn and the secret passage that led out of the district.

Doing his SLLS in the dark shadows as he waited, hearing the fading brawls and battles down the alley behind him and across the nearby streets as more of the gangs realized their prey had slipped the noose, Thor smelled danger in the night.

It was close.

He couldn't quite put his finger on it, where it was at, where it would come at him from... but it was there as he waited in the darkest shadow he could find. His final approach to the rendezvous, just before they'd fade to the hideout, ahead of him in the shadows where no light or torch spilled onto the haunted and abandoned street here at alley's end.

He couldn't see the danger, but he was sure it was there. Somewhere.

He spit dip and studied the old skeletal structure of the burned-out tavern in which there were stairs leading down to a basement, then into an ancient cellar littered with smashed barrels and walled-up corpses never meant to be found but kept there just in case.

They'd reconned this site extensively.

Everything looked on the up and up. But somehow it wasn't.

Everything looked just as it had in the battlefield recons

Sergeant Thor had worked up for the plan to steal the Prize Chest and everything in it.

Once that was accomplished... he was officially "made," as the guild's thieves said in their own colorful patois of languages.

Thor laughed at this. Laughed at how some things survived from the Before where most had not managed to hang on after the catastrophe of the nano-plague that had collapsed and taken civilization down into a long deep dark age.

*Made.*

The lingo from some mob Scorsese movies had survived and thrived among the thieves. Except they said it in Gray Speech mixed with Arabic.

"*Gemacht,*" they would say. And then other thieves would say of one who was made, switching to their ten-thousand-year-advanced Arabic they called *Sandspeak* when discussing what language to trade in, those thieves would reference the "Gemacht" one by indicating "*fi alzili.*"

*In the shade.*

Again, some phrase from the past. But the guild thieves meant one who operated in the dark and was trusted, or *Gemacht,* to do so.

In the shade.

In the shadows.

Thieves and brothers now.

After arriving in the dhow from across the Sea of Riddles and saying goodbye to past companions who were on to other horizons, Sato had taken Thor to the Bloody Bucket and introduced him to the guild contacts there.

They drank and roistered late into the night that night, comely wenches on their knees and one exceptional beauty named Alluria that Thor had yet to capture as the thieves told Thor of all the city offered for one who knew the ways of stealth and a deft hand with a lock.

Treasures could be had in abundance.

The one called Alluria watched him with cool blue appraising eyes and danced away from his attempts to grasp and draw her near for better conversation. She even passed on his intense come-hither-girl no-fail gaze as the night wore on and would continue to do so on many occasions hence, for she served the guild in many of their secret meeting taverns.

He did not think she was made. But that she knew they would reward her with coin if she served them and made sure the beer was cold and the joints of meat the choicest and still dripping with hot juice from the roast pit when served.

She was smart and savvy and knew where her value lay.

Still, he'd caught the fetching beauty biting her lips and appraising his swollen muscles and tall stature. She was a blond beauty with creamy skin and a spritely tongue who liked to laugh and shine. Lithe like a dancer, and at times like an acrobat as she carried impossible trays of drinks through thronging presses of knife juggling, splayed drunken feet, and grasping drunken claws that would try a pinch at her round and shapely buttocks barely covered by a sheer silken veil.

Her taut belly was wrapped in a chain of gold coins. Her ample chest protected, barely, by the filmiest of silk veils. But it was her flashing ice-blue eyes that paled all these other charms when she cast them upon you like some wizard's spell.

That night the thieves Sato leagued with had discussed what Thor might become among them. This step Sato had told the Ranger of in the silences of the night watch as the little dhow followed the stars and long course heading for the fabled City of Thieves.

The Ranger would know that the meeting at the tavern was an interview, of sorts.

"When you reach my city, Warrior, even though you are strong and capable in battle... you will be prey to the jackals that haunt every street and corner. That is the way of the City of Thieves."

Thor at the tiller had merely muttered in the moonlit darkness of the quiet ocean all about them, "We'll see about that."

Hearing the challenge and accepting it as one he would test himself against. For that was his way and even he knew he was at times headstrong about that. And so... he listened to his friend the master thief.

Waves lapped at the side of the boat and the rest of the crew snored or lay deep in sleep as Thief and Warrior took the night watch and kept the dhow on course for their destination.

And destiny.

Sato laughed quietly and then explained how dangerous the city was to all, even the most experienced. Even the most dangerous.

"Imagine a field of battle, Warrior, where the footing is always uncertain, the night is dark, and no one can be trusted. Within the City of Thieves there will not be a flea-bitten inn you can sleep in where you will not be robbed, eventually, for you must sleep, Warrior, even you. There will be no meal you will not taste of and wonder whether it has been poisoned by some enemy you knew not you had acquired that day in your brawling and bloodshed. Even drink offered by a comely and buxom wench dressed in the merest of silks who offers to caress your aching brow and listen to your warrior's tales while she smiles cleverly to herself and watches you succumb to the sleeping syrups she has plied you with for she studied the witch ways of Caspia enough to rob and steal, and you did not know this, for such is the City of Thieves. And perhaps she'll make sure you are sold to either slavers, and there are many of those in the city, or offered to the vivisectionists who serve the wizards that their studies and dark rites may continue without pause due to a lack of corpses or soon-to-be corpses. Some wizards require such, Warrior."

Thor didn't say anything. Only listened and formed his plans. But Sato wasn't dissuading him if that was what the thief thought he was doing. No. Not at all. If anything, he was in fact, *selling* the Ranger. For this was an edge indeed. An edge just as dangerous as vertical ascents and terminal velocity on any hot DZ with tracer fire, high winds, and rocky terrain getting kicked out the door well below minimum jump altitude and good luck having the time to get that reserve deployed should the main fail to deploy.

The City of Thieves. An edge...

In the night, on the distant sea, the moon and stars above by which to steer by, he heard the smaj's dry West Texan laugh.

"*Now you wanna test yerself on Dark Vegas with a heart full of murder in each roll of the dice, Ranger,*" the ghost of the smaj, Thor's constant companion for times such as this, seemed to whisper in the smack of the sails and the groan of the old dhow's ancient worm-eaten hull as the little ship made her way through the night, west of the sun, east of the moon.

"Yeah," muttered the Ranger far away and planning, and Sato knew not why the man had said this thing for the warrior was a strange one indeed.

The thief made a small martial sound as though he were thinking deeply, wondering if all called "Ranger" were as strange as this one.

"You are indeed powerful, Warrior. Your skills in battle are as without parallel as your will. I see destiny upon you and that you are one to lead conquering armies against the strongest cities and take them by your hand and cunning. But the City of Thieves has never been conquered by such as you. Armies, Warrior, armies with legions and war basilisks have gone to the City of Thieves to die with banners waving and armor polished and bright swords glittering."

Sato leaned forward, his voice low and serious, full of gravitas and wisdom.

"Hear me, Warrior. It is not a city that can be *conquered*, as cities are conquered by warlords and empires... it is a place that can only be *survived*, and many times I was certain I would not live to see the setting bloody-red sun over the high western walls of the next day as I dashed through its wild streets, enemies on all fronts. It is, Warrior... the most dangerous place in all the wide Ruin I have ever been, and I say this with no flower."

Thor watched the thief and could see the seriousness on his friend's face. A face that normally had been quick with a warm laugh and an easy friendly smile. Even in the few desperate battles they'd fought alongside the other in the short time they'd known each other, with knives out and dead men flailing and spraying blood, the little thief seemed of a good nature and affable.

And it was the seriousness in his friend's face, the utter sobriety with which what was said, was said, that paused Sergeant Thor for the moment.

Long ago, Thor had made up his mind that there was more to the thief who had become his friend than just thieving. But Sato had played that part of himself close to his chest and the Ranger respected that, for such was the way of Rangers also.

There were brothers, and there was everyone else. And in the hostile environs Rangers operated in, everyone was an enemy.

Surrounded and outnumbered, knee-deep in a pile of expended brass was just Tuesday for Airborne Rangers.

The night wind and the waves slapped at the little dhow, and up there beyond it all the broken-glass wheel of the universe did its slow turn and dance. Careless of the business of warriors and thieves late in the night.

"Do you understand the term... *Death Ground*, Warrior?"

Thor nodded. He understood it as it was used in Sun Tzu's fabled treatise on the art of warfare. *Death Ground* was the worst ground to fight an enemy on. That old Chinese general, Sun Tzu, a tactical and diplomatic genius, had cautioned it was best to leave the enemy a way to flee. If they felt they had no escape, even in the direst of circumstances, if they were on what was known as *Death Ground*, the ground they were likely to be the ones doing the dying on, then they would fight like cornered wolves with no way out but to win or die trying.

Offer them a way out, and even make it a trap, and you and your forces had a higher likelihood of surviving and maintaining your numbers as opposed to fighting cornered wolverines to death and losing a lot of men trying to finish them off.

That made sense to most war fighters.

Rangers understood it all too well. They'd use it against their enemies especially if they'd gotten into a tussle where the odds were disproportionately unfavorable to them and getting worse by the second.

Some third-world hellhole and a pile of expended brass being Plan B. Put a Ranger there and you were likely to get a fight you'd never forget.

A fight for your life, in fact.

Yeah, scare 'em and give 'em a way out.

But Rangers also understood Death Ground another way.

Every battle was Death Ground to a Ranger.

A Ranger didn't want a way out. A Ranger only wanted to kill his enemies. Every fight was for all the marbles because they were always in it to win it and they'd have it no other way.

It must be said twice for this is the way of Rangers and even the creed by which they'd been forged to become tip-of-the-spear killers said so.

*Energetically will I meet the enemies of my country. I shall defeat them on the field of battle for I am better trained and will fight with all my might. Surrender is not a Ranger word. I will never leave a fallen comrade to fall into the hands of the enemy and under no circumstances will I ever embarrass my country.*

Every battle to a Ranger was *Death Ground*. Meaning... someone was gonna die. That's what they were there to make happen. And it was probably gonna be the other guy.

But Thor understood the wisdom of what Sato was saying. The Ranger NCO saw this. Yeah, he could go into survival mode once they reached this City of Thieves, fight his way across the city and keep moving, hitting and fading and getting as much of the city as he could, but for *how long*...?

*How long* until he became enough of a problem, and just being an outsider seemed to identify one as a target to the civilizations of the Ruin who depended on cohesion to fight and hold the thin walls against the dark madness and monsters that was most of the rest of the world, *how long* before the numbers of those who opposed him, deeming him an outsider, could stack enough against him?

*How long, Warrior,* Sato's quiet silence seemed to say as the little dhow continued eastward with the night, heading for that rendezvous where Thor would see indeed... just *how long*?

Constant fights both direct and indirect inside a city he had little intel on and not even a map of, before he made a critical mistake, or just slept, or drank that cold beer the hottie Sato had described to him, and ended up in chains again.

How long before he ended up chained to a rowing bench? Rowing out to sea once more aboard some slave-powered pirate vessel operating into southern and unknown waters?

Or that vivisectionist thing? He'd never heard the word *vivisectionist*, but... he could put two and two together. And that two and two didn't add up to anything good as far as the Ranger could see for himself.

There was wisdom in what the little thief was telling him.

So, there was a way to do this... smarter, not harder.

"What do you have in mind?" Thor had asked the thief in the night as the ancient dhow threaded the wide dark ocean beyond the moon and now navigated by the stars alone.

"My guild, Warrior. My guild is the answer to the problems you will face in the City of Thieves. There you will be under our protection. It is not everything and it would be wrong of me to make it seem so. Even thieves get conned, Warrior. Poisoned, and yes... even murdered. But there will be places where you will be safe as you get your boots under you, Warrior. And this is not to be underestimated on the wild and dangerous bull that is the fabled City of Thieves. My guild will protect you if you render service to our queen. And I am sure... they would welcome one of your mighty talents, for you are no mere warrior but possess many skills a thief prides himself in. But we will teach you more, and better. There will be places to rest, hide, and plan your next steps across the wide trackless wastes to the east, for I see you are headed into that cursed east, or perhaps the frozen north. Some things I see, Warrior, and some I do not, for they are not known yet."

*Places to rest*, thought Thor. Not a bad thing.

Behind the wire. Someplace safe when it was needed.

Even Rangers need to rest eventually. You can fight effectively beyond three days. He'd done that, other Rangers had too, and then some more long days and nights beyond that. But three days with no sleep, minimum calories, and behind enemy lines with everyone gunning for you, that was Ranger minimum standard.

After that... things got bad. When things got bad, eventually someone had to pay the price. And that someone would be him for there was no one else to pay it this far downrange and away from the detachment.

*Edges cut both ways, Ranger*, whispered the ghost of the smaj.

"How do I..." began Thor and took his gigantic hands away from the dhow's tiller, flexing them and checking the healing of the wounds from battle on the Isle of the Fates.

They were healing.

"Join the guild, Warrior?" finished Sato. "It is very easy to join. But to climb, that is indeed another thing altogether."

At that moment, Thor detected an edge. A new edge for him to test himself against.

That was the beginning of how he fell in among the thieves of the Little Guild, and now here, in the dark shadows well past midnight and watching the dark, burnt-out tavern where he would rendezvous in the basement and escape the net trying to close about him after besting the enemies of the Pit, Thor smelled danger.

Perhaps it was just burning narcotic lotus out there wafting away through the threadbare roof and broken walls of the smoke dens.

Perhaps it was death out there in the night.

In five minutes, he would go in and barely escape the trap that came for him with his life. Three guild brothers would die in the ambush the Dark Cultists had planned because someone somewhere down the line during all the planning for the op... or heist as the thieves called it... had *talked*.

But by morning's light the city would be abuzz with news of the great theft of the entire Prize Chest of the Game.

The High Priests would rage.

The eunuchs would covet and spread coin to know just who had done this, and then to have them within their deepest dungeons in chains.

And the wizards... they would plot and do anything for the *yet more power* they constantly lusted after that was the chest and all that it held.

Weapons of great power.

Wands of wonder.

Staffs of mighty magics.

A spell tome thought lost for three thousand years.

Rings, gems, charms, idols, strange and bizarre magical items. And gold, a seemingly endless amount of gold coin in the large chest that was rumored to be larger than anyone ever imagined.

Thor would be *Gemacht*, for it had been his heist planned. *Made. Sune*, as Sato would sometimes say in Sandspeak Arabic. His final test to see if he could be trusted as a thief. A brother. A made man. This was his... operation. His plan. His way.

Adventurer, Ranger, Warrior. And now Thief.

*Gemacht.*

And the reply from other thieves would be *"Fi alzili."*

*In the shade.*

*In the shadows.*

*Brother Thief.*

An edge found, an edge conquered in the City of Thieves.

# CHAPTER FIFTEEN

DOWN THERE IN THE DARK CELLAR OF THE BURNT-OUT old tavern, the cultists came out of the walls as Sato greeted Thor who'd just treaded cautiously down into the basement on a rickety old ladder they'd placed there in the leadup to the heist. Sergeant Thor had followed the Contego blade with the Ranger shank back and ready to bring the death blow as he made his way into the charred ruins making not a sound on what floor remained, then finding the hidden trapdoor that led down into the blackened guts of the place.

He checked for guild marks on the trapdoor just as he'd been taught, then, as Mingo had shown him, scanned and ran his fingers over the surfaces and edges looking for other traps perhaps someone else had come along and planted.

Nothing.

The well-oiled trapdoor opened without a sound and the Ranger stared down into the well of darkness below.

*Stick and move,* he told himself, making a plan in case

someone unexpected was down there. *You're almost out of this.*

He shrugged the overloaded assault pack higher on his back and went down below.

Manadarc, Sura, and Coins were at work on an ancient door that had long been in the ruined remains of the cellar. It had many clever locks that a rival guild had paid the wizards good stolen gold to trap magically for them so they could use this district for their needs and operations without detection.

The Little Guild had spotted the door and markings on a scout for the heist and repurposed it for their needs, leaving it locked and trapped until the time came when they would need to use it. The Brotherhood, the largest guild in the City of Thieves, used the old magicked and trapped door to move about the district around the Pit when they wanted to bring secret cargos in from the docks without the notice of the fat and corpulent greedy eunuchs and their pretty prancing guards always watching everything for their unusually fat and thick bejeweled fingers' cut of the incoming action.

No need to give everyone a cut all the time, most of the guilds had reasoned, and forged their own doors and secret passages into almost every district and alley within the vast sprawling city.

But the Little Guild, the smallest of the three largest thievery guilds, had long known about the secret passage, though because there was a warding owl, a magical creature that watched the high rafters and could not be killed without giving alarm to its master, the passage had never been used by the thieves of Sato's guild. It had just been marked and forgotten mostly.

Until, on the scout, Thor decided to use it.

The guild masters muttered over the deeper, diplomatic, inter-guild politics of such a maneuver, then agreed to the action as if payback for some wrong recently done by the larger guild needed addressing.

It must be said here that although Sato was not the guild's leader, he was not merely among its highest-ranking masters but was universally accepted by all as having the ability to make important decisions in the absence of the guild's true leader... the Queen of Thieves.

Who remained unseen and hunted by almost every faction in the city for reasons that will be discussed later.

Only Sato and Mingo and a few others dealt with the mysterious Queen of Thieves, as much of her existence had to be kept secret in that both the wizards and the other guilds wanted her dead. At any cost.

Teams of bounty hunters, cloaked and helmed, carrying crossbows, were often seen working districts and running down leads on her whereabouts. The standing bounty on her head was two caskets of pure gold bars. An astounding fee even by City of Thieves standards.

But... she was sly and very crafty, and as of yet she'd managed to slip their traps and intrigues and continued to administer Little Guild affairs by secret messenger system with Sato and the other guild masters.

Thor came down into the dank, dark cellar and saw the thin light of the lantern the thieves worked by as they used their bars and picks and detection dusts all across the intricate ancient trapped and magicked door, humming and peering close at its puzzle-locks they were now busy solving by slender probe, crooked pick, a deft hand with fingers that were as keen as ears, or just outright force.

Their costly dusts of detection had dispelled the great thunderbolt spell that had been laid across the door's surface, negating it as slender snakes of electricity fizzled and crawled away and off into the darkness down there in the lower cellar that was the last rendezvous for the final fade from the district.

Open the door and disappear into the port district. That was the plan.

They'd heard the warrior's silent tread coming across what remained of the wreckage on the first floor and down through the dried oak planking that had been the upper basement.

"He's good..." muttered Sura, working at the next lock

along the twisted and carved warding face of the door. "Taught him well in the art of the sneak even though he seemed already naturally adept... but... needs to get better I don't mind sayin'."

Coins answered, "P'rap's 'cause 'e's so strong and large. A warrior's frame indeed that one!"

Coins was called so because he always worked two golden coins across his knuckles and fingers, dancing them as they slithered back and forth end over end, always when he was not busy with some thievery task.

"Bah," muttered Sura and hissed at the damnable door, demanding the light be held closer now that he was to the critical part of removing the poisoned pin, and a deadly poison at that, one that would kill within seconds, deep inside the last lock.

And just as Sergeant Thor came out of the twilight from above, entering the small flickering fellowship of thieves gathered around the tiny lantern and working the problematic door's last lock, the servants of Mistress Hudu attacked as one, coming out of the rubble they'd hidden another door behind.

Quite a trick for their kind...

# CHAPTER SIXTEEN

THE DARK CULTISTS WERE NOT A PART OF THE CITY OF Thieves' messy yet functional organization. In fact they were becoming, more and more by the day, a problem for all three factions continually vying for advantage and power one over the other.

Wizards.

Eunuchs.

Thieves.

And this unseemly lot, worshippers of a great spider-lady god whose name they forbade the mentioning of, had entered the City of Thieves of late about some business that perplexed all who stopped their busy days of honest work and thievery to wonder what new variable this added to the current paradigm of greed, corruption, and endless murder.

The wizards thought the cultists were little more than religious fanatics come in from the Eastern Wastes beyond the vast necropolis that stretched off into unimaginable distances, tired of their nomad tents and dark dusty desert caverns, looking to start a formal base of operations, perhaps even a grand temple to their spider-lady god, or whatever it was they were on about.

That was all. Their leadership could be compromised, or replaced, soon enough, and the wizards could get back to their dark studies and be left alone.

But this must be said here: wizards don't agree on anything. Collectively. There were factions that advocated folding in the Dark Cultists in order to get rid of some of the more venerable holy factions that had grown *too powerful* in the years since they'd established inside the city proper.

These felt chaos was good as long as they came out on top of and in charge of it all.

Or perhaps even using it to destabilize the old religion that was already here and well-entrenched in city life.

A lady-spider god would make a lot of corpses, and the necromancers were always in favor of more corpses, never mind the practically millions lying out there in the shallow dusty east of the city.

When a necromancer is involved, you can never have enough death. Which is why all, even other wizards, regard them suspiciously.

Too much end of the world in that faction, and a frozen wasteland of nether in which there were only squads of skeletons tracking the trackless frozen wastes they believed the world would become, collecting the lost great artifacts of power once everyone was either dead or undead.

Other wizardly factions indicated the Dark Cultists of the lady-spider god should be destroyed here and now, and with all means, money, might, and magic that could be brought to bear. These fanatics were clearly a danger, so said these factions, the more reclusive wizards who preferred to be left to their own deep researches and preferred little change to the cityscape or geomancies therein in order that their pursuits of magical power might further go undisturbed, what with all the magical balances as they were at the current time.

No sense in waking the Eld.

And then... there were the small cabals of wizards, sometimes three to six at a time. Powerful name-level sorcerers with towers, who'd allied in order to wield power over the thaumaturgical councils and covens that comprised the wizards of the City of Thieves.

These... these were open to the possibilities. All of them in fact. They saw that Lady Hudu and her Dark Cultists brought to the city possibilities to shift the balance of power, and a god that was interested in power, and... how they might advantage themselves with it. Claiming alliance, but really intending... manipulation. Always the subtle art of the possible. These small cabals were like the eunuchs and had many tight and secret alliances through the *mandarini*, those who served the chief eunuchs and were eunuchs themselves.

Then... there were the eunuchs also.

The eunuchs were trying to seduce the followers of Hudu with delights of the flesh and purse. "Corruption is the way to go," crooned the high tenor enfanté vizier. "Treat them to grand spectacles of dinner and gluttony at our laden tables. Offer these zealots our finest ladies of pleasure, or even ourselves, then show them how much playing for our side could gain them more of these endless pleasures to consume them, and fat, but not too fat, purses with promises of more. Make these offers wherever you can, boys, to their leaders. Not the mindless blathering riffle-raffle. Can't have everyone having a seat at the table. Unseemly. This has been our way, and it is the way of old. Compromise the leaders and sell out the sheep. That's how I say we will deal with these spider lovers."

And then he licked his fat sausage fingers and watched the towel boys with his greedy pig's eyes practically popping out of his hairless skull as more of everything was brought to his immenseness on that night's feast.

Every night was a feast for the eunuchs.

"So wise," clucked the other eunuchs from over their

heavy and ever-filled goblets, saluting the Enfanté and eyeing him for the slaughter once again. Measuring twice as they did every day, for who knew which day the cut that must be made was coming and the deck of power shuffled.

Perhaps this was their year...

Drowned by a towel boy in his pleasure pool. Hard to do.

Poisoned by some great new delicacies. Harder to do. He had an army of tasters ready at fat hand.

Stabbed to death behind the walls of his crimson-bricked palace, amid the magic hanging gardens on some off-bacchanal night when the assassins could be managed and paid enough to actually dare. Harder, as there were few nights the great whale did not steep himself in grotesque lusts for all to witness deep beyond the personal and heavily armed guard, and the high wall, and the trained best of the best he made sure had his immensely fat back at all times.

It was said he blinded the towel boys with powders so they would not look on the horror of his naked and grotesquely corpulent body. Or be able to stab him to death as he plundered them.

The masters of the three largest guilds of thieves had this to say on the eunuchs' failure to fully recognize the growing problem that Hudu and her Dark Cultists were becoming...

*"They don't know how serious it's gotten."*

The wizards had gained their power because they had apprenticed themselves to power. The eunuchs had gained their power by doing all the little tasks the City of Thieves needed doing, administratively, that the wizards had no time for. Both factions, wizards and eunuchs, had acquired further power by dealing with power. Magic, in the case of the wizards. Or, in the case of the eunuchs who were the administrators of the hot mess that was the City of Thieves, that teeming mass of wild civilization who were those who did their business and lived within the hot, desperate streets, by collecting what taxes they could plunder and maintaining a monopoly on handing out selective violence for what passed as "law." And it was hard to argue that this power, the eunuchs' power, wasn't the equal of the deepest, darkest magics of the wizards on some days.

As for the three leaders of the guilds that specialized in illegal acquisition... they, all three, had gained their power the hard way.

By forging it... *from nothing*.

By starting as the meanest urchins on the lowest streets. Running messages and learning the art of the pickpocket. Apples from the stalls to coin from purses, pouches, and pockets.

A beating if failure.

A chance to learn better if done properly.

By learning every trick of the trade, and along the way a little diplomacy and some warfare, commerce and finance, geopolitics and the price of an egg on Gate Street at any given second, they found their crafts within the guilds and rose to the top.

Deciding what would be done about everything involving the City of Thieves, and even cities distant and unseen, and of course angry wizards and petulant eunuchs and... other, competing thieves.

No guild master took chances with his power. Everything and everything else must be considered and considered twice before launching a heist, or doing nothing and watching, for there were consequences for that too.

Every thief remembered what it was like to live day and night on the streets and starve for failure and dare to dream what better life might lie in someone else's pocket, purse, or pouch.

Thievery started with intelligence collection.

Lesson one, learned by all the masters at the very beginning of their climb up the shadowy rungs of real power, was...

Know who you're dealing with, and what you're getting into, before you reach your hand into someone else's business.

And the thieves knew Hudu and the Dark Cultists were

a far greater danger than anyone suspected.

Wizards had no time for religious zealotry.

Eunuchs didn't understand things like ethics, morals, and codes of honor. Didn't understand that even dark spider-god worshippers had those things even if they were steeped in murder, blood, and poisons.

Ethics, morals, codes of honor...

All those pesky things got in the way of the perpetual snake dance that was power and politics in the City of Thieves, as wizards and eunuchs weighed how best they could turn the newcomers against the other and use them for their own ends. Wizards and eunuchs had no use for what could not leveraged to further their climb to greater heights of power and profligate excess. But what each of those two factions did, sorcery and obscenity, pursued with all the fervor of the most passionate and determined zealot, most of the common folk of the city didn't care for either. Not one bit. No. Not at all.

All the religions practiced in the city agreed on that.

The eunuchs thought the cultists were stupid and ignorant and that no one took them seriously. They said these things to themselves, and they all agreed it was so. Cluck-clucking over their bejeweled wine goblets and eyeing each other for the next dagger they cared to play for the climb upwards among their lot.

They were finished with dark cults. But any street vendor shaken down by the guilds could have told them... *Just 'cause yer finished with the shakedown, don't mean it's finished with you.*

Hudu and her cult were here for a reason. Fact.

Only the thieves seemed to know that the plague of spider cultists that was this new bizarre player, which had gathered first from the sewers, now counted among their members, of late, the houses of some of the most wealthy merchants in the fabled and fantastically rich City of Thieves, Jewel of the South. Their influence spreading invisibly like the silken webs of their spider god from the smelliest fish gutter warehouse to even the inner sanctums of some of the most holy priests of the powerful temples along the main broadways.

Or so it was whispered...

Lately.

The thieves knew things were getting worse day by day and lately they'd begun to go over to the clothmakers' district, weaving through the late-afternoon alleys chanting "*barli*" in the thieves' and assassins' cant so they were not strangled to death by a sudden group of shirtless weavers absently working at their day's work, turned suddenly to what they really did when the hour was late and the moon was fallen beyond the western gates.

*Parley.*

The problem of the Dark Cultists, and Lady Hudu, was getting worse and worse by the day. The thieves knew it to be so.

And now, just as the heist was about to be... successful... out of the walls and black-burnt ruin down in the dark cellar before the magicked and trapped door, the crazed cultists hit the thieves gathered in the cellar like bad meat on the street hits the gut after paying a shaved copper for a meal you should have passed on.

# CHAPTER SEVENTEEN

THOR WOULD'VE BURNED THE LAST GRENADE HE'D brought with him upon leaving the Ranger detachment in the Lands of Black Sleep beyond the River of Night. Or what the world that was, the Before as it was called by the Ruin, had once known as Egypt. A vast spreading desert of ancient tombs and necropolises being consumed by the desert. A land where the necromantic Saur, even though Sût the Undying was dead, still slept and dreamt their dreams of power.

But he'd spent the frag on the were-jaguar at the edge of the black pit to win the One Draw from the Prize Chest.

Otherwise, he'd probably be dead.

The Saur were on hold for now. But they still certainly dreamed and schemed, for the Rangers and their allies had not been able to kill them all. The win had been just smoking their big bad, Sût the Undying himself. A lizard lich pharaoh who was a powerful sorcerer, a cleric to a dark and angry god

188

who was more a devil than anything, and even a warrior that was a legend straight out of the tales of old.

And... he was undead. Hard to kill.

The rest of the Saur had been driven deep under the burning sands down into the cool, carved, dark, ancient tombs and underground cities where they would fester once more. And rise another dark day...

Vandahar had assured the Rangers and their allies of that.

"One should never hope to kill evil, totally," the old wizard had told them. "For then we would have to kill ourselves and erase every beating heart from the Ruin. Why is that, you ask? Because the evil... it was always, and it is even now, in our hearts. Not possessed only by some race by which we measure ourselves better, or defeated in some cause in the moment that seems just... it is always us. And those of us that have chosen not to do evil, as best we can, we can only hope to end it like weeds in the garden, knowing that one summer's morning spent pulling the cursed fiends among our squash and 'maters, is not the job done for all time. The work is ongoing. Always. There will be more weeds of evil tomorrow, and into the garden we must go to see them uprooted and burnt if only to protect tomorrow's harvest. Same as it ever was, same as it ever will be. Tomorrow morning at first light will always come with some new evil."

Then the tall wise wizard blew smoke rings from his long-stemmed pipe as his old and ancient eyes seemed far away on some other matter altogether.

And the old mage was right, Thor had decided in his journeys since.

The Saur and Sût the Undying, a great lich pharaoh, hadn't been the last of it.

Sergeant Thor was beginning to wonder at all of this as the Wand of Wonder detonated her fireball, the resulting overpressure down there in the basement tunnel suddenly crushing Dark Cult skulls as hot flame and blistering heat seared guts and destroyed everything once again.

The Ranger and Sato were fleeing down the dark tunnel beyond the door cracked at the desperate last as the Dark Cultists hit the room like a storm of unclean filth. The screams of their three brother thieves who'd been taken by the Dark Cultists silenced now as the ball of fire exploded, baking, burning, sizzling, igniting, and consuming everything with its plasmatic ignition.

Their suffering ended.

Then the roof of the cellar, blackened and wasted by time, collapsed in a huge thundering finality.

The evil that had surfaced this time, coming through the walls, the evil of the fanatics who worshipped a dark spider god and had plans for the City of Thieves and all who made it home, the evil that had tried to take them all and steal the haul of Thor's prize money from the game, it, or at least its beseeching fanatics on the scene, was blown to bits, burnt alive, and buried by the titanic groan and collapse of a ruin that had once been something else.

Bare seconds after Sergeant Thor entered the shadowy remains of the burned-out cellar of the ancient tavern, seeing the three thieves working by the wan lanternlight at the ancient magicked and trapped rusted door the wizards had set here for the Brotherhood's own passage through the district, the Dark Cultists had struck, flinging their spells and blowguns filled with poison darts and mystical powders at everyone in the room as they surfaced from the rubble like a wild-eyed and many-tentacled thing of horror from the outer dark.

Hissing and clicking their tongues like madness itself to speak in their spider's tongue which seemed a weird and strange unconsidered horror the two who survived would remember later, as it all began at once, destroying the Ranger's plans to fade and finish the heist for this long night.

It was hard to tell how many there were, but even the Ranger had to admit it was a near perfect hit on their part against his patrol base. Even the expert thieves had not known enemies were there, coming out of piles of charred wall and up from the sewer grate that had once fed to the city's byzantine waste management system.

The walls and delicately staged rubble crumbled and there was a series of loud whistling hisses as the cultist blowguns were fired from their hidden ambush, discordant and imminent in their urgency. The three thieves working at the door were struck multiple times and became paralyzed within seconds, their faces freezing into masks of terror as the dawning horror of what was about to happen to them read in their rapidly freezing features.

Sato reacted faster than any and unceremoniously sucked charred ruin to avoid the sudden fusillade of whispering poison darts that hissed and whistled through the sudden battlespace of wan lantern light and clutching darkness being waged by the gloom down there in the cellar. Even the guttering candle inside the lantern itself seemed attacked by dark, mephitic spirits in the next instant and the lights twisted, wormed, and shifted to an insane purple, throwing shadow spiders all along the walls and into the gloom where dozens of red eyes peered hungrily at the ambushed thieves.

This was spellwork by the Dark Cultist enchanters.

Thor caught a dart on the armored pauldron that still remained on his immense frame because the assault pack was there and it would have been too painful to lower the burden and take it up again. The dart strike could be felt through the armor, and it hissed as it disabled some plate and that was a good thing. It tipped off the Ranger some fresh attack was next, instead of the expected escape off the objective.

He hurled the big circular shield up at the last second and caught a dozen more whistling hornets of the poisoned darts which, to him, seemed an impossible thing.

But he heard their rattle-clatter strikes on the other side of the great circular spartan shield as he moved like some titanic hunting cat through the cellar dark seeking not just cover, but a position of strength and superiority to fight back from, now that this was looking more and more like *Death Ground* indeed.

He immediately went into kill mode and slammed the Ranger shank into one of the bare-chested black-greased painted cultists to come for him all at once, plunging the shank right up to the grip and into the ululating man's concave chest.

The murderous cultists chanted and hissed some spidery clickety-clack nonsense about the *Darkness being him and he being the Darkness*. Then the man was dead, thrust from the shank as Thor, bloody, scarred, and beaten, entered a fresh battle like he actually had something left to give, putting wounds and blood and fresh blood and fatigue and limits all behind him.

What else was there to do.

When you're in a fight, then you must fight.

*You gotta get after it, even if it looks bad, Ranger.*

The magicked and trapped door was still blocking the fade, and the room was filled with whispering death and madmen more and more by the second. And even through all this, as Joe would have put it to a bunch of young Rangers just like Thor had once been, as they learned what it would take, what they'd have to blow past, even when the odds were awful and the hopes few and far between, as Joe would have said to them...

*"You gotta get after it. You might only win small or lose big, but if you get after it every day, you have everything."*

Thor slammed the shield into some yapping chungo and caved in the guy's skull, grunting as he did so, "So sayeth the Book of Joe." And selecting the next one he'd kill until there were none left to kill, or he was dead, "Get after it, Ranger!"

Then his roar filled the cellar.

Working the shield and slashing out, he cut his way and shouted what he would to do them, slamming through a room suddenly filled with every form and shape of the Dark Cultists in his charge to reach the door.

Halfway there, two things happened.

One, he linked up with Sato, who weaved his curved talon blades like shiny little murder scythes in the darkness, cutting and slashing as spells magicked psychedelic lights and menacing shadows, the old thief laughing politely and teaching the dead how it was done as he sent them to their deaths, the Dark Cultists who dared approach his good-natured fury, sending them back to the shadow realms they so desperately thought they coveted.

"Come get some!" shouted Thor, kicking one and slashing another who screamed and spun away, spraying blood all over his fellow ululating, hissing, clickety-clacking-like-a-spider's-eight-legs-articulating mad cult members who would press them and stab them a thousand times if they could.

Many died against their defense, but still more pushed through their secret ambush sites. And beyond that, humpbacked, many-legged horrors with large red eyes glared the murder they would do when they could get into the dank little cellar at these who dared oppose the wrath of the High Priestess Lady Hudu.

"It seems that way, Warrior!" hummed Sato thoughtfully as he disemboweled a cultist with a terrific cut, then danced up to the dead man suddenly and quickly, lightly even, and slit the bicep of another man covered in the shining greasepaint the cultists affected for ambush battles and dark rites. Just as that one intended to brain Sato with a light iron mace carved with runes and headed with a pulpy carved spider's body, its eight sturdy legs pounded into crushing flanges, the thief rewarded him with a dangling and useless arm.

Now the man's arm would never work again, and the terrible mace dropped uselessly from his grip as he screamed in horror at what had been done to him.

"You must always protect your attack," laughed Sato at the stunned man, teaching, then deftly shot out the off-hand blade and carved a thin little slash on the man's neck artery.

Dying now, lifeblood pumping out, the man stumbled away from the battle press, hissing that same chanty clickety-clack the rest did about the darkness and being one with it.

"Finish the door, Sato!" Thor shouted, rebounding more attacks with the broad shield he dealt out savagely at the pressing cultists, his fractured arm screaming every time he did so.

But there was no other choice. He fought the waves of nausea and pain, turning them into anger and rage, intent on seeing the cultists all dead even if he never made it out of this cellar alive.

"Got your six. Once it's open..."

Thor heaved out raggedly with the Ranger shank, roaring titanically down there in the close dark gloom of the cellar that had suddenly become a slaughterhouse all at once, splitting a cultist's skull.

"... we'll pull our wounded out and fight our way up the tunnel."

"*Hai*, Warrior," said Sato crisply, and as suddenly as his deadly talon blades had appeared, they were gone and a single pick flashed from the folds of the thief's sash and he went to work on the final lock, confident the warrior he'd only just recently met would protect his back or die trying.

Sergeant Thor had done so before. They had been through a lot together in that small space of time.

Nothing was sure to Sato, but he had come to expect great things from the warrior called Sergeant Thor. And now he trusted his life to his comrade as he bent to the lock, working fast to spring it and heave the door aside so they could escape.

But one look back, one glance over his shoulder as a pin was pushed and the hook of the pick scratched at the bar to pull it aside, as Dark Cultists pounded at Thor's impenetrable shield, massing more and more by the second despite the killing blows traded in return for their efforts, told him they would not be rescuing their own.

Thor grunted and raged at the savage blows being thrown against his shield, his teeth clenched and his body breaking out in rivers of sweat that ran channels through the dirt and blood across his huge triangular upper body.

That was when Sato spotted the giant spider now biting its own in half and tossing the pieces aside to reach them. It was a looming, terrible thing that dripped poisons from its large salivating fangs.

And now there was another of its kind, closer than the other and already in the cellar.

"The dark lady has sent one of her shadow beasts, Warrior. Watch the ceiling."

Thor, intent on deflection and killing where he could, looked up and saw a giant black widow draped upside down from what remained of the charred and burnt ceiling. This one's fangs dripped deadly poison as its legs, all eight of them, delicately, and seemingly impossibly, scrabbled forward even as thick webs spun down from its rear and hauled up poor Sura, frozen and now mummified in webs, his horrible, muffled screams not to be denied. The other hideous beast now trying to get at the lone survivors fighting a desperate defense before they escaped the ambush the Dark Cultists had set for them in the ancient ruined cellar of death.

"It's open!" shouted Sato, suddenly shifting to a stance and pulling with all his might at the dense vault door's mass, the barrier the wizards had placed here to deny all but themselves and the Brotherhood. He grunted breathlessly, "Help me, Warrior!"

Thor pushed his shield forward in a great heave, backing off and stumbling many away from them, spun like a whirlwind twisting, grabbed the massive door, and heaved at it so hard it slammed open on a quick rusty whine and thunderous *bang* that resounded out over the chanting, hissing, and greedy clickety-clack of the giant spiders, and perhaps even others of their kind coming, further off in the darkness of the ambush tunnels the Dark Cultists had secreted here.

"We cannot save them and save ourselves, Warrior!" shouted the thief, taking in the desperation of their situation.

"Run!" shouted Thor.

"Go now, Warrior! I have a gift to give from the queen!"

From the folds of his robe, Sato produced a carved baton with the laughing head of a jester, insane and mad and leering.

"Stolen from the treasuries of the Great Fazaz himself," Sato said proudly. "A wizard without peer."

Thor pushed through the door and hustled down the dark passage into the deeper darkness that lay ahead. Behind him, madness.

Sato stepped backward quickly and spoke the words to activate the magical device his guild had fairly stolen. A wand that generated random magical effects. Sometimes useful. Sometimes ridiculous. Sometimes fatal to the wielder.

"Let this time not be butterflies," muttered the thief, aiming the mad jester's-head baton at the press of wild-eyed cultists and lurching spiders readying for their next push.

Then he shouted the secret word taught him.

"*Shazaaam!*"

And a stream of the most beautiful butterflies ever seen thundered like a waterfall, exploding outward over the press of mad zealots and ravening spiders.

There was confusion. For a moment.

The thief cursed and gave more ground, dancing back up the passage into the dark Sergeant Thor had gone ahead in. Sato shook the fiendish little wand as though that would make it do something better on his behalf than it had done so far.

"*Shazaaam!!*"

A moment later the blast responded and the burning spiders screeched as they were engulfed by a rolling and growing fireball of flaming death. The little Dark Cultists among the heaving giant spiders going to their shadowy salvation.

Sato turned and ran, catching up with the lumbering and badly wounded Thor whose legs were beginning to give out as the pain could no longer be ignored.

The fiery blast pressed at them from behind as everyone and everything was roasted alive inside the inferno the cellar behind them had become. And the wind was driven from them, blowing them forward as the blast sought somewhere to go in the tight space. Their ears popped and it felt like their skulls cracked open and their brains were leaking out as the whole world became heat and pressure, bending reality and testing its limits.

Both found themselves in the tunnel dark, later, facedown in the char and ruin as behind them the cellar, or what remained of the burnt-out old tavern above, collapsed down on those that had tried to ambush them and take their stolen prize.

And who had slain their brothers in the process.

Coins. Sura. Manadarc.

Dead. Gone.

But the final ambush had failed.

Sato and Thor got to their feet, unsteadily, and faded off the X.

# CHAPTER EIGHTEEN

THE TEMPLE OF POESIDIUS, THE EVER- SEA GOD FROM Accadios, was once the boast of the Fish Market district a hundred or more years ago.

But who keeps count of relentless time between the desert and the deep blue sea and all the devils in between?

So it is said in the shadows of the City of Thieves.

Coin in heavy stamped gold had been handsomely spent once and long ago by a notable pirate king who no one remembered even though there was a badly kept shrine just past the fortress-like main gate that led into the district. A pirate king who was the offspring of a maid lost at sea and a deep Tritonian who had captured her foundering ship, taken her off to his lair, and there spawned the child who would one day be the pirate king no one remembered anymore.

Such is the way of pirates...

Then that cruel deep Tritonian had set the then-child, someday forgotten pirate king, adrift in a rowboat, keeping the woman among his vast harem near the reef islands of Al-Aqaba near the mythical island of Ceylos the Lost.

Or so the rumors said.

Stories get suspect south of the City of Thieves, for many who go that way, along the southern routes, never return. And those that do... are never quite the same.

That long-lost forgotten pirate king had prospered in the times of pirates against Accadion strike fleets raiding the ancient shipping runs bringing the fine silks and spices of the Eastern Ruin beyond the end of the Lands of Giants, a largely wild and unknown place, and the city-states there that supposedly lay at the edge of an endless great Sea of Typhoons. Once the silks and eastern goods reached the City of Thieves and profits were made, they were then hauled north by coastal hauler up toward Sûstagul and, from there, distribution along the coasts of the Great Inner Sea.

The trade of these current days paled in comparison to the trade of that age, often recounted by the sages as the Golden Age, among the great city-states of the Eastern Wastes that were now lost, ruined, or haunted.

Now was only a trickle of lone merchants or small fleets under the paid protection of the Scarlet Brotherhood. Nothing so great as the ancient merchant fleets of old and the fabled navigators who were like the heroes of those long-lost days.

But as has been said... that was long ago during what many sages specializing in the history of the Ruin had called the Golden Age. When the great city-states of the Eastern Wastes flourished before the stars fell and before the area was hit, rifted, and became a strange and mysterious place where some said time didn't work as it was supposed to.

Before the Eastern Wastes were called the Eastern Wastes, they had once been a place of mythic heroes, terrible titans, and great deeds done recorded in song and stone.

One can still go see the decaying carvings on the faces of titanic ruins crumbling into the haunted sands. And, if one is quiet, still hear the ghosts out in the desert winds singing just the harmonies of the lost fables, or so the mad who wander those forgotten wastes say.

Strange lost magics abounded during the Golden Age that was, and, in the time of the now, occupied much of the research the great wizards of the City of Thieves spent their time researching, either by exploring the lost libraries and the many dangers that came with such places, or sending out parties of reckless adventurers to obtain some scrap or artifact of lost knowledge, hoping to reach the fabled heights of power that had once made the wielders of magic like the gods themselves.

And it was in these times, almost at the end of or just beyond that Golden Age, when that lost-to-history pirate king had paid properly stolen gold in vast sums, and even a chest full of the fabled pink pearls of the jade city called Lai Pan, which was once a great and fabled seaport in the east along the Sea of Typhoons until it was destroyed by the Greater Morkoth Aahahbagolish'xxeryx the Grasping.

One of the Eld who lived beneath that sea and had surfaced to seek some vengeance on the city, dragging it and all who lived there beneath the waves in one single night.

Some sages say such a place no longer exists or never did and the stories of Aahahbagolish'xxeryx are fables told only to frighten children and sailors. Others say if they are true, then it would be best not to go to such a place as lost Lai Pan.

And so... it is lost, either way.

But none of that mattered anymore, tales of fabled kraken and lost sea kings gone off to pirate the fabled lands beyond the end of the world never to return ever again, of pirate kings whose hoard was spent to build, and perhaps some of which remained hidden within, the walls of an epic edifice that defied all reason for building, and even less reason for being built in the location that it was built in... the Fish Market.

The Temple of Poesidius.

There in the market among the guts and fish heads and weathered folk who made their living out there in the seas beyond the lighthouse and the great sea wall, sometimes going out at dark before dawn and never coming back, having been gotten by the maids.

The fish market district.

The Street of Scales.

A place so... smelly and reprehensible, that even the lowest wizards would not build the meanest tower to consolidate their power within its district, or even anywhere near it. Nor did the two main guilds, the properly recognized guilds and not the Little Guild, neither would bother to run their rackets there where the fishes were gutted and the heads sold for scrap, a cheap stew perhaps, and neither guild would maintain an interest in goings-on within the stalls and along the fishgut-littered way that was the old fish market district and into which a major roadway didn't even run, if you can imagine such a lowly place.

Small mean gangs ran the district on behalf of the locals, and others from other streets were often beaten and looted if they didn't keep to their fish-getting business and be timely about it on top of it. The whole district usually went quiet by three hours after noon due to the early-rising deep-sea fishing required.

The high families, in other finer, more genteel neighborhoods, tittered that they could not be bothered with such a low place, and so servants were sent for the fine cuts of bluefin tuna, fresh oysters for great bacchanals, clams for late-night spicy broths and crusty breads, and of course the lobstrosities and other delicacies that could be boiled and dipped in spiced butters that found their way to the market from the fishing fleet that went out in the morning dark.

The great temple of ever-angry Poesidius lay at the end of the stall-lined market street known as the Street of Scales. The street hedged by the docks that served the fishing fleet and not the main harbor that served merchant ships trafficking the city. The *proper* harbor, for merchants and great warships, was farther south and behind the Hannibal Fortress and her cyclopean seawall that had been extended out into the water all the way to the Island of Pathos and the great light tower there that had been placed by the Accadion emperor Garius the Mad in centuries long past.

It was said that a thousand dead prophets had been sacrificed by Garius the Mad so that his masterpiece lighthouse might give true light to the entrance through the rocks and treacherous sand islands that lay along the shallow approach to the main harbor. Those wise men were now walled up in the saltwater catacombs beneath the crumbling ruin of the lighthouse that was still manned, and there was said to be a shark cult that considered this horror a holy place to them and theirs.

And of course, Garius the Mad's fabled lighthouse was

haunted, and either the workers who worked there stayed, growing distant and silent with the years, finally disappearing some long storm-tossed night, or didn't last long at the Great Mirror, as the tower of light was known to some.

It was a beautiful structure though, ornate and complex with fine gardens that hushed and whispered all about the small island beyond the harbor in the warm offshore breezes that beat the coast.

On the other side of the Street of Scales within the fish market district lay the fishermen, and the mongers, in a warren of neighborhoods that had been built ramshackle and stacked up against the great wall that protected the city within. There was only one gate here, and a great one indeed, adorned by two excessive carvings of some forgotten tuna god. The tuna gods were thought to be relics of some probable Altantari occupation in the long-ago and unremembered past of the city. Each tuna god had once been sheathed in hammered-leaf gold, their great scales pounded and beaten from the purest metal the Mines of Saphir could produce beyond the Shadow Hills deep within the Eastern Wastes.

And, once and long ago, each fish god had had one great emerald that had been its eye. An emerald that must have defied imagining for any such valuable stone to occupy such a great construct in such an epic city. But now the gemless sockets of the tuna gods were all that remained in the misty night as Sergeant Thor staggered toward the cyclopean gate.

Sato, just ahead and on point, saw payment to the night watch there to forget that the two strangers in the night had ever been this way. The guards near their fire said nothing and returned to watch the mist and the harbor below, unconcerned about thieves, more concerned about the ghosts of the murdered coming out of the sea as they sometimes did.

Thor stopped, leaning against the walls of the gate, feeling the blood in his boots thick and viscous, and stared up at the eyeless socket of one of the tuna gods. It must have indeed been a great emerald, for that empty socket had left a gaping pit the size of a small mortar crater.

And of course, the beaten shimmering gold must have been something to see as it sparkled brightly on sunshine feast days when the great white fleets of the Atlantari came back from their distant rovings and far-off conquerings, pennants flying and broad sails buffeting, handsome Atlantari warriors shining in silver polished armor. That must have been something, thought the Ranger as he struggled to stay on his feet and stay conscious, his mind drifting to better days than this one.

Then he looked down at the state of his blood-covered body, the heavy pack on his back no longer even felt, just a dull aching numbness that had replaced the pain and weight. But that was nothing. Every infantryman knows this stage. When the ruck no longer hurts because everything is just numb, feet, shoulders, back, legs, neck. And all that must be done is to keep moving forward until the halt, or you die.

"March or die..." he grunted, his voice a dry hiss of a croak. He needed water.

Still, it must have been beautiful. All that gold had long been peeled away and lost. It must have been...

The Ranger was on the move again as Sato went forward, down the slope of the street away from the gate and toward the silent and dark fish stalls.

Sergeant Thor followed, telling himself he was *almost there*.

Entering the fish market, the two thieves, Thor and Sato, made their way down the hill along the lone roadway that cut a straight steep roll down to the docks before hooking right. Sticking to the shadows, and watching the other shadows along the quiet avenue, they continued on to the looming gigantic temple of Poesidius the Ever-Angry at the end of the street. Up against the great wall of the City of Thieves here where it doglegged out into the waters along the point, or more accurately the wall of the Fortress of Marius the Great, a long-ago Accadion general who'd administered the city and fought campaigns against the dog-men of Ophir.

The Wulfen Legions as they'd been known in the day. The smaller fortress had been erected to house the Seventh Accadion Legion that had never returned from the final campaign against Ophir and the intended sack of Mount Sariyam Temple of the Wulfen.

Now the eunuchs used the once-noble fortress to house their gangs of tax collectors and their squadrons of bright and pretty tax enforcers to do the hard dirty work of robbing by force those who would not be robbed by edict.

The Temple of Poesidius towered over everything in the fish district and even reached higher than the walls of the Fortress of Marius the Great.

Which in the brilliant old tactician's day would have never been allowed.

But that half-Tritonian pirate king had had enough plundered gold and magical artifacts to buy what he wanted from the pouty-lipped Troodo the Fancy, chief eunuch of the day, who cared not for common sense and proper defense but only that his personal coffers might be vastly enlarged, for his debauchers and debaucheries were great even by current standards, which were still quite high.

And what the forgotten pirate king had wanted...

For he was neither devout nor grateful to the angry sea god. He had been rescued by sea-nomadic Mandala Talon Priests after being set adrift by his mad Tritonian father, and then raised in the ways of those perpetual seafaring nomads who were the fabled originators of the talon blade itself, and the keeper of its arts and the dark secrets they guarded.

That he owed Poesidius everything he'd acquired by thievery and bloodshed, which was much... that was just a nice story told to everyone about why the wildly successful pirate built the temple right there, where it was more like a fortress and contained a small private harbor all its own that was covered from the eunuchs' fortress by the temple itself, and so was the approach on certain moonless nights.

You see, the wizards and thieves might shun the district. But the eunuchs never minded how dire and desperate the locations were where they sent their collectors and enforcers. Every ship was watched, and even if you were a pirate... well, you got taxed too. A lot, because of course you were successful. As a pirate, and a pirate king at that, you were either successful, or you were dead down there with the maids.

So you paid, because eunuchs were government and government is greedy.

So...

The temple blocking the Fortress of Marius the Great's view of the harbor, along with the aid of the street gangs who beat any who didn't live there, was a great way to avoid the tax and get into the city what you didn't want every wizard with a scrying stone, or a watching pool, and the thieving eunuchs, knowing about.

For the Temple of Poesidius had had ancient spells lain over its stones and wards across the curving seashell pinnacles where bronze-turned-green sea monsters and silver tridents were carved and intertwined like strange homunculi that were like gargoyles but of the sea, like the dreaming marid genies out there in the deep underwater canyons... and the spells defied the watching stones of wizards and the watchful eyes of the tax collectors who were everywhere at all times, even darkest midnight.

Much of the Ruin's wealth passed through the City of Thieves, oh the irony of that. But of course, when you think about it, why wouldn't it.

And so, the Scarlet Brotherhood of Pirates had taken over the protection of the temple and used it when they needed it to do what they did and didn't want anyone else knowing.

And when it wasn't being used for smuggling or other such activities, then it was merely the temple that did little business, for its lone drunken priest was a craven drunk, so bad that it must be said twice, and whose healings were more dangerous than they were helpful.

Or so it was whispered...

And it was into this temple, high green marble columns

still capped in gold leaf, for superstitions kept the lowest of thieves from daring to peel away what they could, that limping, grunting, bleeding Sergeant Thor and deft and quiet Sato made their way, passing across the rose-colored marble portico, hauling desperately for the great bronze door turned green by the sea and salt long ago.

High above under the great porch of the entrance, beyond its massive steps, aquamarine censers and thuribles shifted in the merest breeze off the ocean where the mists mingled with the sea smoke that came from these hanging pots and bowls of flickering flame.

Sato pushed the door open, and they went inside to the darker darkness, where they found the priest talking to himself on the empty benches, mumbling prayers he no longer believed and wondering if he ever had. A huge jug of the cheapest wine, almost empty and ripe, near at hand as his gravelly old voice wailed out the unaddressed wrongs done to the few parishioners that bothered to come and seek his comforts.

These were his prayers, and he cared not who heard them for he was convinced no one did. He sobbed and then screamed at his stone god.

Into this came the bleeding warrior and the thief.

"Priest, the hour is late and we have desperate need of your services," said Sato, his voice calm within the great empty beauty of the ancient temple. "My brother is dying."

# CHAPTER NINETEEN

"YOU ARE SAFE HERE, WARRIOR... FOR NOW," WHISPERED Sato and eased the giant wounded Ranger down onto a cold stone bench in the shifting aquamarine light coming from deep within the censers drifting in the high reaches of the Temple of Poesidius.

The deep silence of the night beyond the massive walls of the temple lay across the city like a heavy blanket that could not be shifted.

There had been too much death this night, even for the City of Thieves. And the wounded Ranger had been the cause of most of it.

Above Sergeant Thor, up there in the shifting shadow-and-sparkle aquamarine architecture of the temple of the angry sea god, among the twisting sea serpents and great carved pink shells, the light shifted and made it seem as though the whole inside of the temple, the immense structure of the place, had been contrived so that the worshipper... was under the seas.

The temple was silent save for the ragged voice of the drunken priest mumbling his anger at his god for doing nothing to ease the ills the Ruin had thrown at humanity, or the wrongs done to himself.

And then, as Thor's eyes closed, he heard the soft sure steps of Sato's sandals. He didn't feel the pain at all now. He was slipping into the ocean up there... and it was warm. Warm like a bath...

The Ranger sat with a heavy fall. No, he fell over. He'd already been sitting and now he was lying on the floor as the warm sea came and flooded all around him, pleasantly drowning him in its salty embrace.

He knew he would pay for how far he'd gone past his edge, his limits...

He'd been here before.

The recovery would be brutal. If he lived...

His boots were wet with his own blood. He could feel it drooling out onto the floor of the beautiful temple. The place was... amazing. Easily... one of the... wonders...

He couldn't even shrug out of his assault pack. With some difficulty he sheathed the bloody shank, wiping it on his Crye Precisions, just barely. Losing consciousness for a second as he did so and listening to it clatter to the marble of the temple floor.

He should... sheathe...

His hands were caked with blood and his assault gloves were tattered and done for. Finally. Whether that was the nano-plague doing its invisible work on every piece of modern gear and tech from ten thousand years ago before the world was called the Ruin and it wasn't a Bronze Age hellhole filled with monsters and magic, or whether it was just the hard usage he'd put them through along the way from the Savage Lands of what was once France to now halfway down the Arabian Peninsula in a place unreliable maps marked as the City of Thieves... who knew anymore.

He could hear Talker, or, no, Vandahar telling him this city was a jumping-off place for expeditions to cross the gulf and enter the Lands of Black Sleep to plunder the tombs of the lich pharaohs and the Saur priests.

But it was so much more.

Violent.

Angry.

Dangerous.

Beautiful.

Breathtaking.

Savage in its extremes.

New in every twist... and turn...

He must've passed out.

Passed out when he tried to unstrap the sturdy shield

that had taken all manner of blows and broken his forearm in the process. Broken it more than it was already broken.

He must've passed out when he thought to do so...

Now, assault pack off, Sato was getting him to his feet and leading him into an inner cloister to the right of the great looming statue that was the god's embodiment in the main sanctuary.

To Thor, the stone colossus that loomed up from the bronze-cast waves to the heights of the sea... or ceiling... its features were like those of the Sea Elves he'd seen carvings and statues of, lost in the Sea of Riddles.

The Atlantari, back on the Isle of the Fates.

The next thing he remembered was the great, fat, messy, wild-haired, reeking, drunken priest standing over him.

"He's dead," the middle-aged but wrecked priest growled raggedly, and began to sob and wipe snot from the great red blossom of his large nose. He was fat and his hair was wild and gray. But... his eyes sparkled like dark gems full of swift fury and sudden rage. His garb was dirty, and even in his swoon Thor could tell the man had thrown up on himself at some point in the evening. There were bits and flecks of it in his beard and on his fine robes.

Or what had once been fine.

Now the symbols of his office were threadbare and the stitching to the ancient cryptograms was beginning to fray and come undone.

He smelled of his sick too.

"*Hai*, you drunken lout," said Sato crisply, and struck the priest swiftly with a deft backhand. "Dead he should be, faithless pig... but he is not... yet. This warrior's will is greater than the death demons that come for him even now. Now... work your spells and magics. Make your bargains, pray that he will swing his sword again, or my brothers will haul you out to the deeps where whispering demons wait for your soul and send you down to your damned sea god. *Hai*?"

Sato's voice had reached martial thunder and crescendoed at the last, bouncing and reverberating across the innards of the sea god temple.

The struck priest wept anyway and wiped a great tapestry of snot from his nose, then heaved his wicker-basketed jug of cheap wine up to his great fat and chapped lips, intoning a great gusty gasp at the end of his long gulp instead of some healing prayer that might save the dying Ranger at the last.

The incompetent priest grasped Thor's broken arm and indelicately hauled it up.

Thor grunted in rage and forced himself not to pass out as he reached up to strangle the wreck of a human being with his other bloody glove.

He was sure now one of the fingers on it had been broken. But he would...

The priest, with Sato's aid, firmly resisted Thor's strangling grasp and forced the bloody hand down on the sacrificial altar where once great tuna and dolphins were sliced up and offered to the angry sea god for favor in fishing, war, and perhaps a child.

As Thor's eyes fluttered at the intense pain from the priest's indelicate probing and ham-handed handlings of his broken body, he smelled dead fish and saw mermaids up there in the frescoes along the ceiling, watching and waiting to drag him under like they'd tried to at the battle for the citadel along the North African coast.

The Lost Coast.

The fat, drunken priest was suddenly sober-eyed and suspicious as he babbled an incoherent sentence to the thief.

"So, we're gonna sacrifice him now and perhaps the pool will reveal the wreck of some great treasure ship then..." the priest rumbled.

Sato growled, and it was a frightening sound.

"No! No, you stupid excuse for a man of faith. You must heal him now before he goes too far into the night realms. We want him to live."

The priest dropped the jug, and it smashed despite the wicker basket that protected it.

"I was afraid..." He burped loudly. "... you would say that."

Then the priest sighed and wiped spent tears and drying snot from his face.

"I cannot do this."

The next growl that came from Sato was like that of some night predator out there in the dark warning that you were intruding on its hunting grounds. Its kill. And... that you would be next. The growl trailed into his next sentence.

"You must, priest."

There was no *or else*. But it was definitely there.

"It is impossible for me!" shouted the angry priest, seemingly oblivious to the dangerous ground he trod on and the predator he stood next to.

Sato's blade came out as the thief pivoted and flashed the cutting edge of the talon, landing it right where it would kill on the priest's jowly neck.

"Then..." he said in a low hushed whisper, "I will cut your throat myself and save the guild the long row out to the deep trench to send your fat body down to your careless sea god. Say the prayers now. Make the healing, call in your markers, do you understand? If he dies... you die, priest."

The priest began to shake, got sick, and fell to the wet ground, for the floor was always wet and cold in the Temple of Poesidius.

Down on the ground, heaving still, the ruined priest bleated out his tale. Sobbing at first, growing cold and stony as he went along as though too dead to relive all the pain and horror again this night, for he had already done so in the hours of drinking in the dark shifting aquamarine light alone. As he did every night. It was a sad tale, and a wretched one it was indeed.

"A priest in the Accadion Navy I was once. An expedition ship. We went as far as Kungaloor... then, though we never should have... beyond the end of the Ruin. All the way to the Islands of Death. They are real. I have walked their cursed shores, thief, and wished ever since I never had.

"Lost the ship... we did. A hundred of us went into the waters and the sharks were hungry that night and for the next three that followed as we bobbed on the surface of the deep beyond the tell of maps. Oh... how hungry they were. How very hungry. They begged, thief. The sailors I served begged that our god, my god, would see us to a safe harbor as we clung to wreckage and paddled toward a horizon with no harbor, no ship, no sirens and their songs to guide us by. They begged, and I prayed. Oh, how I prayed. Prayed prayers for weather and wind and fair sailing... the ones that had always been heard before. The ones I learned. The ones I believed, for that was what I do... did. Healings, too. I never was good at such, but I did it as it was my oath to care for gashes and cuts and sometimes the scurv... or even the southern plagues and pestilences, if they were less than they could have been."

The fat faithless wretch got to his knees and stared up at Sato.

"I had faith then, thief. The faith I had when the flaming arrows hit the sails and the men screamed and the decks were awash with our blood in battle. And other times too. Even... even then, there, beyond the edge of the Ruin... even as the sharks and the other... the darker... the darker beasts of the deeps... the unholies that make the seas their home, the home of him, our god... even as they took the crew one by one and the complement of the *Odyssey*, good and fine ship she was, went screaming down into the roil and froth of how a shark will take ye. Biting... the death roll. Then... drag ya under 'cause it's a devil. All sharks is devils."

The priest began to crawl away from the altar, waving his hand about for some other bottle he'd left on the floor that perhaps he might draw from for a little bit more of the poison that had taken everything from him.

His shaking hand wavered even as he did so.

"I care not for your tale of woe, *borracho*," hissed Sato, spotting the bottle the man was making his way toward.

Sergeant Thor heard all this from far away. His blood running out onto the cold, salt-smelling block of an altar they'd laid him on. His eyes were closed, or he'd gone blind. He could no longer see either way.

The swift, staccato strikes of Sato's sandals crossed the cold wet marble ahead of the crawling priest who would have sold his soul right there to reach the three-quarters-empty jug first.

The priest wailed as Sato snatched the jug away and hurled it against the wall of the temple with a savage grunt. Then the thief deftly backhanded the larger man and sent him sprawling across wet marble, tumbling into the salty block where bloody tuna had been offered up to appease the rage of a sea god. The wretched priest bellowed at the wrong done him, raging at all the indignations and injuries... ever.

Sato followed the great disgusting pile of a priest and hauled him to his feet by his filthy collar, slapping him repeatedly, again and again, threatening death and worse in his terse martial speech.

"I care not what you do to me!" cried the priest. "I care not. Do your worst! If he dies, then he dies! All men die! *All* men die! All of us... *die*, do you hear me! Who is this one that he should be different than the rest of us cursed to try and to die all the same? We are all, all of us, lost sailors adrift in a sea of faith, being consumed by the demons of the deeps. Who is he that he is different?"

So cried the Priest of Poesidius.

"He is a warrior!" shouted Sato suddenly and right back in the fat man's face, his usual patience and discipline lost in the moment. "And he saved my life and the lives of others, and I will do so for him for we are brothers, priest, brothers to the bloody end. Say your prayers, or sell your wretched soul to the nearest devil you can find that will buy it for cheap... but he lives, or you die *this night*, and badly. And if that is not enough to scare you, know that I am from the east and of a clan that once journeyed into the Hells to get their revenge against a foe who did us a great injustice. Thirteen masterless warriors entered those realms of death to see their blood oath done against the evil demon Goru. I will make that journey, idiot, on your behalf, and I will find you in the hell they have placed you in for your faithless sins. Then I myself will drag you to the worst one I can carve my way to even if I have to slay a thousand devils. Do you understand, priest? I will take you to the worst hell of all the hells if the warrior dies."

Cold. Shocked. Silence. Followed.

"I do..." whispered the wide-eyed priest hoarsely and now suddenly more sober than he had been in his drunken endless pity and probably more so than he had been in many woeful pitying drunken days if not months. "I believe... I do, Master Sato. I know of your deeds and know that you would go this far to see my end more miserable than my life has been since the seas beyond the end of the world where I lost my faith in a god I still serve. But..."

Sato was in the priest's face, his visage grim, cold, uncaring, sure, death itself. His teeth clenched in a contained promise of titanic rage. Fists bound up in the filthy robes of the unclean priest he could have easily throttled at that very moment had he so chosen.

"But... *what*," hissed Sato in the great vast silence of the gigantic temple beyond the intimacies of the altar of good luck at sea.

The priest trembled. Shaking.

"We must use the eels... for my prayers are no longer heard."

Sato spoke slowly. "Then use the damn eels, idiot."

# CHAPTER TWENTY

His name was Caius Poesidius. He had, once long ago when he was a young and slender man of faith who'd intended to share the news of his god... taken this name, the name of his god, back in fair and sparkling Accadios.

But that had been long ago.

Now a fat, wild-haired wreck, a great bulk of a ruined priest, his barf-stained robes wet with the seawater on the floor of the sea god's ornate and empty temple, he dragged, with the help of Sato, the immense half-naked battered and bruised body of the strange blond-haired, blue-eyed warrior into the Pool of Slyphira and Silvanyia.

The holy eels of Poesidius himself.

The pool lay in front of the tall statue of the sea god that reached into the very aquamarine heights of the "undersea" temple. The god's carved physique only half hidden by the delicately worked-stone net draped over his cut pecs, ripped abs, and broad shoulders that supported the great pinnacle blue dome of the edifice. A massive trident Poesidius raised as his oath of his office. Or so the temple builders and long-dead priests had mandated that their god be portrayed in the crafting funded by the murderous pirate king's hard-stolen plunder.

Thor was either passed out or dead as the two men, thief and priest, worked their way toward the sacred pool where the two servants of Poesidius lived deep in its depths.

They dragged the lifeless Ranger through the cold seawater that fed the pool, the shifting greenish-blue lights playing across the walls and themselves making it seem as though they were all down there under the waters of the ocean, swim-walking through wonders reserved for the gods.

The bottom of the pool, at least here, for it was wide like a great pond children might swim in, was shallow and filled with soft pure white sand.

Sand said to be from the sacred atoll of Poesidius himself.

In the center of the pool lay a deep grotto, and down there the two holy eels slept and waited for their services to be paid for. Each undulating and biding their time until their services should be required, and more importantly... payment in prizes and trinkets offered down into the sandy and fantastic grotto beneath the grand temple that gave way to the sea itself along the harbor and then out into the Sea of Riddles and its cobalt depths.

"This will not be..." The ruined priest sighed heavily, sucking in a great breath and heaving his bull's shoulders and fat gut to get more air to confess what needed to be confessed now that time was short and soon things would become blasphemous and unholy. His hands trembled, whether from fear or drink, the thief did not know. "... easy," finished the gasping priest.

"Nothing worth doing ever is, priest," grunted Sato and heaved at Thor's inert form. "Now summon your devils to do the work your god won't."

The priest ran his trembling hand over his unshaven jaw, then anointed himself with water from the pool by merely grabbing a handful of it, splashing it across his face, and running it through his wild ash-gray and dark curly hair, quickly mumbling a prayer that must once have had deep meaning for him.

"Something..." began the priest haltingly like some beggar getting ready to lay the touch of a needed thing on a passerby for some spare coin. "S-s-something of great value. That's all they'll take these days, the two damned whores. One... of the reasons... I don't court this type of power."

And then the priest ran out of words and just stared at the thief, his eyes finally revealing how pathetic his state was, and that yes... he knew it too. Knew how far he'd fallen.

Sato reached into Thor's assault pack and retrieved that

shining, burning-from-within diamond from the midst of the shimmering gold coins that lined the interior of the assault pack the Ranger had brought with him from across the Sea of Riddles and the aftermath of the battle with Sût the Undying himself.

"Will this do, priest?" said Sato, gripping the diamond in his weathered fist. Its light sharper, brighter than the shifting cobalts and aquamarines of the temple deeps.

Caius Poesidius nodded like a fat man suddenly shocked to life, running his trembling hand across his suddenly agape mouth. Startled at the shimmering beauty of the perfect baseball-sized diamond that seemed to have some strange firelight coming from within.

"It's..." mumbled the fallen priest, and the thief cared not for what he said next and instead opened his fist and offered it up for his friend's life, remembering some wisdom his long-suffering mother had told him about the price of great treasures meaning nothing when weighed in the balance against family.

*Strange,* thought Sato. *I have only known this warrior but a short time, and how swiftly I trade a lifetime's fortune for his life now.* Then he remembered their time on the Sea of Riddles and the strange island and their desperate battles there against the claws of death that had tried to drag them all down into blackest oblivion. This... Ranger... had never failed to lead, fight, and get them all through no matter the odds. *And...* the thief thought, watching the priest's awestruck eyes lit afire by the diamond's brilliance, *there were times when the odds were impossible and still he did not relent.*

Sato held out a diamond that would have financed an orc khan's raid deep into the Cities of Men for all the fantastic plunder held behind high and mighty walls.

But the wayward priest did not reach out to pluck the gem from Sato's grasp.

Sato continued to hold it out while still keeping the Ranger's great head above the shifting waters of the pool there deep within the aquamarine dais beneath the golden steps of the sea god.

The priest turned suddenly, desperately, fear and loathing in his voice, staring down into the depths of the grotto at the center of the wide pool of worship that served this temple, and called out, "They come now! Damn them!"

And for a moment there was a triumphant roar in that once-holy man's voice that must have comforted frightened sailors and encouraged hardened Accadion soldiers going into action in some desperate sea battle beyond the limits of the maps where things get strange and often weird, and where only courage and teamwork and a great deal of luck might see them to safe harbor someday. Some call to prayer and last confession before the steel clashed and blood ran. Some appeal for victory, perhaps, or at least honor in death at sea.

"Give it to me," he said rapidly, his trembling hand out, his gaze remaining fixed on the grotto deep, where two long and slender shapes writhed their way up out of the blue depths down there.

Sato thrust the fantastic diamond into the unworthy priest's trembling paw and stared down into the depths of the deep area of the pool which seemed to go at least three levels below the temple floor of the main sanctuary of the sea god where the pool of worship lay.

There were ruins down there. And dark caves. All things of interest. But what drew the thief's gaze was the vast amount of treasure that lay along the wavering bottoms and the sand and half-buried ancient tiles of the grotto, even as the two dark sea serpents slithered their way up out of the depths.

Chests filled with silver and gold. Ingots and coins. Some small and shimmering, others large and flat like beaten discs. Other chests filled and overfilled with gems spilling out onto the sand-washed frescoed bottom of the pool. And weapons that seemed of great renown. There were even large pearls and a small idol whose eyes gleamed with red gems and must've been the precious object of some lost tribe or civilization, plundered by some adventurer pirate who'd traded it there to escape the curse the wronged had laid on the scallywag for stealing their god. And there were other treasures down there too numerous, varied, and tantalizing for a thief to take in all at once.

"By the Hawks of Ahora," mouthed the usually inscrutable thief, "*it's a djinn's fortune down there!*"

"That's their damned tithe," roared the angry priest clutching the burning gem. "That's their cursed price for the energy they will give me since I lost my faith, Asmodo take them!"

Suddenly out of the water both sea serpents rose, each having a head of sharpish and once-regal elven beauty now turned cruel and crafty... envious and covetous of what pretty or special thing they might have next for themselves.

These were the Holy Naga of Poesidius, and they were terrible and alien as they rose from the sacred pool dripping water and hissing together, their austere visages and sinister charms glaring down on the men in the shallows of the pool like a black-hole ray of doom.

But something happened.

Even as Sato moved to protect the lifeless Thor, standing over the Ranger's body and daring these devils to attack, the priest rose to his full height, ripped a small silver trident from off the leather thong about his great fat neck, and thrust it out at the two naga like it was a savage sword he would defend himself against them with to the last, daring them to profane his office.

For one last moment... he was a priest again.

And the man he'd once been.

"What trade bring you, Caius?" hissed one of the sisters coyly, seeming to laugh even though there was no sound of it in the electricity-filled air between them.

"*Yesssss... what bring you to us... priest?*" crooned the other.

They were known as Slyphira and Silvanyia, the water naga. One leading the question with an almost stentorian demand that was melodious and imperious in tone, the other murmuring the same words in an echoing hiss.

"Yessssss... what trade you, priest, for our power?"

"*Yessss... our power.*"

# CHAPTER TWENTY-ONE

CAIUS POESIDIUS, A WRECK OF A HUMAN BEING AND A poor excuse for a priest for anything calling itself a god these days, thrust the flaming diamond that seemed to burn even brighter here in the contrived underwater darkness that threw aquamarine shadows, emerald lights, and cobalt depths all across the great cathedral of Poesidius.

The gem burned like a bright sun that could not be denied and the naga sisters' greedy eyes were suddenly aflame with ravenousness and the desire to possess it even as their austere features seemed to consider violence by force if necessary.

"Drop it," whispered Slyphira.

"*Yes...*" hissed Silvanyia. "Drop it into our grotto and we will fill you with our dark powers, Caius. Come, priest... take hold of us and your fill of our desires."

The enraged priest turned back to the thief holding the dying Ranger's head above the waters of the pool filling with

Sergeant Thor's drifting blood from a dozen wounds handed out by now-dead enemies in the Pit and the battles from there to here.

He was pale like a corpse.

"Be ready!" roared the priest desperately. "If I do not die from their embrace, then perhaps I can cleanse his body and heal his wounds. He will live... if he survives what comes next!"

The faithless priest dropped the sunfire gem and watched as it shimmered and twinkled in its meteoric descent, like some star fragment burning up as it came through the skies. Then the dazzling and lovely gem came to rest lightly, swaddled in the pale sands of the vibrant crystal water of the pool deeper down below. The priest then waded closer to the deep grotto's edge, his filthy robes dragging and flowing in the ebb currents of the naga sisters' rising from the waters of the sacred pool.

"Goooooooood..." crooned the first sister.

"*Yessssss... goooooodddddd...*" echoed the other.

Then they rose up out of the pool and coiled about the large fat priest who'd called storms from the sea to destroy enemies of the Accadion warships at broadsides with catapults and massed arrow fire.

They entwined about him, and he screamed like the dying sailors and warriors he'd once ministered to as they lay bleeding out on the bloody decks of those Accadion warships, a thin line of defense between consuming evil and the Cities of Men.

They slithered all about him, almost delicately, seductive even in the cruel grip of their grotesque undulating bulks as they laughed and chanted unknown words in dark languages full of hisses and fated promises.

Caius Poesidius's eyes rolled back into his head and he shook suddenly and violently... then began to weave his hands like waves coming and going on the shores of unseen beaches, imitating the healing spells of his religion, a sea god's worship, in which he no longer had the faith to believe anymore.

But the power from the eels would make the Na-No weaving so...

The eels laughed cruelly as the priest began to groan aloud.

Then the power was there, and it surged through him all at once as the hands of the fat wretched man who'd once been a faithful priest made the symbols of the waves of his god. As he'd once done. Drawing in healing energies, his mouth mumbling by rote the prayers he'd been taught and could never drink enough to forget.

One sister hissed and crooned to the captive tormented priest within their writhing coils that his god was nothing but a trickster demon from the outer dark who'd played a cruel joke on all his worshippers. And that the demon cared not if they lived or died, or if the harvest was great, or if loved ones would return from the sea or battle. She laughed, high and mirthfully, at this. But there was no love within her croon.

"*Yesss...*" the other moaned. Their power would supply where the demon playing at a god, Poesidius, would not, and in time... this temple would be theirs if the priest would but yield to their power and let them transform him.

Suddenly strange visions of that possible future played like some long-ago reel from a movie across the waters of the pool despite the froth and churn of their considerable writhings.

Yield to them and become their chief prelate. Greatness. Worship. Hoard. Slaves.

He shook his head back and forth at them so hard it was like he was being slapped from side to side, screaming, "No! No! No!" over and over again in all the languages of the seas and far-off ports he'd ever learned in his service to the Accadion Navy.

And then the priest thrust one fat, bloated, red hand from their coils, cupping it as though he were drawing water up to drink. And perhaps he was. Electric water like a phantom upside-down waterfall rushed up from the pool and formed not only within but all around his cupped hand.

His next hand movement was slight. Nothing more than a tic. The twitch of a man gone too long without the precious bottle that both sustained and drowned him all at once. But the result...

Wave after cascading wave of healing energy crashed forward, flowing all over the dying Ranger floating in the pool.

The priest screamed at the eels' laughter which was hollow and like vast giants roaring hushes at one another as he held and directed the power to heal, their voices fighting one another and finally crescendoing as the priest collapsed into unconsciousness within their surging coils.

And...

The wounds of the Ranger began to heal within the waters of the pool and the onslaught of the rushing energy. Drifting stormfronts of blood thinning to a trickle until the churning waters became more placid and showed it no more. As the eels released Caius Poesidius, gashes healed. Slices closed up. Even some old scars seemed to fade as the now almost visible waves of energy shimmered between the at-once-more-conscious priest and the hulking sniper in Sato's arms within the pool.

Ghostly angelfish appeared like images of light and swam their lazy patterns over Sergeant Thor as the arm that was broken was made whole as though it had never been snapped in fiercest battle.

Curses hurled by dying foes, taught by tribal witch-men and adulterous fortune tellers to those the warrior had slain, faded away as the angelfish nibbled at them and the priest's energy surrounded the wounded man and brought him back to health.

Then... just as suddenly as it had come... the power of the eels faded and Thor heaved upward by the chest as though dragged up from the very gates of death and gasped to life, sucking air and roaring titanically, his ragged bloodcurdling cry ringing out over the upper vaults of the grand cathedral of Poesidius.

Sergeant Thor coughed and heaved and Sato patted him on the back, whispering and reminding the warrior he was alive.

Slyphira and Silvanyia descended back into the pool slowly, crooning and hissing their blasphemies to the priest that soon, the more he drew from their terrible love and power... that, "Soon you will be ours, Caius."

"*Yesssss...*" echoed the other. "*Sooon.*"

The priest thundered like a runaway bull for the side of the pool, dragging his massive wet-robed bulk to clear its edge and instead falling over and drifting there in the water a great sloppy mess, his towering god rising high above him in the sea up there as he murmured apologies and cursed himself for the faithless wretch he was.

"Soon you will be ours, Caius."

"*Yesssss...*" echoed the other. "*Sooon...*"

# CHAPTER TWENTY-TWO

BY DAWN, NEWS HAD SPREAD THAT THE ENTIRE PRIZE Chest had been plundered and its fantastic treasures and seemingly endless coin were gone completely missing. By early golden light before the day would become unbearable, breathless tales, baseless speculations, and outright lies had entered the markets as another sweltering day's heat began to grow along with the murmuring babble of trade, exclamations of thievery, and not occasional wail of murder along the vast sprawling streets of rising palaces, looming temples, and sunburnt slums.

The High Priests were said to be in a rage, and the Pit had been abandoned by their servants. This was both dark and concerning, for tradition and superstition held that much of the city's luck and wealth had something to do with the games of death inside the Pit and the High Priests' holding of such rites and ceremonies.

Powdered and perfumed eunuchs, freshly bathed and

constantly fanned, dispatched teams of hard-eyed armed heavy enforcers, dangerous mercenaries loaded with sharp weapons, long drooping mustaches, and jangling gear, and seasoned shrewd-faced inquisitors to get right to the very bottom of "this wild rumor" spreading like wildfire across the eunuchs' city that some oaf of a murderous winner of the game had managed to plunder the Prize Chest by craft, magic, or guile.

Somehow.

Even though it was considered impossible and there was surely some other explanation for this madness.

Omens and rites were considered and conducted by the various temples. Bulls and goats were slaughtered. Black smoke rose from the temple of the Old Religion.

The day entered noon and pounding hammers rang out on white-hot forges while vendors in the food stalls sold their goods cheap now that the day was long and hot and produce was going unripe in its swelter. These merchants thinking it best to retire to the striped pavilions near the splattering fountains for a hot, roasted, and trade-route-spiced sand-brewed *qahwa*, a honeyed sweet, and perhaps some little shade to hide in near the whispering palms to listen to the latest on the great robbery done last night at the Pit and what this meant for all.

The latest...

No sure sign of the chief suspect, the northern barbarian, sometimes called "Ranger," sometimes called Sergeant Thor.

The thieves' guilds were out with fast messengers in taverns and dead drops to find out just who, exactly, was involved, for surely so great a heist had to be one of their own and not some wild and savage warrior oaf in service to none of them.

A reaver.

An adventurer.

A common thief.

Made thieves exchanged insults between the guilds and cabals, then quickly flung accusations, and soon enough daggers and caltrops were also flung and small bloody street battles broke out, even as all involved declared their innocence.

The Dark Cultists were said to know something...

Many who had converted in recent months had seen to their morning work and were suspiciously absent by afternoon as the fresh relief of a breeze from off the sea came to surge across the city, blow sand, and make the palms dance as they hustled and hushed at its behest.

Both a eunuch and a wizard, low-ranking but... involved, as they say... were strangled, and it was then clear, as it had been before, that the assassins were interested in that shiny and glittering pile the wild northern Dire Man had somehow stolen or been involved in the stealing of even though all said he was practically dead after the battle at the Pit with the demon that had caused much murder in the city throughout the years.

*Hadn't there been a deafening explosion sometime near midnight?*

The dead, stabbed and strangled, had their pockets rifled and their secret hideouts tossed. Necromancers were called in to find out if the dead had known the truth before they'd perished and just what exactly they knew about the great robbery of the Prize Chest and all its fantastic treasure and hoard, and had been holding back on the other side of the black veil of death.

Many wrongs were committed in the absence of real information as the thieves turned over every source they had if just to know what had happened at the Pit, and afterward, for knowing was... as clever thieves and warriors say... *half the battle.*

Eunuchs watched.

Thieves listened.

And the wizards...

Wizards plotted, for there was much power in that stuffed chest, and, because the old bargains were now null, that power could be had now that the chest had been plundered.

Its power was up for grabs.

And if one had power...

Then... one could rise.

# CHAPTER TWENTY-THREE

THREE DAYS LATER, IN THE MIDNIGHT GLOOM surrounding the tower of Osirex the Wizard, three appointed by the Council to see an end to the chaos the northern barbarian had caused all across the City of Thieves since the night of the Game, gathered. They were to obtain the contents of the Prize Chest that had been so skillfully looted from the High Priests of the Game.

The powerful wizard Osirex was there because of course he would be, for it was his tower they had gathered in. It was he who was a direct representative of the High Table that led the wizards of the city.

Osirex's tower lay in the southern district near the Gate of Lions and along the main way to the grand vizier's palace from which the eunuchs were allowed to rule and control the city, taxing it as they liked and making sure the wizards were left alone to their deep studies and arcane researching into the dark mysteries of the various branches of thaumaturgy they practiced.

Every form of magic was practiced in the City of Thieves, for—a little-known secret—it was really a city of wizards and always had been. The thieves were there, and were allowed their profit, in tacit exchange for their service in keeping back bands of reckless adventurers, or haughty generals seeking fortune and glory by gaining some fabled artifact locked within the towers of wizardry, and even kings needing all the power they could get to wage their next war against their fellow sovereign, for just a little more of what they already had enough of.

According to some, this was said to be the reason for the alliance between thieves and wizards.

The wizards with their artifacts of power and magic drew to the city the wealthy, the adventurers, the... marks. The thieves did the intel work, made sure the plundering expeditions were fleeced and left penniless, murdered those who couldn't be dissuaded, and acted as a kind of fence for the wizards to hide behind where the cyclopean walls of the city that went for miles were not enough to protect them from those profiteers who would loot their towers and ruin their valuable and dark research.

With the thieves' guilds doing this invisible work and the eunuchs administering the populace, the wizards found the city to be a paradise in which they were well kept, quietly feared, and allowed to raise their arcane sanctums high into the night sky in which to delve far and wide into the deep magics they'd spent their lives researching, acquiring, and wielding.

And occasionally, they'd spend the lives of others to get all that needed doing for their power to grow and continue to grow into dark dimensions without end, done.

As it was whispered, all forms of magic were practiced within the City of Thieves.

Elemental magic.

Wizardry.

Necromancy.

Summoning.

Elven.

Tribal.

Runic.

Illusion.

Osirex was a mighty wizard, climbing high in the most powerful of the schools of magic, learning spells that bent the Na-No and accomplished the great wonders and mighty magics by which he was known and feared. Osirex was very clever, and had ambitions little known but suspected by the High Table and even the Five who watched him with a cautious eye but knew they had need of his skills and willingness to do what needed to be done. A natural leader among wielders of magic who usually abhorred leadership of any kind at all costs, as it interfered with their secretive plans and constant researching for more power in their schools of study, Osirex was, as murmured among the High Table that oversaw the wizards of the City of Thieves, a *comer*. In this year or next he would be made a Council member, and someday he would be one of the Five whose word, and power, was near absolute among the many wizards who made their great towers, small towers, libraries, inner sanctums, and even the deep dungeons few knew about, all throughout the City of Thieves.

Each wizard's tower was a fortress of might with summoned, or hired, minions that rumors said were often monsters captured from beyond the walls, beyond the wastes, or simply... beyond. Each tower could be filled with deadly mind-bending illusions or lethal traps so that the powerful wizard, no easy foe on a good day for an army and a warlord with tactics and skills, could be left alone with his hoarded scrolls and costly reagents collected for the next great uttering of some damnable spell which would unlock yet the next tumbler in the great and grand locks of knowledge and mystery all wizards seemingly set themselves to know first, eyeing one another as competitors and enemies even though their alliances were mutually beneficial to their survival and continued acquisition of yet more power.

Even the meanest necromancer's hut out near the cemeteries and great death valleys and burnt hills filled with uncountable graves and fallen stone markers, once a mighty battlefield lost to time around which the City of Thieves had thrown itself up to the west of, near the Sea of Riddles, was not to be trusted.

Even in these mean magic workers' huts there were...

Halls to nowhere.

Pits to other planes of existence where survival was almost impossible.

Magic, mad, monstrous "chests" with poisons that looted the mind and turned a plunderer into a living dead.

And even mirrors that entered other worlds from which there was no possibility of return.

To tempt a wizard's tower, even for skilled thieves as they said among themselves and murmured it so, was to court total destruction in ways even the grimmest veteran of tomb and dungeon had not yet conceived.

*Better to kiss a python or love a devil,* was the saying, *than to steal from a wizard.*

*But imagine the fortune in glory if one did,* whispered those same thieves.

So of course, daring and desperate thieves only robbed the wizards when they went rogue from the guilds or were working for other rival wizards.

Very desperate.

And then of course, there was the tried-and-true end of many rogue thieves... joining up with the grand expeditions into the temples and pyramid tombs of the mighty Saur in the Land of Black Sleep, beyond the River of Night. These were often financed by the wizards, for the plunder and power contained in the average Saur tomb could lead to the prized secrets of endless life, and endless power.

It was within Osirex's tower that the three had gathered, appointed by the High Table of the Wizards' Council to deal with this... *barbarian problem*... as Sergeant Thor was being referred to by the wizards of the High Table and even the Five who talked with their eyes and thoughts and wielded the darkest and most well-kept secrets of their mighty and powerful disciplines.

The City of Thieves, after three days, was in crisis. The game was changing. Power was loose and wild in the wind.

And other, darker interests had become involved in the three days of murder, inquisition, savagely desperate street battles, and total chaos.

And of course, there were rumors of one greater than them all watching events unfold.

The Dreaming Sorcerer himself.

Some called him Tuth Evol.

"*Tooth Evaall*," it was only ever whispered, and the

name, to the few it was known to, and even the powerful Five, was said to generate such fear that even then rarely was it ever whispered loud enough to be heard.

That is, if one wanted to live long and gain power. Whispers only, please. And really... not at all.

Osirex's tower, which lay along the Street of Gold, was high and slender at its top. It was said that on moonless nights the sorcerer himself could be seen atop his high black tower, opening gateways to other worlds up there among the glittering lights of the stars and the spinning wheel of the galaxy beyond.

The grounds around the tower of Osirex were walled and well protected by mephitic homunculi that assumed the forms of stone during the day, their wicked eyes ever watching the thronging streets beyond the high walls in protection of the powerful one that had bound them. At night, it was said, the little imps cavorted among the rich gardens and patrolled the walls, occasionally snatching a working girl or an urchin who'd stayed out too late in the night for their master, or themselves.

These taken were never heard from again and whether they became the prizes and playthings of the homunculi, turned into statues themselves, their suffering frozen in stone among the labyrinthine gardens, or were taken deep into the dungeons of Osirex by the savage Ape Men who served the powerful wizard... was not known.

The Ape Men.

Not true gorillas like those in the east who had come to study the way of bushido and the blade, but more like their savage predecessors. It was told of Osirex that when he was a young and journeying mage of some talent, he had gone into the emerald south beyond the Red Desert to obtain, train, and bewitch the Ape Men in order that they serve him and him alone throughout his dark and arcane career.

These powerful beast-men wore red cloaks and sometimes a belt with a crude weapon they favored for their savagery when their fangs and claws and brute strength could not rip an intruder in two.

Their fangs were vicious and dripping with animal malice, and other than their roaring snarls and hoots, there was no language they spoke that was understood.

Yet they obeyed, protected, and acted as a praetorian guard for the powerful wizard Osirex on his way up the Twilight Stairs of Power deep inside the councils, both lesser and greater, the path definitely leading all the way to the High Table... and perhaps even the mysterious Five, whether those there liked it or not.

Wizards resent those that would replace them. Great lengths are gone to, dark pacts sealed, that they might not fall and see their damned studies continued by another.

Sometimes the Ape Men who served the sorcerer used a crude weapon. Obsidian flint knives were their favorites. But they had little need for these as they could rip a powerful warrior's arms from his sockets if they so chose, easily, snarling like the wild feral beasts they truly were. At the bidding of their powerful and arcane master, Osirex, they could do this.

The sorcerer wasn't, as some other workers of arcane magic muttered among themselves, merely their master, a powerful sorcerer on the rise, but their leader. Their god, even.

Some say this.

But there were two others gathered there in the nepenthe of the late night when even the City of Thieves itself must sleep and pause from the wildfire of rumor and chaos the Ranger had caused in their midst.

One was Baalubrozz, correctly pronounced *baal-you-bross* in polite eunuch company, with which the summoner had affinities and secret alliances, or *bay-lub* for short among the wizards who were often frank and terse, insulting even, an altogether crabby lot.

They did this to demean him, for they despised him. Then again, they despised everyone not themselves.

They were rude with most for they considered all, even their fellows and the occasional sorceress or witch that managed her way up the ranks, beneath them.

They hated warlocks. And they hated the witches of Caspia with a passion. There was a great secret thousand-year war between the wizards of the City of Thieves and the witches of Caspia few knew about. But many bounty hunters and assassins had profited, or died, much from this conflict.

The wizards considered everyone beneath themselves.

Less than.

Inferior.

A mere counter to be used in the grand game, the real game, for power *unlimited*. Which is what every wizard craves. Power beyond the gods themselves.

Always.

So, in the Black Tower of Osirex that night was the summoner Baalubrozz, Osirex, and another.

And that other was Mandelf Tallhat, as he was sometimes known. Or, as he was known most often... the Smoke Wizard.

Baalubrozz was short and fat with pig-like eyes. He would have grown a wizardly beard or even a sinister goatee like the one the powerful and crafty Osirex sported, but he could not. His skin, fingers, and every feature was pudgy. He was a summoner with the face of a cruel and spoiled child. A binder and bargainer with demons or any dance of devils he could make pact with for more power. Piggy little Baalubrozz wore every possible magic item and powerful artifact like some little girl wearing all the costumes she'd accumulated, fairy princess and temple dancer, and a host of others, all at once in one hot chaotic mess. The summoner had collected and crafted many items of great power, imbuing some with bound spirits, others with jewels that drew the powers of the Hells. From the Staff of Wizarding, sleek and made of some stellar metal, ruby gems gleaming from its brass-cast demon's head, to his Robe of the Elements and Shielding Cloak of the Great Garhazzugazz, Gray Dragon of the Ice Hells, he ended up looking a little more than comic already. Then he sported ten gaudy magical rings, each set with a fantastic jewel from the Kingdoms of the East containing an imprisoned wraith sorcerer of the Jade Eye. Each jewel garish in the extreme and more sparkling than the last.

If there was some new treasure or artifact of power in his presence, the toad-like summoner licked his fat wet lips and coveted it immediately as much as he lusted after every fine sugar delicacy the eunuchs laid before him, or whatever fleshly delight he could conquer and command for his wicked pleasures.

He had a high-pitched squeaky voice, and he was altogether unaware of how annoying those of the High

Table found it.

But he was very powerful, and he had made many deadly compacts with dark devils and trickster demons.

Where the summoner was short and fat and gaudily adorned with wizardly drip, the Smoke Wizard, Mandelf Ravenshair, another name he was called long ago for he was very long-lived, Mandelf was the opposite. Tall and carved of face, his ancient gray beard, dirty and barely kempt, flowed down onto his soft multicolored and greatly faded robes.

He held and often leaned heavily on an old, gnarled oak staff he called *Tree Father*. He wore a tall yet floppy-brimmed wizard's hat that was gray though it might have once been some other brighter, gayer shade.

He had no drip.

Only a long-stemmed pipe carved of yellowed ivory constantly wafting the sweet and rarest of narcotic lotus: Tyrian Lotus. The pipe was spellbound and an artifact the powerful wizard had labored twenty years to craft, journeying as far as the Dire Frost Ice Giants' frozen fortress of the *Helkarakse* to learn the Spell of Neverending from the hearths of Curuni the Cold. After that he'd gone into the lost east, to the Islands at the End of the World to find the Lost World, itself a mythic island, and there obtain the narcotic Tyrian Lotus giving off its vibrant blush of pillowing purple smokes that made visions and dreams real.

Or so it was rumored.

Mandelf was... an illusionist.

Any who had ever thought to best him at his sorceries, thinking his powers were merest fictions and little more than pretty, or terrible, lies, had paid deadly the price for such mistakes. Even among the High Table and the silent Five there was no illusionist that was his equal. This was a fact. And a deadly one at that.

But the Smoke Wizard had no yearnings, a rare exception among wizards, for powers over councils and control of the High Table of any sort. His desires were for the dark and whimsical pleasures he sought, and the unlimited endlessly wasted days of oblivion and lore were the only power he wished to acquire more of at any cost.

Often, he spoke seldom. But sometimes he was given to great and long rambling rants on the natures of anything ranging from the obscure to the aesthetic. He would hold forth among beggars, highwaymen, and even sinister traders he drank with in the cool back lots of some of the seediest taverns, staying late into the night and weaving mind-spinning visions with his softly smoking pipe as he held forth and held court among the entranced in the wasted and ruined outer districts of the city.

The Five had insisted the vagabond Smoke Wizard be involved in this crisis, and Osirex had obeyed, for there were some commands that just had to be.

Osirex stepped down off his obsidian throne in the Grand Hall that was his reception area along the lower levels of his black tower. It was here he received audiences, which he seldom did for he was more interested in acquiring powerful spells and thereby greater power.

At any cost.

The two wizards that had come to the tower of Osirex, one short and fat, the other tall and gaunt, purple haze drifting away from his fabled long-stemmed pipe like a murmuring kraken's snaky tentacles, had gotten the unspoken message when they'd been ushered into the midnight receiving room where the floor was mirrored black marble flecked with gold, and the thick and heavy crimson curtains spell-woven with castings of spells of Silence to protect the conspiracy and prevent attack by enemies pretending to be allies should they think a spell of power, words of death, or even spell-wrought fireballs or a forked lightning strike would see Osirex dead and his house and tower open to their looting.

Wizards often fought duels over some tome or staff. And these contests were winner-take-all, to the death, and rarely announced.

The Council appreciated that the weaker spellcaster had been culled, and power consolidated. And... now they knew better who to watch.

Osirex had fought five such duels. Three of the wizards were dead. Two were in places where they wished they were dead.

Osirex's robes, like his throne and the thick and heavy curtains that lined the chamber, were black leathers and blood-red cloth. Arcane symbols in gold and silver, each a ward or a bond, radiated quiet menacing power on a low guttural hum to the knowing of such warding arts in their stamp and design.

Osirex stood before his arrived guests, fellow conspirators, hands on hips, black Cloak of the Vampire splayed wide, a rare artifact indeed, flaring behind him, then gestured that they should sit at the grand table and the fine spread he'd had his unseen servants, spectral beings only there in shadow and shade, prepare for the cabal ordered by the High Table.

Fat little Baalubrozz's eyes went wide at the cold fish plates on ice and the towers of oysters, chilled and salty sea fresh, that had been laid out. The rotund little chimp of a sorcerer went for the nearest seat just as Osirex had foreseen in the planning when gazing into his crystal ball at how his plots should be laid.

Once in the large chair, feet dangling, which too had been the intention of Osirex by design, the greedy summoner

Baalubrozz reached for a crusty loaf of fresh sourdough, tore off a hunk, steam rising, and ran it through the fire-pepper butter the unseen staff had whipped up and flaked with southern salts for the tasting.

Baalubrozz muttered something, either grumbling about the size of the chair and knowing Osirex had done that on purpose, or that the bread and butter was the finest he'd ever eaten. No one could tell. His wide and fat-lipped mouth was too busy working around the wad of food he was trying to compact in order to swallow it all at once as it passed his many chins and went down the short wide frog's pipe that was his throat.

Then the summoner began greedily reaching for the prized oysters, slurping them down and tossing the shells onto the floor like he was some machine that was made only to do this. And as fast as it could possibly be done.

By that time the tall and gaunt Mandelf had taken his seat at the far end of the fare-laden table and began to work at his fantastic and mythical long-stemmed pipe, inhaling it solely for its narcotic pleasures as he settled himself in and prepared to listen to, as best he could, what would be required of him so he could get on with the important business of the dreams and sorceries he was busy researching in the late nights of taverns and the alleys where he sometimes slept because he'd lost his way back to the crumbling tower down by the outer walls and the sea he was known to keep a thing or two in.

With both guests seated, Osirex moved to his own elegant chair, tall-backed and much grander than the other two chairs at the long table. Osirex's sparkling black eyes took in the other wizards as though he were appraising gems he might trade in for a better, brighter gem that would make him, and him only, greater.

Or a cow he might buy and slaughter.

As if all knew this and he didn't care that they did.

Then he smiled cruelly, stroked his black goatee, and spoke, his voice rich and just as cruel as his eyes.

He began to implement his scheme from the very first.

"The High Table has a problem. A problem named... *Sergeant... Thor.*"

He gave a small, cold, cruel laugh.

"And we, my fellow wizards, are the Council's answer to the problem he has made of himself. Now... how shall we kill him and take the best of what he has stolen?"

# CHAPTER TWENTY-FOUR

"IMPOSSIBLE!" SHRIEKED THE FAT LITTLE SORCERER Baalubrozz as he licked the cream from his fingers the unseen servants of Osirex had brought out to bring the war council to a close.

Cold sweet cream in which had floated ripe mangos and swimming honeyed snakes, living sorcerous creations that curled about the delicate slices of mango like tiny pythons and exploded with honey and cinnamon in each bite. Over this final sweet delicacy from the table of the powerful wizard Osirex, fresh mint had been chopped.

"Impossible... I bet it wasn't so... because *he* did it!" screamed fat little Baalubrozz. "Impossibly so! But somehow this stupid Dire Man managed to loot the most valuable Prize Chest short of..." And here the fat little pig-eyed sorcerer looked about, as though a dark and huge wolf that wasn't just a wolf was somehow loose in the shadows of the audience chamber of Osirex. Then, cautiously, slowly, he whispered the name of the one not to be whispered. But if the name had to be said aloud then it was best whispered about. Or so it was said truly by those counted wise.

"*Tuth Evol himself,*" whispered Baalubrozz.

The reckless fat little summoner looked about as though expecting some horrific beast from the outer dark he had no truck or sway with to come roaring out of the darkness all at once to consume him. The bulging little pig eyes darted about here and there, searching the shadows.

When the whispered horror did not surface and murder them all, Baalubrozz smiled smugly as though using the much-feared name, and getting away with it somehow, had accorded him a new amount of power the others had dared not grasp at.

There were three wizards at the table.

Old Mandelf cleared his throat and sent a necrotic purple ring over himself. This was a minor warding spell against latent curses affecting the room, and since it was wordless and derived from the powers of Mandelf's magical pipe, the spell-woven curtains of Osirex had no effect over this.

Cruel and dead-eyed Osirex watched the fat little summoner get away with his daring invitation to bring down destruction on them all, then smiled a smile that never matched his heartless glare.

"Yet it is so, Baalubrozz. And my... sources, let's just say...

inform me he is no mere... *Dire Man adventurer* as you say... come down from the north come to wreak havoc, loot and plunder and wench until his parts fall off from the diseases of the whores and the rabble that sully themselves with such. Nay, he may, in fact, be one... out of time."

Osirex let these words hang in the air, for they were indeed important and each of the wizards knew what they meant.

*One from not somewhere else*, but from... *some time else*. The history of the Ruin was rife with such legends and rumors that, in the course of wizardly research and study, had proven to be all too real, time and time again.

It was clear the ancient past of the Ruin, whatever it was in the Before, had come forward in time to play at their games of power.

"Well..." coughed Mandelf and drifted off murmuring to himself about some such matter that had once been great and vastly important. Spells and magic incantations and the lore of artifacts could often be detected in his seemingly incoherent murmurings, and it was said of him that while the Smoke Wizard often seemed confused to the point of babbling, there was always some rich thread at work in his seemingly lotus-induced mutterings, and that even now, his brain like a vast great infernal tome, was pulling together the arcane and unseen strings of the problem at hand... for a solution.

If... it could be detected.

Three days now and no sign of the treasure. The city was in an uproar. Mysteries of the great Dire Man could not be authenticated even with scrying stones.

The High Table of the Wizards' Council in the City of Thieves knew this, and so did cunning Osirex who had set one of his imp scribes capable of shadow-walking near at hand to record by mimic everything the Smoke Wizard had to babble, incoherent or not. Osirex himself might parse over these meanderings later and see what bits of power could be gleaned and gained for him to use for himself and himself alone.

The Council was as much disturbed as the city was out there in the night.

That vast and powerful treasure was loose in the wind, and the only lead was a murderous northern savage who was actually... one of the strange and powerful warriors called Rangers who had done Old Sût himself to death in the Land of Black Sleep.

And that was thought to be impossible.

Osirex's power lay in the working of great spells of might and powerful incantations of magic, but he had also built an incredible intelligence network all across the city in the form of shadow servants and paid commoners serving in every grand estate, for he was crafty and on the rise within the Council and he meant to rise higher than even the High Table, and even the Five, and yes... even that whispered name.

His network was so vast and far-flung that even on the ships at sea, trading to distant ports of call, and among the great expeditions rife with thieves and porters who dared the haunted sands of the Valleys of the Kings and Priests of the Saur to go tomb-busting in search of wealth beyond imagining, even there he had ears to listen and report.

It was only into the Great Eastern Wastes and the Rifts of Madness deep within that distant land where the powerful wizard was blind, but so was everyone else, for what happened there in the Rifts was unknowable and... *uncertain.*

Still, Osirex collected what ghostly rumors he came across that made their way out across the long abandoned and haunted trade routes from the ruins of the once-fabled cities of the lost Golden Age of the Ruin.

"Impossible," huffed pudgy Baalubrozz again at Osirex's rebuke and correction that they were dealing with someone "out of time" rather than merely the oafish yet wily northern savage the rest of the city considered responsible and in possession of the fabled Prize Chest. The fat little summoner looked about at the ruin he'd created of the meal that had been set before them all at the behest of Osirex. Nothing was in reach of his small fat arms and fingers, and he thought it unseemly and unwise to go digging through the other wizards' portions to sate himself yet further.

For the summoner... enough was never enough.

Then Baalubrozz smiled knowingly, a grotesque sight due to his malignant cherub's face and greedy pig's eyes, seeming unconcerned with the problem of the looted Prize Chest for the moment, or even the capture, torture, and murder of the one called... *Sergeant Thor.*

No. Baalubrozz would treat himself to one of the houses of delight before dawn. He would order that three of its finest beauties be brought to his private rooms there.

Then a breakfast to choke the mad emperor himself.

Then dark sleep within his circle of power.

Then...

"The problem is, the real problem, Baalubrozz my ally..." Osirex continued after the silence of what it meant to each of the three to be dealing with a man out of time.

Osirex the Wizard.

Baalubrozz the Summoner.

And Mandelf. The Smoke Wizard himself.

"... is not the *imminent* murder of this... Thor..."

Osirex chuckled cruelly, for he loved the misfortune of others and it often brought a small mirthless laugh out of him that never reached his black glittering eyes. The chuckle was a small and loveless sound like a dry winter's wind knocking at the shutters on the coldest and darkest days of the year when the light grows brief and the nights long and cold.

"The problem is not the killing, though... that's what the High Table has tasked us with. Is it, boys?"

Fat Baalubrozz looked up like a greedy child caught with his stubby little hand in the cookie jar once again and with no intention of listening to the scolding or obeying the command to cease that was sure to follow.

The summoner giggled.

Down the obsidian table where the remains of their feast lay, the hooded eyes of Mandelf the Smoke Wizard looked up from their deep considerations, suddenly startlingly clear and focusing on the haughty and imperious Osirex at the far end of the table.

As though intent on every word being said, for what would happen next... was of great import to them all. And even others who shall not be named.

In the darkness around their meeting feast, mephitic little shapes shifted, flitting this way and that, moving among the muffled curtains so softly and deftly it was as though they weren't even there.

But a sorcerer knows. A sorcerer knows what's there even

though it cannot be seen by normal eyes.

"You see, boys..." continued the powerful and cunning Osirex, feigning camaraderie, "it's that chest... that's the real problem, isn't it? Not some warrior who was merely the cat's paw for the game that's being played."

Neither of the other wizards said anything, for what was said had been what each had been thinking, exactly.

How to get that chest, and keep it. For themselves.

That was the problem.

"The Wizards' Council has decreed that this... *Thor*..." Again the dry cruel chuckle of Osirex. "Need perish if just so the chaos he has caused to flare within these walls, the slaughtering clutches of guards by teams of mercenaries, the dispatching assassins and thieves one against another like some butcher seeing to the day's cuts, stops. The whole system of the city seems gone mad with getting what he has somehow, as Baalubrozz would have it, *impossibly* taken. Stolen. The thieves' guilds, which this... whatever he is... seems not allied with... the guilds have stopped talking one to the other, and that means only one thing..."

"War in the streets!" shouted Baalubrozz joyfully if only because he'd guessed the answer and shouted it first and faster than anyone else.

He loved to be right.

"Quite..." murmured old Mandelf, unusually sober for

the moment. His magical pipe lay unconsidered in his long twisted and gnarly fingers as its narcotic smoke drifted and wisped away. Imps in the rafters sucked at the wafting poison, trying to inhale as much of the dreaming lotus as they could.

"Even I know..." spoke the sagely Smoke Wizard, his eyes beginning to go otherwhere, "this business 'tis not good for... business... if our acquirers of hard-to-find reagents and sought-after artifacts suddenly go off a-slaughtering one another pell-mell... well... it's not good for business. This Dire Man has caused much confusion in the days since the looting of that chest."

Then Mandelf went off about the lost tomes of power the Dragon Kings were rumored to have curated in the long dark years of the first of the Ruin. And all the great spells that once could be conjured from them that were lost, or in deep hiding, now.

"And of course, there are the eunuchs..." taunted Osirex and let that tantalizing hook hang in the late dark before early dawn beyond the walls of his powerful fortress. Earliest morning was not far off now. Perhaps forty-five minutes.

"*Sons of orc whores!*" screamed Baalubrozz apoplectically and suddenly for no clear reason.

Bodies were cooling in the streets out there.

Whores and lovers crept by them.

Thieves rolled dice in the raucous backrooms with a cold beer, eyeing their night's haul.

Life in the City of Thieves was beginning anew. Again, as it did yesterday. Again, as it would tomorrow.

"Ha!" mumbled the once-more-addled Smoke Wizard as suddenly his lavender and necrotic haze made visions of the eunuchs triumphing through the streets of the city, their toyboys and slaves in full bacchanal. The towers of the wizards in flames and being looted by an angry populace.

This would be so, could be so, if the thieving eunuchs gained the chest first.

"You show rightly," murmured Osirex from over a jeweled goblet he'd taken up from near at hand. He eyed his "compatriots" like some salesman on the Street of Delights offering his most tempting beauty for cheap. "You show rightly, venerable Mandelf. And yes, summoner... indeed they are sons of monsters. The balance of power in the city is... *in question*. It must be we..."

And there was so much implied in that *we*, but really Osirex meant something, someone, else.

Him.

"... who gain the chest. There can be no other solution."

The cruel wizard nodded at the illusionist with a small sneer he had not the guile to hide, for it was his true self poking through.

That true self that hated everything and everyone not him.

"The illusion of the Smoke Wizard is prophetic. And a delicate vision at that. However, this... *Ranger*... and he seems one of those... indeed... from the *Before*... if such a thing can be believed... has managed the heist or at least had some hand in it. But it's indeed clear, thanks to the powers of Mandelf, that if that Prize Chest and whatever he's done with it, falls into the hands of the eunuchs, then the balance within the city shifts, and my own crystal ball shows what your smoke confirms. In time... we wizards will be driven from the city in black smoke and flame. Or... we will see it burnt with our own magic flames of apocalypse and all... will be lost."

Osirex smiled briefly at that.

But again, that smile never met his eyes.

"The Prize Chest of the High Priests of the Game must fall into *our* hands," he continued, "or all will be lost. That is so. But... let us not talk falsely now, companions. An opportunity presents itself... for we three..."

*For me and me alone, fools*, thought Osirex and was able to mask this truth from the summoner and illusionist he conspired with this night.

"Now... if *we* were to obtain the chest... we would become..."

"The High Table!" gasped Baalubrozz breathlessly again, satisfied he'd guessed another answer to a rhetorical question and sussed where things were going first and faster than anyone else.

Osirex smiled patiently and the summoner was satisfied his peers at the table thought he was indeed some kind of tactical genius who had solved all their problems and was sure to plot a course that would gain them success, and himself... diabolical glory.

"Yes, summoner. In time, with the haul of the stolen chest as... our war chest... we would steer the High Table and..."

Both wizards watched Osirex and at the same time dreaming and envisioning exactly what he did not say to them beyond the words that were left to hang in the heavy silence of the black and symbol-covered curtains of the wizard's audience chamber.

*All would bow to me and despair.*

Each thought.

An ancient phrase found and inscribed on the earliest rune-walls of the Dragon Elves deep in the Savage Lands. Wizards who delved into the damned destruction of those ancient First Empire elves... knew it well.

It had been their... creed.

And they envied it. Plotted the course of their powers by

it. Dreamed it might be so of themselves.

Then Osirex told them the lie by which they would wave their banner, assuming the authority and secret cabal the High Council had entrusted them with to see to this problem of one called Sergeant Thor.

The story for public consumption, and not the truth at all. No. Not by a long stretch. For such is the way of wizards.

"And ensure the balance... of the city. Of course," murmured cruel Osirex to his fellow conspirators as the schemes, games, and graspings for power within the City of Thieves continued once more.

Same as they ever would.

*All will bow to me, and despair.*

Thieves slept.

Sorcerers dreamed.

Eunuchs sallied forth to unfold their plots at first of day, oiled and fresh.

And once again, a new day began in the City of Thieves.

# CHAPTER TWENTY-FIVE

THE RANGER SLAMMED HIS FIST INTO THE DRUNKEN brute who'd tried to take the comely girl off to his mean hovel, roaring that she was his somehow, and not that of the handsome and jacked Dire Man savage from the north who was free with his coin and drinking the best the tavern had to offer with all that prize money he'd stolen from the High Priests.

"I know you da one!" the brute had shouted just before the Ranger punched him. The ugly lout fancied himself the shining knight of the long-lashed doe-eyed beauty on Thor's arm. "You da thief everyone's lookin' for. And now I know. And soon *they're* gonna know. Come back wit me now, Mazzi! Come back if you don't wanna get kilt wit dis one!"

Mazzi, the shapely raven-haired wench in gossamer-soft robin's-egg silks and kohled eyes with long lashes, laughed lightly as the big man claiming her went down and Thor swiped up the battered tankard he'd been served all afternoon in, draining its cold beer dry once more in one huge and terrific draught.

He was playing the goat now. And cold beer and wenches was part of the act.

*Sometimes,* he thought, eyeing the soft curves of Mazzi and her come-hither eyes in the late afternoon of yet another tavern, *things swing your way.*

If the ghost of the smaj, his constant companion, said something in that laconic east-Texas drawl the senior NCO of the Ranger detachment spoke with, Thor ignored it as a serving girl, a dainty beauty, young and red-haired with peaches-and-cream skin, green eyes taking him in, refilled the drained tankard.

The pours in this tavern, *The Acrobat's Perch* it was called, were known for their excessiveness across the City of Thieves.

The oaf swore more promises of revenge as he tried inexpertly to get to his feet, with one hand attempting to stem the flow of blood coming from his large red nose.

Both the lovely wenches batted their eyes hard at the Ranger, sensing now after the oaf's revelation, or insinuation, that this handsome stranger might be indeed the wanted man the entire city was talking about, a wanted man with tons of coin.

The legend of the haul was growing exponentially as the

wildfire rumors raced across the City of Thieves...

And it was not often an opportunity like this fell into their silken laps.

"I think not, bruh!" roared Sergeant Thor titanically at the lumbering oaf. Everyone in the tavern laughed heartily at this as the lout sat down once more, rubbing his busted nose as he plopped down hard on the common room floor littered with sawdust and smelling of roasting meats and the perfumes of the other wenches among the customers. He began to cry, for he was drunk.

Sergeant Thor had said this in the patois of the city but kept "bruh," and everyone seemed to get the meaning and find the new word most amusing.

All eyes were on the perfection of the jacked and towering warrior they called Thor now that they were certain they would be his boon companions, and perchance... some of his fabled gold would fall their way, at least a few coins, maybe even more, before he was slain by the many forces now gathering against him. Those forces were scouring the city daily, following a trail of bodies and leaving a trail of bodies in their relentless wake.

It had been three days since the temple heist.

Since the Pit.

Since the game of slaughter and death.

All the City of Thieves was abuzz with the deeds of this

strange and seemingly unbeatable warrior who'd somehow bested those in the Game and taken not just the personal reward he could haul forth with his great fist, but it seemed, if one believed the uproar and the buzz that seemed to be on the lips of everyone in the city that hot, hot, simmering summer, that the whole chest had been looted down to the last gold coin.

Stories spread. Rumors abounded. Tales were traded and suspicions freely aired. Speculations were wagered on, and of course... plots laid.

The Ranger was on the move, according to the plan. The impression that the treasure was somewhere close at hand where he could get to it was made abundantly clear as he spent freely at taverns, inns, and gambling dens. Bevies of buxom beauties on both his massive arms as he spent and lost money like a Spec-4 getting his reenlistment bonus on a Friday afternoon and hitting the clubs by five.

At this rate, that soldier would have been busted by Monday. But the more the Ranger spent, hitting every tavern as he crossed the city, the money seemingly appearing from nowhere, it seemed to many he had almost an endless supply of the gold coin.

No one noticed the small pouches of gold coins handed off to the Ranger by this merchant, or that porter, or this servant girl, as Thor left each tavern, gambling den, or inn, seemingly drunk and fed, a girl or two in tow.

It was Alluria who made the handoffs most often.

The guild had trained Thor in the art of *the pass*, the exchange in public of stolen goods or valuables that needed to remain unseen. This was the specialty of a master thief called Asabie Alriysh, a wily dark-skinned little man always smiling at everyone and greeting most with a patter of chatter about weather, the wrongs of the eunuchs and ills of the wizards, or reminding these prospects to watch out for thieves as he looted their coin purse, unnoticed, from one pocket and placed it in another of their pockets so there was no loss.

Just to show Thor how it was done.

Asabie Alriysh meant *Feather Fingers*.

And Alluria the serving girl had learned well. Thor would clock her in the market or along some street, and the girl, carrying a jug of water on her head, or laundry, or a large basket filled with the day's produce for whatever inn the guild had her at, slipped past Thor, placed the stuffed coin purse in his pocket, and grabbed his butt quickly and deftly not lingering beyond an unnecessary second.

Sometimes she would distract whatever wench was on his arm by misdirecting her with her eyes, or exclaiming how beautiful she was even though Alluria herself was stunning, and then whisper only so the Ranger could hear, "The common whores you sully yourself with, thief."

Then she'd smile and the passing crowd would take her as though she'd never even been there. Thor belt-swapped on the gold coin and went on his next full-auto "drunken" spending spree as more kill teams of hired sellswords, bandits, and drunken dandies needing a quick score tried to relieve him of his fortune.

Never mind the pros the factions were sending at him with friends and sharp weapons to bring to bear against him.

The coin he spent reinforced the lie the Little Guild and Thor wanted everyone to fall for. That he was a lone wolf who'd gotten lucky and gotten rich. His luck was going to run out and why not be there when it did because no doubt that pile of treasure was somewhere nearby and near enough at hand to get at.

As one prince of thieves told a mover and shaker among the eunuchs amid a clutch of cooing and clucking *mandarini*, "Iss like this, Fauntly..." for that was the name of the eunuch who managed festivals and sweetmeats on the Streets of Brass and Copper, and by *managed it* is meant taxed, stole, and looted every stray coin he could get his fat fingers on, "Iss like this, Fauntly... we thieves view the Big Coin, and really when you take apart like we do iss all connected so iss all one big fat purse of the finest coins rolled up into what we call the Big Coin. We view that Big Coin as being in the possession of one single person at a time. Maybe among many, but usually like... iss under the control of one. See me? You got that Big Coin, well pop pop and all dat, you can control all the rest of it as it moves about in the city here-like... see me?"

The eunuch, all ears and perhaps even eyes, for this particular prince of thieves cut a dashing figure in his fine cloaks and tight leathers.

"But here's the thing, Faunts... that Big Coin is always movin' about and all. Sometimes this chap's got it. Other times the next boyo is runnin' the stack. We thieves... we know this, and, wasss more important... we accept it. Sometimes... iss even our turn, Ol' Faunt, see me, right? To run the stack of the Big Coin. Every dog gets his bone."

Fauntly the eunuch murmured softly that he did understand this method of viewing the local economy. The eunuchs had similar, more refined ways of putting it, but yes, usually someone chose the winners, and the dead. The powdered and corpulent eunuch sipped sweet cold wine from his golden goblet. His simpering boys nearby in the open-air drinking place they were meeting this particular prince of thieves in for an information exchange regarding "that Dire Barbarian Thor Problem," as it was known in eunuch circles, fanned him with great feathers from some strange and exotic bird. Nearby, a great southern warrior, dark-skinned to the point of being a glistening black, shining with sweat in the heat, armored in gold bands and cutting an impressive and stern figure, held a cockatrice feather whip in thick leather-gloved hands.

Beautiful as it was, the cockatrice whip, it could turn a man to stone with the merest caress of its feather lash, for that was what the cockatrice could do. And so that was why here in the Street of Daggers, a dangerous but not the most dangerous alley in the Ruby District of the City of Thieves, not one of the locals molested the fine eunuch in his gorgeous cool white perfect silks and pearled turban as he stroked his thin curling mustache and listened to this particular prince of thieves get on with what exactly was going on with regard to the guilds and "that Dire Barbarian Thor Problem" he'd been sent out into the heat to attend to.

"Sometimes..." repeated this particular prince of thieves, "iss even our turn, Ol' Faunt, see me, right? And we accept that 'cause even us thieves hafta note that fair's fair and there is, in fact, honor among thieves."

The thief suddenly flung a dagger that hadn't been obvious before and landed it at the foot of a local urchin boy trying out for the guild that ran the Ruby District and was tasked with stealing something off this particular prince of thieves in order that he might advance and receive training.

But the prince of thieves didn't make it easy. Even if you

were an orphan raised on the streets of one of the most dangerous and deadly streets in the Ruin.

If you'd asked him, he would have said why. "'Cause life ain't easy."

There are, and it has to be said here, many princes of thieves in the City of Thieves. It's more of a guild rank than anything, but generally it goes right to their heads and it is said, in quiet quarters late at night among the wise, that perhaps this is by design.

*Whose*, the question that is asked next by those attending and wishing to know wisdoms late in the night. *Whose design is this by?*

*Why*, the answer would be, *the wily old craft guild masters themselves,* comes the thiefly wisdom. *The unseen ones. The ones that are in power and wish to remain so. Unseen. For that's real power. Ain't it?*

"But this Dire Man lout who got the whole chest," continued this particular prince of thieves to the eunuch in the heat of the day under the fans of the simpering boys who wanted to be elevated to *mandarini*. "This savage, and beat us with a maul if we knows how it was done, Fauntly... but he's sorta messed up the whole system now when you think about it, and that's why everyone's scheming to get 'im."

"How so," murmured the ethereal Fauntly, the mover-and-shaker eunuch. Or, as he was known locally, *The Devil*

*Himself of Copper and Brass.* Especially by those he taxed, they called him this, and worse, behind his back, spitting, swearing, and making their signs to ward off various evils and bad lucks.

As if such things can be so powerful.

"Well, see here now, Faunts... this prize money that was in the chest. It's in play now and it never was before. That's fine. If it woulda been any other bloke that gots his paws on it... fine. Someone got control on him, and control is everything. But this one... this one that calls himself Thor and others say is a *Ranger* whatever that is... ain't no one got control on him. And he's got the Big Coin and it's in play and everyone up to the wizards themselves is worried for what that means for them and theirs. It's chaos, Faunts. Pure chaos. And this may seem a wild and lawless city down here at the edge of the known world, but we both know the world's a whole lot bigger than anyone thinks it is. Ya hear of those Fire Giants in the Ganistan? If that's what's out there beyond the edge, then I ain't interested in anything beyond the walls here. But it's a lot bigger and far more dangerous than those behind walls care to admit. The Ruin that is, see me? I'm off track here, Faunts... but don't you notice... people'd rather believe the lie, than admit the truth. Know why?"

Fauntly sipped and murmured something to the effect

that he did not know why. Which was a lie. Eunuchs knew more than even the wizards about the way the Ruin really worked. They just didn't go around sharing it with anyone else not them. Information lost its power when it was known by all.

So the eunuchs were listeners, for in the gathering of what was said, and the keeping and protecting of it, there was much, much power, and perhaps even more power than possessed by those wizards had who sought the Arcane Realms and delved the Abyssal Fortresses for lost and forbidden spells to bend the Ruin to their cruel wills.

"Well, I'll tell ya, Faunts... truth is damn scary. And most people... don't like to be scared. So... they don't like the truth. See me on that?"

Fauntly sipped a little more and murmured about the heat being *simply too much*. The lad who'd been frozen in place by the dagger at his feet was released with a signal flick of this prince of thieves's manicured hand, allowing him to understand he had failed and could try again. Another time. Not this one.

This was done in thieves' cant hand signals the lad didn't know. But he would learn. And that too was part of the training.

The caramel-skinned urchin with blond hair and green eyes, and threadbare clothing, scampered off into the trading press along the street. A failure, and unseen, once again.

"Are you scared?" asked the eunuch. "Are you frightened of this man Thor? He seems dangerous. Many have died already and the numbers..."

This particular prince of thieves looked afar off, out there in the press, to the other side of the market, the wall, and the sea beyond. Other places, other cities. Appraising the traffic and selecting who he would target tonight for robbery. Who could lose so he could provide for his guild, and himself. And then there were the wenches coming out on the roofs. Dressed in silks, fanning themselves after their morning baths. Readying themselves for a long night's work.

A few beauties eyed the dashing prince of thieves and indicated no one played for free, but perhaps a fine bauble, a sparkling gem, some noble lady's comb... and well, a few minutes' pleasure could be spent.

This particular prince of thieves looked back at the eunuch, his mission accomplished as the guild master had made it known... *Find out what the eunuchs know and make sure they know the one called Thor is a problem.*

Job done.

The eunuchs were scared. They'd said as much. They knew that whoever got their hands on all that loot the stupid warrior had heisted was going to be the Big Tuna in the City of Thieves for some time to come.

They'd send their guards and assassins now, those vile fanatical scumbags, at him. At the one called Thor. Perhaps the thieves could cut themselves in on some of the take in the chaos that ensued if they did the scouting or located his stash.

He didn't seem to be allied with anyone. He seemed reckless, and frankly stupid.

You don't get to be a prince of thieves by being... stupid.

*Seemed.*

This Particular Prince of Thieves thought about that word and what he, and all of them, were being sold as this Dire Man savage, or *Ranger*, whatever that was, went through the city like feed through a goose.

And this Thor... he'd left a lot of dead so far. Many were missing after the Pit. Those who made their living robbing the winners.

Gone. Just... gone.

"Yeah..." he said softly. Whispered it so the immense brute with the whip of feathers that could turn you to stone, the one glowering at him even now, didn't hear, and frankly, this particular prince of thieves didn't mind if the man did.

*Sometimes you have to be honest about these things.* Some warrior passing through had once said that to him. But he couldn't remember the man's name. Just that he was tired and his pack was large and he'd seen and done many things.

He had that look in his eyes.

"Yeah, Ol' Faunts... I'm scared to death on this one. That... Ranger... whatever that is... ain't just chaos pure and terrible, he's death itself, Faunts, see me? Fifteen dead since he surfaced after the Pit. Prolly more, and that's not counting the dozens who vanished the night of. And of course... winning the Game. Granted those fifteen were mostly probes by the wizards and us. But that man has killed all what tried to take what he stole fair and square and real stupid from the High Priests themselves. And you know what, Faunts..."

Long pause.

Commerce in the marketplace.

The bray of donkeys being driven through.

Wind chimes among the whores' high houses where the breeze cools them as they wait for the night and the men who will pay. Hoping... someone will love them.

A merchant shouts that he has been robbed.

A snake charmer plays his hypnotic flute and a cobra hisses and strikes at a screaming chicken.

Wares are offered.

The end of the world is bleated.

A thousand conversations that make up life, small and petty, sometimes meaning so much more than what is actually said, swirl and pass like the tides out there beyond the great fortresses and the sea walls.

"No. I do not know what," answered the eunuch who thought he'd kept his cards close to his chest on this meeting.

The thieves didn't know anything. That would be his report. And... they were...

"Iss gonna get a lot worse, Faunts, see me? This Thor's a fire, Faunts. Not just death maybe even. But a fire that could consume us all if it gets out of hand and the Big Coin ends up where it shouldn't. I got that feeling, Faunts. This one's different. And a lot of us are gonna die finding that out."

*The thieves are scared.*

That would be his report.

Then, as smoothly and easily as he'd appeared for the late noon meeting with his contact among the eunuchs, That Particular Prince of Thieves was gone out into the trading press along the street. Disappeared as he picked three pockets just to remind himself that he still had skills, and that death would have to measure twice and cut once if it was going to come for him.

Even if death was a *Ranger*... whatever that is.

And to give himself some confidence for all the death, chaos, and fire coming, he mumbled to himself, "Yeah... fire, iss headed our way, Faunts." He'd whispered that just before he left. Then he was gone like a ghost in the dark.

"See me?"

# CHAPTER TWENTY-SIX

BY THE TIME THE NEXT BATCH OF TREASURE HUNTERS tried to corral the big blond-haired blue-eyed and tatted Ranger everyone wanted the truth of the heist out of, their luck had already run out long before they knew it. Like every other killer, wizard, eunuch, or cheap sellsword assassin in between all those devils and the deep blue sea beyond the walls, they wanted, one, to know how it had been done. And two, they wanted Thor dead.

It was best that the one called "Sergeant Thor," who was now everyone's target in a city where murder was as casual as "good morning," be left to die in some alley or sold off to the ghouls down in the cemetery districts that were always looking for a fresh corpse to do some work on.

But that afternoon in yet another tavern, by the time this latest batch tried their luck in the late afternoon at the drinking and roasting place near the Street of Sighs and Pleasures, just off a small twisting alley ending in a wide courtyard where the middling bards and desperate players would come in the evenings to entertain with songs from the west and plays by Ascal the Blind, always hilarious and filled with misdirection and comic beauties, this latest batch of killers' luck had run out despite the numbers, coin in their pockets for services about to be done, and the belief that when they got up that morning someone else would be dead.

Not them.

Now, their luck had run out. Long before their first member entered the front door and scanned the room, murderous eyes landing on the giant Ranger.

The tavern was called the Dancing Goat. It was known for its coffee by day, served under a wide red, blue, and gold striped pavilion out front in the courtyard, and cold barrels of frothy beer in the evenings, brought up from the cellars where a minor drunk of a wizard had lain frost spells across the floor to keep the beer cool during the long hot nights of murder and revelry that clung to the city like the tight bodice of an ample serving wench.

Sergeant Thor had gotten the signal after the three fights in two gambling dens and one tavern, probes really, that the wizards were sending in a major push next, right at him, to try and either abduct Thor and torture him to find out just how exactly the great Prize Chest of the Pit had been plundered so expertly, and where exactly all its loot was, or they were just going to kill him, wait until his corpse was buried out in the eastern necropolises of the vast and spreading city beyond the proper walls, then dig him up later and get some answers with the help of a dead-whisperer.

A subset of necromancy specializing in the revelation of information from beyond the grave.

A necromancer working at the behest of the wizards involved in this particular cabal would cast *Talk with the Dead* and they would get the secrets they needed to know out of the big brute the city was all abuzz about, in death if he was not willing to part with it in life, or if he failed to survive the afternoon attack-and-capture and perhaps some heated iron in from the forges applied firmly to skin and eyes to bring forth what they wanted to know.

All options were on the table as teams of armed men converged on the Dancing Goat all at once. Those on the street knew a murder about to happen when they saw one, and got busy shuttering their businesses and bolting their doors.

Fights had a way of spreading, and this "Ranger," if the stories of the last few days were to be believed, was no easy target.

In fact, he was a very hard target.

The gambling dens were now taking bets on the body count before he went down, and small life-changing fortunes were to be made on some of the higher numbers.

Such is the way of the City of Thieves.

One way or another... they were hellsbent to find out.

Five came into the rowdy inn that smelled of beer, smoke, and roasting meat. Two heavies. Men carrying large reapers' axes who usually spent their days dispensing local justice for some byzantine infractions in the tax code on behalf of the ever-clutching eunuchs.

And sometimes not even for an infraction. Sometimes the eunuchs just wanted your property and the best way to get a deal was a discount payment to your widow, or perhaps she could be drowned in the sewers or off the rocks near the Great Lighthouse. Her call. You were dead anyway.

Either way... they'd get what they wanted which was the only rule the greedy eunuchs who administered the City of Thieves lived by, and these two brutes did the beheading in this district.

They were capable axe-men and they knew their bloody trade.

Now... the strangling, if it came to that for the widow, and perhaps even her children if they couldn't be sold to the flesh pits, or some merchant, was done by the assassins. The eunuchs had paid blood money to the assassins' guild to go in with the two brutes on this one against the one called Thor.

Messengers were in the streets, and the eunuchs running the op would be apprised when the deed was done. So sure were they this would work, that a grand bacchanal feast had been thrown together on the fly complete with young boys and tons of lotus. Within hours of the death of the Ranger, the eunuchs would be cavorting and celebrating at the estate of Nuzom the Vain, a shifty snake of a eunuch who dared dream big, and that he might rule over the eunuchs in time with victories like this and a dark and unknown alliance with Lady Hudu.

Again, it was surprising none involved were aware, even the despicable tyrant Nuzom the Vain, that their luck had run out and that the wild and chaotic Thor was about to end all their plans, and a lotta lives in the process.

So sure were they that impending victory to the "Dire Barbarian Problem" was imminent, that defeat was wholly unconsidered.

A lot of spilt blood was about to teach them otherwise.

The fourth to go in with the two axe-men and the assassin was a knife-thrower of note called Bullseye by all the locals. This was a warrior of some renown who specialized in certain methods of delivery of death. Bullseye marked an upping of the game for the eunuchs. Local celebrities, let's call Bullseye that, were starting to get recruited on Day Three after the spectacular looting of the Prize Chest, to get the dirty work done before some other faction, wizards or thieves, got their hands around the muscled throat of the one called Thor the Ranger by some bit of luck and got the prized answers to the riddle out of him...

One way, or another.

So Bullseye and his expertly weighted and shiny knives came to play in the afternoon of that day ending as both oafs with the reapers' axes kicked open the door like they were breaching huts back in the 'Stan.

Bullseye had once put twenty knives into a warrior who made the mistake of challenging the man to a duel. And that was twenty knives before the guy even took two steps toward him. The idiot had cleared leather on his blade and suddenly Bullseye, moving like a blur, made his knives appear all across the body of the idiot warrior no one remembered the name of anymore.

Now the two chungos, with the reapers' axes up and ready, kicked open the door *like they were breaching huts back in the 'Stan.*

That was what the Ranger thought, back to the wall, across the wide room and drinking another cold draught as the tasty wench on one arm massaged his swollen bicep, tracing the ink there with one long delicate finger and cooing with each curve and twist in the design. Making the case that she was his... *no price asked this night, stranger.*

On the other arm was a redhead, tall and strong. Almost as tall as Thor himself. Almost. Her jade-green crazy eyes flashed and watched his, staring long and uncomfortably, but kinda cool, as she sat back on her hands and forearms making sure the big sniper got a good look, and a very good look at that, at all the wares she had to offer him.

She wore little other than gossamer silk to cover the best parts.

But it was those eyes. Crazy eyes.

They were kind of entrancing. In a weird, dangerous way. And yeah... they had that... *edge*... to them. He could get into that. Her eyes reminded him of the Fate he had once known. And the nights they had spent together.

But the banging open of the front door of the Dancing Goat by the two oafs with reapers' axes out and ready to do the killing work told him all he needed to know as he tore his gaze away from the fiery redhead and clocked both operators coming for him now.

These guys were pure death-dealer.

The lithe and comely brunette on one arm screamed, suddenly and hysterically, backing away like a cat on a hot tin roof from the clear and intended target of the two executioners, the man the whole city wanted dead in so short a space of time.

"Knew this was coming..." she said hysterically and got as

far away from trouble as she possibly could. As fast as she could.

Thor stood and reached for the sword that he'd laid on the drinking table with his pile of tantalizing gold coin and the roast meat and cheese they'd brought out for him.

The redhead on the other arm, quick as a panther, grasped the sword and flung it away from Thor, holding on to his arm like a sinister pale-skinned python in the next moment so he couldn't draw the shank on his thigh to defend himself. She was laughing wildly.

Then, madly, she tried to kiss him before he was slaughtered by the men who had paid her well to keep him occupied while they made their attack.

She was the fifth in their attack force.

A warrioress from Caspia, skilled in scimitars and armor, one of their spell-working skirmishers, she possessed those skills and the skills of grappling that had once been known as BJJ.

Or what Thor and those of the Before would have called Brazilian jiujitsu.

In Caspia they called it the Cobras and Matadors.

Instantly her shapely long and powerful legs and thighs twisted about his, entangling him as her powerful creamy white hips locked about his back and tried to control him.

"Wench!" Thor thundered and with the one hand he still

had free, drew the punch knife from his belt at his waist. "Off me now!"

Then without waiting, he plunged it right into her alabaster throat, long and slender.

The look of shock and sudden horror on her face as her plan to take a share of whatever they could peel off his body after the two headsmen got done with him was replaced by frozen rage as she went limp and slithered off him, choking on her own blood as she died.

Luck, it had already run out for the assaulters. The problem was, most of them didn't know it yet.

Attempting to curse him with the spells taught her by her witchy grandmother back in the mean streets of Caspia beneath the shadows of the mountains of Umnoth, the comely redhead only gurgled instead, and death took her.

Free of the treacherous wench, Thor scrambled as the first death dealer had already reached the long table the Ranger had been at and smashed his axe down on it, sending coin and roast fowl in every sudden direction.

"*Ahhhhh!*" screamed some rando who'd been in the tavern just hoping this would happen and seeing his chance to get in the action. He was a sailmaker down at the port who owed money big-time for gambling debts he could never ever seem to pay off.

The rando came at Thor with one of his cutting sailcloth

knives out, wicked and razor-sharp, hoping to stick him in the gut or the kidney as the big Ranger scrambled for the stair leading up to the second story where the wenches kept their rooms and others, a few, were offered for a night's rest.

The Ranger reasoned he could fight from there better and take them one at a time. But the rando, sharp canvas-cutter knife out and dripping juice from the roast fowl he'd been working at and biding his time for just such an attack, was in his way now. Thor kicked the man in the nuts, drawing the belt knife low as though ready to thrust it up again at anyone who came for him next. When the sailmaker with the bad debts instinctually bent at being kicked savagely in the sensitive place where he'd been kicked, the Ranger turned slightly to let the man, in intense pain, impale his face onto the sharp belt knife, then scream suddenly as he recoiled away in horror with a pulped eye.

Death dealer two, with the second reaper axe out and high, saw the escape attempt the Ranger was making and moved to cut him off, slashing down and wide with the axe to bisect Sergeant Thor should he continue his course.

Thor went down on one palm, low beneath the sweeping shining scythe of the headsman's axe, and kicked the man's legs out from under him in a savage twist and sweep.

The giant went sprawling and Thor was up and leaping for the narrow corridor of stairs leading upward into the high darknesses of the inn suddenly turned bloody battle and screaming injury all at once.

Flung knives, sharp and small, followed Thor as he made the stairs and fell back up them, and the first giant filled the entrance to the narrow stair with no room to swing his axe.

The Ranger turned and pressed both hands against the sides of the corridor leading up, swung his legs upward, and rocketed one boot right into the man's face.

The crunch of the headsman's nose was terrific and resounded out just below the screams of the sailmaker running from the tavern, holding the bloody and viscous drool that was once his eye, along with the shrieks of the wenches and the bellowing innkeeper.

The headsman on the stair, blind and braying, sent both beefy paws to his broken and blood-spurting nose, and backed away. The other headsman pushed past and raised his own sharp axe, a weapon he was expert with and took much pride in, over one shoulder and made to attack upward, intent on chopping the axe overhead into such a tight place as the badly illuminated darkness the Ranger had chosen to fight them all in.

It was a good plan, and even though Thor had the high ground it wouldn't matter against the huge and heavy gleaming axe in the twilight of the stairwell.

That was when the fourth member of the assassination

squad sent by the eunuchs seemingly materialized out of the dark and slipped his silk strangling scarf around the great head of the Ranger from behind, instantly cross-knotting it and strangling Thor even as the strangler pivoted and kicked one of the Ranger's knees out from under him.

The assassin was a second-story man and had gone in through the wenches' open windows to come into the battle from the stairs.

Thor grasped the cloth that was strangling him and knew it was woven so well it would not rip. Silently, behind him, grunting, the spindly little naked torso and turbaned slender man held on for all he was worth.

Below Thor, the second headsman raced up the stair, axe raised high and ready to strike.

The Ranger suddenly folded forward, turning himself into a ball, and flung the man off his back and right into the savage downswing of the executioner's axe.

The strangler screamed as he caught the swift chop of the axe right in the belly and lay beneath the headsman who seemed incredulous that his axe had ended up in the man on the floor.

Thor stood as the strangler grasped the axe and tried to pull it out of him while at the same time the headsman tried to do the same. They ended up struggling against each other, and the Ranger swiftly drew his shank off his thigh and thrust it right through the headsman's throat in the chaos of the tussle on the stair.

Both men were dead and dying, dimly aware that their luck had run out when the messenger had come with this contract sometime in the half-light before dawn.

The other headsman, the one with the smashed nose, blind from his own blood, had by now run away from the inn, knocking down sprawling whores and smashing aside early drunks to get free of the folly that had been the attack against the Ranger.

The knife-thrower called Bullseye reached for more knives as Sergeant Thor made the floor of the inn once more, weaving to dodge and scramble forward as the expert's blades were tossed. Thor flipped tables and tossed chairs to intercept the quickly hurled bright blades as they came at him. Then at the last, close to the point of close-quarters combat with blades, Sergeant Thor, using a chair as a shield, both bashed the renowned knife-thrower over the head with it and stuck the shank in his abdomen, running it clean through to the back of the man and past the spine.

Then, just as savagely as it had gone in, the Ranger yanked the blade out and stood over the knife man as the killer fell backward onto the filthy ruin of the tavern floor, whimpering pitifully and little in keeping with his dangerous reputation in the city.

The battle was over.

The luck had run out... for the other guys.

The Ranger wiped the blade on the dying man's knife-laden vest and hissed, "Who sent you in?" using port-speak which was a mixture of Gray Speech and ancient Arabic. There were some strange words in there, things Thor had learned along the way. Words Talker, the detachment linguist, had relished. Words the sniper just used as yet more tools for him to take on the edges he found, and then ended up killing his way through.

That didn't bother him.

"Who sent you?" he hissed now at the dying man on the floor, his voice not a ragged gasp but a low hiss. He breathed through his nose, calming himself. The inn was almost vacant now. Everyone had fled the chaos and bloodshed.

Only the sweeping boy, cowering behind the bar, remained.

The dying blademaster on the floor whimpered again, looking around hysterically and wide-eyed at the ruin that the one called Thor the Ranger, the target the eunuchs had sent him and the others for, had made of him. Them. Their plans.

Unbelievable.

Unexpected.

But... no longer in doubt.

Truth flickered in the knife-thrower's eyes, replacing the horror of his injury. His bloody hands shaking, he let them fall from his belly, useless now, trailing his own guts and gore as he did so.

Bullseye looked at Thor.

Thor heard the cocking of a crossbow behind the bar. In the darkness there where the kid who swept the floors was. A skinny, nothing of a boy who'd never get farther than driving a broom across bones and vomit day after day. The whores teasing him.

Everybody has to take their shot. Thor didn't fault him for that. He'd dismissed the kid when he walked in. Now... he had some respect for him. He could respect the kid drawing down on him.

He thought perhaps that might be the voice of the smaj. The voice of warning and reason and edges. The voice that challenged him to come back and Ranger with the detachment.

*Where you was meant to be, Sar'nt Thor.*

Or perhaps it was his own.

Everybody's got to take their shot. Right?

The dying man watched the hulking Ranger above him, mouth working, unable to answer the asked question. Staring death in the face.

Death itself asking the question he could not answer.

Didn't matter, thought Thor as he saw the dark shadow of the sweeping kid rising from behind the bar. The wizards, or the eunuchs. They'd sent this bunch. This was all part of the plan. His plan. Draw fire. Keep distracting them from what had really happened.

And now the boy behind the bar would take his shot too.

Or was the kid simply defending his inn? The place where he worked. Defending the whore who didn't even know his name he was in love with.

Or maybe he was getting ready to fire on the second set of bad guys Thor would have sent in to clean up after the first attack. That would have been how he and the Rangers would have done it.

Not everyone all at once.

*Everyone all at once...*

As good as that sounds, that's amateur hour. Too many people in one area and the chances of failure increase. Assets get lost for no good reason.

The principle of mass, coordinating all combat elements to attack as one, must be effective. You can't throw everything all at once at one target in a confined area. Gotta be ready for bad guy number two. Gotta exploit the weaknesses.

That's why he kept shifting to inns. Spaces were too tight to be hit with too many all at once. Out on the streets... now that was a different story.

Who knew why the kid picked up the crossbow behind the bar...

Thor pivoted and fired the shank overhand at the dark silhouette behind the bar with the crossbow. When he got it back later, after Bullseye's eyes had gone otherwhere, he'd find that he'd drilled the kid right in the forehead as the bolt got fired into the bar once the sweeper boy's switch got flipped.

Thor turned back, looking at the dead blademaster on the bloody floor. Knowing no answers would be forthcoming there.

"Doesn't matter," he grunted, getting to his boots. Covered in blood and spatter once again. Just him and the silence of the empty tavern.

No wounds though.

The cat-like brunette came out from under a table.

"Where do you go now, Dire Man?" she asked, trying to be seductive as she stood, but he could hear the tremble of fear in her voice. That close-to-death-just-seconds-ago tremble that can't be hidden. Even if you want to. Even if you need to. Badly.

Sergeant Thor went behind the rough bar and gained back his shank, again wiping it on the dead, this one staring up at where the thick blade had landed right in his skull.

He took up an empty tankard and poured a half draught. It was cold and frothy, and he downed it just to remove the taste of the blood and their fear from his mouth.

The inn was a slaughterhouse.

This had been the plan. Keep shifting inns. They would attack and attack while the heist got more and more buried. The thieves of the Little Guild would stay away and watch. They would send messengers when they could. But for now, in the City of Thieves and on his own, Thor had to survive as the powers that be started to turn up the heat on him in their desire to know, exactly, just what had happened in the Pit. Never knowing where this whole plan was going. Just reacting.

That's the way Rangers liked it.

Thor set down the tankard.

"Where go you now?" she said again, standing shakily beside the ruin she'd hidden under. She was a beauty. Someone had cut a scar on her neck once but that only seemed to make her sexier to him.

Across the broken rubble she made her way smoothly as though such battlefields were not new to her. She stepped over the dead redhead from the witches of Caspia.

The redhead's glazed green eyes stared in anger, or horror, at some fate she'd been ushered off to.

Such sights were nothing new in the streets of the City of

Thieves.

Thor began to pick up the gold coins that had been spilt in the chaos.

"Another inn, girl," he rumbled in the quiet darkness between them. Evening twilight would come soon. The players and bards would arrive for their show under the striped canvases to perform once again their bawdy tales and heroic lays.

Poems of humiliation and verses of innuendo, of course paid for by duelists one against the other.

But they would find there would be no place, or customers, to play to this night.

That was standard in the City of Thieves.

"Another inn, girl. Show's been canceled tonight."

A strange thing about the Ranger. He'd never liked the movies back in the Before they had all come from. He'd liked real life. Real adventures. But here in the Ruin, he'd found he liked their little street plays. It helped with the language. Taught some history, or lore, as Ranger Wizard PFC Kennedy would have called it. Helped him to understand them more.

And he needed everything he could get, everything he could collect, if he was going to survive the edges here.

Ain't that right, Sar'nt Major?

Even a play about love and blood with rhetoric. He'd

seen some about love and blood. Some about rhetoric and blood. But the blood... it seemed compulsory in all of them.

And he didn't mind that.

"May I go with you, one called Thor the Ranger? Go with you tonight wherever you go next? I am not dangerous."

Thor smiled and extended his bloody hand. The shank in the other.

"Doesn't matter if you are, girl."

Then they left there and went out into the late night.

Wizards fumed.

Eunuchs plotted.

Thieves schemed.

Assassins chanted.

The City of Thieves went on with its mad and bloody ways, for such is the City of Thieves.

And wizards plotted...

# CHAPTER TWENTY-SEVEN

IT WAS LATE MORNING THE DAY AFTER THE SLAUGHTER at the Dancing Goat the whole city was abuzz about. That outright brawl and rout by the big Dire Man savage Thor, and other fights and chases that had taken place over the past few firestorm days, were on everyone's lips as business, trade, thievery, and murder continued unabated. It was becoming more and more abundantly clear, powerful factions within the City of Thieves were now willing to spend big on teams of desperate killers to get their hands on the strange barbarian who'd stolen the entire Prize Chest the night of the Game in the Pit, or sometime shortly thereafter.

The High Priests were now missing too, and fast-spreading whispers in the fruit and nut markets at the height of the day indicated they'd gone deep beneath the city into the ancient catacombs and lost areas there. And... that they might not ever return.

How this "Ranger" was not dead already was quite the

mystery. But informal and formal bets seemed to indicate he would be soon.

Meanwhile...

Baalubrozz had whored and debauched his way straight through six houses of pleasure until he collapsed from pure exhaustion in the worst of them all sometime after a hot dawn in the company of three of the worst the city had to offer.

The shambling "palace of delights" was little more than a ramshackle, rundown, leaning, three-story collapse of a house where the worst and lowest-priced girls offered their services to... anyone.

The next haboob sweeping out of the Eastern Wastes would surely knock it down soon enough.

In the top room of the wreck of a whorehouse, what "the madam" of the establishment had called *The High Palace*, the corpulently squat little summoner lay face-down on a broken bed surrounded by three ugly whores he'd paid sometime before dawn.

The whores slept too. Either from exhaustion or... depression at the low estate they had fallen to.

One snored.

That one could have been pretty had someone not taken a knife to her face. She was young and lay failed on the collapsed bed away from the summoner in a death-like sleep.

Her slender hand flung across her face as though to ward off yet another terrible day of being her.

All her days were terrible since what had befallen her, had, well... befallen her.

Then there was the fat one on the floor with the bowl of grapes she'd devoured. She lay back, her flesh rolls on full display, her painted fleshy mouth wide open and drool crawling down the sides of her puffy cheeks, running through the cheap makeup she tried to sell herself better by if the drink was much and the lighting not so bright.

She didn't snore so much as gurgle.

This was how Baalubrozz hunted, summoned, and did his evil magic.

It wasn't even dark, shadowy, or black. The spells he wove were purest evil. And to call forth what he did... evil in its most corrupt form... he had to get as close to it as he could.

He had to become it.

Baalubrozz had learned over long years along the twisting and midnight trek that was the acquisition of his power, that debauching and debasing himself was how he worked best in controlling the spirit realm and binding the demons and the occasional devil he'd trapped within his rings in order to do his bidding.

Summoning was a dangerous business, and you had to be

clever. You were dealing with innate liars and deceivers in possession of, and in thrall to, huge amounts of power. The summoner who'd taught him said you had to be half mule-skinner to deal with these diabolical beings. And that guy got sucked into a magical circle he'd made the mistake of assuming could protect him as he explored the Ninth Plane of Hell.

So after that, Baalubrozz took his old flesh-bound tomes and taught himself, now that his master would never return from the endless suffering he'd banished himself to.

He got good at what he did even though he was... who he was. Let's just leave it at that. He learned, he survived, and... he became that which he sought to master.

Osirex knew just how to use him, and the wretched little bastard of a summoner was both flattered at that, and resentful.

The night before, Baalubrozz had gone to the Pit as ordered by Osirex, in order to cast his spells of detection, scry with his Ring of Seeing, and let forth his minor shadow demons to find out just how exactly what had happened in the aftermath of the Game, the One Draw, and then... the beautiful, yet vexing, theft of the fantastic Prize Chest... had happened.

What had become of all that loot in the Pit?

The detection spells revealed nothing.

Whether that was because some greater more powerful magic was at work in the area by dark and unseen forces, or no magic had been used in the heist, was not discernible, and that vexed the malevolent cherubic summoner much as he stalked the midnight crumble of the Pit, his shadow demons flitting about and murmuring malevolently.

The Seeing Ring saw nothing.

And still the shadow demons just flitted about and tittered about, not knowing a thing.

Not very likely.

They were lying to him...

So he opened a gate to a particular hell with a demon lord he'd done some work for and sent them there to think for a while about how they could serve him better.

Now he was alone in the quiet ruin of the old place and he wondered, sensing some greater, deeper, darker power below... whether his shadow demons had possibly grown too afraid to tell him what had happened.

He sniffed, spit, blew his nose, and hawked a loogie onto ancient, blackened ruins.

There was something deeper, and darker, here.

But this was not part of his mission. Not today.

He needed to finance an expedition and go deep. Hire a hundred men to die making their way deep so he could find out who, or what, was down there.

Talk to it.

Trap it.

And if not... do a deal with it.

But that was all for another time...

*This lot of unseen dark servants are getting difficult to work with, these shadow demons*, thought Baalubrozz. The imps sharing not so much as an intimation on the fate of the Chest and how it had been looted. And really... where all the loot had gone. Perhaps it was best to leave them where he'd sent them off to, or just plain banish them straight down to Tartarus, which was as far from the Hells as Heaven was.

Then he'd go Hell-diving and planewalk into one of the Hells and entrap more shadow demons to serve him.

Again... that was a problem for another time.

The Seeing Ring saw nothing.

The shadow demons mocked him and would do nothing.

And his spells weren't... or... were, working. He just didn't know.

Hard to tell.

Baalubrozz was chaos, and yes, wholeheartedly evil. Had to be to acquire the terrible powers he wielded, or the devils and demons he worked with. Having been thrust into the cabal with the insufferable and lawful, and evil, but yes lawful, Osirex, had somehow played with his magical powers. And the summoner did not like that now that he was away from the leader of the cabal.

And don't get him started on that drugged-out illusionist. Mandelf Stoned Hat or whatever his name was. That one was so old he'd probably die at any moment.

And illusions... that's not real magic. That's tricks and games. No real power there.

The summoner hated pretenders. Maybe he'd let something dark and wild loose on Mandelf and see how he liked it when the dark forces showed him some real nightmares he couldn't trick his way out of.

*Again*, he almost yelled at himself in the lonely midnight emptiness of the Pit from which the High Priests had disappeared, *another problem for another time.*

Find the one who stole the contents of the chest. Do that by finding out either how it was done, which he could not, or finding where the northern oaf had run off to.

The latter question had a ready answer. Apparently the Dire Man savage was storming gambling dens and taverns left and right. But where had he gone *right afterwards*...

That was the knowledge he needed to know.

And there was strong magic in the answer to that question, suspected the diabolical little summoner.

Baalubrozz needed chaos. Debauchery, and definitely some deviltry.

"This is gonna be dirty," he mumbled to himself, trying out a wild little cackle thinking of the trouble he'd need to get up to, to do some real summoning and get some real answers. "So... time to get real dirty."

So... in the absence of answers at the scene of the crime, he'd gone off whoring. First starting at the finest establishments until he was thrown from there by rough guards who knew not with whom they dealt. He'd slit one of the prized beauties' throats in the lantern-lit jade-lotus-smelling suite just to sell her to a devil lurking about, but the establishment had heard her screams and rescued her corpse. The devil got mad and was gone.

Baalubrozz drunkenly hurled a small purse of coins at the guards and stalked off, laughing madly and hissing angrily at shadows.

Then he went through more pleasure houses all day long and through the heat of the night, feasting and debauching as fast, and as much, as he could. Getting weirder and wilder at each new stage, handing out drugs and drink, potions and powders, and even the erotic syrups of Caspia, to girls all too willing to do anything for some more coin.

In time he was chased from the establishment, this one and that, every house he waddled and perverted his way through, or the whores died and none of the others would cavort with him after that, running and clutching their silks from his bloody rituals and impromptu erotic scrawlings.

So he went south, along the city wall where it's dark, in the late of the night, finding streetwalkers and paying them as he went, cackling as he forced mushrooms and psychedelic herbs on them, laughing wildly and madly as the dying whores expired in the silent streets they had just walked, yet more of the flotsam of death among the alleys and trash of the City of Thieves.

Toward dawn he found the three-story ramshackle, a red lantern out front, brooding in the night silence and sleeping whores waiting in the lounge. The place with the "palace" at the top and the whore who was really ugly and snored, and then the beautiful whore who had been marred by someone's knife, and the fat whore whom he could never feed, drink, or drug enough to get her to die so he could sell off her soul to a wandering devil or a passing pack of working demons off and on their way to make more mischief for mankind.

It was hot and the sun beat through the slats that barred the window. The room smelled awful. He didn't know how much more he had in him, and how much further he could fall.

If anything, he needed to rest up for a day and break into his nepenthe syrups and go really wild and wicked. Anything could happen then.

He would literally be out of his mind.

But... that always worked.

He'd tried... everything.

He was passed out when the knife-cut whore began to talk, croaking like a door opening slowly in the night, in her sleep. He awoke, groggily, his head ringing, his body on fire with sweat and drugs and syrup of curst and witchy Caspia, and the rising heat of yet another hot, stinking, grueling, hell of a day in the worst section of the city.

Her voice was a dead croak, and before he could slap her and tell her to, "Shut it, wench!" he rejoiced because it was not her talking.

It was... someone else. And that someone else slowly croaked...

"You rang... summoner?"

# CHAPTER TWENTY-EIGHT

BETWEEN KNIFING DRUGGED-OUT WHORES AND GETTING thrown out of orgies in some of the finer houses that would have made even the Blood Emperors of Accadios blush, Baalubrozz had stopped, in desperation, at a little-known curious feature in the City of Thieves. This was before heading south along the city wall and finding the ramshackle palace and the whore who began to croak at him.

It was a much-forgotten architectural feature called the Fount of the Watcher, and it was hard to find but could in fact be found along a very good street in a very fine district of the City of Thieves. It was an old feature, a simple carving mounted on an alley wall with a stone basin beneath it.

The carving mounted on the wall was a manticore's head from which water must have once come from its mouth, fed by one of the nearby cisterns. Except... there was no cistern nearby that served the fount. And... the basin was... empty.

Always had been. Always would be.

And normally in a city, any city and not just the City of Thieves, the fountain would have been filled with trash, or eventually some plant or vine would have taken root in it.

Or it would have crumbled. Or broken. Or just... been removed.

It lay in the small street that ran alongside the Temple of Mûmmron which was little more than a heavily fortified bank for some of the more wealthy in the city. There were guards along the front street, for there was vast and incredible wealth within the deep vaults of the temple.

But the side street was cool and dark and Baalubrozz was frustrated. So he'd gone to the fount and made his offering to try and see if the... it wasn't exactly lore, or superstition, there was definitely something at work and it scared many... but to try and see if whatever it was could be of use to him and his quest to find out how the barbarian Sergeant Thor had done the deed and where he'd gotten himself off to.

And... where the loot was.

Baalubrozz would kill to know that answer right now. But he'd kill for most things as he was quite murderous and so that wasn't really saying anything.

But...

Whispered custom among the wizards was that if an item of great value was placed into the open mouth of the stone manticore, from where water had presumably once come to fill the basin and refresh the populace, whispered custom and ancient tradition said that the Deep Watcher, an ancient thing that supposedly lived in the great vast underground reservoir beneath the city, that this thing, whatever it was... would hear your petition for help... and perhaps aid.

Even the locals were known to make petty offerings and claimed things happened on their behalf, but generally it was baked honeyed cakes or coins left in the basin.

Now... those were always gone by dawn.

Cautionary note.

Most of the wizards agreed that, yes, there was an ancient ocean far beneath the city, perhaps some great cavern that gave into the Sea of Riddles. And most of the wizards were convinced this Deep Watcher was most likely of the Eld, and it was best not to mess with the Eld. It might even be... they whispered... an aboleth.

Which was something no one wanted to deal with, as those things psychically enslaved almost everything they came into contact with. Very powerful beings that liked to be left alone with their slaves in deep, dark, watery places.

But no one really knew. Whatever detections and knowings had been cast or sought by summoning or fortune-telling... indicated that whatever was down there was indeed... deep, dark, and weird.

Even for wizards.

The fear of disturbing the Deep Watcher, especially if it was a long-sleeping Eld, or, shudders, an aboleth, was so great among the wizards, and few in the city knew the true nature of the fount, but so great was that fear that perhaps it might be of the Eld that the wizards had issued a High Table edict, rare, for wizards did not like control of any sort, other than what they were controlling, but they issued an edict that the abilities of the fount were to be avoided.

Any who did...

Would become a pariah among the wizards and would be banished into the Eastern Wastes where such must go.

The locals were just doing superstition rites. Nothing would happen. The locals had never read the *Infernium Malefica* and had no idea that to conduct true business with the fount, one had to sacrifice something of great value.

The locals possessed nothing of value. And if they did they would be relieved of it quickly.

This is the City of Thieves.

To do this thing, as far as the wizards were concerned, was beyond the pale, and that was saying something for those who delved even the reaches of the Infernal Fortress for yet one more spell, or the knowledge of a spell.

The fount was off-limits.

*May the Rift consume them*, was pronounced by the High Table.

So no one, no wizard, did this. It jeopardized their place in the city, which for wizards, was quite safe and valuable. To be sent into the wastes was to be... perhaps... lost forever.

So, no wizard dared.

But then... Baalubrozz.

Of course Baalubrozz.

Of course he would be the one to do it, because it served what he wanted right now and that was the very nature of his both chaotic and evil existence.

Osirex had wanted a detection of what had exactly happened, and if Baalubrozz was to continue to be allowed a place in the cabal then he was going to need to accomplish his task.

The summoner hissed, growled, and spat at this.

It was clear the pompous twit Osirex was playing for control of the High Table, and Baalubrozz didn't need that kind of enemy.

He also didn't need Osirex, or any wizard, thinking they were better than him.

Why, if they knew what the rings on his nine fingers, he'd sold one to control a major pit fiend once, could do...

They... would... fear... him.

Period.

Fact.

Just like the dead whore he'd watched strangle on her

own vomit, for the Death's Breath mushroom he'd fed her had been too much for her system.

Her lifeless body lay at the mouth of the alley.

She'd once been a sailor's wife. He'd died in some battle out in the desert, she murmured as the drugs began to take hold of her. Her children were at home, waiting for her, she'd mumbled also.

Baalubrozz was going to send some men around to collect those little brats in the morning, if he remembered to, and have them promptly sold to the flesh pits.

The devils would notice that wicked move and hear his requests for summons and help.

But right now, standing before the fount, he had little to work with and much to do. Yes, he was going to the other houses of pleasure and delight, and yes, he was going to show them what real evil lusted like...

But why not. Why not dare?

He slipped the Ring of Saurozz from off his pinky finger. It allowed him to transform into a werewolf. He'd battled his way through the Seas of Mist to reach the Isle of Werewolves. He'd lost many demons and even a pit fiend lord in the process.

Those wolves were tough.

That ring had cost him much.

He'd even been planning to use it at one of the inns later.

Turn into a howling bloodthirsty beast and have a bevy of beauties locked in a room with him, then go full beast...

Then... show them.

Now he held the costly ring and sneered in disgust that he wouldn't be able to do that little bit of horrific evil. He had to trade something valuable, so the legends of the *Infernium Malefica* stated, and the fact that he was going to do such an evil thing with the ring... well... to the right entity... that made it more... attractive.

He cast about the shadows hoping some devil was slouching by and in the mood to make mischief.

Nothing.

Just him.

Baalubrozz sighed, muttering "Needs must," and put the steel ring carved in blood runes and adorned with the opulent moonstone beyond value into the manticore's gaping stone mouth, the dead sailor's wife cooling at the entrance to the alley in the pale moonlight behind him as he did so.

Then Baalubrozz straightened up and because he was a summoner of renown, he expected that immediately an audience from a powerful and mostly unknown dark and very dangerous force that went back to the primordial mysteries of the early Ruin, would respond promptly.

Nothing happened.

The squat little frog-eyed summoner looked upward and cursed the heavens and reached out to take the ring back...

It was all just superstition and myth and of course the dolts at the High Table would fall for it!

But when he looked into the manticore's mouth... the ring was gone.

# CHAPTER TWENTY-NINE

"YOU SUMMONED ME... SUMMONDER?" CROAKED THE KNIFE-marred girl. Her pale, frail hand still thrown across her tormented face.

He had used her much.

She'd passed out and he'd hoped she'd died.

Now she was speaking... in that... *other voice*.

Shaky and sweating, the naked summoner, not a pretty sight, got on all fours and loomed over her like a leering fat snake getting ready to strike.

"Who... are you?" he asked quickly, uncertain. Feeling something dangerous in the air now.

Behind him, on the floor, fleshy and holding the bowl of skeletal grape stems resting on her fat rolls, the fat whore began to talk in that same "other" voice as the knife-marred girl who just lay there.

"The Watcher... in the Deep."

The fat little summoner's mouth worked open, frog-like

and made even more so by his bulging beady eyes. He twisted around, caught up in the cheap and dirty linens that the hideous madam of the house, an ancient crone more witch than pimp and covered in far too many cosmetics, had been so proud of.

Now he was on the edge of the bed, staring at the fat whore who was now talking... *Other*.

"I have a question!" shouted Baalubrozz like a man desperate to be free of some trap he'd gotten himself into. He was almost lunatic, and his body had broken out in a cold sweat because he was close to something diabolical and that excited him and scared him. And this was a man who worked with devils and demons after all.

Long pause.

Then the third whore, the ugly, *ugliest*, whore, lying half on, half off the bed, began to talk in that same cold voice as a titanic frog's croak from across a far canyon when distant thunderstorms begin to pile on the horizon.

"I hunger... summoner. I hunger... I am the Watcher... in the Deep. And... I hunger... summoner... oh... how I hunger."

Frantically, quickly, Baalubrozz barked his next question.

"I gave you the ring! What more do you want?"

"I hunger... summoner. I hunger," the thing croaked through all three women.

Baalubrozz swore.

"All right... then... what do you... hunger... for?"

It was never food. It never was with these things.

The girls, each in turn, began to tell him in that... other voice... what the Deep Watcher wanted.

Baalubrozz agreed to the terms.

The Deep Watcher accepted with a final... "Good, then... ask what you seek aid of... now. One question... summoner. Then I will answer... for the Deep Watcher... watches. The Deep Watcher... knows."

Shaking and sweating, Baalubrozz worked frantically at the sudden problem presented him. There were so many things he could ask for right now, but he had a feeling, like a *Wish* spell, that this could go horribly wrong if he asked amiss. It was best to keep these things simple.

Complexity invited irrecoverable damnation.

What Osirex had sent him to do was find out where this barbarian Dire Man had gone off to. Where the treasure was. And yes... how it had been done.

But...

The ramshackle leaning collapse of a house was silent.

Downstairs in the decrepit house of pleasure someone began to cry. Softly. Out on the hot, swollen streets outside merchants shouted their wares on offer. Steel was pounded. Animals complained about the heat.

But... what the High Table and Osirex wanted was... the treasure.

I've got it, Baalubrozz thought feverishly. I'll ask where it is, right now, go get it, keep the best of it, or at least a few of the best wands and rings for myself... who are we kidding I'll take it all! he thought wildly. I'll take it all and overthrow the High Table myself... if this stupid thing will just tell me where it is right now!

*But...*

What if it's only there *right now?*

And when I go there... *it isn't.*

Waste of a question.

"Keep it simple," the tormented sweaty little summoner murmured over and over to himself while the entity calling itself the Deep Watcher waited silently to answer his interrogation, silently, through the whores all around him.

Don't, Baalubrozz thought to himself, try to get it all in one bite. That's the way you usually do it and you know how that goes.

*Don't be you right now!*

Follow the trail. Step by step. If you follow the trail, stay on the trail, the real trail, of this warrior... which no one else can seem to follow... then. Eventually. You will find him, Baalubrozz.

And perhaps...

All of it. For you. Think of it! You and you alone, Baalubrozz.

"Where..."

Got to get this right. His mind scrambled like a line of warriors collapsing and trying to hold together the defense.

The thing wanted him to blow it. Damnation was possibly... just seconds away if he blew this.

"Did this... *Sergeant Thor*... go? Where did he go after he left the Pit and escaped in the alley where everyone went missing. Where did he go after that?"

Silence.

A long silence.

The soft crying downstairs stopped.

The noise of the city beyond the rotten walls of the whoring den did not.

Then the knife-marred girl got up, like a zombie, and Baalubrozz had worked with his fair share of those, gathered up the foul and disgusting sheets from the night about her like a sarong, a covering of her ruined self, and walked out of the hot-sweaty, stinking room.

The fat whore on the floor croaked, "Follow her, summoner. Follow her."

The knife-marred girl went out into the streets, and fat little Baalubrozz almost lost her by the time he got all his wizardly gear and chaos assembled across his frame.

She walked up three streets and just collapsed in an intersection, and no one cared as carts and animals were driven past.

From there a seller of pots and pans... a dark-skinned southerner... in that *other voice*, suddenly bade the summoner from nearby to follow him.

The man's eyes rolled white, he went all zombie, and then he began to walk off in another direction.

That one went another few blocks before falling over. No one seemed to mind another body in the streets of the City of Thieves.

Baalubrozz wiped thick sweat from his head, noticed his pudgy dirty little hand was shaking, and seemed to surge forward at a standstill, inner conflict racking his body in spasms as he waited to follow the next zombie.

Surely there would be one.

He could hear a high, lonely whistle, twisting and slithering inside his brain. Just barely.

The city was ethereal and dreamlike in the heat and haze as the summoner stood there for a moment, unsure what to do next.

Farther up the street, a fine lady waved at him, beckoning him slowly like she was in a trance. Her eyes wide and alien. Baalubrozz approached her and she said in that *other voice*... "Follow... me, summoner."

And this went on. And on. And on. Crossing the city.

A sellsword.

A scribe.

An urchin.

A cart man.

A wench.

A fishwife.

A blind man.

A priest.

A drunkard.

And others. They led him on a winding chase through the city until the last one, a woman who was poor, her face mean and hard. A black eye. Her clothes sewn and well kept, but... life... life had not been good to her.

Not easy at all.

She was not a zombie. Her eyes were full of imperious frozen... rage.

Standing in front of the tuna god's gate at the entrance to the Street of Scales, she pointed down the way toward the Temple of Poesidius and said...

"He went there, summoner. The one you seek went there."

But this voice was not the voice of *other*. It was deep and rich. An accent like the people of the Red Desert. And when it had told him where his target had gone, it laughed. A full

335

belly laugh, high and haughty, and just as it had started, all of a sudden and all at once coming out of the poor woman's thin and twisted mean mouth, her frozen anger etched on the lines of her narrow loveless face, it was gone and the woman merely turned and walked off into the constant crowd.

Baalubrozz turned and stared down the street at the tall and impressive Temple of Poesidius.

Then...

He rubbed his hands together like some comic player playing the villain and planning mischief. Like some child ready to eat all the sweets that had been laid out before the party started, before anyone else, ever, could have some.

He would get his answers there next.

One way... or another.

"Yes," muttered Baalubrozz to himself. "Yes, I will."

# CHAPTER THIRTY

IN THE HEAT OF THE DAY, THE RANGER SAW THEM ENTER enter the cool of the tavern he'd chosen for his next fade. Each and every one of them was ready for a fight because they had that look that it was going to happen. Some were afraid and just there to die as meat shields, others were certain and killers like any jungle cat.

Thor read who was who and made ready to move.

The Ranger shoved the buxom serving girl away from him as the ambush started to unfold.

It was part of their act. The buxom Alluria had come to deliver a message at just the last moment, direct from Sato himself, that the eunuchs had hired expensive mercenaries to come settle matters with the Ranger.

"They got here fast," muttered Thor and readied himself to hand out some pain and suffering. These guys meant business and he could sense there was some planning he wasn't seeing.

He was right.

A warehouse near the caravanserai had been prepared to torture the answer to the riddle of the stolen Prize Chest out of him within the hour.

Blond Alluria scampered away, shifting through the drinkers and making for the back door, a serving wench no longer important now that a fight to the death was about to go down on this hot afternoon in the City of Thieves.

There were thousands of serving wenches out there in this city alone. She was just another.

How many fights had it been? In only three days. Some major. More minor. Countless more skirmishes avoided, Thor's would-be attackers scared off, warned off, dodged, or simply... thought better of a bad decision looking worse by the minute. He was tired. And truth be told... he was a little drunk this afternoon. Running, hiding, setting ambushes, interfacing with various elements, eating and drinking and fighting... it was catching up.

"Hadn't been expecting one this quick..."

Just hours ago, there'd been violent slaughter done when thieves from the Brotherhood had come at him on the Street of Cobras where the rug merchants did their business.

Alluria had barely gotten to him in time, got him to shift over three streets and run into the QRF team, tear through them, and get out of the net the larger guild had thrown across the district.

Some arrow fire from the archeress Seringa had aided his escape and taken down a few in the doing of.

"Oh well..." he sighed there in the shadowy tavern where he'd hoped to catch a little breather and maybe even a quick catnap. "Time for someone to die," he then bellowed, rousing himself.

He picked up the tankard and drained it, flexing his bare powerful hands after he set it down. His assault gloves were more than done for, they were done and gone, having come fully to pieces as he'd grappled with the team of blocking thieves who'd cornered him in the shadows in an alley off the Street of Cobras. Beating each of them senseless with powerful blows from his fists and using the walls to bash a few senseless when they wouldn't relent and kept coming at him with sharp knives out.

He moved through them like a bull. Getting caught in a swordfight was a great way for them to get more on him quickly.

Stick and move.

Stick and move.

Keep moving and get off the $X$. That was the plan for today. He didn't have to do this much longer... but for right now, that was the way it was.

Inside the cool and dark little tavern room, the big

mercenary, their leader no doubt, smiled and walked into the tavern.

Thor knew the look. It was confidence, and the guy had lots of it probably because he had reason to.

Still...

"You got that right, stranger... time for someone to die," the mercenary shouted back, locking eyes with the Ranger still sitting at the big trench table in the common room. "And that someone is called... Thor."

Comely wenches scattered, emitting small worrying cries as they fled. Drunks slapped stacks and threadbare pouches of coin in various denominations down, instantly making their bets on the outcome.

"Certainly is..." grunted Sergeant Thor and went to reach for his blade, finding... that it was gone.

Fine... he'd do it this way.

Then he roared and lunged right at the big mercenary.

Thor was tired of fading. He needed a good workout.

# CHAPTER THIRTY-ONE

EVERYONE'S GOT A PLAN UNTIL THEY GET PUNCHED IN the face.

The hulking Ranger rose from the rough, wooden long table in the common room of the dirty little tavern. Outside, life went on in the Street of Brass and Knives, so named because it had once been the favored place to obtain shining brass cooking tagine-like vessels and ebriks for roasting brewed coffee, but had long ago switched over to blademaking after a particularly long war between the thieves' guilds, ending in one no longer existing.

Inside...

Someone, or someones, was about to die.

They'd come with a plan and were running their game now. All elements locked and loaded.

The Ranger smiled as he began to fight.

*Everyone's got a plan until they get punched in the face.*

That's what Sergeant Thor was thinking as he rose up to

meet the clear challenge he was being offered once again, to either tell them about the treasure and die. Or... just die.

They'd get it another way. Alluria had hipped him to the necromancers on standby to make his corpse talk. Those ghouls commonly didn't move around until late at night and then kept generally to their procurement work. That they were seen on the streets, in the heat of the end of the day, was the tell that someone's paid force of killers was about to make their move.

The Little Guild had been developing and running that intel, updating Thor and all elements as fast as the urchins could reach Alluria and the thieves who watched over her. Then she'd move into the location, running some variation on her disguise, to update Sergeant Thor.

Sato instructed the Ranger to know that death didn't bother certain interrogators of the necromantic persuasion and that given the right circumstances even the gates of death would yield to the right questions.

Thor laughed. He loved enemy plans. And like every Ranger... he loved ruining them even more.

*Everyone's got a plan until they get punched in the face.* But sometimes... that worked both ways.

Whoever, thief, wench, or urchin, someone had managed to lift his blade just seconds before the mercenaries came for him. These called themselves the Black Tigers. Now they'd make their play to find out where exactly the fantastic contents of the Prize Chest were, and how exactly they could be gotten to. Bonus round for figuring out how the stupid northern Dire Man had indeed done... well, the deed.

The Black Tigers needed a win, so they'd taken the work.

They'd find out sure as the blaze of noon every day how the deed of heisting the chest by no means anyone could detect, had been done.

They'd taken the contract from the wizards and spent the last of their war chest hiring several types of killers, meatshields, support, and the necromancers seen moving close by to dark and secluded areas where they could do their damnable rites.

But as it was being said, that punch in the face... *it works both ways.*

Thor stumbled, mentally and operationally for just a moment at the loss of his primary. But because he was a Ranger it wasn't a long moment, as it was for some...

The Black Tigers and the chungos they'd hired should have appreciated the break. After all, it was the last moment they were going to have, and so that, to them whether they appreciated it or not, was a kind of bonus moment in which they got to live a little bit longer instead of the moment less it would have taken had the Ranger been able to get his bare hands on the pickup blade he was using as his primary at that moment of the ambush in the tavern. It was a blade of no description and he'd taken it off one of the dead of the last bunch to try *King of the Hill*, the king in this version of the game being the finder of the secret of the heist of the Prize Chest, with him.

They were dead and their bodies were being sold to the vivisectionists, or the necromancers.

Both always were in need of fresh corpses.

Contego out fast and ready, the Ranger lunged for the snarling brute commander of the assaulters who'd made his clever yet braggadocious announcement upon entering the tavern, that someone was going to die today.

If Sergeant Thor had known the mercenary's history, he would have said the man was probably within his rights to brag a little. But he didn't and took it personally as he went after the dude with the Contego like a bull gone mad and ready to kill anyone stupid enough to get near it.

These were Black Tigers. No easy targets. Mercenaries from Skeletos, or rather warriors for hire who'd begun to work together as a company hundreds of years ago in the civil wars between those warring city-states that had racked the region of Skeletos through much of her turbulent history. The wars of that region were little more than proxy wars between the ruling tyrants of Accadios and the upstarts of Caspia vying for a little bit more of the thin power available to the Cities of Men clinging to the coasts of the Great Inner Sea behind their strong and high walls, for much of the Ruin was overrun by monsters, tribes of demi-human monsters, and even nations of magical and twisted yet fantastic beasts the Ruin had revealed.

Mankind was the minority in the Ruin. Its cities, behind those high and impressive walls, were the only area where they were the apex predator. So of course, they ruined each other's lives and did their best to screw their fellow humans out of every last gold coin.

The Black Tigers were some of the most feared mercenaries to hump dirty dusty packs of heavy armor and deadly weapons of all varieties from this war to that slaughter.

They generally wore black leather and some reinforced armor where they could get it, or get what they had, repaired. Their specialty was surprise attacks and deep raids into enemy territory with little backup and nothing more than a plan to cause chaos and destruction in the enemy's rear.

They were quite good at this self-reliant type of war work. Until... Ganistan.

This particular company of the Black Tigers had recently come from service down along the southern coasts working for the Princes of Uran against the gnoll chieftains raiding out of the deep desert from the distant cliffs and high valleys of the region no map and only tale called Ganistan. Their number going forth against the dog-men had been a hundred and fifty, and they'd made it as far as the Old Trade Route into Ganistan, slashing and burning dog-men villages as they went to take the pressure off the raids against the coastal cities of Uran.

Then they'd been surrounded by several clans of dog-men and attacked near a high mountain pass. Ten had survived the slaughter and five had made it back to the sea, fighting the whole way back across the edges of the mysterious Eastern Wastes.

And barely surviving.

The five who'd made it were the hardest and best that particular company of the Black Tigers had ever produced. They'd have to be to have survived the Gnoll Passes of Ganistan and the strange demon-haunted sands of the Eastern Wastes to make it all the way back to the City of Thieves along the Sea of Riddles.

Rank in the Black Tigers was simple.

Cutter was a regular line warrior skilled in both close-quarters combat with a variety of weapons, and ranged combat particularly with the powerful short bows they used for skirmishing. This man usually wore black leathers, dusty and worn and personalized with armor purchased or picked up off the dead that was of note and valuable.

They moved fast and light and were capable of fighting alone or in teams. They wore a simple black-and-gray-striped rag, cloth, or silk about their upper left arm. Usually a swollen bicep cut, scarred, and tattooed with either ancient wounds or strange snake-like inks that were of uncertain origin.

Three of the five Black Tigers who'd survived the horrors of the Ganistan campaign in service to the fair Princes of Uran were cutters.

In the passes of the gnoll chieftains they'd become hardened combat veterans and they were silent and haunted-eyed by the horrors they'd witnessed and heard there. Many of their captured brothers were cooked alive at night as the dog-men yapped and tore them to shreds after the day's battle.

Next came the sergeants of the Black Tigers. These wore their unit cloth on the upper bicep, but it had a sewn red slash along its folds denoting their rank. These men were older, harder, more scarred, more inked, and seldom laughed other than to express sarcastic surprise at whatever hard horror they'd been tasked with dealing with next if they were to collect their pay and survive.

They also seemed to never sleep, as though that ability had fled them when the red slash had been sewn into their cloth. They watched the night and waited for the shadows of past enemies to come and try to settle old scores.

There was of course a warlord of each company of Black Tigers.

Between the warlord were the captains in any given company, usually four, but all those had died in the high rocky valleys of Ganistan when the snows began to melt and the barking mad dog-men rained down arrows from their high rock-wall fortress and charged in waves with flailed weapons against their moving line.

The warlord wore a cloth with three red sewn slashes.

These were the ranks of the Black Tigers, and they were simple for the men who simply killed for pay.

The big mercenary who breached the inn to begin the assault, capture, and/or killing of Thor was one of the three cutters. The warlord, who was nearby, had a lotus-addled necromancer in a warehouse near the closest cemeteries ready to interrogate Thor's corpse and find out all that was needed to know if things went that way.

The cutter to lead the assaulters was the one most likely to make sergeant next. Had this bunch of the Black Tigers not been reduced significantly among the tribes of the wild and savage dog-men far beyond the reaches of civilization... where only idiots and madmen dare what riches can be gained from the lost and buried empires rumored to be in those lands... it would have taken him longer. But he'd survived and survived what all soberly agreed were impossible odds. So... taking some stupid northern savage in a tavern with an assault element, a support element, snipers on the street, a blocking force out back, and a quick reaction force ready to move in...

That wasn't anything to him.

He'd stacked dog-men in Ganistan waist-deep. He had survived where many had not.

Black Tigers generally sported long drooping mustaches.

Their eyes were always dead, haunted by what they'd seen and done. They wore black grease under those tired Ruin-weary eyes as if to emphasize their death to the cares of this life, and anything you could possibly throw at them.

"Time for someone to die!" shouted the burly man with the drooping brown mustache and the mournful hooded eyes he'd often applied dark grease under to make himself look even more of a murderer than he already was.

His name was Skodt, and one of the other cutters rode herd with Skodt on the band of pick-up sellswords they'd brought with them for this first part of the trap laid for "Thor the Ranger" as some in the city had taken to calling the man who'd mesmerized them all with his feats of battle and theft.

Some. The tag on the target shifted from one walled district to the next within the city, depending on what deeds and rumors were currently spreading about.

Skodt pointed the hefty bastard sword as he ran and shouted, "Get'm, you worthless dogs!"

The *worthless dogs* were the sellswords hired from the quiet and shady alleys and back lots along the Streets of Brass and Knives. These were a rough and badly assembled lot, and they began to die as soon as they attacked the Ranger in the tavern.

The first, a tribesman from the Red Desert who'd come across the seas and into the port looking for this kind of work, ululated the traditional war cry of his people and went swinging a heavy wooden club, polished and shiny, adorned with the tribal markings that denoted him a *manslayer*.

The Ranger surged away from the table, planted his lead foot, and using the Contego as a boxing extender, threw a wild haymaker just as suddenly as the glistening dark tribesman had surged across the food-littered and grease-stained floor of the inn that smelled of the miasma of cooking smoke that hung across the low upper rafters where hams cured in the cool shadows.

Two more of the pickup sellswords were fast on the heels of the black tribesman and didn't seem to mind that their target, Sergeant Thor, had just slashed out the lead man's throat with the wild edged-haymaker that stopped the man's bloodcurdling tribal war cry mid-ululation almost as soon as it had started.

Blood sprayed in every direction as the slashed man dropped his polished jungle-wood club and clutched at a throat that would never be repaired unless there was an extremely powerful battle cleric nearby.

There wasn't.

The Black Tigers' battle cleric had been caught and roasted by the dog-men of the passes months ago. Then gnolls had hung his weapons and holy symbols over the entrances to their caves, throwing his shattered and gnawed bones outside among those of the many others who'd dared their passes and paid the price for doing so.

That had been a dark day for the company, and after that things had gone from bad to *much, much worse* for the Black Tigers.

Today was going to be remembered as such by those who survived the Ranger.

Thor jabbed hard after the throat slash with his off hand, a powerful shot that slammed into the nose of the next man on the heels of the ruined tribesman gurgling in his own blood and dying. The man twisted and landed across a still-upright table within the inn as everything and all involved devolved into total chaos and desperate screaming all at once.

Wenches screamed or shrieked.

Merchants shouted for the guard.

Drunks groaned on rusty notes that another wasted day had been ruined.

Innkeepers were nowhere to be seen, as they'd been paid to bolt the back and side doors and pen the target in for the slaughter. The staff of this inn, having done so, had then gone down into the cellar and barred the trapdoor to protect themselves.

The sellsword with the smashed nose was a fighter, and swung on Thor anyway despite the blood gushing from his nose and the inability to see through eyes turned to waterfalls.

He grunted hard and struck out at the Ranger. Thor dodged the blow, fully in control of the battle, adrenaline clearing the buzz of food and too much beer to dull the pain of the wounds and sore muscles he'd taxed to the extreme over the last few days of brawl and street battle. He weaved the hand gripping the Contego over the attacker's weapon, redirecting the blade toward the other wild-eyed warrior coming for him, a large-nosed Caspian with two knives out and ready to slam into Thor's ribs should he have managed to get in behind his intended target had the target chosen to go after someone other than the Caspian.

Instead, the Ranger redirected the machete-looking blade of the other man right into the Caspian, pivoting his whole body, grabbing the man's outstretched swinging arm, and pushing the blade center mass and deep into the double-knife-carrying Caspian's chest.

No one looked more surprised than that guy at what had happened so fast.

Blink of an eye.

Plan... meet punch. In the face.

And...

It had happened so smoothly. The titanic giant they were facing knew what he was doing and his movements were swift, economical, and utterly brutal.

The stabbed Caspian opened his mouth and nothing came out as he died instantly, the machete-like blade run right through his foul and greedy heart. His head went back, his eyes rolled white, and Thor side-kicked the leg of the man he had control of, shattering his knee with one suddenly sharp and definitive thunderstrike of his combat boot.

Machete Man screamed bloody murder, fell to the floor, and got trampled by the five other pick-up sellswords.

Skodt and Splittnose, the second cutter, shoved into the brawl hoping for a chance to cause so much confusion they could just jab one of the spears they'd carried in at their prey. Just stick him in the guts, or the kidney, or perhaps even the heart, and get this settled before the other elements of the Black Tiger company came into play.

Get a bigger share of the purse, if so, more than likely.

The warlord was known to do that. On occasion.

But Skodt also had it in his heart to get the info out of the big murderous Dire Man himself and disappear and see if he couldn't find where the loot from the heist was. Or just rifle Thor's corpse and take what the brute had intended to spend on whores, dice, and beer.

These were ridiculous ideas.

Now, seeing the violent ferocity of the uncaged panther they'd come for, Skodt admitted to himself, as he watched Splittnose get stuck in the guts and run from the bar trying to keep them in as he screamed, Skodt admitted he would be satisfied with just pressing the big savage and letting him fade to the ambush they had waiting in the alley out the back of the inn they were supposed to be pushing him toward as all five sellswords went in with all they had.

Thor, seeing the odds weren't just bad and getting worse, they would shortly become suicidal... more were pushing in the front door of the tavern to get at him and some of these even had bows... Thor faded to the shadows at the back of the inn, leaving a wake of bodies and blood, kicking chairs and knocking down tables, slashing wide with the Contego and slicing with the shank he'd deployed because it was getting thick and too close.

One man got his head split for his brave efforts and went down on the floor. Still, the odds were bad.

And now they were gonna get much worse.

# CHAPTER THIRTY-TWO

Seargeant Thor didn't gamble at all that the back door to the dirty little inn was locked. He'd been betrayed by enough owners of establishments in the past three days to operate on a *trust no one* basis.

Include the denizens that frequented these seedy drinking dives, and the treachery was flat-out baked into the MRE vanilla pound cake on this one.

Sergeant Thor raised his booted foot as he throttled the big cutter, Skodt, who'd dared follow him down the shadowy little passage to the back of the inn and the piss lot where drinkers emptied their bladders. With one swift strike he smashed the back door to the inn, and it opened suddenly and terrifically whether it wanted to or not.

It practically came off the frame.

The Ranger swung around savagely and jammed the shank into the guts of the cutter he was holding by one of his thick arms in the powerful grip of his naked fist attached at the end of that jacked and tatted limb.

The strangled and now run-through cutter gurgled as his guts ran out on the floor and he got tossed into a heap, watching the hulking shadow of the man who'd just slain him run for the hazy daylight of late afternoon and the piss lot out back of the tavern.

Some endings are not as heroic as the hero.

Thor emerged into wan hazy daylight filtering through the spartan olive trees that were often planted in the small side streets, squares, and sometimes even the enclosed back lots of the many merchants that choked the City of Thieves at every available space within the cyclopean walls.

Beyond the walls was nothing but danger.

The men from inside the tavern pushed past the trail of dying and dead heroes the Ranger had left in his wake as he took sudden leave of the drinking establishment.

These were more sellswords. Desperate, hungry-eyed killers who'd never managed to make, or maintain, any kind of allegiance to anyone with power. They'd kill for money, and sometimes for fun. Yeah, the target was dangerous on this one, but the reward was fantastic if the tales and offers were to be believed.

Such killers as these sellswords were the flotsam that collected in every city where violence was a kind of rule of law that kept things relatively orderly even if the ruler, or rulers, or governing cabal, were little more than petty tyrants. Such flotsam killers like the sellswords still had their uses. Even for the wizards that had financed the Black Tigers' assault force to hire these for the push into the real ambush that lay out back of the inn and was led by Carhorse Goblinslayer, the sergeant with one red slash on the coarse gray-and-black-striped rag that marked him as one of the Black Tigers.

There were still more sellswords waiting for Sergeant Thor out in the piss lot and they'd come in fast before intel could reach Thor.

Still, the Ranger wasn't surprised. Of course they'd be here. He made up his mind to go through them like a particularly bad case of food poisoning.

Carhorse Goblinslayer was a wily old coot who could still swing a sword faster than most young'uns who tried the mercenary game, and had a lot more fifty-year-old-man muscle to put behind it than most of the rascally young and lithe sellswords who'd never live to see what thirty had to offer.

Carhorse worked a longsword one-handed and a wicked dagger in the other hand in the style known as Accadion Death Dance. Where he'd acquired the style and pedigree of his swordsmanship was never known, only that he had, and that, it didn't matter what direction he was facing, he could still kill you any six ways he could stick either blade into you. He wore black armor, the skull of some giant one-eyed creature fitted neatly over his head as a kind of fearsome war helmet, and his wild, long, dirty gray hair sprang from underneath it. His armor was light with some iron on the shoulders and his look completed by a long light-gray cape that looked ragged but was actually fine silk and magicked a bit by a Caspian witch woman who'd imbued it with a misdirection spell that often confused those who found themselves at close blades with the wily old Black Tigers NCO.

Many who faced Carhorse had lost their focus in single combat against him, tricked by the whirl and flash of the ghostly cloak and then suddenly run through by Carhorse's old notched longsword, or the wickedly sharp dagger that was his primary for the actual killing that needed to be done.

As he would have told any one of the Black Tigers under his charge, when asked, "Sword's jes' fer defense... keepin' off me, and all. *Sheila*... now she do the death just as she always done fer me!" And then he would hoot and holler like that was some hilarious joke that had been told had the hearer only known more of the tale and who Sheila was.

*Sheila* was the dagger.

He often muttered to himself about his past misdeeds as a young warrior in service to some warlord or another, muttering, "Bad old self," over and over and, "That was me then. Bad old self," he would say and never explain.

Sometimes he'd just swear. Sometimes he'd hit someone.

Sheila was a merchant's daughter he'd never come home to after the wars. She died. So he named his killing dagger after her and went off across the Ruin, fighting wars and doing hard deeds that needed to be done by one who didn't mind the work, and liked the pay enough to do it.

He was strange. And he was deadly.

He and a group of young men who'd taken the blood oath of the Black Tigers and drank from the silver cup they carried even despite the relentless mass wave attacks of the dog-men in Ganistan, were waiting out back in the "piss lot," as the tavern and its patrons called the back area behind the inn.

This was the real ambush.

The push from inside the inn by the assaulters, led by the now-dead Skodt, had merely been to canalize their target, Sergeant Thor, into a channel right from the back of the inn and into the real ambush waiting in the late afternoon shadows of the piss lot.

Had Thor managed to push past the assaulters and go out the front door, a dozen archers were arrayed all about the street and along the low and high rooftops to put immediate fire on him.

These were managed by the third of the three cutters, who was excellent with the short, curved skirmisher bow the Black Tigers considered basic kit.

The sniper was good enough that he had survived the unending treacherous ambushes from the high cliffs of the dog-men who wanted to take the survivors deep into the warren and caverns and show them the dark dog gods they worshipped down there... before the feast.

Everyone forgot what his name was and called him Bullseye. The archer sniper could fire two arrows at the same time at any one target, and he could do it fast. Especially in a pinch. That was how good he was. And if Thor had gone that way, out through the assaulters, beating and killing his way out the front door, then he would have died by the Black Tigers' best archer, or the other eleven hired from the city guard who specialized with the weapon and were good with the powerful longbows the city put its faith and trust in against the various desert raiding gobs, hobs, and orcs that came suddenly out of the wastes to the east to take what they could from the edges of the city at bloody dawn, or dying red-rust-hued dusk.

And sometimes there were other, worse monsters, lurking out there and willing to come and terrorize the walls in the dead of some late night.

But the Ranger, assessing the trap and the hit on his

person, now playing the role of High Value Target, had faded for the rear as had been his plan all along. The front was a death trap for sure.

All the inns he'd stayed at, drinking, dicing, wenching, and generally carrying on like the guy who'd just won the lottery of all time by stealing the Prize Chest, had been scouted thoroughly by a large and silent wine slave hefting a massive clay amphora in the weeks leading up to the heist. Scouting the inns. Scouting the back lots, and the adjoining warrens of small desperate neighborhoods that clung to these drinking places like small foreign countries all to themselves within the great and eunuch-regulated districts of the city.

This inn, past the piss lot, gave way to the blacksmiths who served the weapons merchants along the Street of Brass and Knives.

The blacksmiths were large men like the Ranger. Often Dire Men come down from their frosty realms to do trade among the cities of the south. Sometimes there was even some strange beastman that seemed human but had been the product of the orcish raids deep into the Cities of Men, who labored silently at a forge and sold what crude weapons he could craft.

There were dwarves of the deserts here too, farther into the blacksmiths' small neighborhoods behind the tavern. Small and sturdy, red-skinned to the point of being almost black, or cinnamon, they had beautiful blue eyes and dark curly hair they kept long. They kept to their forges, did little trade or truck with anyone not themselves or purchasing their fine weapons, and made sure a certain level of security was there for those who had the coin, or raw iron, to trade.

Sato had led the Little Guild's chief negotiator, Az-Azim as he was known, a courtly gentleman with no thieving skills other than having once been a diplomatic spy for Uran, with an actual letter from the mysterious Queen of Thieves herself, and a small cask filled with gold coins, to pay for the security of the great Dire Man Thor as he was known, should he need to flee through the Desert Dwarves' district.

The Desert Dwarves had eyed the letter suspiciously then agreed as one, eyeing the cask of gold with a greedy glitter in their sapphire-blue eyes, that they would honor the agreement. To the letter. The dwarves would be alerted once Thor was in the area, and if he needed to fade, then they would take him through their secret tunnels to the docks and there he would have either eluded predators or be on his own then.

Spit was applied to calloused hands, big and little, and a deal was struck between dwarves and thieves. The cask of gold coins closed and handed over by the venerable Az-Azim, a handsome man who looked every inch the wealthy and wise sheik, or imminent sage, from his manicured goatee to the sparkling white silks he dressed in.

So, when the Ranger had chosen this inn for this part of the plan of the fade, he had an escape route and that was where he needed to go now.

*Just like ya do*, as Sergeant Joe would have said.

All the Ranger had to do was get through the baked-red-brick dusty and crumbling old wall on the other side of the small piss lot, cross three streets of blacksmiths he resembled to some greater, or lesser, extent, and lose any pursuit in the process of moving among them and their great smoking forges as weapons were pounded to red-hot killing perfection. Then reach the Street of No Return which all knew to be the unofficial kingdom of the Desert Dwarves within the city.

That's all he had to do.

Carhorse Goblinslayer and six new trainees for the Black Tigers stood in his way.

The trainees had polearms and spears. Perfect for new guys. All they had to do was stab and thrust and maintain their line, as Carhorse saw it. With the range of those long and formidable weapons even a killer like this Dire Man could never get close to them.

They'd stab him to death, then hack him to pieces.

And Carhorse Goblinslayer had had them stabbing and thrusting one for a week before the desperate battle in the piss lot.

Not because of this... *Ranger...* who now occupied every waking greedy thought of every denizen of this cursed city from the lowest beggar to the most princely of the thieving eunuchs, but because the warlord of the Black Tigers had wanted it so.

And now the warlord wanted this man dead. And wanted it done by Carhorse.

The future fortunes of the company depended on this contract.

Seac the Raven, warlord of this particular association of the Black Tigers who'd almost been done to death by the gnolls in the high passes of Ganistan, was waiting nearby with this reaction force of trainees, former mercenaries and pit fighters given to fighting men in front of bloodthirsty crowds baying for a little bit more blood on a bloody day. Same as it ever was. And Seac had wanted the new men with Carhorse Goblinslayer trained in the use of the defensive pike also, because he was intent on going back to those cursed cliffs and high passes of the dog-men for all the great treasure hordes the escaping force had gotten glimpses of deep in the warrens of the gnolls when they'd been forced to flee that way.

He was going back because they'd seen, down there past the crude cities of the dog-men deep underground, the

SGT. THOR: THE CUNNING

remnants of some greater, older civilization down in the dark and ghost-haunted fortresses their ancestors had built deep down there long ago.

Places that radiated magic, and power.

Seac the Raven, a Mourne Elf and mercenary warlord from the end of the world, was going back for those things. He could smell the magic down there.

Or such was said of the Mourne Elves.

And... of course... for revenge. That didn't need to be said. The company had been greatly wronged and Seac himself had gone south to assassinate the Prince of Uran who'd failed to pay on the contract that had slaughtered almost the entire company.

Revenge was a given with Seac the Raven.

But of course it would be, for he was Mourne Elf. And to that lot, revenge is like the blood-pumping blood that moves through the heart for that tribe. It pumps through their veins with every beat of their black hearts. And he needed a lot of fighters to go back and face the horrors there so the Mourne Elf could have his plunder and revenge. It would take time to recruit and train them all up. It would take a war chest. Hence the new, the untried, and the undependable. Within these, those that survived, Seac would take the uncut gems and turn them into killers. Into Black Tigers.

Then it would be time for repay what was owed.

Settling up.

Paid in full.

Revenge.

# CHAPTER THIRTY-THREE

THOR THUNDERED INTO THE PISS LOT AT CARHORSE Goblinslayer and his pikemen. Six new guys with a week's training who had recently begun to hit the taverns and tell the local wenches they were elite mercenaries with the Black Tigers now.

They had no idea they were about to get utterly wrecked.

To say the ambush was not a surprise was not an overstatement. Generally, Sergeant Thor had found that those who'd come to take the loot of the Prize Chest had been rather simplistic and straightforward in their approach even if they thought it was really clever to have a couple of guys in the inn or on the street before the "surprise attack" happened.

Years in the various sandboxes of the Before with the Rangers had honed Sergeant Thor's senses to smell out an ambush before it happened. There was a nervousness in the air that day, and right in the AO as you got closer, that couldn't be helped. Call it *whatever...* but some part of you picked up on that certain fatal something-real-bad that was going to happen next, or real soon, and those who'd ignored such warnings hadn't liked the outcomes.

Thor had learned that locals with dead eyes and thousand-yard stares who were doing their best not to pay attention to you were the surest giveaways.

Once it started there was only one way out. Acceptance.

Accept... this dance is gonna happen. Is happening. That the people who've come and set up IEDs and emplaced machine guns and maybe some wonky mortars on demand or even RPGs to throw down once the defense turtles and freezes on the *X*, getting themselves killed in the process, to distract from the unexpected direction the real ambush is about to come from... accept that they have come to make all these things happen to you.

They are... *committed*. And they know it.

Spot that and you were halfway to spotting the kill box you'd just walked into. Accept it.

And if you're wrong... who cares.

And if you're right, then you just got an extra second or two to do something.

Accept it and then kill your way off the *X* because that's the only way out.

Thor had been drinking that afternoon to numb the pain

of wounds and batterings over the last few days and keep moving.

Which was the plan.

The drinking in the taverns and letting the wenches coo and rub his muscles and try to steal his coin... that was a kind of rest for him.

It gave him a moment to refuel, surrounded by them. They were tripwires in and of themselves. If he didn't spot their ambush, if he didn't realize he was on the $X$, then as it started to go down, they would let him know. Scream, yell, or disappear as the dead-eyed killers started to surround whatever $X$ he found himself on that day. As soon as some dirty desperate killer with a bad sword decided to make his play for the kingdom and all the prizes that popped out of Thor's dead body...

... or whatever they thought would happen...

The beauties on his powerful arms drinking his beers and casting long dark lashes at him would scream as it went down. And for him, reasoned the Ranger, there was a certain rest in this, these moments, when he could drink and study their barely clad bodies, and try to watch the shadows, the seedy characters in the room, and all the secret ways into the inn where some group, eunuchs or wizards or any other of a dozen opportunist factions who wanted to front the coin to get a group of thugs and killers together and try to take what he had fairly stolen, and kill him doing so, these moments it was like he'd thrown tripwires out with flashbangs and even claymores of a sort.

All he had to do was set up the approaches, clock the defenses, and have a way out. Taverns were just another kind of patrol base.

And Rangers lived for patrol bases.

It was a pleasant kind of long halt.

Thor had interfaced with Sato when he'd gone to the back lot to piss and Sato had come over the wall and dropped down in the shadows behind an unkempt and wild tree, passing info and updating Thor on the situation within the district.

They smelled trouble.

There were necromancers moving in, curse their foul kind.

But...

"I fear, Warrior, they will not relent from the prize we have stolen out from under their out-of-joint noses. The High Table has formed a cabal of powerful named wizards to answer this question. This... becomes more serious by the second as we play our game. Do we still follow the plan for the prize we have stolen, Warrior?"

Thor guffawed and burped as he pissed. Heaving his shoulder to button the fading and threadbare Crye

Precisions he wore, bare-chested for the day was hot and the heat relentless.

The sweat ran constantly.

"No one's gonna steal what we've fairly stolen, Sato. Stay on mission."

Sato was already fading into the early afternoon shadows, this being a few hours before the attack.

"Fairly stolen... Warrior. You are truly a thief like me now."

Then he was gone.

Now, as Thor entered the back lot and took in a number of young men arrayed in a battle line with polearms and spears all across his front, as they began to advance on him at the call of some hoary old warrior, Thor roared and dared them to come die on his shank now.

This was not bravado.

This was cunning.

They hadn't expected this.

The men with the poles were young, and other than perhaps a mean dagger on some worn leather belt at their waists, they had no other kit of even the most basic warrior, or fighter, he'd faced so far.

Their beards were scraggly. Their eyes hard and determined to be brave. Teeth gritted too tight and trying to make sure they were getting this right as they advanced, sharp edges forward. Waiting for the command to "Thrust!" from the Black Tigers' NCO Carhorse Goblinslayer near the tree Sato had delivered the intel update from.

They were new and barely trained. He could make use of that.

They advanced swiftly but in unison and Thor could see the tremble in their grip as they came at him.

Right on that knife edge between fear and bravery was where their minds hovered and he could read it in their wide eyes. The worst place for a real warrior to be right now.

A real warrior wants to be cold and thinking, looking for advantages to take and quick concise cuts to be made to see the end of the battle quickly and himself walking away with little damage.

Winners and losers could be figured out later when the corpses got counted.

Kids envision something else.

Something desperate.

Something dire in which to display that true bravery they know they must have deep down inside... somewhere. Along the way, as mercenaries, warriors, or whatever, those illusions die if they survive, and if they do, cuts and scars teach them how to get it done better next time, smarter, definitely not harder.

They weren't there today.

And Thor guessed rightly in that the old grizzled warrior at their back would use them up, get them killed, if just to face Thor wounded and thereby have a better chance at the glory he thought he was going to get out of this fight.

The Ranger intended to disabuse the old man of that notion.

Along the way, these kids could have become masters of the human condition, understanding men and why they do what they do even though they'd wish they had none of the experiences that had led to such wisdom.

Why some run.

Why some fight.

Why some pass out after getting shot at.

And why some smile as cold as ice and think nothing of the blood on their hands even if their pants smell like their bowels.

They would have learned those things.

After that... it's just a job, a kind of work, and there's a way it gets done.

But these men... they wouldn't live long enough as the warriors they'd told those wenches they were, to find out.

Thor roared like some angry caged animal that had been cornered, full of menace and real harm, daring them to come at him with all their civilization and tools and weapons and agreements and superstitions and even beliefs...

They would die because he was a predator unlike any of them.

They felt that. And it checked them.

They weren't the trappers... they were the trapped.

The line of advancing polearms and spears in the fetid little back area of the wretched inn, the piss lot as it was called, faltered at his sudden and unexpected battle roar.

Carhorse had even encouraged the untried youth that perhaps this outcome in the ambush would be something else for them. He'd seen men calc the odds, drop their weapons, and extend their palms with a smile as if saying, "Hey, tried my best. Jig's up. You got me."

"Then we run him through and make sure to get those spears," he told them, "in here between the fourth and fifth of his ribs 'cause that's where this demon's heart is." So hissed the wily old battle hobo on the long days of thrust and chop.

Then Carhorse had snickered to himself and muttered his mantra about his bad old self.

Some, if not all of them, would die. He knew that.

And so the youths had expected, according to the lies they'd been taught, that cornering the big tiger that was the Dire Man might just end for them in victory and then it was back to the taverns and the wenches, Asperia and the voluptuous Tintinnabula herself, to tell of their particular daring during the killing of the savage the whole city was talking about.

But... that's not what happened. No. Not at all.

Thor roared, Ranger shank out. A big chunk of sharp killing steel ready to deal some death. Nothing more. Nothing less.

The line faltered.

Three on the left hesitated. One on the right too. Just stopped.

Two advanced at the center.

And one, the bravest... Kel the Rash, roared back at Thor because he was a scrapper and charged even if it was just him.

Thor sidestepped the thundering polearm, maneuvering the barely trained youth with one powerful hand, pushing him past himself. Kel the Rash, not tempered as he was—one day he might have been a fierce warrior had he survived Thor and the Battle at the Piss Lot as it would come to be known —stopped, rebellious at the hand that had guided him and his long weapon forward in a useless thrust into open air, pushing the youth forward. Powerful was the impression on the hot-headed youth's back, for Thor was jacked and the kid's adrenaline to murder was high. Kel stopped and pushed backward...

And the Ranger drove his shank right into the kid's brainpan at the occipitals.

This was easy for a cold professional. Easy effort. Easy kill. There's no resistance at the base of the skull and the blade sank in, savaging the neck, switching off the rash youth who'd decided to play warrior hero games at the pro level his first time out.

Despite the encouragement of Carhorse Goblinslayer who'd merely counted on the youths to waste time and wear out the killer he'd been sent for, Kel was down and the big Dire Man who'd looted the chest was in and among his new guys, hacking at them with that savage swinging chunk of steel like a werebear disturbed in the night.

It was horrific what the Ranger did to them at close quarters, never stopping, always moving. Too close now and inside their ability to bring their poles and spears to bear on him.

They tried to raise and use their weapons defensively. This would be ineffective as they were not made for this kind of combat. The swinging Ranger shank disabused them of this fantasy, and they went reeling away from savage quick ruthless cuts Thor handed out to vital areas and wherever he could land the blur of a weapon in one of his hands.

The last of the youths who would be heroes later with the wenches, just ran away.

Screaming.

But by that time Carhorse Goblinslayer had already put

two dirty fingers into his mouth and whistled the order that let Seac the Raven know the ambush had gone south, just as he'd known it would, just as he'd intended other than their prey being wearied and potentially "gut-stuck" by one of the "heroes" with the pikes they'd handed out, and that it was time to get ready to come in and cut off the target's sprint for freedom as the target was gonna try to run back the way he'd come.

The NCO would hold him here for a bit.

"Well Hells o' Suth..." Carhorse hissed to himself cantankerously and drew the nicked longsword and *Sheila* his killing razor. "They don't pay me enough for this kinda work."

But that was just his act. Grumbling about the work. He'd perfected it over many years leading hard-bitten killers into no-win situations. In truth... Carhorse Goblinslayer was looking forward to this fight.

There were rewards.

And if he could put this... Ranger... down here, and now... who knew what the big dumb savage was carrying on him from the Prize Chest? Ain't nothin' Carhorse was gonna go on about once he had it stashed before the others got there.

The wily old mercenary NCO went after the Ranger Thor for all he was worth.

# CHAPTER THIRTY-FOUR

FIRST PASS DREW BLOOD AND OL' CARHORSE LAUGHED wickedly at his good luck until he saw that the Ranger had cut him good and cut him deep and hard on the arm carrying the old notched longsword he'd used for defense in battles both desperate and unfair.

Which he generally preferred.

The Black Tigers NCO had been in enough bad spots to appreciate a good ambush and the occasional massacre in his, and his boys', favor.

There was... a fair amount of blood coming off the cut arm now that he looked at it.

"See what ya done there, boy..." he muttered to himself and spit into the dirt, ignoring the pain now that he'd witnessed the wound.

*So be it then*, thought the old warrior and went at the big Dire Man they'd all come to kill. Hacking overhead with the notched longsword and keeping back the wicked dagger for the cruelest cut he could make at the soonest opportunity possible.

Sergeant Thor had come into the piss lot, been charged from all sides forward by the inexpert pikemen, and dealt with them quickly. One of them had been strapping a small sword, a short sword, a good though by no means quality or even magical one at that. He'd pulled it from the sheath at the kid's waist, unused and unconsidered as the Ranger slaughtered his way forward to reach the old red sunbaked brick at the back wall of the dirt patch behind the tavern, stuck the kid hard in the ribs, pushed him away to die, or try to live, that was up to him... then watched as the last pikeman fled and the rest bled out on the scuffed and scarred dry dirt where much processed strong drink had been finally spent onto the ground there.

He was already breathing heavy when the black-armored, skull-helmeted old man came at him afresh with sword and dagger.

Now, wielding the stout little blade, Thor recognized instantly that he was dealing with a swordsman of skill, if not a lot of it. The man hacked overhand hard, but the dwarves who'd trained the Rangers as best they could with hand weapons had taught that many fighting styles used this approach to distract from the deadly weapon in the seeming off hand held lower and back and out of the way. Even

Otoro the strange enigmatic gorilla samurai who'd disappeared after an epic battle at Sûstagul had taught them strokes and cuts in the Ruin form of kendo the powerful gorilla samurai used. And also, powerful throws to dispatch and finish enemies on the battlefield.

Though who in their right mind would attack an eight-foot-tall humanoid gorilla carrying blades that cut steel like warm butter and severed orcish heads effortlessly in the maelstrom of battle, making the typhoon of a warrior seem like a poem whose sole purpose was to extol beauty and strength combined with a disciplined animal ferocity, the Ranger did not know.

The overhand cut was the distraction, Thor's mind grunted at him as he weaved the short sword up, twisting and shifting this way and that, giving ground as he batted away the old man's flurry of gasping and guffawing attacks.

The old coot muttered and howled as he attacked, and the Ranger blocked that out for the distraction that it was.

Some limit at how much combat could be asked of him, his body... how much running, fighting, and killing... he could do... it came now and Thor pushed it away, giving more ground knowing the rope-a-dope was coming soon enough, arms aching as he kept up his own assault against the old warrior's powerful downstrokes, steel ringing out in the dreary, bloody, hazy red courtyard at the back of the bar.

More would be pushing from behind, coming from the slaughter he'd left them to deal with in the bar, he told himself, patient and waiting for the trick he knew the old man was about to play on him as quickly, more and more, he ran out of room to give ground in their battle.

Then the old warrior whirled, his gray worn cloak suddenly becoming a shifting, distracting kaleidoscope of colors, all the colors in the immediate area...

The red worn brick.

The yellow haze in the sky at the end of the day above.

The black smoke of a hundred cookfires starting toward the evening meal by which the city was governed.

Even the heat waves coming off the blacksmiths' forges farther out and over the streets he must cross and escape through in order to avoid yet another killing stroke from surely another team of ambushers that had to be coming in even now.

Time was running out.

The colors before his eyes blended and oozed. The black leather, burnt face, cold steel flashing, and wild gray hair of the old desert fox who'd thought he was about to play the greatest trick of all and stick Thor with that wicked little sharp pigsticker he had down and low and out of the way as he shifted and spun... playing his combat tricks. Running his game.

Thor shifted hands with a flip of the found weapon, deftly catching the grip in his other fist as the man spun and all the colors blended near the spellworked cloak, all the colors of the Ruin in that courtyard which only one of them was going to walk away from in this frantic battle without honor or humility.

Then...

Eyes finding the horizon, almost soulless like a shark's eyes, ignoring the spin and chaos of the world as any paratrooper learns in the maelstrom of exits from aircraft, Thor brought up the weapon he'd stolen off the dead, or dying, kid just moments before... and plunged the blade in a wide and savage arc right into the ribs of the wily old coot, driving it in deep and hard as the old man tried to play his tried-and-true killing trick.

Feeling bone crunch.

Lungs puncture and collapse.

Warm blood instantly flowed down Thor's fist because the blade was wide and not long.

Suddenly Sergeant Thor's beard and ice-blue eyes were close to the old mercenary's, even as he went up on the tips of his combat boots, but out and away with the wily old trickster on the Ranger's pickup blade, sucking it in for all he was worth to avoid the savage strike of the old man's pigsticker as it had tried to come for him.

"Damn you, son," hissed the old man knowing he was done for when it was over. "I'll... see... you... in the Hells... someday..." he gasped.

Thor pushed the mercenary warlord off his blade and watched him backpedal, ungainly, and then go sprawling in the dirt badly as he coughed and could not catch air ever again.

"Yeah, maybe... but not today, old man."

Then like some jungle panther or stalking house cat, he was up and over the back wall of the piss lot easy and fast and moving into the streets of the blacksmiths' quarters for escape through the Desert Dwarves' secret tunnels.

# CHAPTER THIRTY-FIVE

The Ranger ran, arms pumping, one hand holding the bloody short sword. Women screamed, gathering their children close at hand as he sprinted past them like a hunted beast out in the wild.

Powerful legs heaving forward.

Worn boots pounding the old streets of the City of Thieves at the end of the day as the noose that had been set for the thief began to close.

The first of Seac the Raven's three elements that comprised the expensive quick reaction force the mercenaries of the Black Tigers called blockers, came thundering hard and fresh down the first line of stalls the Ranger-turned-thief raced down, heading toward the forges and tent pavilions of the Desert Dwarves deeper into the district where the metalworkers beat and pounded at weapons day in and day out and sometimes late into the hot nights, their hellish forges glowing bright red and throwing hot flame and sparks everywhere in the shadowed darknesses between the pits and the leering moon above.

Moonblades on those nights fetched great amounts of silver and gold.

Thor took another route now than the one he'd initially intended, tracking the five runners on his heels and assessing their ability to intercept him. These were skirmishers, and their gear and kit were light, as were their weapons. There were others with spears and various smaller hand-to-hand weapons. They wore leathers or little else and came at him swift-footed, seeing the direction change he intended and cutting him off through other lines of stalls on intercept angles that would bring the Ranger face-to-face and knives out soon enough.

They were running him down.

The first one came in fast, and Thor merely grabbed him and flung him onto the hot coals of a glowing forge nearby.

The man screamed, flesh sizzling, and the blacksmith heaved the wailing man off his task at hand and went right back to stoically beating at the chunk of steel he'd been intent on in the seconds before the interruption.

Thor darted in another direction moving swiftly and tirelessly as the hunters closed in on all sides, some ululating strange cries and hisses that meant something to one another.

Skidding to a halt, Thor ran smack dab into a wide tent, open and revealing within fine weapons and stout northern beauties in furs and silks. A giant of a man with dark hair and a long drooping mustache smiled broadly, as did the beauties, seeing the jacked and sweating Ranger come skidding to a halt in front of the tent where the merchant proudly sold his deadly wares.

The two men on his heels cared less for the impressively tall and muscular merchant in the red rich robes nor the voluptuous beauties that served as his marketing within the fabled city.

The first hunter hurled a spear, and wily Thor dodged it easily and returned the favor, flinging the bloody short sword right in the man's chest after it tumbled savagely and landed solidly anyway.

The struck man seemed as surprised that this had happened and sank to his knees to spend his last few precious seconds trying to remove the blade from his sternum.

Then he fell over dead.

The other, a bald-headed man with chalk-white warpaint made of thousands of dots and a leering grin of gold teeth, shook a small snake off his arms that anyone would have mistaken for some piece of contrived jewelry and flung it at Thor, there before the merchant's wide pavilion of weapons and lovelies.

Then the chalked snake handler advanced with his sword out.

Rangers don't mind snakes at all, and Thor caught its writhing, twisting form even as it tried to curl and loop its tail about him.

It was black-over-yellow striped.

Nothing to worry about, and the hunter only used it to frighten his prey so he could get close just as he was doing now with the narrow-bladed sword he was getting ready to martially thrust right into Thor with a savage war cry and all.

Collect reward and get drunk.

Anyway...

Thor crushed the head of the snake and flung it aside, then grabbed a spear from a nearby rack as the chalked savage came in at him. He thrust it out, forcing the snake handler's blade to the ground, and delivered a fierce kick with one boot to the man's jaw.

Broken or whatever, the chalked man went down, lights out, and Thor turned, looking for a way out of this trap as more hunters ran through the forges and markets all around like wolves on the hunt.

Behind the Ranger, the giant northern merchant bellowed in some language Thor didn't understand and picked up a double-bladed battle axe that was neither large nor small. Both blades of the fearsome axe were like those of

Thor's tomahawks, curved and wicked and with definitely that northern flare.

The merchant was taller than Thor and he looked more warrior than seller of swords.

The northern merchant bellowed at the Ranger in some harsh Scandinavian tongue turned Ruin language long ago. Of all the languages the Ranger had collected since finding himself in the Ruin, this was not one he'd had time to master or even gain basic proficiency in.

Only Vandahar, the strange Gandalf-like wizard who'd allied himself to the Rangers, had used it, rarely and in those times only to himself... muttering about the differences between the times he fondly remembered and the dark times of now.

Talker had said Vandahar's name, in those northern languages, meant *Wanderer*.

Seeing that Sergeant Thor did not comprehend the Dire Tongues, Ulfvaang the Steel Merchant, come down from the Dire Frost, tried instead the trade tongues of the city.

These... the Ranger knew. Although often with some difficulty.

"Brother, take a good weapon now!" he said sternly to the Ranger. He was holding out the fine double-bladed battle axe.

"Your foes are upon you now," continued the powerful

red-bearded Dire Man, "and you have been so long in these lands you have forgotten our ways! Take it now, boy. Take it now... and slay."

The impressive merchant warrior smiled slyly.

More of them were coming quickly...

Thor lunged for the blade and nodded, muttering, "*Shkran.*" *Thank you.* The form of Arabic that passed for a trade language here in the deadly deep along the desert coast of what had once been the Arabian Peninsula.

And then he was gone and more of the hunters followed him quickly, deeper into the markets as the day died a bloody-red ending of smoke and hammering in the heat.

Soon, it would be night. And the cool stars would be out.

The epic northern beauties within the weapons merchant's tent laughed, watching the handsome warrior go with their hungry eyes. And the warrior merchant turned and shouted at his wicked daughters, telling them to get back to polishing weapons, and themselves, wishing he were the young wolf that had just come into their tents.

As he too had once been on other days not this one.

# CHAPTER THIRTY-SIX

THOR MANAGED TO MAKE THE TUNNELS, FIGHTING A running battle that ended right at the line of heavily armored Desert Dwarven warriors the hired mercenaries had no intention of tangling with. Each dwarven warrior was carrying at least five well-made weapons and they had the look, and the scars, of knowing exactly how to use those deadly, shining, razor-sharp weapons of all varieties. Never mind the series of hashmarks on the hafts of the axes that could be seen.

The dwarves threw up their line all coming together from every direction among their forges and tents and the Ranger passed beyond their barrier and was quickly hustled into the secret tunnels beyond the reach of immediate pursuit, on his way to meet Sato at the rendezvous on the other side of the tunnel that led from the forges and pavilions of those strange and quiet dwarves to the loading piers where great galleys and massive cargos came out of the distant wastes to the east by heavily guarded caravan, or from farther distant into the unknowable southern seas for transfer to coastal ships hauling north to Sûstagul and then overland and into other galleys doing trade along the Great Inner Sea.

As he emerged into the early twilight of the docks, he smelled smoke in the air. Ships were on fire. Fireballs slammed into galleys along the quay and even merchant vessels come into port to deal with their cargos. The pyrotechnics were cast by small bands of twilight bastards surrounded by combat teams of sellswords leading a running firefight up through the docks and burning ships.

A rumor had spread that the Ranger barbarian was headed for the port, and small armies from either the wizards or the eunuchs had run smack dab into each other trying to suss it out. Combat had begun instantly.

Smaller vessels were casting off, going to sails and trying to escape the growing conflagration and combat. Medium-sized warships, moored farther down the docks, sent massed arrow fire arching out across the bloody end-of-the-day sky at the attackers swarming forward. The arrows landed with thick wooden *thock*s among other ships or along the piers.

The eunuchs had sent messages up the coast for more mercenaries, and these were just arrived in the port of the City of Thieves, come seeking the bounty on Thor, now thrust into the brewing war between the factions.

Sometimes there were screams when the arrow fire found a target.

Merchants ran clutching chests and navigational charts, while grimy bare-chested sailors tried to put out the spreading greedy fires alight aboard their vessels as two of the cities' factions now engaged each other in a battle neither side had expected when they'd come looking for Thor, or been hired to do so and were just entering the city.

Both had come looking for the Ranger now watching from the shadows on the near side of the secret dwarven tunnel that led here. Instead they'd found each other, and either hard or harsh words, backed by well-founded suspicions, had led to the clearing of leather scabbards and the casting of sorcerous flamestrikes and fireballs. Whatever had gone wrong... it was full *gone wrong* underway now and only one side was coming out of this.

One way or another.

"Ahhh... Warrior," mused Sato as the two men watched the bands of twilight bastards and their armed mercenaries attempt to take out a ship full of archers and more heavily armored mercenaries with web spells, sleep spells, and cold hard steel to be dealt out with no quarter.

Massed arrow fire answered and slaughtered one twilight bastard advance, but by that time two other elements of sellswords and bastards had managed to take the target ship and now the clang and clash, amid the desperate roar of combat, had engulfed a second ship where more archers were rallying to support by fire. Nearby, a triple-decker merchant galley was aflame across the sails and upper deck. Sailors and fire brigades could do little, due to the ongoing combat, to save the wounded vessel, and it was clear she'd burn moored.

Another ship in berth nearby had already burned to the water line. Men were seen swimming away as sharks raced into the bay to take what they could.

"... A rumor spread just an hour ago that you were headed here, Warrior, instead of where you were. The wizards sent their bastards and guards and promptly ran into a force the eunuchs had assembled to scour the district, putting everyone on lockdown. I suspect the wizards were at their scrying stone and saw some hint of your escape. Both sides had their informants and threw everything they had on short notice into the harbor. This is the sad result..."

Some cargo within the burning triple-decker trireme suddenly exploded amidships, sending flaming debris in every direction. Furled sails turned into roman candles and there was no saving the immense ship. The losses would be total.

Still, the fight on the nearby galley continued unabated.

"This is fortunate for us. The city is becoming too hot

for you, Warrior. It would be wise to move to the second-to-last position now."

Thor wiped blood from his bicep and grunted as Sato handed him a new old-worn-out rucksack. The pack of a dockworker. It was filled with bread and wine and a rough cloak that would cover Sergeant Thor's immense frame. A wide-brimmed straw hat woven in eastern rice farmer fashion would hide his clear features if he kept his head down and "labored" under the comically overstuffed pack the guild had prepared for the next part of the fade.

Thor knelt and dressed quickly in the costume. "I'll go there now. We wait three days as you suggest, Sato, and then we'll move to final."

"*Hai*!" Sato said and grunted. "If all goes well then no one will ever suspect what has become of the treasure."

Then for a long moment the two men, warrior and thief, were quiet there in the shadows of the alley. Beyond, out in the port, magic crackled and snapped, swords were broken, choruses of arrows sang in their crossing of the last light in the sky, and ships burned as spars snapped and hulls groaned, crackling and hissing at the water's misty embrace.

"This business will engulf the whole city, Warrior," whispered the thief softly.

But Sergeant Thor answered nothing in reply to this and was soon gone down along the docks as the night's darkness came and the fires from the burning ships made the shadows darker and the bonfires of the galleys brighter and more hellish.

Within the hour, the swift-moving Ranger would be beyond the city and following the port road south to a small village along the beach.

Sato watched him go, watched the battle on the war galley, which was now completely on fire, then turned at the titanic slow groan of the trireme merchant ship as her spine finally broke and she flopped over into the waters of the harbor where bodies floated.

Along the docks the clumped shadows of the motionless slain in battle, bastard and eunuch mercenary, lay like small piles of rubbish.

By morning light much of this harbor would be burned, and the fire, as the winds came and went off the sea, would spread slowly among the districts leading toward the deeps of the City of Thieves.

The next few days would be smoke and ash.

And to some it would seem like the end of the world. And the end of everything they'd ever known.

Wizards worried.

Eunuchs shivered.

Thieves plundered.

Dark Cultists whirled and chanted, celebrating the

coming of their dark spider-queen god in the last days of smoke and ash.

# CHAPTER THIRTY-SEVEN

SEAC THE RAVEN WANDERED THE BURNING DOCKS AT midnight that night.

His company was slain now.

Only one other remained. The archer. The slender yet muscled archer, a quiet man, the air of a hunter about him, following behind his commander in armor, wrapped in his Mourne Elven cloak as though in grieving despite the heat of the blaze coming off the burning ships and now engulfing the port warehouses nearby.

Burning ash drifted through the air.

The archer could smell smoke. And further south, the salty cool fog coming onshore. But here it was gray smoke and few stars above.

Many dead along the docks.

Many arrows broken and shattered and still sticking out of bodies, buildings, and piers.

Burning ash drifted through the night. Landing on the

last of the Black Tigers in the City of Thieves, then flying off like fire-fey, weaving and dancing further into the city on the night's wind to see what mischief could be found and made alight.

The archer wanted to tell his commander, the Black Tiger sergeant, the man who'd led them into, and out of— no small feat there—the deadly passes of Ganistan... the archer wanted to tell Seac the Raven that it was time to go now.

That this contract was lost.

Everything was a mess and if there was going to be the Sixth of the Black Tigers, which was their company, then it was time to leave this city and find young men daring or dumb enough to sign the blood oath and then find some battle to sell the company to. Some side desperate enough for mercenaries. Some lost cause to fight to the death for.

Some field of war other than this cursed and doom-haunted city in which one man had flipped the tables and caused it to light itself on fire.

The Ranger.

A devil.

A phantom.

A killer without peer.

Anything, to the archer now, was better than chasing this demon-murder phantom called a "Ranger" through the streets of a city known for its larceny at all levels.

This was bad.

Time to go.

There was no winning this one.

But the archer, who was deadly enough to be called Bullseye, said nothing, for he could tell the shadow of his commander was like a stormfront. And a dangerous one at that.

# CHAPTER THIRTY-EIGHT

The large stevedore with the huge worn pack on his shoulder was yet one of many fleeing another fast-brewing conflict that had erupted within the city. This time in the port. This time with fireballs, arrow fire, and more dead.

The conversations Thor passed, along the way south and out of the city, disguised as just another large bull of a man who loaded endless cargo day after day, doubted whether either side, eunuchs or wizards, had gotten their man yet, or if they ever would.

"This... Ranger... he is like the revenants from the open graves beyond the Old Tomb out in the cemeteries beyond the walls. He is mist. He is shadows. He is something none should mess with. Like a viper in a basket."

Or...

"I heard he was killed in a gambling den and that when they went to find his money it was all spent. Now the wizards don't believe the *mandarini* and are out for blood, thinking those painted-lipped whores are just stealing it all for themselves like they do all our coin and call it taxes! It will be war. More blood in the streets... mark my words, Jozato! Mark them. This will be a war the City of Thieves is finally conquered by, where all others have failed. Mark them, Jozato!"

Whether the long-suffering Jozato marked them or not was not known to the Ranger. He moved swiftly beyond them in the shadows and the dark, his road-eating stride taking him swiftly along the column of refugees fleeing to other parts of the sprawl within the walls.

In the night, heading south along the port road that led to the massive Dragon Gate between the sea and the wide southern desert beyond the cyclopean walls of the City of Thieves, they were all just shadows to him. Shadows carrying what they could to get away at the last moment, away from a fire now consuming the port district.

Behind them the sky glowed a hellish orange as the night got deeper over the port.

The Dragon Gate was closed for the night, but the guards of course had a small door open, and for the right flash of coin one could pass beyond its barrier and into the south and the night.

Alluria, dressed as a laundress and carrying a basket of

ripe and dirty linens, sidled up to the Ranger and whispered her information. Her shapely form was revealed by the way she'd tied her top and allowed her goods and taut belly to show while her hips undulated beneath the long wrap she wore. She balanced her load perfectly and it was an excellent cover, as the tantalizing allure of her beauty impressed the guards to want to do anything for her, and the precarious bundle of piled mildew-smelling laundry seemed, in an unspoken way, to be some horrible unclean mess that could befall them if she was touched, or jostled, in the slightest.

She was but a humble washing woman and perhaps the woman of some hard-working man who'd found in her a treasure that could not be purchased.

Thor noted that the disguise was quite clever. The beauty carrying the stinking laundry was just like holding a hot steaming cup of coffee on a crowded subway platform with the lid off. People just got out of the way for you like they normally didn't. That hot coffee, whether they recognized it or not, actively sent the message that one misstep and it could end up all over them. No shoving, jostling, or bumping. A wide berth was given, for the mildewed laundry was overpowering.

Guards didn't want stinking laundry dumped on them even if she *was* a tasty treat they wouldn't mind trifling with. So she went along and wherever she wanted, quite unmolested, using her beauty, protected by the foul load she plied.

"Clever girl," whispered Thor as he clocked her among the refugees at the gate, making her way toward him.

She slipped through the dark and came alongside the hulking "stevedore" approaching the mass at the gate. Ahead, guards waited for coin, and if it wasn't offered they merely muttered a gruff, "Gate's closed for the night," and directed the refugees to spaces off in the dark where they could sleep under the wall.

A few showed the right coin and slipped past and through a cluster of guards with pikes, making for the small door that was quickly opened and shut just as rapidly.

The fee paid, the stranger passing through and on about their business beyond the city walls in the night out there.

This was by no means safe. Life for a human beyond the walls of a city, in the Ruin which was more monster than man, was a dangerous proposition.

"Well Well has already made the arrangements, Warrior," whispered the seductive Alluria, her voice filled with intrigue and adventure. She was having the time of her life. The Ranger could tell that about her. And he liked her more for that than her obvious sensual beauty and ample charms. In a way... she was a kindred spirit to him. She was beautiful enough to be married off, or bought and sold, for such was the civilization of the Ruin. She probably didn't get much of a chance to get caught up in the adventure of things. "Pass through and go to the gate, Warrior. They are paid already. Do not say anything because they are on the listen for your atrocious accent. Seriously... one called Thor... thieves are masters of dialect and languages. It's half the job, you big piece of meat."

Thor listened to her and spotted the guard who seemed to be in charge motioning the other guards regarding the big Dire Man savage they'd been paid to pass as he and the washing woman slowly approached their gaggle of a checkpoint. He gripped the battle axe under the coarse robe that covered his frame just in case things didn't go as smoothly as Alluria had indicated they would.

There was always another way. Violence opened a lot of doors, contrary to popular belief. Ask any master breacher in the regiment.

"What do you know of thieves, serving girl?" the Ranger rumbled. "Last I checked, you just fetched drinks and passed information from this one to that one."

She gave a pouty *humph* and hissed a, "I know a thing or two 'bout thievin' some don't, Warrior. See ya 'round, Thor, if they don't slit your throat in the sand and fog."

Then she winked at him.

The guards began to part as he approached, and the

laundress peeled off from the Ranger. But not before she whispered a last, "Be a shame if they did. One with your physique could make a good living among the *mandarini*. They like big boys. Ta, Warrior. Maybe if I get rich, I'll buy you for myself."

Alluria didn't speak the cant. This was all in port patois and the Ranger thought it had been a bit cheeky for her to keep engaging as he reached the chokepoint and made ready to pass through without incident, or kill them all, smash the door open, and double-time it off into the sandy reaches beyond out there in the night.

Muscles relaxed and ready to deal death if the deal at the gate went sideways, Thor passed through the clutch of guards who were keeping their side hustle quiet and lightless.

With little fanfare and the soft creak of the small door...

Somebody should oil that, thought Thor, the NCO running an operation kicking in for a moment.

... then he passed through the gate to the other side of the wall. Heading south in the night, the moon low over the sea. The offshore breeze moving the seagrass in waves here and out there under the moon's silver light.

He found the coast road and began to walk the seven miles south through the sand dunes, and in time, the quiet of the fog.

It was lonely and it felt good to the Ranger to be away from the city.

# CHAPTER THIRTY-NINE

THE SAND AND FOG WAS IN INN IN THE SMALL FISHING village of Hook's Rest.

This was seven miles south beyond the Emerald Dragon Gate that was the southern exit from the City of Thieves.

Thor covered the distance quickly, ditching the useless pack but keeping the coarse robe and his battle axe. He still had his knives, the Contego, the shank, and the punch knife.

*Mjölnir*, his assault pack, the Pearl of Fate, and his remaining tomahawk and some other gear that had survived were safely hidden back in Shadowrun, the neighborhood deep within the City of Thieves where the Little Guild ran things and basically watched over an area of the city neither guards, eunuchs, or wizards unfriendly to the clan would ever enter.

It was a safe haven.

His rifle and the strange pearl were safe there.

Now on the move south and watching the nearby dunes

and the tall waving seagrass in the night, hearing the crash of the surf out there on the coast off to his right, the Ranger moved quickly through the fog and the darkness.

He avoided the beach. Smugglers were down there getting ready to load their small boats and shift cargo into the city, hoping to avoid the eyes of the eunuchs and perhaps gain more profit.

The smugglers were a rough lot, and he didn't need another fight, another slaughter, another clue for those pursuing him to follow.

The other danger on the twisting road through the dunes and fog was bandits.

No one would miss slaughtered bandits. If it came to that, the packs of jackals and other carrion feeders, even the buzzards of the southern desert that roamed the sands and hills to the east, would do away with bodies that had dared try him by noon the next day.

No one would miss dead bandits.

But right now he didn't need a surprise attack or an unseen arrow suddenly in the back. So he humped the road fast and got ready to move off it if need be. He'd bury himself in the sand, or hide in the tall waving grass, undulating like the surface of a silver ocean under the moon's light.

Within two hours he made the village of Hook's Rest

and found the quiet inn they'd scouted.

The Sand and Fog.

For a long moment, near the fish-drying racks at the edge of the sleeping fishing village, among chimes made of driftwood, the Ranger studied the inn from the dark there and waited for the shadows of some ambush that had been sent there to wait and watch for him.

The village was quiet.

There were many such villages along the coast road, and he'd passed through three of them before reaching the target of Hook's Rest.

The inn was quiet and even the smell of food on the night's wind was missing. There was light from the few windows. Smoke from a hearth inside. But no raucous roister or bellowing fights suddenly erupting.

The Sand and Fog had been chosen for this reason. It was a quiet inn and rarely visited. A small poor family ran it and Sato had assured Thor the inn had little to nothing to do with the guilds or much of the city.

They were considered poor and of little consequence.

Thor waited.

Watched.

Listened.

Smelled the night wind.

He pulled the small pouch full of coins that had been

secreted in the pack. Ten gold and a handful of silver.

A fortune in an inn like this.

Along the back of the inn, a small candle came to life behind a crude window. Thor watched. Soon, a small figure bent near the candle, silhouetted through the bad glass. Thor's keen eyes could see it was a child. And watching further, he could see the child was holding a book.

Reading it in the night.

He waited longer, listened to the village fall asleep, then just at the last, as the innkeeper, a man called Omir, began to close up the shutters, the Ranger strode swiftly and business-like across the sand, walked up the ancient sun-weathered wooden slates that served as steps, and opened the door, slipping inside quickly, light spilling out across the sand outside briefly for a moment in the dark and foggy night.

Nearby a dog did not bark, and the small fishing huts and a warehouse remained dark.

Nothing had happened.

No one was seen.

And the night moved on toward its later watches.

# CHAPTER FORTY

OMIR, THE KEEPER OF THE SAND AND FOG, WAS A medium-sized slight man with handsome hardworking features and a well-kept goatee.

He was young.

His mouth opened almost on the verge of protest, or giving alarm, seeing the huge Dire Man northern savage he took Sergeant Thor to be, enter his inn at the end of the night when usually no one did because of the road and the bandits.

Thor watched as the innkeeper's eyes flicked toward the stairs where the family's living quarters were. As though the innkeeper had thought, *If this man is a robber, I will cry for help*. But then his eyes seemed to say... *But to whom?*

Thor towered over him.

Omir had a wife. Two daughters. And a son. The boy was a reader of books.

The Little Guild had done their reconnaissance of the

inn well. Even Thor had come here one night to verify that the inn that was the second-to-last fade before the heist was done.

Thor held up one massive, scarred hand.

The universal gesture for *Friend. Peace. No harm intended.*

Omir watched the warrior that had entered his... life. Uncertain. Studying the fine gleaming battle axe the big savage carried.

"I have come for a room tonight," said Thor in Arabic.

For a moment the innkeeper seemed not to understand or comprehend that this was even an option. He was waiting for the battle axe to swing for his skull and wondering what would become of his family. These types usually never came to his inn. The lands south of the City of Thieves were quiet and lonely. A powerful holy man wandered the sands along the coast, and it was said the monsters were kept at bay by his presence. Though he had not been seen for weeks now. Still, his fearsome reputation was enough to keep the coast quiet, and safe.

Then, suddenly, Omir nodded. Still uncertain. But understanding that perhaps... this Dire savage just wanted a room. For the night.

Omir could do that.

Thor opened the pouch the guild had prepared,

pickpocketed wealth from within the city, and shook the coins out onto a scrupulously clean table. They gleamed in the candlelight there along the rough wooden table.

The standard price for a room in the inn was two silver.

What lay on the table... was... *life-changing money.* To Omir. Not by itself. But... it could be put to use.

Then...

Husbands for his daughters.

Books and maybe schooling for the boy who seemed to have the gift for such things.

A new dress for the love of his life. His wife. The girl who'd once taken a chance on him.

Dreams that had been nothing but gossamer hopes before this night.

Omir nodded. This was... probably too good to be true.

The oldest girl, her name was Asora according to the developed intel, came running from the shadows behind the bar, talking fast and picking up the slack. She was barely in her teens.

"Come, come... sit while we have your room made ready, friend." Her manners were polite and her eyes wide and welcoming. "Come, come... my father, he runs the finest inn," she said proudly. "And now you will see how good we take care of our friends."

Omir came to life suddenly at his daughter's bravery.

"Yes, yes!" he exclaimed. "It is late, but we have fresh red fish stew still warm in the pot. Perhaps hot bread and a drink before you sleep the best night ever. What is your name... friend?"

Thor stepped over the bench at the lone long table and sat down. His size and muscles as compared to the small size of the bench and table made this funny to the girl. She covered her face to giggle and her father told her to see to the room in their tribal speak.

She nodded obediently.

Omir left the coins on the table, went behind the bar, and disappeared into the dark kitchen. Within moments he returned with a bowl of aromatic and spicy fish broth and some warm flatbread spiced with fennel.

He was proud of what he served the Ranger, and Thor could see it by the way the man set it down with a flourish.

It smelled like real food. It reminded Thor of better days, long ago. Which is the magic of a meal, sometimes.

Mingo, who'd done the scout of the inn, said the red fish stew was exceptional and that if the inn was known for anything, it was in fact known for this dish.

Even the bandits didn't bother the place because they did trade in the village and liked to sneak into the inn every so often for a bowl of the stuff and a quiet drink.

Omir placed the food on the long rough table along with

a utensil, then went to draw a cold beer. He returned and set it down in a small cup, apologizing he had nothing bigger to serve it in.

"You... uh... Northmen like bigger... tankards. Horns. We... we do not have that. I am sorry. I... will..."

He said all this as though the air in the room were made of crystal and that if he said anything wrong... it would break. It would disappear. He would fail. The stranger and huge Dire Man would leave, and those beautiful coins, shimmering on the table, would disappear.

As would the hopes and the dreams.

He could not believe so much coin was in his inn.

The Ranger swept up the small cup and downed it. Then began to eat the stew. He was starving and it was delicious, and he only realized he was starving as he ate it, feeling himself let down a little. Safe, finally. That had been... a long fade.

Omir refilled the cup and sat down. Directly across from the Ranger, his eyes darting to the shining coins for a moment. In the shadows behind the bar two females, the younger daughter and Omir's dark-eyed wife, a chaste and fine-looking girl in a dark robe, watched from the shadows of the kitchen.

They whispered but Thor could not tell what was said between them.

Probably something about the coins. Something about him and his strangeness to them.

Thor finished the bowl and swiped up the small drinking cup again, emptying it in one go.

Omir raced to refill it again and sat down once more, saying, "Do you... I have heard... forgive me if I insult, my friend... do you drink your brew from the skulls of your enemies as I have heard your people do?"

Thor gave the man a long serious look.

Omir seemed like he was going to faint or die right there. He had offended!

"Only on holidays," rumbled the Ranger, then laughed a little and Omir relaxed, leaning back and actually wiping sweat from his dark brow.

Then Sergeant Thor spoke. "Take the coins. You have a small cottage down near the cove."

This was not a question. It was a statement.

Omir, suddenly confused, nodded and did not take up the coins. His eyes flicked to them and then back to the big Dire Man at his table.

Things were... curious. Suddenly there wasn't just a mystery in the air... but danger. The cottage was for the fearsome holy man when he passed this way. Though he had not been seen in weeks.

"Yes, my friend. But no one ever goes there. It is simple."

"Take the coins," rumbled Thor. "I will need it for the rest of the week. No one is to know I am there. Bring me food. If anyone starts asking about me, tell me, and I will leave and trouble you no more. You will receive more coins. Can you do this?"

Could he?

Omir was no fool. He knew he was being caught up in something. He could... bring destruction. Or... those books, husbands, the dress for the love of his life who had dared marry him on the promise of his dreams.

Dreams that had not...

For a long moment, Omir studied the hulking strange man across from him, seeming to understand who he was.

A dangerous man.

A daring man.

Something he, Omir, had thought he was when he'd taken his chances and dared, dared to make this inn. Even smuggled a little to get the coin. He had dared.

But this man...

Maybe he did not know the details. But he was dealing with a man who was nothing like him. Or anyone he'd ever met.

A very dangerous man. With much coin.

And...

That by making this deal...

Omir was entering dark waters. Like some pirate. Risking it all for profit. Betting... his family, his treasure, on perhaps...

Betting for that better life he had promised them all without ever saying a word.

Husbands for his beautiful daughters.

Books for his smart daydreaming boy.

A dress for Asami. The girl who'd become a woman and taken a chance on him, the least in their tribe. A dreamer just like his good son. All the good things he'd ever dreamed of for them lay on the table, gleaming gold, between him and the dangerous man on the other side.

A chance to dream.

A dare.

Omir closed his eyes and said some quick prayer.

Then opened them and nodded at the Ranger.

"It will be so."

# CHAPTER FORTY-ONE

The summoner looked around at all the chaos and carnage wrought inside the Temple of Poesidius.

It had been one of the goriest, most relentless battles Baalubrozz had ever been involved in.

No, he realized on second thought, a post-battle adrenaline crashing into a kind of pleasant high... it had been more than that. He had been in a real struggle for life and death. He'd come that close. He'd burned every spell. And he'd looked the damnation he'd sold himself for right in the face, always thinking it would come some other day when he was too tired to debauch anymore. When he'd sated himself on every pleasure the Ruin, and all the other worlds than these, had to offer. Or... perhaps he'd cheat his sealed fate...

There was no look on the summoner's face.

No sigh of exasperation at what had been wasted in spell and summoned dark force.

No disgust at what had not been obtained. Answers.

Power unshared.

The temple priest had been torn in half.

The drunken lout...

Fool.

Idiot.

Slave.

Several demons lay slaughtered on the floor where Baalubrozz had summoned and then flung them right against the surprised horror of the two sacred naga whores... *that had been quite a surprise...* that had surfaced just as he tortured everything he wanted out of the boozy wayward priest for what information he knew of the thief, and warrior, who'd stolen the entire contents of the Prize Chest.

That he'd been working with one of the guilds... that was clear now.

The two sisters, the sacred naga whores, their snake-like corpses now lying half in, half out of the pool... were dead. One's head was missing. The other had slain several of his minor demons and the pit lord he'd summoned to boot.

The pit lord's smoking corpse was still on fire in a corner of the temple, and the reek from it was foulest sulphury hell and horrifying pestilence the likes of a pit where human waste is burnt. The creature's massive bat wings had been ripped from its body and the fiery hell blade it wielded had been sundered in two.

The broken hilt still glowed red hot, black sulfur rising like snakes from the fracture where the dark magic of the forges of the Hell Giants had been most powerful.

The cost to the summoner had been... *enormous*.

Baalubrozz had come back to the Temple of Poesidius the next night after being... *led*... to the temple. The entire day in preparation, he'd done his black rites, made his diabolical symbols, arranged his bargains, and done his devilish deals.

You know... just in case.

Baalubrozz thought the fire elementals he'd brought along, summoning them in a dark alley just near the temple steps, would be enough, but he'd committed the summoning of the pit lord to a handy serpent-blood-inked scroll, just in case too.

The minor demons were there to torment the priest who'd probably died of a heart attack sometime during the not-long-enough torture.

That was when the two naga sisters appeared, convinced their gig was ruined.

Baalubrozz had tried to bargain with them. At first. They got cute and wanted more treasure and half the haul of the Prize Chest the summoner was after, and... were willing to tell Baalubrozz right then and there where it was and where this... *Ranger Thor*... could be found that night.

If...

If he'd submit to a *geas* and be bound to the terms of their cursed, one-sided deal wrought by the powerful binding spell.

The insult. How dare they?

He'd flung the demons and the elementals at them right then and there as he sputtered with rage at their cheek. Then it was a brawl the summoner thought he easily had the upper hand of from the get-go. But as the two sisters' powerful magics chewed through his forces pretty quickly, that was when the pit lord scroll got read off pretty darn quick and that smoldering hell-fiend appeared, completely dark with rage he'd been bothered at all, and was immediately and rather unceremoniously ordered, forced really, into battle by Baalubrozz.

"Deal's a deal, Dark One!" the summoner had screamed apoplectically as the sacred water naga flung a typhoon within the temple, summoned straight up out of their sacred pool, right at Baalubrozz who'd just cast *Wall of Fire*, *Shield*, and even *Earthquake* right at them to save his skin as his minor demons got massacred and returned to the deepest of the Hells.

All the scrolls he'd read off badly because he was busy dodging the dire eels the two sisters had sent at him through the flooded temple, shrieking, hissing, jaws wide with needle-sharp horror teeth, serpentine scales crackling with live blue electricity.

By that time Baalubrozz was flying above the rising flood waters inside the storm-tossed temple, hovering in the salty air, watching his demons get drowned and torn to pieces by tiger sharks surging in through the fracture caused by the earthquake spell.

Those imps were dead all across the floor of the gaudy temple.

The waters inside the temple were receding now, after the battle. The earthquake he'd cast, trying to fracture the pool, had fractured the very foundation of the edifice and collapsed half the temple floor into the waters of the grotto below the whole temple.

Chewed-up demons and dead sharks twisted and turned in slow motion down there among the aquamarine depths turned inky.

The statue of Poesidius had crumbled, the head smashing and dazing the summoned pit lord who'd just lopped off the head of the lead hissing sister and was preparing to strike a fiery blow against the other. With the powerful nightmare fiend dazed, the other sister, somehow, immolated the demon with a powerful staff curled within her twisting coils as the battle raged.

All hell had broken loose then, and that wasn't enough

to get the summoner's answers, or even kill the last sacred naga...

There would be hell to pay. That was for sure.

The demons would be pissed and plotting against him down there in Tartarus. Calling in favors and making bargains Baalubrozz might not be able to buy, or protect, his way out of. There was surely a dark debt coming due for all this.

That was the problem with working with these types of entities. They held long grudges.

And of course Poesidius himself, that fiend would be really sore, putting it mildly, that the summoner had done this to his temple and his sacred naga...

So...

That was gonna be a problem too.

Baalubrozz stepped over the dead naga, avoiding the disintegrating body of a leech-like demon he'd summoned that was turning to maggots writhing in the bloody and black waters on the tuna-and-sea-god-hauling-a-net mosaiced floor of what remained of the temple. The massive stone image of the god, the head specifically, was lying on its side and gazing at Baalubrozz like a baleful promise of how much ill will that demon bore him.

The summoner stared down into the Atlantari face of the dead naga that still had her head. He tore the now-

425

worthless Ring of Death off a fat finger and finally gave fully into his simmering rage, hurling the now-useless trinket at her.

The once-powerful artifact, the Ring of Death, was now spent. Its last charge expended on her. Baalubrozz had been meaning to hire a band of reckless adventurers to quest for a Titan soul that would allow him to extend its charge, a dangerous and long quest few ever returned from, but he hadn't gotten around to tricking someone into doing it, what with all his busy research and constant debauching.

That was no longer an option. Once fully depleted, it could be recharged no more. Its powerful dark onyx gem was sucked dry, burnt to its core. Useless.

But things, Baalubrozz reminded himself as he began to savagely kick the dead sacred naga in the face, destroying her austere beauty further, could be different.

He could be... dead.

Down somewhere real dark and very deep paying for all the diabolical bargains for power he'd made.

He really needed to get busy on that *Undeath* research. That was the only way to avoid the fate he'd sealed for himself, regardless of what the followers of the Hidden King blathered on and on about, or so Baalubrozz told himself.

He could be... *worse than dead* if he hadn't burned that Ring of Death at just the last second.

She'd given him the space to use it, calling out her dead sister's name and then naming herself, saying she would revenge her sister's death upon the summoner.

*Naming herself...* in the process.

Which was just what the Ring of Death needed.

That had been the ticket.

Names were powerful.

So he'd burnt the last charge in the ring and named her and... then she was just dead.

It was really that easy. Simple. Powerful ring unless it got depleted completely. Then it was... dead. Ironically.

The battle had been easy at the last. The summoner laughing and jeering as the naga's heart exploded, him hovering and spitting at her over the dying storm within the temple floodwaters as the powerful magic faded.

Except... it took several scrolls, twenty dead demons each with a whole host of problems that opened up upon destruction, a major pit lord completely smoked... and a lost artifact Baalubrozz had betrayed a whole band of adventurers over when he was just a young summoner masquerading as a wizard and making his way up the levels of power to become the powerful summoner he'd become.

For a moment, rage abated... Baalubrozz wondered if that long-ago party was still lost deep down there along the Endless Stair beyond the Mountains of Umnoth.

Still going downward.

That had been... years and years ago.

*It's a long fall*. Words an old summoner he'd betrayed had once said to him.

Baalubrozz shrugged as if to say *Oh well*. Smiled and began to giggle in the aquamarine dark of the temple. He broke off some coral on a railing nearby and cut himself with it.

His left eye was twitching.

The stress was incredible.

The failure clearly catastrophic.

And even after all that, Baalubrozz had no real idea where this Thor was. Or how he'd done the deed of plundering the Prize Chest.

Which, he had to be honest about, was killing him. He needed to know. More than anything... he needed to know how it had been done. There was probably much power there.

But...

"Curiosity killed the black cat," he sighed in the vast mausoleum silence of the place after ceasing his insane gibbering and giggling.

Then he answered himself nonsensically. "I know. I know. I know!"

He was no closer still, and in fact, given the time spent,

much further away, from the capture he'd been tasked with, and the haul he would betray the wizardly cabal for.

The summoner passed by the dead demons and the marred and destroyed beauty of the temple. The priest still lay in two pieces, the treacherous imps having gone mad with fiendish glee at the man's suffering at the last.

But now the old wretch of a priest, what was left of his face, had surrendered to some impossible... *smile*... or even... peace.

Baalubrozz swore at this.

He would have sent a fusillade of magic meteors right into the dolt then and there... but he was out. Plain out. He was completely out of spells...

... out of luck...

... out of power...

... out of answers...

And...

Out of time.

Osirex wanted a report soon. The morrow's evening.

It was almost dawn now.

He spit at the smiling priest but missed the corpse.

Then he left, muttering, "Someone else will clean this up. Someone... always does."

And then he was gone.

# CHAPTER FORTY-TWO

IT WAS LATE.

Somewhere Baalubrozz was disappointing Osirex who was enjoying the failure of the spoiled little greedy brat of a summoner much, while Mandelf merely looked on absent-mindedly, stoking his lotus pipe and seeming to think of all the wonderful, and terrible, things he had forgotten.

The High Table... would not be pleased with the three of them. Each of them knew that.

But right now, among these fellow cabal-ers... there were opportunities in others' misfortune.

For such is the way of wizards.

But... that was somewhere else in the City of Thieves this night.

It was late...

In a vacant lot where some structure that had once been part of the port had burnt down, Seac the Raven sat before a small fire, roasting a chicken.

Nearby, a gypsy man played a wild and sometimes mournful song on his stringed instrument. His old hag of a mother sat watching the roasting chicken, fat sizzle-dripping into the fire, with the one eye left to her. The faded silks and ancient colored scarves that wrapped the old crone fluttered in the breeze coming off the waters beyond the sea wall.

Other parts of the city were on fire now.

But much of the city still was not.

The gypsy played and the moon rose, the wind shifting the smoke and ash further into the City of Thieves.

Out there in the darkness, circling the perimeter of ruined and blackened destruction like a shadowy wraith, the archer tread softly, stealthily, keeping watch as the commander, once-sergeant, now warlord by default, Seac the Raven, got his intelligence on where the target was now.

Got his intelligence the way he would get it. Gypsy and bones and sad music calling.

The commander would not relent. The archer knew that.

The commander was a Mourne Elf come down long ago from that strange and last of the elven kingdoms at the end of the world, right at the edge of the known Ruin where no one much goes, and few ever return from.

And few here knew of a Mourne Elf or would ever see one in their lives. They were more rare than the big savages, hulking northern Dire Men, come down out of the Dire Frost in the unreachable north where there were giants and dragons.

Little was known of the Mourne other than two things. They had little to do with the affairs of men or dwarves, or even other elves... and revenge was a powerful force for them.

Very powerful.

It was said there was a great, secret war between the Mourne Elves and the Black Prince in the Crow's March. But those regions were so distant and unknown and information about such a war between shadowy elves and armies of werewolves and vampires with legions of skeletons, zombies, and all manner of undead was so strange and bizarre that many in the south considered this little more than a fairy tale told to frighten children.

Or just a fable to explain the sullen and brooding Mourne Elves when rarely they appeared among the southern Cities of Men.

But... these two things... they were true about them.

Little to do with others.

And revenge.

Mourne Elves were given to long silences for they knew the power of words and the power in a name. Revenge was survival and not just a fetish or a passing fancy to them. They were indeed locked in a long war, a death struggle really, against the Black Prince of the Crow's March himself, for it was said that once that diabolical fiend slew the Last King of the Mournes, the world would end.

Badly.

So the Mourne had taken up the tireless burden of fighting a war against enemies that could not be easily killed, or even killed at all. The Dragon Elves, and it was said even the dwarves, had abandoned them. Men could not stand before such foes as werewolf or vampire for they had no magic in them and were not considered allies in the death struggle against the Black Prince.

Thus... it fell to the Mourne alone to prevent the end of the Ruin.

And that was no easy task.

Slay a vampire and can't find the resting place... the fiend returns to the field of battle soon enough.

Werewolves come in many forms, and they breed like flies. Find the pack leader and you can kill them all. Don't, and you and your formation can get overrun and turned into lycanthropes fast enough. If they don't make a meal of you first.

And the undead... well, the necromantic priests of the Black Prince love old battlefields where their fallen have been buried in great mounds. The Savage Lands that lie between the Mourne Elves and the Crow's March are littered with such ancient piles and barrows no one knows tell of. The priests can have an army at your flanks, or in your rear, within the span of a long moonless night.

It's like having an army ready to go at a moment's notice wherever you want, fighting for those dark servants of the Black Prince.

And... there is that prophecy. That end of the Ruin foretelling.

The last king of the Dragon Elves, he who betrayed the Mourne, had said it would be so and would be a curse upon them for not just all time, but time beyond time... eternity... if they were to fall in their battle against the prince upon his cobalt throne.

And so, if you are Mourne you learn to fight with two silver weapons at once because your enemies outnumber you, always.

And you learn to keep short accounts on your enemies, abiding no long-standing feuds to occupy your time and resources because you have to concentrate on preventing the end of the world. All the time.

Seac the Raven had become a mercenary long ago. For reasons no one knew, nor would he ever tell. And he had come south. Or been sent. Or banished.

Who knew?

But he was still Mourne Elf.

The Dire Man had destroyed the last of his company.

He would have his revenge on that one.

And the dog-men of Ganistan... they were owed deeply.

Yes... he would see that debt paid, the warlord commander of the Sixth of the Black Tigers vowed, and cared not who heard so.

The chicken was roasted and Seac deployed a small sharp silver dagger, sectioning it up and passing some to the old lady, leaving some for her son as he worked his strings and made the keening heartbreaking solo virtuosos from long ago come and play on the night's hot wind among the drifting ash.

The wind whipped at the long dark hair of Seac, dark-haired like all Mourne, for once long ago they would have been of the Irish and the Spanish when the Ruin was the Before.

Long ago in the Before few ever knew of.

Before the world became the Ruin. Before it was the way it would be. A place of werewolves, and vampires, and terror... and a thin line against madness, death, insanity... and the end of the world.

A very thin line.

They ate, the old toothless mother gypsy gumming the meat to death, picking the bones clean and laying them down before her.

The wind whipped at Seac's long dark hair and the ruddy face it tried to cover.

There was a scar from long ago that ran the length of one cheek. A rope burn about his neck too.

He watched the old woman and his face was purest hatred, or so some said. But that was a trick of his race and the scars he'd received in battle. He was merely studying her and waiting for the revelation she would give him soon enough.

The bones cleaned, the archer in the dark somewhere out there watching over them, the son of the gypsy witch began to play a plaintive wail of a song, a heartbreaking dirge, at the merest nod from his old crone of a mother.

She began to do her fortune-telling trick in the night as the city burned and all hell began to break loose.

Her work.

Her magic.

The strings rose and rose and would rise no higher but did.... and continued to do so. The song rose until the strings and the sound they made became one with the night and the ashy smoke in the air rising from the fire. Wild and dancing, the gypsy son twirled and played like he was consumed by the fire raging in places out there across the city.

Out there the city burned.

Wizards plotted.

Eunuchs searched.

Thieves listened.

Lovers embraced as though they never would again.

Old men in quiet hovels grieved for their lost loves, watching the empty plate where she once was.

The gypsy woman shrilled suddenly and shook like she was having a fit once the cleaned bones were laid out in the dirt before her.

The music climbed and she heaved up spit and spat on the bones in front of her.

The music climbed, crescendoed, and died.

Then... as her gypsy son wandered over the strings softly now, barely, so softly it was like the background noise of everything that could not be heard... the old crone bent down into the dirt where the moist clean bones lay, studying something... watching something...

Seac leaned close, a half-eaten drumstick in one slender hand. Fascinated.

He would have been beautiful if not for all the wars, battle scars, and hard years on the road he had seen.

He had slain werewolves in a battle no one would ever read of.

He'd slain a vampire deep inside an old haunt that had once been a terrible fortress in the Age of Darkness when the

Delta Kings ruled the north.

He had seen terrible things.

And wonderful things too.

The wind wilded, the strings moaned, and the old woman told Seac, muttering as she did so, peering up at the battle-scarred Mourne Elf with her one remaining eye like a twisted homunculus of what she once was when she was a wild dancer girl, young and free and picking pockets and twirling away from the many lovers who would have her...

"He is south, Black Elf. The one you seek. South... in the sand and fog."

Seac the Raven was on his feet instantly, hand on the hilt of his silver blade.

The archer was coming in from the firelight. Six months running and fighting in the mountains of Ganistan had taught the archer to know when his commander got one of those feelings that death was imminent and it was time to move fast or end up dead and spitted on the fires of the dog-men.

"But..." hissed the old crone. "He is death... that one, Mourne Elf. No thief or robber that one. No... he is death. That one."

# CHAPTER FORTY-THREE

TWO OF THE GRAND MASTERS OF THE THREE LARGEST guilds within the City of Thieves arrived for the urgent meeting late in the night at the fine inn tucked away in a better district than most.

This was on the Street of Gold. The inn lay among the granite and sandstone edifices of the ancient temples that were now banks, the priests and their armies guarding the vast hoarded gold of the eunuchs within and keeping the constant debts of the wizards accounted for.

The meeting had to be here. Had to be now. Usually such a meeting was held in the lower haunts of the city. The grand guild masters of the thieves preferred these dens and taverns, but now such places were either overrun by constant street battles between the factions hunting Thor, or under threat of fire raging across portions of the western part of the city adjacent to the docks.

But now, here on toward midnight on the day and

evening after the first big battle at the port, in an old quiet tavern's upper room the bankers used for their plottings, hearings, tallyings of interest, and meager meals while they loaned or repossessed, both of the two major guilds' masters arrived for what was called... *Dinner*.

Tumo the Breaker, master of the Smugglers of Sand Street.

Ramour Widebrim, master of the Brotherhood of Thieves.

Where Ramour had lost touch with his early start in filching and thieving, now looking more a dandy and rake in his tailored finery, cutting a dashing figure indeed even down to the pearl-handled slender blade he lay scabbarded on the table of meeting, his opposite in the other guild Tumo the Breaker had not.

The leader of the second-largest guild was a thief's thief if there ever was one. A real working-class burglar, as all widely agreed, and he hated Ramour Widebrim with such a passion that he always got drunk late at night and silently plotted ways to kill the man.

But Dinner... had been called. And so there would be no assassinations. Just questions and answers.

Times were desperate.

Times were bad for business in the business of thieving. Alarm, fire, and warfare were spreading within the walls because of the heist of the Prize Chest. Calm needed to be restored so that thieving, real actual thieving, the day-to-day picking of pockets and rooftop burgling, could get back to being done by the simple thieves in their respective guilds.

And the Little Guild too. The other, lesser guild whose master had not arrived yet.

"She's probably died of the coof," muttered Ramour.

Out there, the eunuchs had small armies of sellswords and twilight bastards crawling the city.

The wizards and their own armies, sometimes magical, sometimes just as many mercenaries as they could get their hands on, were out in force too and looking for this *Thor the Ranger* who'd looted the Prize Chest, impossibly, down to the last coin.

Who knew how that was done?

If either side ran into the other side while out looking, ran into them as they scoured the city, ran down every rumor, chased every lead, or leads, which seemed to spread like wildfire from one district to the next, of this... *Sergeant Thor*... then battle immediately ensued between the two sides.

There could be only one winner. The paymasters of both sides had made that clear and offered enough coin for it to be so.

Bounties were up incredibly on anyone working for

either side, by both sides.

Instead, the result was that often it was either an outright slaughter for one party or the other, an ambush in the streets being the favorite here, or both parties got entangled all at once and were ruined for further operations what with the dead and wounded, not to mention the damage to the street and area merchants either by violence or sorcery.

None of that mattered though, to the wizards and eunuchs that is. Even as the city burned, mercenaries, pirates, and bandits, and every thug, killer, and anyone handy with a weapon was flooding into the city because each side was spending big to get their hands on all that loot that had been inside the Prize Chest.

Losses could be replaced.

Both sides were betting big on the outcome of where that treasure, and this... *Sergeant Thor*... was.

"Know how it was done, Tumo, my boy?" asked Ramour nonchalantly as he picked at one delicately manicured nail he'd just had worked over by one of his girls.

Both were mere shadows in the lone candlelight provided. The room was opulently furnished by the bankers, swaddled in red cloth and deep velvet and fine appointments all about. It was the perfect room to meet in, for it had been made impossible to hear anything said in the room beyond the heavy burnished doors.

And what was being said tonight... was serious. And not for public consumption.

"Like I'd tell you, Fancy Man," barked Tumo the Breaker.

Ramour looked over his curled mustache at the squat Tumo who sported many knives and huge brawny arms. Tumo's specialty coming up through the guild had been vaults.

Breaking into them. Hard work. Much reward.

The guild master still broke vaults. No easy work cracking into them and hauling out the loot. Experience was a must.

Ramour's eyes were dead like a shark's as he stared at the smaller wider master thief who specialized in breaking into subterranean vaults.

Each of them was... the best of the best in their profession.

You didn't get to be a grand guild master without being so. Maybe among the effete eunuchs and *mandarini* you could rise. Or with the wizards you could ensorcel your way up the chain. However that happened. But to be a thief, you had to do it the hard way.

You had to put in the work.

Each of them had.

Ramour was both an assassin and a thief. And in fact, he

had done time as a duelist too. He'd also been an acrobat, and... incredibly, he'd survived three expeditions into the Valley of the Priests and Kings as a humble thief disarming traps among the haunted sarcophagi of the Saur and looting vast ancient treasure rooms, avoiding the curses that came with such dangerous work.

Tumo had done five trips in.

For perspective... it was the rare thief who crossed the gulf and went beyond the River of Night more than once to plunder those cursed and haunted tombs of the Saur.

Once was enough for most.

"You know the rules, Tumo, my boy," reminded Ramour pleasantly. "Gotta tell all if we come to Dinner..."

There wasn't going to be any dinner. *Dinner* was just what they called, in thieves' cant, a very important meeting between the heads of the guilds.

Tumo scowled.

Then, "Where is she?" said Tumo, deadly serious.

"*Tsk tsk*... Tumo, my boy. If you're thinking what I'm thinking... then... no. We cannot kill her. No matter how badly *you know who* wants her dead."

The word among the guilds was, the Dreaming Sorcerer himself wanted the Queen of Thieves dead for some unexplainable wrong done him. That was why the queen was seldom seen, even among her own guild members. The reward for her death... was quite high.

Short of the Nether Sorcerer... the Dreaming Sorcerer was said to be one of the most powerful wizards among that kind.

But no one knew where to find him, and it was clear he did not even need to make his refuge among the wizards and their strong towers in the City of Thieves, for so great was his awesome power.

Again... Tumo scowled and failed to answer the original question.

Ramour returned to the inspection of his finely done nails. And, as if on cue, both could hear the tap of a cane in the hall, coming down the passage from the stairs that led up to the second story of the very fine inn on the Street of Gold.

"No bother, here she comes now... and then, Tumo... you will answer, just as I must, or... bad things happen. And the last thing this city, and the guilds need, is us going knives out for each other over an old tradition broken by someone as stupid as yourself."

The *tap tap* of the cane and the ancient steps of one very old grew closer.

"No," hissed the breaker at the other guild master. "No, Fancy Man. No one knows how it was done. Even you, 'cause you asked me if I did. No one knows, and it's probably gonna be the death of this city because we can't figure it out. Ponces and smarties killing 'emselves just to get at all that wonderful loot. Half the city's on fire now, Fancy Man. So no... I do not know how that savage Dire Man appeared in the city all of a sudden, roisted and drank himself silly, then up and went into the Pit, slaughtered his way to the chest, and then, after the One Draw... looted it down to the last coin. Maybe he didn't even do it. Maybe it was someone else that did it in the long dark after..."

The old woman was at the door, turning the latch. The tap of her cane silent as she did so.

Some said she was blind.

"He sure has been spending like he's got it all, don't you think, Tumo?" asked Ramour Widebrim. "Half the treasure's got to be in most of the taverns and among the pretty girls if what's been told is even half true."

Ramour smoothed the fine and fancy cavalier's hat he'd placed on the table. Admiring the ostrich feather he'd just paid handsomely for to adorn it, having ruined the last one in a duel with a now-dead jealous husband.

"Who knows anything, Fancy Man," hissed the other thief.

Then the Queen of Thieves turned the latch at the door and entered the Dinner that had been hastily arranged at the last moment.

# CHAPTER FORTY-FOUR

SHE WAS AN OLD, OLD, VERY OLD WOMAN, THE QUEEN OF Thieves was.

She was seriously old.

She was frail and papery and what could be seen of her moved as such.

She'd been a fixture of the city for longer than anyone could remember. Once her guild, the Little Guild, had been far bigger, or so some thought.

Perhaps that too was a lie. There were many lies, misdirections, and false information in the City of Thieves.

With some difficulty, the old woman who was the Queen of Thieves sat in the chair that had been set for her. This one, like Ramour Widebrim's, had arms. Tomo the Breaker's did not, and that had been done on purpose because Ramour had spent a little extra coin to make sure the slight would happen and was sure his rival would be greatly irritated by it.

"So..." began the old, old woman. Her face was hooded. But surely it was horrible, thought each thief, so that was for the best. But you could see the dim image of the old woman, her heavy powders to cover the canyon of her lines, just barely by the candlelight in the room, beneath the cloaked hood. Her hands gloved to cover the gnarled fingers and age spots beneath.

She was of the old school when thieves wore such getups as cloaks and hoods and gloves as a badge of office, formally, for such meetings.

Things used to be that way. Now, they were different.

Her days, mused Ramour, were soon coming to an end anyway. Then... he would sweep the rest of her guild into his and be done with Tumo and his bunch shortly thereafter.

A small war. Of course.

A little bit of murder. Why not?

Ramour Widebrim was no stranger to such things. When he'd taken over as guild master, his guild had been three guilds and his one of the smallest of the three. Ten years in the City of Thieves had seen big changes since.

"... let us not talk falsely now," uttered the tired old Queen of Thieves, her hag's voice a croak.

Silence.

This was part of the ceremony. Almost like it was a religion.

Ramour rolled his eyes at the formality and said with very little emotion and much impatience, "For the hour is late."

Then he glared at the swarthy vaultbreaker Tumo.

The best in the city.

Sullenly, Tumo echoed what Ramour had spoken in response, and the ceremony of treaty and true speech was begun among the thieves there at the Dinner.

Little ceremonies. Old ways.

Under the conditions of the meeting no lie could be told among thieves now, or else...

Here, there was honor.

To lie now was to invite both guilds, and all your enemies within your own guild, to blacklist you.

And that usually meant the end of not just your thieving, but breathing.

Then you got sold to the vivisectionist, and one in particular who was also a necromancer.

So the fun didn't just stop in a quick death.

This was a serious meeting. Serious stakes were on the table. And so there were serious consequences.

"We..." she began haltingly. Clearing her old lady wreck of a voice.

*How old is she*, Ramour wondered. She'd always been a part of the tapestry of the guilds within the city. Had been when he was but a little runt running messages, picking pockets, and occasionally getting a second-story job to flip a lock for the burglars back in the day.

She'd been there even then.

"... we did not steal... the contents... of the chest."

She said this defiantly. Like old people do when they're not interested in an argument or what idiocy you try to pass off as intelligence at them.

They've seen it all.

Including your stupidity.

Silence.

Both of the other guild masters stated that they, and theirs, had not stolen the chest, or its contents.

"The city... burns... now," the old woman said after these affirmations. "Soon... if the wizards have their way... it will burn right... to... their tower doors. They would be fine... with that."

Tumo shifted uncomfortably. Her voice, and the place, annoyed him. He fingered one of his sharpened picks and thought about just doing her in right here.

But... guild war.

"The eunuchs will allow everything... everything, I say... to burn," whispered the old crone because that was the best she could do.

Again, she cleared her throat and gathered her strength.

"They... wish to rebuild it... in their image... now. New taxes. More... plunder. But... above all that... they want the magic of the haul... within... their grasp. For it was great. And for either side... to have it... now... that side... would have the advantage... over the other. And soon after..."

She coughed dryly.

"There wouldn't be another side," finished Ramour and glared at her. This was becoming tiresome. The thieves had worked out the *why* of all this desperate search for the treasure of the chest.

Whoever got it would be in charge and probably kill the other. That had been coming for years.

It wasn't complicated.

The thieves' plan was just to steal portions of it along the way. And continue... business as usual.

This stupid old woman didn't need to—

"The people... neither side care for... them," she continued. "They will... let them burn. Their markets and shops, their houses... their dreams, and... hopes. The treasure that was in... in the chest... that is all that matters to wizard... and eunuch. Nothing... else."

"Yeah, *and,* you old crone?" Tumo swore petulantly. As in... *We know this, aaaaand?*

The Queen of Thieves favored the thief with a serene dismissal of quiet contempt.

"The people... are us, breaker. You... were once them. They... are who we rob. The merchants, the traders, the craftsmen, the poor... all of them. Sometimes... we rob a wizard... but... you know what that... invites. Not without reward... but much risk. Of... course."

"I know. I *know*," Tumo practically shouted. "And the eunuchs just rob it back from us in the taxes we have to pay. Got it. Again... *Aaaaand*?"

"To your point, my Queen?" said Ramour with much false sweetness. He was, he had to admit, enjoying watching the old hag torture Tumo. But, as was said, the hour was late, and he had operations to oversee and stolen gold to count.

Ramour... hated the breaker.

His manners were atrocious. Like one lowly born.

Spoiler... they'd both been born on the same street within a year of each other a long time ago and were related though neither knew this because their mothers were both working girls.

It's a small world. Sometimes so small you don't even know it until you see the hand in your pocket.

"If the people burn... then who will become the next batch of urchins to train as thieves, masters? If they burn... who will we rob, and... extort, and provide... all the other... services... we guilds... do?"

Long silence.

Ramour turned to Tumo.

"Well, she's got a point there."

Both men turned to the ancient Queen of Thieves wishing she'd just die right there and let them sweep up her action.

"So, what do we do then?" asked Ramour pleasantly.

Tumo unconsciously nodded along, for her wisdom had suddenly captured him. Whether he liked it or not.

Spoiler... he didn't.

"We stay... neutral. If the wizards kill the eunuchs... we become... the second most powerful faction... in our... city. If it is the other way... again... we rise. But..."

Both men were as still as stone gargoyles. But inside she was awakening them to her wisdom, unconsidered wisdom.

And seeing the possibilities it provided them, and them alone.

"If both wizard... and eunuch... perish... well then... that would just leave the three... of us... would it... not?"

Ramour's mouth fell right open.

Tumo's already was because his nose had been broken so many times before. That's an easy way to identify a vaultbreaker. Broken nose. Goes with the job. He was not, in fact, stupid. He just had his particular view of things. It was harsh and utilitarian.

The old crone laughed at them both now, her voice a dry

chuckle in the rich silence of the opulent room in shadow.

"And..." she continued after her ancient delight.

*Wait, what? There's more?* each man thought to himself. Truly it did pay to listen to these crusty old elders, occasionally. If you had to. Then...

Well, *then...* that was another thing. The elders couldn't hang around forever. Know what I mean.

"... we cannot let them win. One... or the other. Both must lose. And we must appear to have remained uninterested in the affair."

"And what do you suppose we do? Wage war now? Ally with those freaks the Stranglers and start slitting wizard and eunuch throat? Hoist the black flag and spit on our hands?" asked Ramour, who would never spit on his hands.

Ever again.

"No, we thieves... we do not work harder... we... work smarter. Do we not?" she reminded them.

No thief had ever not heard that from some old burglar planning a job.

Each man was silent again for the moment.

"*We* know where this... Thor... this... man is."

Tumo swore suddenly.

Ramour plotted and eyed the old crone that was the Queen of Thieves with a newfound respect he wasn't sure he could stomach much of.

But the game was afoot now. He thought of that Prize Chest.

"Under the terms of... *the Dinner*... you old hag... was he working for you?" sputtered Tumo.

She ignored the direct question.

"We... shall save the people, our people..." she continued, sure in her position as the Queen of Thieves, "... the flock we fleece, the flock that becomes us... and... to do that... we will aim this... Dire savage... right... at both the eunuchs... and... wizards too."

She suddenly began to cough and then experienced a long coughing fit they had to wait her out for. Finally, she spit some unclean and unseen glob onto the floor in the shadowy gloom of the room late in the night and cleared her wreck of a voice once more.

But by that time Ramour was ready again.

"Under the terms... you old shrew... you must answer. Was he, or is he, one of yours? Is this all some big, and I must admit, admiringly even, some elaborate scheme of yours, you wretched old hag?"

The ancient Queen of Thieves stared at the silver fox of a guild master.

"My death approaches. Soon, it won't matter. Do your worst, whether he is, or was... I won't tell you. I... like letting you think he was... it should make you afraid if you have half a brain, Ramour Widebrim. I also like letting you think he wasn't. But that's for reasons I'll... never... tell. So... run out there... while the city's half on fire and get every thief to turn against me now... the blacklist... and tell them I've got a plan... that saves their city, and their tomorrow. In a month... or maybe less... I'll be dead. So it won't matter. I tired of this life... long before you were born, Rammy the Runny."

That stung hard.

Ramour had been called Rammy the Runny as a mere urchin. Running messages and wiping his perpetually runny nose. He was always sick then. Always cold. He slept in the street. He was always... hungry. Always cold. Always alone. Even in the desert.

He hated the name.

He'd gone to great lengths to erase the memory of it, in other minds, and in his own too.

Tumo the Breaker laughed out loud, muttering the ancient nickname over and over, again and again as though memorizing it for future use.

Ramour winced and picked up his fine hat for something to do with his finely manicured hands. Then threw it across the table in disgust.

"So what would you have us do, you old shrew?"

She was up from the chair with some difficulty now, grunting and groaning and making a show of her old bones barely moving. Then *tap tap tap*ping her way toward the door once again.

"Do nothing... until you hear from me. Stay out... of his way and this... warrior... this Thor... he will solve your problems by violence and action where you will not. And... all you... have to do... is nothing but wait... for the pieces, including myself, to fall... and then... it will all... be yours. Not just the Prize Chest, but the haul of the action we can acquire once wizards and eunuchs are sufficiently weakened from their war with one another."

She made the door.

Her bony shoulders heaved. She sighed a gurgle.

"Indulge an old thief, masters. Once I was like you. I violate the terms of Dinner... for... reasons. Spare the blacklist and let the hand play as it will... now. You will divide the city among yourselves if you aid neither sorcerer, nor... eunuch. The die has been cast... already. Farewell... on this side of the veil, brothers." Then she croaked the farewell of all thieves in the gloom of wavering candle and thick silence. "Easy locks and wide pockets, fellow thieves."

The latch turned, and she was gone from their presence.

# CHAPTER FORTY-FIVE

THERE WAS A KNOCK AT THE OLD COTTAGE DOOR DOWN near the cove. At the end of Hook's Rest.

It was morning. Early morning. Fog turning to sea mist and golden sunshine. The Ranger in the twilight between rest and the images of the heady days that had preceded the breathing space behind the wire he was allowed for this moment.

The knocking was angry, and it reminded Sergeant Thor of that first drill sergeant at the first of his army career, not even in basic training, formally yet. The repo depot.

The repo depot drill sergeants.

The drill sergeants in charge of getting the new recruits ready to start actual basic training with the drill sergeants they'd be assigned. Then the shark attacks would commence. The real ones.

A trash can rolling down the aisle in the dark before dawn. A harsh bark refined by cancer sticks and Drano telling you something to the effect of *rise and shine, princesses*, this is the rest of your life.

Welcome to Hell's waiting room.

The bleary-eyed all around Thor as a young recruit, staring around in disbelief as some demon in a crisp uniform came thundering down the aisle between the bunks, promising death, pain, and suffering, and not necessarily in that order.

What... exactly... had they gotten themselves into? some must have wondered. Thor did not. He knew, had asked for the toughest contract he could get, a RASP contract, and got himself ready for whatever came next.

In the twilight before full wakefulness, the young recruit that would become Sergeant Thor had already been awake. Waiting for this moment. He'd known it was coming. And now he was...

... *becoming*... along that new edge, then, that he'd found to test himself against.

*What you will one day be, you are now becoming.*

Those were the thoughts in the twilight between sleep and the chaos of the fade off the Pit and through the City of Thieves. Days of fighting, nights of drinking, gambling, and girls... all with a wary eye toward the door that could open and the ten hardened killers that could come looking to collect at any moment.

He was the goat. The lure. The... misdirection as the treasure of the chest got further and farther away from eyes, real and magical, that could still locate it.

It was... almost gone now. Twenty-four hours and it was over. Then what?

That was tomorrow's problem, Thor had thought as some angry badger banged at the door to the cottage, clearly seeking a redress of some unknown wrongs.

The Ranger sighed heavily and willed his tortured muscles to get ready for whatever came next. Mind the healing wounds if you please, boys.

Now the knocking at the slight cottage door, rapid and harsh, accompanying a grumble of some old man no doubt, impatient and angry, beating his fists against the weathered wood like a fifty firing six-to-eight-round staccato bursts and the whole nine yards to run out.

"Come on out, sunshine... outta my cottage now!" barked the old badger. "Ruin's 'bout to end, and you're in there sleepin' on my bed and all!"

The bed the innkeeper and his wife had provided was soft. Very soft and free of mites. The sheets clean and warm against the cool of the misty nights down there in the isolated cove at the end of the small fishing village. Beyond the dunes and near the high rocks where the surf crashed and swirled. Near the tide pools.

Farther up the beach, the small fishing boats of the little village had already gone out with the morning dark and would be back later with their nets full. By noon. Then they would be back, and the day's haul would be attended to, and processed by all within the village, for this was the reason of the village.

Fishing.

The Ranger had helped with this work after Omir had assured him none in the village would speak of his presence to any outsider.

But in the hours leading up to the return of the small fleet of beaten old rowboats, and in the hours after the gutting, skinning, cleaning, and salting, or drying, Sergeant Thor had wandered the sands south along the coast, and in doing so had gained two little constant companions from the inn.

Two followers. As it were.

Two children who were full of questions, races between the two or with Thor himself, a desire for things to be explained and fish to be speared or butterflies to be captured. He didn't say much. They talked endlessly.

A village girl and a boy. The innkeeper's two youngest children.

He taught them to spear fish in the shallows near the tide pools.

They showed him the caves and rocks along the cliffs when the tide was out and brought him food from the inn when it was time to eat.

He told them stories of the world the way it was in the Before. The way it had once been.

The boy explained things he had read in the few valuable books he had access to. He asked the Ranger how many books there were in all the Ruin.

"I don't know," rumbled Thor as they waited for fish in the shallows. Thor poised with the spear. Shirtless and wet from the toss and turn of the surf and the spray coming off the cliffs and watery destruction there. "More than can be counted," he offered the innkeeper's boy, who was called Hammatt.

The boy's eyes went wide at the thought of this, and he grew silent as Thor waited patiently, like a statue, for the fish he would spear. The Ranger could feel the boy's yearning to read them all.

The girl who went everywhere with the boy was silent. A listener, but a doer. She climbed, swam, and challenged the Ranger to footraces in which she won and threw her arms out to cross the finish line they had agreed upon at just the last moment. Putting everything into those last few steps as the Ranger "ran" to catch up.

The boy asked the Ranger to tell him everything he ever

knew.

Thor smiled.

"That would take a long time," Thor told the boy. "And I don't know as much as some, or as much as I would like to."

The small boy with the dark brown eyes and a book in his hand considered this as they sat atop the cliffs, the girl attempting to catch the butterflies that collected and danced there among the waving tall seagrass on the cliff above the cove.

"Me too," whispered the boy as he saw all the books in the world in his imagination.

Those days beyond the city... were *idyllic*. This was the rest the Ranger needed after all that fighting, running, and fading, after the long march across the Ruin from the Savage Lands to the City of Thieves. And then the crossing of the Sea of Riddles and the things that had happened within its mysterious gulfs.

Those days beyond the city were the opposite of the days inside that fetid hellhole, and Thor had long conversations with himself about what he would do next. After the heist was done and the treasure safely beyond reach of those who would kill to have it for their own power.

He had wanted to see a city, that had been one of his goals as he'd crossed the Ruin with the Rangers. He'd wanted to see it alone. Without the Rangers as he'd seen Portugon in the west. They'd been on a mission there. No time, or room, to really explore. He'd wanted to know what it was like to walk ancient streets as one of the people of those times. These times. The Ruin.

He'd had ideas about the experience, before actually doing it...

Now...

Now he wanted nothing to do with cities. Or wizards and eunuchs, for that matter.

"Nothing but treachery and corruption," he muttered to himself near the tide pools, the two children watching him, a spear he'd cut and sharpened himself from some driftwood in his hand. They watched as he plunged it downward and skewered the fish there.

The children cheered for the success of this.

"Let's go catch a butterfly now," the little girl shrieked.

So they went. And of all the things the Ranger could do, he could not catch one for them. And neither could they.

And Thor had fast reflexes.

But still it was fun. Fun to try. Fun to watch them try. The children were so intent they practically levitated by force of will as they sought to capture one of the tiger-striped drunken beauties that waffled and wobbled carelessly, or carefree, among the wind-driven seagrass in the heat of the day.

Those days were the opposite of all days before these.

They were special. He knew, even in them, that they were rare, and he would remember them for as long as he could remember.

The heist was almost done now.

Every day someone from the guild back in the City of Thieves would come south and apprise him of the growing chaos and tempest within the city. Wizard and eunuch were now at each others' throats. Metaphorically, but occasionally literally, street battles turned to small wars between both factions with the thieves of all the guilds keeping out a weather eye on events as they unfolded.

The caravan district, the many caravansaries along the edges of the city at the eastern and southern edges, had burned the night before.

Other parts of the city were on fire. Temples burned up in a night. Fires in wizards' towers that no one dared put out due to the inherent danger of such places. Traps, magical beasts, doors to other planes of existence.

The Temple of Poesidius had cracked in two and collapsed into the waters of the fishing port.

The Fortress of Marius the Great was a burnt-out hulk now. A great battle had been fought there the night before. Hundreds of mercenaries were dead.

The eunuchs' opulent and crass palaces were either the sites of major battles, being turned into garrisons to sally forth from, or... constant bacchanals of food, lotus, and sex as the *mandarini* and the eunuchs celebrated their sure victory, or just the coming of yet another day of the life they chose to live.

And the treasure... it was gone. No one had any idea where it was, and dangerous rumors abounded as to its current location. The worst thing that could happen to someone was to be the subject of one of these wild and often scurrilous rumors. If so... in short order... desperate killers and hard twilight bastards were going to be showing up to find out the truth of the rumor. And they had a way of using extreme violence to get the answers they wanted.

Then they started killing each other and anyone else caught in the middle.

The city was turning into an orgy of bloodshed as eunuch and wizard decreed no limits to get what they wanted by any means possible.

And news of the Dire Man savage, the one called sometimes *Ranger*, sometimes *Sergeant Thor*... gone too now in recent days.

All was proceeding according to plan. And now... the plan was winding down...

Then came the hectoring *knock knock knock*ing at

morning's light, sea mist in the air, golden sunshine burning off the fog.

Another day of spearfishing, work, and catching butterflies. Or so the Ranger had thought in that twilight between dream and reality.

"Catch a butterfly before it moves," the little girl would scream just as Thor, huge and hulking in the grass, made ready to grab the little flying drunkards.

Then... the little drunk flying caterpillar would just wobble away, unhittable, uncaptured.

"Ruin's end is upon us, one called Thor!" shouted the old man beyond the flimsy door to the cottage out there in the sea-mist morning gold.

The Ranger got out of the soft bed, padded across the wooden slats that served as a floor for the cottage, and opened the door, shank behind his back.

Because you never know.

Especially in the Ruin.

It was the holy man.

But the Ranger didn't know that. Yet. He would learn who he was dealing with soon. Now he only saw a robed man, bald with flying gray hair from the sides of his large head. He had a salt-and-pepper beard. He was short but his demeanor was fiery, and he had the carriage of one who was used to hard work. A smith perhaps.

His upraised fist had been poised to hammer at the door once more when the Ranger finally opened it to him.

"What are you doing in my cottage, strange one?" barked the old prophet into Sergeant Thor's face.

"Rented it. Mine until the coin runs out." Then the Ranger moved to close the door.

The old man slammed his paw of a hand into it and grumbled about something. Promising to get to the bottom of something else, then looked up and glared at Thor.

"Walk with me. Down to the water."

Thor raised his eyebrows as if to say, "Really?" Then was just about to close the door and throw himself back onto the bed until the kids came for him and made him climb, or race, or catch a butterfly before it moved... impossible... or just fish or tell stories about Rangers.

They wanted to know who Tanner and Talker were. They liked those stories. Or the two brothers on the "gun team." Or Sergeant Kang who made explosions. Or the captain who could become a tiger. Or many of the other Rangers he would tell them about.

And even the history of the Rangers and the wars they had fought in and the deeds they had done before his time.

They wanted to hear all about Rangers. And the Before. Especially that. And then the little girl would shriek, "Catch a butterfly before it moves!"

And then they would do that. Except he would fail, and the drunken flying caterpillar would get away no matter what plan was tried to capture them.

Sergeant Thor knew it was all coming to an end. Had known it must. This was just rest. Healing. The wounds closing up, scabbing over, becoming scars. The mind refocusing after all the constant fade and fight.

That was necessary.

*Rest is fifty percent. Other half is fight to the death.* That was straight out of the Book of Joe.

But lately, there had been more fight to the death, than rest.

So for now, here in the little fishing village, in the days just prior... it had been rest. Finally. Just for a bit.

Everything comes to an end...

But even in the half sleep, dreaming of a girl he'd once known that had been an actress in Hollywood, she was dead now, dead even before the Before had ended, reconciling what could not be reconciled as he sometimes did, that *knock knock knock*ing of the old man had been...

A signal?

A doom bell?

Something...

A warning.

A call.

Reality coming back to assert itself.

Rest was over now. Soon, he'd be back in it. Just like when you got the call back in the battalions. *Leave's over, Rangers. World's on fire and needs our help one more time.*

And then you were standing up, hooking up, and shuffling out the door of a C-130 at an improper altitude of nine hundred feet, jumping onto a hot DZ in another third world hellhole.

Everything comes to an end.

*Knock knock knock*ing...

"Catch a butterfly before it moves."

Then the old man staring up at him hard and asking him to walk down to the water and listen to what the prophet had to say because this was about more than beds and cottages by the sea.

Reality needs a word, Ranger. The world... is in trouble. Again.

The Ranger took a deep breath, then followed the old holy man down to the water's edge to get his brief.

# CHAPTER FORTY-SIX

"FIGURED YOU'D BE DOWN HERE BY NOW. JUST DIDN'T think you'd be in my cottage," began the old holy man.

The Ranger said nothing to this and merely let the cold sea run across his bare feet. He'd sheathed the shank.

"I'm the prophet around here, y'know. Serve the Hidden King and all. You'd think some things... like my cottage... would be sacred enough. But that boy Omir..."

The old holy man was silent for a long moment, staring out to sea and breathing heavily through his nose, calming himself as his mouth twisted this way and that.

Then...

"... he just wants better."

The prophet turned to Thor.

"Five nights ago, I was out in the deep desert. East of here. Got a message from my god. A vision. So I started out for here 'cause an angel showed me this is where I'd find you. Been walking for five days and nights now. Ready for it, I'm gonna give it and you're gonna hear it. That's my job. Rest is up to you. Got me?"

The old holy man seemed almost angry about this. Then his face softened after a moment's pause.

"Sorry. I'm rash. Man of unclean lips. What I got to tell you... it ain't good. Not at all. It's bad. And I don't like it as much as you ain't gonna like hearin' it. Sorry. Sometimes that's the way things are."

Thor stared out to sea, considering all he had not seen beyond the limits of his eyes. For a moment just wanting to stay here, right here, and also go out there and see it all.

*Yeah*, he thought to himself. *Just like back in the batts when you got the call to stand up.*

That bad DZ was somewhere ahead. He could feel it now. This was just like that.

And where some men might be afraid of that, saying it to himself reminded the Ranger of why he Rangered. He lived for that DZ. The real bad one. The one with tracer rounds coming up through the air and the *get it on* right after the hitting the ground and dodging the incoming.

Testing yourself against its edge...

*Fine. This is what I was made for*, he thought.

Sergeant Thor had accepted this long ago. About himself. About the world and others who chose not to jump when they found the edges.

And now, the Ruin had a message for him... and yeah, as Ranger Wizard PFC Kennedy used to tell them when explaining what the Ruin might, or might not be...

*Embrace the fantasy.*

Just a riff on the operator maxim *Embrace the suck*.

Thor had done that too long ago. It was the only way to survive in the Ruin. Stop not wanting to accept monsters and magic and just get down to the business of killing it before it kills you.

Embrace orcs and trolls and war giants and magic and elves and dwarves and magical weapons. Then put rounds on target from his rifle *Mjölnir*, or the two-forty, or the SAW, or even a Carl G if you had one handy and the Forge had cranked out a new launcher and some rounds. You just embraced the weirdness of the fantasy monsters and magic and then did whatever it took to put that snarling, fireball-casting, sharp two-handed swordsman in ghost armor fantasy down and walk away the winner since it had dared try you.

That'll learn 'em. Violence works both ways. Be the monster the monsters are afraid of.

The Rangers had done that.

Thor had done that.

So...

"Give it to me," rumbled Thor at the holy man as the sea

mist faded and the day's sunshine broke through and began to rise. "Tell me what your god said."

The holy man seemed taken aback at this. Usually people just liked it when he healed or blessed them. They liked the goods and prizes. They usually didn't like the messages. Not at all. Usually... they found something else to do when he showed up with a message. Or got angry about what was said within the message from his god.

That was pretty typical.

So the cranky old holy man, he smiled and laughed a little at the big warrior's *give it to me straight* attitude. In fact, he liked the Ranger a little bit more now, though he'd made up his mind on the long walk out to Hook's Rest not to like the one called Thor because he'd probably caused all this, and now here the man was sleeping in the old holy man's special cottage, and the cottage and its soft bed really were special to the old prophet.

Some things... to a holy man... were sacred.

"But I know," he'd told the wind and the night as he walked those five days, "that's me and not you."

He rolled his wide bull's shoulders and ran his calloused old hand through the wild remains of his hair, readying himself to deliver the message. And a painful one it was at that.

"All right then. A dark elven warrior called Seac the

Raven just sold you out, this location in fact, to the eunuchs last night. They've hired a huge force to come south and hit you sometime in the late morning tomorrow. But... that ain't gonna have a chance to happen."

The old man stepped back and peered at Thor with one eye to see if he was processing all this from the start.

The silent Ranger watched the sea and remained immobile like some lighthouse waiting for a ship to appear out there in the morning's golden mist.

But he was listening.

"What's gonna happen first," continued the old holy man, "ain't much better. Two wizards, really bad fellas... I mean like... think of the worst person you know... and it's these two ahead by a neck... but each in different ways... well, they're gonna come down here late tonight because this Raven fellow... he also went and sold out your location to the High Table, that's the wizards' council in the city. The wizards already have what's called a cabal... to deal with you. They don't need to hire mercenaries and spellswords. They're gonna come down here with summoned demons and phantasms that'll make yer hair turn white. And then they're gonna torture this whole village just to find you. They're gonna kill everyone."

The old man looked toward the inn.

Then...

"Everyone. You hear me? They're gonna kill Omir, his wife, their eldest daughter, the younger daughter too..."

*Catch a butterfly before it moves.*

"And the boy," said Thor without emotion. His teeth gritted.

The old holy man shook his head.

"No. I'm afraid they're gonna sell him. Slavers. Your friend... Sato... he's going to rescue him. Sure. But... the boy, he won't be... I'm just gonna say... he won't be the same for the rest of his life. Your friend the master thief will lose an eye doing it. But he'll get it done. Read me. This is all gonna happen, Warrior. Unless..."

The old holy man stood back. The wind took his robes and tossed them back and forth and for a moment he looked helpless and lost in a world that was too cruel for his kindnesses to ever matter.

"All this will be ruined. What you've started... it ends this way. If I was the young man..." He opened and clenched his fists uselessly. "If I was... I once was... I'd go... I'd try to stop... these terrible things. Save this little family, this village, the whole damned... but I'd die trying because I never was a warrior like you. I'm just..." He was going to say something else. Then he took a deep breath, argued with himself for half a second, and muttered, "I'm just one who listens. That's what I do. That's all. And then... I go say what I'm supposed to say. Okay?"

The surf rolled in and slammed against the cove further down the shoreline. Up near the inn, the back door flew open suddenly in the wind and the boy and the girl came out. Then they were running toward the Ranger and the holy man. Shouting Thor's name as they did so.

*Catch a butterfly before it moves.*

"You said... *unless.*" Thor's voice was cold. There was no emotion. And even the holy man shuddered to hear what he heard in such an absence. "You said these things would happen... *unless.*"

The old holy man gathered himself and nodded soberly.

Then he reached forward and put his hand on Thor.

Uncertain at first. But it was warm and solid. This was his real magic. The magic, or the ministry, of touch in hard times.

Underrated.

Incredibly valuable. Ask any lost soul adrift on the seas of life and tragedy.

"Unless. Yes. The Hidden King wouldn't have told me what would happen, this time, unless He wanted something done about it. He made you to be a warrior whether you believe in Him or not. Strike first and save Omir and his family, and this village. That's the *unless.* Hit them before they attack. But even I see the hour is almost too late and the odds... hell, boy, those ain't even odds. All the eunuchs and all the killers and horses their ill-gotten coin can buy. And those two wizards... they're hell on earth. It's walking damnation. No... I'm sorry about the message, kid. But those ain't even odds. And like I said... it's getting late. I moved as fast as I could. But this was as fast as an old man could get here, curse me."

Then the weathered holy man looked at the running children coming closer, and the inn, and his whole body shook as the visions he'd been shown came and made him afraid for them once again.

The children were almost to them by the water.

The boy carried his book.

The girl raced like the wind.

The Ranger felt the hidden *Mjölnir* in his hands.

*Catch a butterfly before it moves.*

But the hour was late, and everything was against him.

"Doesn't matter," Thor muttered to the wind and the sea.

# CHAPTER FORTY-SEVEN

THE RANGER RAN NORTH.

He had to move fast now for there was no time to spare. Seven miles back to the city gates, wide open in the late morning and he was through.

The city was in worse chaos.

Smoke.

Fire.

Dead bodies in the streets. Street battles down other main streets. Towers being stormed. Fortresses taken.

There was the clash of steel and drifting ash on the wind but even with this chaos the city still did trade. Shops were open. Whores winked. Thieves stole. Tribesmen drove their herds in for slaughtering.

Caravans made ready to get on the long road to other and distant cities.

Thor wove through the cacophonic chaos and disorder and made it to Shadowrun. He took the Little Guild by surprise and demanded the guild sorcerer be brought to him as he went to the inn where they met for planning.

"What do you have planned?" asked Sato after Thor related what the wandering holy man had told him would happen.

"I'll strike first and draw them off their attack on the village tonight. That's the only thing I can do."

"Well, well... and what are the names of these two diabolical sorcerers who will attack the village this night?" asked Well Well.

"The old man told me they were called the Smoke Wizard and someone named Baybrozz."

Sato seemed suddenly sober at this news.

"Both are known to us, Warrior, and the knowing is not good. This *Baalubrozz*... the one you speak of... he is the Devil incarnate some say. The violence done to the village in the vision you have related would definitely be in keeping with his trade. The Smoke Wizard is a more enigmatic figure, and little is known of him other than that he is considered very dangerous. A bender of reality from what I am told. How will you stop their magical attacks before they begin?"

Thor rubbed his beard for a moment. He was thinking of where he'd hidden his weapons within the narrow twisting alley that was Shadowrun. Planning. How fast he could get at them. How he would attack effectively at one point to cause a disruption in their attack.

"This Baalubrozz is... arrogant," said one of the thieves. "He's the kinda wizard who welches on his debts and blames you for whatever's gone wrong. He got three of us kilt on an expedition out to the Rock Fortress of Surulain. They said he was a coward. He values his own hide, but he won't back down from a fight if it's a poke in his image of himself. That's what was said by Feen."

Thor considered this.

Their plan was to attack tonight. He'd developed a plan to pin them before they could wipe out the village. Now, with this intel... perhaps it would work.

He cleared the table and started arranging forks, bowls, an apple, and some scraps of bread for his sand table.

"I'll take them out. That draws them off the village tonight. I'll need messengers here, here, and here as I move. A bunch of you on standby to hit them if they make the walls tonight and go south. That means I'm dead and we have to stop them from taking the village. Use poison."

"How are you gonna get them to fight here before they go south?"

Thor studied his sand table on the rough wood of the main room dining and drinking table. Someone had placed a sweet date to indicate where Baalubrozz's tower was. Thor picked up a dagger and planted it right through the flesh of the flaky fruit and into the table with a hard *thock*.

"I'll give him a call and tell him I'm coming at him. That'll turtle him and stall the linkup between the two wizards. Perhaps we can get that one next as he waits for the other. Maybe not. Taking out one stalls their plans. That's our move."

"And then the eunuchs, Warrior?" asked Sato. "The holy man said their force would ride south at dawn. Tonight, in the palace of Nuzom the Vain, they are said to be throwing a big revel in anticipation of the strike against the village. Many of them have gathered in alliance for this, throwing in their personal fortunes to finance this expedition against the village and to run you down there. But they revel at the coming of a new hour, so this is nothing for them. They will drink and be drunk awaiting news of the slaughter of the village and your capture."

"That guy's palace they're going to party at tonight. Good. Then they've done half the work for me by getting together in one place."

Sato looked confused for a moment in the aftermath of Thor's sketch of the operation. "I am not sure what is... *party*. But they will be acting per their usual terrible selves, Warrior. And together, many of them, then they will be surrounded by their best guards, and the palaces of the eunuchs are said to be like small fortresses unto themselves.

How shall we strike at them then by surprise? We are not an army, Warrior. We are humble thieves. An attack of this type is beyond us."

Thor smiled slyly.

"We'll deal with them shortly, Sato. Now... where is your wizard? I need to send a message."

# CHAPTER FORTY-EIGHT

BAALUBROZZ WAS BUSY ASSEMBLING BLOOD-INKED offensive scrolls he'd carry to the inquisition this night.

*Magic Meteor.*

*Hold Victim.*

*Thunderstrike.*

*Words of Pain.*

*Entangle.*

*Cause Horror.*

The sun was at the mid-afternoon position, but because of the fires in the sky, the light over the city was a bloody murderous red and that made the summoner very happy as he did his final prep for the murder and interrogation he intended this night by which to redeem his reputation and prove to the High Table he was everything the smug Osirex was not.

The summoner was in the great study at the top of his foul eyesore of a tower. A level above this was his great summoning circle used only for the most dangerous and darkest of rites on full moons, when fiery fiends and dark entities could be drawn forth at the midnight hour.

Just an hour ago he'd promised sacrificed virgins to a cabal of devils that would appear at dusk and accompany him south, so he had little need of the illusionist Osirex had forced to go with him.

The idiot Mandelf was probably drunk and smoke-addled in full by now and he would be of little use once the fun started.

Baalubrozz was going to turn that village into a living plane of hell and suffering the likes few who had not visited such places... would ever know.

And their suffering was going to be delicious.

Perhaps, with the blood rites and dead raisings—he had scrolls for such, costly but the best that could be purchased from the necromantic scribbles of Underwatch—he'd get a clear ghostly trail of this Ranger that would lead him right to the... the prey he hunted... by dawn.

Then he'd be a dead man.

Was already a dead man, giggled the summoner to himself and wiped his sweaty hands on his robes.

All he needed was a few dozen corpses to make that happen.

The village would provide this if they'd had contact with

the big oaf in recent days. So... all the better.

On a raised dais within his study, the scrying pool suddenly emitted a delicate sound like a wash of stringed instruments.

Someone was trying to contact him.

He didn't have time for this. But perhaps it was one of the major devils, the unnamable ones he had sent out petitions and offers to...

One of those, and the Dire savage would be dead within hours.

Delightful. Wickedly... delightful!

Baalubrozz waddle-ran up the marble steps of the dais and peered into the scrying pool, passing his hand over it to invoke its dangerous incantations, murmuring quickly the words of power that brought forth visions he had used to enslave many, many times before.

Scrying was a dangerous business. Look too close and it was a battle of temptations and wills. And so far... he'd never lost.

Many never knew they were getting much more than they bargained for when they dabbled in such communication magic.

The summoner practically giggled at that. Perhaps he could ensnare one of the Lords of Hell someday. Imagine that.

He peered down into the pool and saw...

The face of the one he hunted!

Blond. Blue-eyed. A warrior. Some scars. But a hard and dangerous look. A real... character.

Unconsciously, Baalubrozz recoiled expecting some devil or another powerful sorcerer who had something to trade for some help on offer. The High Table was watching this night and betting big on it. By dawn the eunuchs would launch their pitiful raid, but they would be cheated because he, Baalubrozz, would bring victory to the High Table in the darkest of this night.

Not feeble Osirex who was "managing the situation" from his tower, or Mandelf the dumb, merely along for the ride for reasons the summoner could not fathom.

Illusions were little more than tricks played on the weak-willed.

Tonight, that one was going to see the sorcery of the Hells unleashed!

Still... the fat little summoner recoiled in horror at the vision of the Ranger. Even his chubby little dirty hand grasped the obsidian-flint sacrificial dagger he'd attached to his robes and Belt of Demonic Protection for this night's haunt beyond the walls. He grabbed it in sudden fear for reasons he knew not why. He had always been afraid of warriors. Real warriors. He'd made it a point to poison or entrap them, even if they were on his side, or under his pay...

Then...

Baalubrozz changed and smiled like a cat before its prey down at the image of the Ranger in the scrying basin.

The idiot probably thought to bargain for his life now just in time. Somehow... this idiot knew it was Baalubrozz, destroyer of temples, summoner of devils, master of demons, who was coming for him this night.

The simpleton.

Baalubrozz would let him beg a little. He would hear a feeble petition. Then...

"Heard you were lookin' for me," rumbled Thor within the image in the water. Working dip, the Ranger turned and spat some off into the darkness of wherever he was.

Baalubrozz giggled.

"Not anymore... Ranger. I know exactly where you are. And now, I'm coming for you... Ranger. You know that, don't you?"

*Ranger...* He'd used it as an insult.

Thor said nothing and watched him from the scrying pool.

"You know it will be bad," continued the summoner. "Very bad. For you. And for them down there in that little village."

The summoner was in full control now. Confident.

Superior. In charge. His prey was afraid and trying to act tough in order to cut some better bargain than the one he'd chosen for himself when at first this all had probably started as some lark. Some drunken bet in an inn of such low men. Why else had the slave communicated? He was trying to save his wretched life... or... perhaps... someone else's worthless existence.

Interesting...

Baalubrozz would find out, exactly, just whoever that was from the man's dead corpse, and then he'd kill them too. He'd pay off the devil debts with the one this... *Ranger...* sought to protect.

Inside... he laughed like a madman gone drunk and wild in a midnight tempest.

He'd already made up his mind to do so. So it would be done. Their fate was sealed. Whoever they were.

Baalubrozz smiled smugly at the thought of his unspoken fatal promise.

Then...

"You need to come see me... Thor." Now he was playing with the Ranger, baiting him.

Thor said nothing still. Just worked the dip and watched Baalubrozz like some cold-hearted predator from the deep woods beyond the walls of man that did not know love, or mercy, or anything but... death. And the hunt.

The summoner failed to see this.

"Come see me," crooned Baalubrozz softly. "Now. It won't save you, Ranger. Won't buy your way out of this. But... perhaps... that one you're trying to keep out of this, Ranger... perhaps... I'll let them live," Baalubrozz lied.

Sergeant Thor said nothing, and for a moment that bothered the summoner. Irritated him. The impudence of such behavior.

Baalubrozz narrowed his eyes to slit, becoming the serpent he so wanted to be. Cold. Death itself. Poisonous. Utterly fatal with one strike.

"That is my offer, Ranger. And it is my only offer. Bring yourself to me. Now."

Thor's shoulders moved, suddenly, slowly, moved like he'd just taken some long deep breath, calmly through his nose, and only his shoulders had reacted to the great draw of the bellows that powered him.

Then...

"I'm coming for you. You're my special project now. Baal-you-bruh. See ya real soon."

The image wavered, then the Ranger was gone.

The summoner was gripping both sides of the scrying basin. Knuckles turning white with rage. But he was in control. *Yes, I am in control now*, he told himself. And very calmly he whispered, "Yes. Come now. I'll be waiting for you... Ranger. Right here. With every... thing... I've got."

Then he suddenly pushed the basin over in a savage rage and it smashed into a thousand delicate shards as the summoner began to laugh loud and wildly like some wicked thing that had completely, and finally, lost its mind forever.

Certain victory, at last, was at hand, thought Baalubrozz as he went insane.

# CHAPTER FORTY-NINE

OSIREX, SEATED COMFORTABLY ON A PALANQUIN AND surrounded by one hundred heavily armed mercenaries, loaded personally with his spells, was borne across the city as fast as the half-naked bearers could run.

Bad news had just ruined everything, and it needed to be confirmed before plans could be made.

The mercenaries surrounding him kept up the pace even in armor as the bearers ran and Osirex worried the powerful Wand of Fire he carried.

It was dusk, and in the east the purple of night was alight with the various fires still out of control across the vast and wide city.

The day was done.

And much bad had been wrought in it. If the rumor of what had happened was true... *then perhaps all was lost.*

In the west, the sky was bloody red, and wasn't that appropriate for what had just befallen them all.

The High Council would not be pleased.

And then... then there was the problem of... *him*.

The Dreaming Sorcerer would not be pleased.

The bearers arrived in front of the main gates of the Tower of Baalubrozz and found them wide open. Smashed open. Blown inward. Former slaves and servants were now running from the gates, running straight past the tall and gaunt Smoke Wizard in the bloody end of daylight. Mandelf stood calmly within all the chaos and confusion, nursing his magical long-stemmed pipe and watching the looting of the summoner's tower.

Locals from around the district, and even some minor hedge wizards, were now daring the chaos and entering the tower to take what they could: books, tomes, scrolls, mirrors, tapestries, sheets, pots and pans, small chests, everything the summoner had once owned.

Osirex in red and black leathers never minded any of this and surged from the palanquin once it was down. The captain of his guard rushed forward to protect him, but the six feral Ape Men who guarded their master whirled and snarled at the veteran mercenary captain. Fangs and gorilla claws suddenly out and gnashing. Red cloaks swirling.

They could have rent him to shreds had they wanted.

The captain, hand on his broadsword, drew away from the fierce praetorian guard, well aware that the Ape Men were more than a match for anything he and his men could stand against.

Osirex pushed past the flow of looters coming in and out of the tower of the summoner as Mandelf expelled a great blast of necrotic purple smoke and followed, muttering...

"That damned savage came here and slew him, Oss. He's dead. There... inside. The audience chamber on the main floor."

Osirex and his apes made the steps, the apes mauling and maiming, swiping at any who dared approach the leader of the cabal ordered by the High Table as he passed the great bronze doors marked with many obscene images and went inside.

For a long moment he stared at the dead body of Baalubrozz. There was a hole blown in the summoner's chest. Bloody guts had sprayed out on the rose marble behind him and were still wet in some places.

Two dead demons lay scattered in pieces across the floor. Each of their foul heads blown clean off.

By something awesome and terrible.

Were there other dead demons out there by the gate and the small garden and statuary before the tower? Osirex wondered, trying to push away thoughts that this... what had just happened here to the summoner... had ruined everything they'd planned.

There would be no attack against the little village to the south. No blood trail leading right to the target. Instead, impossibly, the target had just appeared out of nowhere and attacked and slain the wizard who would lead the expedition, spoiling everything they'd arranged to get the treasure of the chest. Finally.

Now... it all lay in ruins like the guts of the summoner on the rose marble floor of his tower. Something terrible had attacked him savagely, and violently.

Now he was no more.

"But..." Osirex began. "He should have been on the move already. You two were to link up beyond the gate and go south, Mandelf."

The Smoke Wizard stoked his pipe and looked over the rim of it at all the blood and guts chaotically strewn across the entrance hall of the summoner's last stand.

To the illusionist it was like the twit of a little summoner had been taken by clever surprise all at once. And so had his demons.

Which... served him right.

Idiot finally got what he deserved.

"My crows..." stated Mandelf, clearing his throat rather roughly, "informed me he had not left the city at the appointed time. I was beyond the gate and sensed... *trouble*... so I came here immediately and found him slain."

For a long moment the wizard Osirex's mouth worked open and closed like some fish starving in the bottom of the boat it had been caught by. Starving for water. Starving for life. Beyond the love of everything known.

This changed... everything. It did.

Suddenly, even with the snarling apes hooting and screeching all across the chasm of the tower, their animal snarls and feral shrieks rising, casting themselves about the dark upper reaches there in the summoner's inner sanctum... suddenly the wizard began to feel something... different... had happened to him.

Something unwanted.

Something new, and yes, wholly unwanted.

Instead of hunting...

Instead of being the hunter...

Seeing the maimed body of the powerful Baalubrozz... yes, powerful. He had faults but he was quite, *quite powerful*... Seeing him dead and staring sightlessly up toward where the hoots and insane howls of his ape guardians landed...

Osirex knew he was *the hunted*.

"Come," he said to Mandelf quickly, unable to tear his eyes away from the ruined summoner even as his feet wanted to run and his bowels to loose. "The devils will come soon to collect their owed debts. We do not want to be here for that business."

They left the summoner's looted tower and the night came on at last.

Wizards cowered.

Eunuchs reveled.

Thieves went dark.

And the Ranger... stalked the night.

# CHAPTER FIFTY

*DID YOU HEAR THE RUMOR OF WHAT HAPPENED LAST night?*

This was said much in the streets of the City of Thieves that next boiling hot, hot and growing hotter smoky black day as the east turned all doom and apocalypse with the drifting miasma of destruction from the burns still raging across sections of the city.

A powerful wizard was killed, many whispered. Slain in his own tower, others confirmed.

By whom?

Rumors abound. No one knows.

But that's not all... there's more.

Fires still rage out of control all across the city. Ill omens were seen last night I say true, seen too in the brooding sea and the leering moon. Have you heard... there are black sails on the horizon. They come in with the morning fog, getting closer and closer over the last few days. Some say it'll be a sack by the Scarlet Brotherhood one of these nights when the fog is thickest. Then they'll sack us to the last coin and take the children off to Kungaloor and the markets there. Some say it's a fleet of an old Accadion Navy lost long ago in the Sea of Riddles... *come to have their revenge on us.*

What more could happen to us? How much worse could this get that has befallen us? This, the end of the city! What next?

Well... let me tell you for there is more. It's all hush-hush... but the *mandarini* are running around saying it never happened... and this is what I heard anyway...

Go on...

Last night at the estate of Nuzom the Vain...

Oh, I hate that one! Such a pretty boy and so evil. He taxes and taxes and it's never enough and next year they say he will indeed be the grand vizier of the city and there won't be any coin to be shaved in this whole city he won't want his piece of! Curse him.

Well... he's dead now!

That's what I heard too... how did it happen?

Oh... that's... pardon me I hope you don't think me ghoulish and all... but that's one bright spot in all this bad luck.

No, feel the same way I do. Curse 'em all. Curse every wretched thieving administrative eunuch living all fine and high, sporting obscenely while we're all broke and burning in the streets and our homes, they got what they deserved last night from what I heard tell of it. Good and hard! No love lost there on that bunch. So, what happened? Do tell. Go on... pins and needles... as they say.

Ah... as I heard tell, sometime around midnight one o' the big pretty boy slaves they have, a new one no one had ever seen before, well, this big strapping bloke took it in his head when they got all drunk with wine and were getting ready to get up to their usuals... well he locked 'em right there in the pleasure dome of Nuzom's spread. Then... he killed 'em all with a fine old battle axe like Rogar sells down in the bazaar with his northern beauties, and then he just disappeared like a ghost that wasn't never there at all.

With what you say?

A battle axe! Sharp and pretty I heard. Like them big northern barbarians use. Or at least that's what I heard it described as such. I mean... he didn't kill all of 'em. There were about twenty of the fat fops in there licking their fingers and doped up on lotus hookah and sweet date wine like they likes... the poofs... and this was just before they had the slave boys brought in... one of 'em survived until morning, supposedly... but died after dawn from blood loss due to the fact that his arm was missing at the shoulder and the bleeders couldn't get him under control. Bad death that kind... ravin' and all.

He... killed them all? This... slave?

There were guards in there too. As the story goes, this big brute locked the doors from the inside, but some said he had help on the outside because it was spiked like thieves do when they want to block an exit. Then this big boy drew the ol' battle axe and told them to prepare themselves to fight right then and there.

That's incredible! I wish I woulda been there to see them get what they had coming. What did they do then? Probably begged for their lives. That bunch has never done an honest day's work in their life, much less scrap.

Well, again this is what I heard happened next. But they started laughing at him. The guards drew their blades on the big slave and thought to cut him up right there, there were five who could stomach what the ponces do in there when they get up to their usual debauchery, sick and twisted it is or so I hear tell... so they had the odds and Nuzom ordered 'em to kill the big murderous brute right there and have done with it so they could get on with the boys.

But that didn't happen?

No. Not at all. You know how that Nuzom speaks. Pretty words and all, but his voice is a wreck from all that lotus smoke and sweet liquor. They say he spends big on his beauty potions and unguents, and even spells, dark ones, to stay... young...

He looks like a ghoul to me, if you're askin'.

I know. The magic ain't working and now it's *really* not working because he's dead and all this mornin'.

So go on... what happened?

Well, Nuzom, he shouts, "Fool... what fear we from such as you, a slave... you're locked in here with us now. Guards... slay him quickly."

And?

From what I heard the big fellow just laughed like a frost giant and said, "I think you're wrong about that, eunuch. It's you who's locked in here with me! And now... you're about to find out what that means..." Then...

Yes? Then what?

Then they were all dead. Guards first. Some of the eunuchs who fancied themselves tough because they had drugged slaves to beat and hold their pretend gladiator fights with on occasion... they tried to defend themselves. *Tried* is a way of putting it generously from what I hear tell. Then... after that... soon enough, they was all dead and that suits me fine.

So what happened to the big slave after that? Was he really a slave at all, or just some assassin sent by the wizards to finally deal with the eunuchs?

That one escaped. Just gone. Faded off into nothing like

a morning mist they say. And all the eunuchs are now at each others' throats due to there's an emptiness among them and power's what they live for. A couple of the more powerful ones who weren't even there sent their own private armies after each other just after dawn this morning and now more eunuchs are dead even beyond the ones in Nuzom's opulent pleasure dome, which is on fire now for reasons no one can explain.

Who will run the city now?

Don't know. Guess we'll have to, and that will probably be fine even with problems. At least we get to keep our taxes and spend it on something else besides them and their wickedness.

And the brute who did this... There must be some news?

Like I said... that one is gone. But... there's a rumor I heard, and I can't tell if it's true or just too good to be true. A juicy one.

Go on then. I can't stand the suspense at this point. This is too much. Dead eunuchs, no taxes. Whoever that slave was... I move we make him King of the City of Thieves based on just last night alone even if he's some sort of lunatic degenerate with a battle axe. He'd probably do a lot better than the eunuchs.

Oh ho, well if you think that then... well then, this is where it gets better. But it's just a thing I heard so... take that for what it's worth.

Oh please... it can't get any better than Nuzom and his ilk slaughtered.

Oh, but it does. Dead tyrants is good tyrants as they say and all. Word is, it was actually that big Dire Man who raided the Prize Chest that done this to the eunuchs last night and set them at each others' throats blue dawn. Word is... that was the one did it last night. And he's on the loose and has a few other scores to settle this day.

Oh... my...

Yup... it's just a tale, but that's what I heard. Thor the Ranger. He's the one that snuck in disguised as a slave, locked himself in with the lot and just a battle axe. Then slaughtered them all. Can you believe that at all?

# CHAPTER FIFTY-ONE

"WHERE DOES THIS END, WARRIOR?"

In the quiet dark of the bar in Shadowrun, Sergeant Thor cleaned *Mjölnir* and readied himself for the next pump. The last actions on the objective... then... it was time for the fade. He replied with only his usual silence to his friend the thief, for he was intent about his business now.

Weapons readiness.

Rehearsing the plan. What he intended to do. Actions afterward.

Then he would go out there into the last of the day, heat and bloodshed abounding without relent, and make his way toward what was most likely an ambush, a very dangerous animal, frightened to death and waiting for him to show, and haul it from its lair. Then Thor would kill it.

Dangerous animal.

Dragon, of a kind.

The one called the Smoke Wizard.

What was coming next as he spent some of the precious last remaining lubricant to coat the various actions of *Mjölnir...* would be very dangerous.

He checked what he'd done by performing a function check, running the bolt.

*Mjölnir* ran as smooth as butter and again the Ranger had to marvel. Many of the weapons the Rangers had brought forward in time to the Ruin had broken down and needed to be replaced. M4s, 249s, Carl Gustaf recoilless rifles, all save the lone M105 anti-materiel rifle he'd scratched the name *Mjölnir* into, all the weapons and gear from the world the Ruin called the Before had broken down. This strange land made of something between *Lord of the Rings* and Kennedy's game of Dungeons & Dragons did this for who knew why, or how.

*Mjölnir* had not failed even a little and showed no signs of the nano-plague, or even wear from the heavy usage the Ranger had put it through in the crossing from the beginning of this strange tale to here, now, a high noon of sorts in the City of Thieves.

This night would see the end of what Sergeant Thor had set himself to do.

It was not done even though others thought it might be.

The game had changed. Gone into extra innings. And that was their fault. Those he'd set himself against. They...

had crossed a line. And now they would pay for even planning to do so.

Just as the first wizard Thor had smoked had, when the Ranger sniper had breached the door to his tower, violently, then put a Raufoss round right through that squat bug-eyed pig-freak's chest. Then he'd done the two weird demons that thought they were his guards.

Three rounds and some improvised explosives.

One down, two to go.

For daring to even plan what they'd thought to do to get at him and what he'd stolen fair and square.

The Ranger caught himself and permitted a grim smile as he made ready to get it on, thinking, *You're starting to think like a thief*. Sato would have laughed at his "stolen fair and square."

"Now you are one of us, Ranger," the master thief would have chuckled.

Even the Queen of Thieves had sent Sergeant Thor a message through the guild's hedge wizard that what he was attempting next was neither needed, nor part of the original plan. The wizards were cowed. Let them be before an all-out war was provoked between factions of thieves and wizards, for the old alliances would not hold under such circumstances. So her message was related.

Thor thought otherwise. The message was not sent in

SGT. THOR: THE CUNNING

full. They were not afraid... *enough*.

So to her, the guild leader who remained in shadow and whisper and whom he had not directly met, the Ranger also had replied with only his usual silence.

Things were moving to an endgame now, but it was time to make sure that on the other side of this heist, the city...

... yeah, the City of Thieves, had a chance.

The powerful had gotten a little too carried away with their power. This wasn't the fault of the plan, or the Ranger. The plan, his plan, had only revealed their faults and their callow tyranny.

People here, in the Ruin, they had no idea what a Gadsden flag was. Now they were gonna learn why you didn't treat those you ruled over as mere pieces on a board to be tortured for either pleasure or gain.

If you were gonna lead, as far as any Ranger was concerned, then you were gonna serve those you led, or you weren't gonna lead anymore.

One way or the other.

And this night, "other" was in effect in the form of *Mjölnir* and the loaded-for-bear Raufoss rounds he had in his assault pack.

The chest rig had finally given up the ghost of being functional after the battle against the were-jaguar in the Pit. Like the assault gloves, it was shredded. Gone.

He was almost ready now. Sato put down the throwing star he was sharpening, laying it down with a flat snap against the polished wood of the table in the quiet inn.

"This wizard, the one they call the Smoke Wizard... he is no mere worker of magic, Warrior. He is ancient, and dangerous. The wizards are at the eunuchs' throats now. And the eunuchs are at each others' throats. The treasure is beyond their reach, and we have succeeded at all the goals we set to achieve. What do you hope to gain now, Warrior, among the carvers of tombs where this master of illusion hides and waits for you to come for him?"

And still... silence.

"Why settle the last two wizards in the cabal the High Council ordained to solve their problem in this matter, Warrior? You invite death now. Even the Five must know the treasure has passed beyond their reach. The plan... is done, Warrior. We have stolen the greatest prize the city has ever seen, and no one is the wiser in how it was done. Your plan was simple, and brilliant. Let us drink now and revel as thieves do when the work is done. Let me return to my wife who is a shrew and a harridan but loves me even so. Let me die a happy man and not by your side fighting the powers of hell. I have fought them before. I have seen many such as yourself perish. And if I have to bury you, Warrior... if I survive where you do not... then the meeting of my beautiful and angry Song Li and myself... shall be bittersweet. For we, you and I, Warrior, have been through much together in so short a time. I do not court such sadness in this life, for it is hard enough. Pass this by, and live, Warrior, and so shall I."

Thor looked up, satisfied he was ready for the hump to the hit.

He heard the smaj's voice in his head within the long afternoon quiet of the bar, asking the Ranger about edges and whether what Thor intended, the mission the Ranger had set himself to, whether that was because of some "noble" reason, or whether it was just because it was an edge and the Ranger, like all of his kind, wanted to see if he could look down into that black yawning abyss that had consumed others, stand at the yawning chasm of that edge, and...

Survive where others had not.

The Ranger knew he could go then and that Sato, his friend... he had a friend in the Ruin that was easily worthy of being a brother to any Ranger... he knew the thief would execute his actions faithfully and even to death, without Thor ever answering his question.

He knew that about this man he'd met on the slave benches of a galley lost at sea. Been shipwrecked with. And fought titanic forces to escape with.

He knew that about Sato.

And he also knew that Sato had earned an answer. In all

those battles, back to back, knives out, the thief had earned his right to ask, and to have an answer from the one he called "Warrior."

The Ranger.

"When I was down at the fishing village..." Sergeant Thor rumbled in the dark of the bar hidden among the twisting alleys and pleasant little streets of Shadowrun where the ancient olive trees curled about the taverns, merchants, and homes. These fine old trees were some of the oldest in the city.

Here, the fire had not come. Yet.

Here, the families and friends of the Little Guild were safe. For now.

"I finally understood what was at stake here," Thor said in the cool shadows that surrounded them. Their packs and gear on the table. Alluria off delivering some final message to all elements that the last actions were underway already.

Well Well tying up some loose ends because loose lips among trusted allies had almost compromised the plans at points. Now those holes would be addressed. Now those infractions would be settled by the pleasant and polite Waste Man working quickly with his sharp knives and murmuring soothing comments as the deadly deeds were done.

Silence in the bar at noon. Thieves were out, listening for truth and lies, navigating the future somewhere betwixt the two. Women kept the little children close. Merchants did what trade they could even as the city burned.

Beyond the invisible walls of Shadowrun, walls made by blind alleys and the sides of vast warehouses or old and noble palaces, or even one of the minor fortresses, rumored to be old and long haunted, the city waged war with itself wherever it could get its hands on one another. The promise of the treasure in the chest had started it all. But it hadn't really. It had just revealed what was bound to happen. Any Ranger could have seen that. The avalanche that one loose stone, or one trap released, would set in motion.

And like any Ranger, he'd built that into the fade. Using it both to obscure his fade where others would not dare to go, and to ruin his enemies in the process.

This was as old as Ranger School and the very difference between Rangers and other tip-of-the-spear military units. Rangers didn't just kill you in their surprise attack from some unexpected quarter and everyone's-asleep-middle-of-the-night, they also killed you when they disappeared like the ghosts and haunts they were and you thought you could get some revenge on them for doing what they'd done to you.

BWAHAHAHA!

You followed them at your own peril, regardless of what they'd done to you and all your pretty little plans.

Their plans to kill you didn't end after they killed you the first time. They counted on the follow of the fade and planned accordingly.

Measure twice, cut once, when dealing with them. Now the wizards would learn, just as the eunuchs had when Thor had locked them in their own dome of horrors.

Murder and mayhem reigned out there in the City of Thieves.

The fires could not be quenched and just burned themselves out. Or would continue to burn until they were all gone.

And all involved and still involved, sensed that yes... it was bad... but perhaps power could still be had in the prized and dusky jewel that was the City of Thieves. *All* the power... in fact. It was still possible to grasp it. If only...

"I realized, down there in Hook's Rest, it wasn't just a heist anymore, Sato. A heist to be *made* by your guild. My test. A... challenge to see if I could pass. I know life is cheap here. I know that the powerful will always... always, abuse those who are just trying to live. Like Omir and his family down in that village. The powerful aren't like him. They live for power. To get what we took, fair and square. They were going to destroy them, Omir and his family, their way of life, their children, and there was nothing anyone could do about it. It was just gonna happen, Sato. I realized that down there when someone came to tell me what would happen. What has *been* happening. For too long."

Thor returned to his rifle, adjusting some bit for what he intended next. Getting it ready for the long carry across the burning city.

"I am sorry, Warrior," Sato said in the silence of the pause. "I may guess that... the Before... where you came from ... things were different then than how they are here now. Perhaps the strong and wealthy watched over the poor and those who tried to build something better as all simple folk have always done. Perhaps you were better than what we have become in the millennia since. I wish it were so still, Warrior. But this is the way of those who want power in the times we find ourselves in. It has, in my life, always been this way. We thieves know that, and we count the cost of who we steal from. For there is always a price. Always. I am glad it was different in your time..."

"It wasn't." Thor's voice didn't rise. But it was final. A rebuke. And it fell between the two comrades awkwardly. Thor watched his silent friend and then continued. For a moment he felt bad, but he pushed that away because there was no room for it. There was only room for the truth now. Nothing more. Nothing less.

As Robert Rogers had ordered...

*You can lie all you want... but don't ever lie to another Ranger.*

Sato by his actions had earned the right to be considered as such.

"It was just as bad," Thor grunted in the darkness. "Maybe... it was even worse, Sato."

Silence.

"And so, this is why you intend to take out the last two wizards," Sato said cautiously. "To settle some wrong from your own past, Warrior. Or perhaps..."

Sato fell silent when he knew what he would say... would land directly on target. The Ranger looked up at this pause. Thor put *Mjölnir* down on its bipod, satisfied it was ready for the next fight. A fight that would come soon. A fight to the death against powerful magic.

The Ranger nodded.

"I think I understand now, Warrior."

Thor shrugged into his assault pack. The last tomahawk attached downward along its length.

"You sought to wander away from your brothers... the Rangers. I apologize if I offend, Warrior. You sought to wander and find adventures by which you might test yourself. But those... Rangers... this is what they do, as I have heard tales from Sûstagul, and from the Before. When there are those that would crush and hurt the simple folk, like Omir and his family, like those in the village, it was your job to go, and... help them. Help those who cannot fight...

tyrants.

"And now... you are confronted by what made you into what you are, a warrior without equal, and what you want to become, a free thief and explorer, a wanderer, a reckless adventurer. But you saw the people of the village and their vulnerability to the tyrants the wizards and the eunuchs have become, treating them not as humans with lives, hopes, and even dreams, Warrior, but as mere pieces in their games of power... and you want to save them from that fate.

"Is this correct, Warrior? Is this why you now go into the eastern district of the city to root out the Smoke Wizard himself even though all within our guild, your guild brothers, feel it is unwise and to court death to do so? This is not the way of thieves. We take, and then we disappear. And we live another day, accepting there will always be such tyrants as these. We are not assassins, Warrior. That way lies madness. Even if you do want to help the people in the village, and all like them, this is the path of revenge, revenge and death. It is not our way. The chest has been plundered. Now we seek the shadows, Warrior."

Thor picked up the heavy, brutal anti-materiel rifle he'd scratched *Mjölnir* into.

Then he smiled and turned toward the door of the tavern.

"*Help*... that's not what we did, in the Before, or now in

the Ruin, Sato. That's not what Rangers do, my friend."

"Then what did you do, Warrior?"

Thor walked toward the door, a hulking shadow in the quiet dark of the empty tavern.

"We showed up and we killed bad guys, Sato. And in doing so... made the world a better place for those just trying to live."

# CHAPTER FIFTY-TWO

IT WAS A LONG HUMP ACROSS THE CITY OF THIEVES ON that final, last, hot afternoon as the game of hide and seek, steal and take, came to an end. The skies above the sprawling city inside the cyclopean walls that meandered east to west, north and south, boiled with black smoke here and there, finally rising into the gray and white cumulus over distant broken mountains of ancient granite.

The Ranger threaded dark alleys now to reach his selected target just after dark. *Mjölnir* on a sling, one hand on the extended bipod if he had to steady it and go suddenly to close-quarters battle right there in some desperate and mean little fight in a dark corner on the route to the penultimate hit against the cabal of wizards that had been formed to deal with him. The Ranger stayed away from the raging street battles, crossed linear danger areas quickly, pied corners as he threaded those dark mazes of death between the inner walls and main broadways, and finally continued on, moving through burnt-out buildings and shattered palaces where once the wizards and eunuchs had issued their orders, made their decrees, and cared little for the local populace beyond how they could be used to further the ends of their "betters."

There were bodies here. And more all along the way.

There were also teams of ragged foul-smelling collectors, hooded and furtive, out working for the vivisectionists, the necromancers also, for some trades did not cease their dark interests even if total war between the various factions was underway and showed no signs of relenting any time soon.

It was as though the end of the Ruin was at hand, and life went on all the same.

Across the city even the siege engines had been drawn out from storage and were now being flung against some hardened point of some opposite number tyrant in yet another effort to gain all the power that could be had now that so many others... were dead.

Sato had been sent on ahead to the tower of the last target to scout entry into that fortified and well-guarded walled redoubt, the Tower of Osirex. Well Well and Alluria were in tow. Thor was on the move to root out the Smoke Wizard who'd turtled in a decrepit part of the city. Once he was dead, the final hit could commence without the worry of support from the deadly Smoke Wizard.

Sato's words in the inn still haunted Thor, and he tried to put them away as best he could now that he was on the stalk and headed into the southern and eastern reaches of the city, an area that was notoriously dangerous and hard... and desperate.

And often, like many other men of decisive action, and deep thinkers, often one and the same, Thor hadn't had the right words at the time to tell the thief why he'd intended to put the last two wizards down before calling it done.

Even if the plan, the operation... the heist was now considered successful. The treasure gone beyond their reach. The plan never exposed.

Even if...

He would leave the city soon. That had always been part of the plan. The last phase of the fade off the objective. It had always been the last step.

But now he had a special project, and two line items to cross off before he would leave this city.

This was his way. And it was not the thieves'. Though as brothers, even unwilling, they had thrown in to see it finally done.

But...

What the Ranger had not been able to convey to Sato was that... he, Thor, wanted to give Omir's family, and the other families, the city itself, a chance against these tyrants.

A chance to be free of their unchecked tyranny.

Something for the tyrants to fear before they tried it next time.

And this was the way. Thor's way.

Ahead, the sun began its fall behind the walls. Shadows lengthened. Silence fell over the city and the black smoke continued to boil.

It was only a pause.

The fighting would resume shortly.

And the only thing Thor had been able to think of, on that long run up from the village of Hook's Rest, after the message of the old holy man, hustling as fast as he could to hit the wizards' cabal hard and hopefully destabilize the two sorcerers who would push on the village... was that people like them, them and the third wizard and all the wizards and even all the eunuchs, the only thing they understood was... *fear*.

Kindness. Love. Respect. That was beyond them.

They couldn't be reasoned with regarding those concepts.

But fear.

They knew fear.

Used fear.

So... the Ranger would teach them.

With fear.

To fear.

Sergeant Thor ran, making his plans and hoping for enough time to start hitting them hard until they pulled back and started worrying about their own skins.

There would be a ghost among them. A vengeful spirit. A wild animal that would come out to kill if they dared what they had dared.

After hearing the holy man's vision of what would happen should Thor not intervene, the Ranger had decided right then and there that the heist was done. Now it was time to teach those in power a lesson about the abuse of it.

Someone. Someones... would need to die.

The cabal would do. The eunuchs too.

And if he did, if Thor taught an effective lesson, a hard lesson, killed their best and broke their stuff, then perhaps... in the future, the next round of tyrants to try... wouldn't. Perhaps. Maybe they'd be a little more afraid to go smoke whole villages of unarmed people just trying to live their best lives because the tyrants wanted a cut of what had been robbed and couldn't just live and let be without getting their snout down in the cut of the haul.

They'd learn because he'd set himself to teach them. Come hell or high water. The heist was done. School was in session.

That was the last gift he could give this wretched, and

beautiful, and mysterious city.

The village too.

The boy and the girl.

"Why do you have to leave?" the little girl had asked as he got ready in the cottage, fast, to be on the move after the dire words of the holy man. To save their lives. Unable to tell her and the boy who stood with the big ancient used book in his hands watching like an owl in his silent way.

"Why do you have to leave, Thor?" she asked again when he didn't answer her.

He'd had an answer for her. But it wasn't one he could tell her because children didn't need to know how awful the world can be. No. Not yet. Let them, for a little while, have that thin wall of safety, a warm-in-your-bed peace, parents, and butterflies that cannot be caught, fishing and running, let them have that. Even if it is an unmanned wall ghosts and monsters try to cross.

But there are men on that wall. Every day. And this is what they do. What he would do.

Back in that cottage he'd bent down next to her tiny face and long dark hair.

He could tell her anything and she would believe him.

Sato wanted a world where there were no tyrants. Even though the wise old thief probably knew no such world ever existed.

There's no harm in wanting a better world.

It's noble to want that. Noble to want better.

He, the Ranger, wanted a world where everyone, most everyone, could have the luxury of innocence the little girl had in her eyes and tiny heart-shaped face as she asked him why he had to go now. But really, she was asking him... to stay.

*Why do you have to leave, Thor?*

So soon.

Too soon.

Please stay.

There is only one chance for that world where the young can have at least a little time to be innocent. The only way that world exists is if... there are hard men willing to do hard things in the dark of long nights when the illusion of a wall is all that keeps the madness at bay.

If there are Rangers on that wall.

The smaj said nothing in his head now as he stalked the chaos and ruin inside the burning City of Thieves, closing in on the stonemason yards south and east inside the city. Where the grave markers are carved and where desperate and ruined men hide in dark corners seeking to avoid the judgment they deserve.

The old sergeant major said nothing as the Ranger closed in on the hit and darkness came over the city despite the hellish lights from the many fires.

But he could feel the senior NCO nodding, as if to say, *That's the way it is, Ranger. That's the way it has always been.*

One last time she'd asked him as she followed him out the door of that weathered old cottage by the sea. The owl-faced boy saying nothing because what was happening, an ending of sorts, had never been written in all the books he'd read so far. Which wasn't all and nearly enough, but someday, when he was a venerated, wise, and kind old scholar, he would read one, and understand what had happened that day in his youth, in the wind and sun by the cottage.

Thor could tell from the look on the kid's face that he did not understand any of this now. Thor gave him a look, checking in with him and telling with just his quiet, massive rock of presence, that someday, the boy would understand.

And then it would be... all right. Then. But not now.

"Why do you have to leave, Thor?" she asked again.

He turned to her before leaving. He had to go. Clock was burning. Failure was not an option.

Then he bent down, kissed her head, and whispered, "So that you can stay."

Then he was running north back to the City of Thieves, running for her life.

# CHAPTER FIFTY-THREE

THE THIEVES OF THE GUILD SHADOWED THE INFAMOUS Smoke Wizard after the events at the tower of the summoner.

The old illusionist was clearly spooked, and he hustled himself off to the southern edges of the city, to old haunts he knew well. It was clear he knew he was on the defensive now, and anyone coming after him should expect traps, resistance, and a determined enemy in a fixed position.

Army standards are minimum seven-to-one for this kind of opponent. Thor didn't have seven other Rangers, and the Little Guild was stretched thin.

So he'd go in alone and allocate more resources to the primary hit which would come next after the Smoke Wizard was taken off the board.

But old Mandelf Tallhat had turtled. The master illusionist had gotten Sergeant Thor's message, loud and clear. By those still-active channels of communication between the city's factions, it had been made clear that the wizards had definitely crossed a line, and the one called Sergeant Thor was now out for blood on the cabal daring to attack the village of Hook's Rest.

The wizards were on notice. This news, this message, was stunning, but with much quiet sobriety and respect, it had been transmitted. Even the Queen of Thieves, who had supposedly seen everything, was said to have croaked, "Well, that's a new one."

The eunuchs had paid already. Their ranks were clearly decimated, and yes this is the correct usage of that word. The eunuchs and their *mandarini* had lost roughly ten percent, maybe even a little more, in Thor's surprise attack on Nuzom the Vain's pleasure dome. But the loss had been borne by the movers and shakers in the higher echelons of the order of administrative eunuchs.

Many who administered other aspects of the city were still active and waiting to see how the dust settled and how they would conduct themselves on the other side of the conflagration running wild.

Now to the wizards...

The destruction of the cabal of three would pay for the wizards' hubris and callousness in their treatment of the populace. That was the message, the *offer* it might have been possibly considered as. Take it or leave it. The Ranger was coming for the three and that's the way it was going to be.

In the past any kind of threat to the wizards would have been met with mocking derision and cold, contemptuous scorn among the powerful masters of magic and thaumaturgical might that were the wizards of the City of Thieves.

But this... *Ranger*... he had clearly proven... capable. Wizards might be arrogant... but they are not stupid. The threat carried weight, and the bodies of the High Table and the Five grew soberly quiet in response.

Make of that what you will.

And also... nothing was said to the effect that they would not brook this type of insolence from a mere lesser. They were in fact... brooking. And that the threat was allowed to be made without outcry was... as has been written... stunning.

They were clearly afraid of this *Sergeant Thor.*

Furthermore...

They answered nothing in acceptance of the terms of the slaughter Thor had put forth as payment for their daring to plan what they had plotted against Omir and his family and the village.

So... they still had hopes the cabal could possibly eliminate the upstart Ranger and then they could take credit for this and maintain their tenuous grasp on power. Perhaps even cement it now that the eunuchs had been dealt such a crippling blow.

They were, smartly, or so they thought, hedging their bets.

Thor entered the grave-carvers' district to hunt and kill the Smoke Wizard at just after twilight. The city, even as it burned, made the night beautiful and even dramatic. But out here in the much-forgotten neighborhood of low men and work no one wanted a part of, there was a sinister air of waiting that hung over the unreal silence. The air was dry, and the heat was fading as the night came on.

This was one of the lowest districts of the city. The work here was dangerous, working with stone and the cutting inherently so, and dangerous also because the graves out there in the vast spreading necropolis east of the city were not always so quiet as one might assume the dead to be once they were... dead.

There were some plots and regions out there beyond the walls in the fields of the dead where armed mercenaries or hired reckless parties of middling adventurers were needed in order to install the remembrance stones and complete the final rites so the dead could be forgotten.

And often the occupants of those unquiet graves weren't so quiet and had a nasty habit of crawling forth, or floating forth, and then seeping through the broken rents and cracks in the zigzagging, badly maintained high walls that guarded this edge of the City of Thieves, seeking life to feed the endless hunger the dead so required.

It was a district that was quiet in the mornings from the ruinous hangovers and the bleak resignation to yet another brutal day in the worst work and neighborhood the city had to offer, and quiet again in the late afternoons after the carving, cutting, chipping work was done, and the drinking to forget began once again.

Those who remained here after dark were either so lost to drink and nightmares, or they served those wretches the smoke and drink they'd paid their meager coins for. Anyone of decent family, or trade, hustled for the other walled neighborhoods closer in to the better districts long before the sun reached the top of the western walls, making the minarets of the towers cast long shadows like accusatory fingers seeking to lay some endless blame at what had been done now that the day was over.

It became especially quiet when the doors were locked, the windows shuttered and barred, and even the taverns and inns grew tentative as night came on and the haunted souls drank their drinks, listening to what soft songs and murmuring tunes were played by what ruined bards could still hold a chord and remember a lay, and all watched the doors and kept one ear to the too-quiet streets outside for hints and warnings of the things they did not want to hear out there moving along the walls, or shambling up the streets, or rustling on the rooftops.

Journeys through the streets of this district, in the hours after darkness fell, were kept quick and accompanied by a bright lantern that always seemed to struggle against the gloom, and also these small forays were best done as little, and as quickly, as possible.

The Ranger entered the outskirts of the grave-carvers' district at twilight, threading a ruined wasteland of wrecked stone too unusable for the fine graves paid in handsome coin, and quietly passed between old skeletons of buildings where the carving was only done during the height of the day.

On the stalk the Ranger moved cautiously from shadow to shadow, scanning the darkness ahead with his razor-sharp eyes and testing the night with his senses.

His high-value target didn't lie too much further along, and the air grew colder as he approached the area.

It was full dark now and the moon provided little light as the sky was filled with black smoke from the fires that still raged out of control further into the city. To the west the city looked alive even with small angry fires, illuminating the great palaces and mighty fortresses along the walls. The street battles had resumed, as had what trade there would be, bitter duels resolved before death snatched the chance at final revenge, or love for why would love wait even if it was the end of the world, or lust because why not, or... simple luck.

Of course, there was always that.

Soon the City of Thieves would put out the fires, count the dead, see who was in charge now, and continue on just as it had through would-be conquerors past, lost armies long ago and buried in the great barrows at the furthest edges of the Fields of the Dead, and other past tyrants who'd thought themselves greater than the City of Thieves.

Thor approached the main street of the grave-carvers' district, which was little more than a disorganized collection of ramshackle buildings grouped together and surrounded by the stone-cutting yards. Few families lived here. Most were either innkeepers or the wretches who carved stone. All were haunted and silent. Unseen beyond their barred doors and shuttered windows as the Ranger stopped in a deep shadow and took a knee in the warm sand of a half-collapsed building's skeletal innards, acclimatizing to the district. He could smell the scent of some greasy stew on the wind.

And dead bodies.

The wind had come up in the late afternoon as the Ranger had made his way through the ruined and fire-blasted streets in the eastern part of the city. Now as night fell, the wind and sand blew in through the open rents in the great and crazed wall that guarded the eastern edge of the city.

Out there beyond the wide and mostly empty grave-carvers' district, the wall looked like some long-forgotten sentinel in quiet shadow.

That wall and the wall alone guarded the city here, for even the guards would not man the wall due to the undead horrors that lurked out there in the eastern necropolises. And it was said even the hordes and the monsters beyond the wall would not try the Fields of the Dead if they were to invade the city.

So the wall and its towers and guardhouses were mostly empty and silent, and the cracks and rents had grown year by year with lack of watch and upkeep.

The smell of rot and death, ancient and new, came with these intermittent gusts from off the desert, and the scent of such things within the sudden blasts was as thick as the sand and grit picked up off the wastes to the east.

Thor donned a shemagh he kept in his pack and studied the landscape for ambush and cover he could use.

The thieves who'd shadowed the Smoke Wizard had said only that he'd come here after the termination of Baalubrozz the Summoner and had turtled in a rickety old bar at the end of the street.

The bar had no name, and it was reputed to be a lotus

den of the lowest sort.

For ten minutes the Ranger watched the lifeless buildings, knowing, feeling really, that there were some in there, hiding and waiting out the night.

He raised *Mjölnir* and scanned the street ahead and the buildings on thermal.

Nothing.

The buildings were lit up hard from the heat of the day, but even now that was fading.

He landed the powerful thermal sight on the leaning building at the end of the street that was supposed to be the drinking establishment, and the lotus den, and even as he did so... smoke, purple and deep black and light gray within the thermal image, began to billow and flow from the inn, coming through cracks and even flooding through the front door of the old place.

At first it was little more than tendrils of mist and then wisps, but within seconds it billowed and piled, growing and feeding, and as the Ranger watched it, he felt the wind grow silent now and the world was filled with a heavy silence that seemed almost... like death itself.

He lowered the rifle and co-witnessed the street with his own keen eyes. Taking in every detail now.

The wind had stopped, nothing moving or swaying or groaning under the relentless winds of the vast spreading desert of death.

The wind was gone now, and the air grew chill with an edge in it.

Now the small hodge-podge collection of ancient buildings and the worn track that passed for a street that moved through them, was filled with a heavy purple mist that hung over the area where his prey was rumored to have turtled.

*So*, thought Thor, *this is the battlefield.*

His eyes grew used to the dark... then... as he studied the target building where the Smoke Wizard had turtled... the front door swung slowly open. Slowly.

He was expected.

Fine then, thought Thor, knowing this was a type of tactic to cause fear. To check him. To get him to run. He could practically feel the fear coursing through the air all around him. The guild's hedge wizard had warned Thor that illusionists work primarily in fears.

But unfortunately for the Smoke Wizard, no one had told him fear doesn't work on Rangers.

In fact and instead, it's like... it's like a siren for them. A call they cannot resist when fear rears its ugly head. Like a dare. Or a trick.

Or a challenge they must accept.

Then... in the night growing cold with the purple mist

that hung over the ruined center of the wasted district...

... the Ranger did the opposite of what almost every human being in Mandelf Tallhat's vast experience had ever done. The Ranger got up out of the shadows he watched from and advanced on the inn where the wizard had sought to hide, and to protect, himself from death.

And death in the form of a Ranger with a rifle came for him anyway.

# CHAPTER FIFTY-FOUR

MANDELF TALLHAT INHALED FROM HIS LONG-STEMMED pipe and stalked about the shadowy ruin of the wrecked inn, vacant and alone save for himself, for he had driven off its usual denizens by casting a powerful weirding spell that revealed their worst fears, right there in the bar now, and drinking next to them.

Smiling about what the figment... vampire, werewolf, demon, wronged foe, murdered lover... was going to do to them shortly.

And then the Smoke Wizard set himself to casting his wards and traps in their absence. Illusions.

A lone flickering wax homunculus of a candle all that remained to watch with him.

Mandelf never minded the solitude. He had his smoke, and his many madnesses he kept muttering to himself. Black things never meant to be heard. Damnable memories never meant to be recalled.

The Ranger who came for him tripped the first glyph out there in the dark, up the twisting track that led to the tavern. Mandelf had etched it in a bit of cracked stone out there in the hot afternoon, a piece of marble tumbled away from some ancient grave marker cut long ago and now lying on its side from the frequent quakes that rocked the deserts and the Fields of the Dead to the east, next to an open grave giving way to a black tunnel leading down into whatever went on beneath the death fields beyond the walls.

The glyph activated a phantasmal predator from the... *Other*... and suddenly the image of a many-tentacled horror burst from the old leaning shed where one of the carvers kept his tools just near the stalking Ranger coming for the old illusionist.

Locked and barred was that old shed.

Mandelf inhaled deeply from his pipe and giggled wildly a little bit in his old cracked and ruined voice as the tentacled horror seemed to burst the locks on that shed, throwing great deadlights and weird noises all across the sands and track the Ranger had made his approach through.

Snakes that were tentacles slithered and rattled like a thousand rattlers disturbed and angry, and the tentacles, with something like great elephant ears at their ends, and filled with horrific suckers, surged toward this mysterious warrior who'd come to kill Mandelf.

"Good... very good," murmured the drug-addled wizard with a bizarre smile, and then his mouth fell open and he had to catch the pipe as it suddenly dropped away as the Ranger pivoted and fired his giant Wand of Destruction, or whatever that huge staff he carried was, center mass right into the illusory "horror" Mandelf had conjured within the shed.

The illusion collapsed instantly and Mandelf swore in a language that had not been used in a thousand years.

The wizard scrambled for the window to verify what his discharged spells had just told him. He pushed aside the tattered curtain in the tavern window and watched the dark figure of the Ranger coming down the street once more.

"Fine then," muttered old Mandelf like some miser miner angry at a recalcitrant vein of gold that would not yield up all it had for him to take, and blew smoke from his pipe after a great stratifying inhale, a holding of the breath for a moment, his eyes closed tightly shut. Then he exhaled and gathered the expelled smoke, casting it out the window like a hurled grenade.

Magic words went with this act.

All around the Ranger the sudden angry flames of hell leapt up through the hot sands now cooling in the night. Gaseous fissures opened and cracked as lava poured forth from these great rents in the sands all around.

At the same time Mandelf began to hurl phantasmal bolts at the Ranger. Each was like being hit by an angry burst of sudden fear and anxiety that chilled the blood and made the feet heavy.

Thor shrugged through the bolts and shifted position for cover.

He stopped, raised his thermal scope, and confirmed all this fire and lava pouring forth was yet another illusion, then, quick as a lick, he pulled *Mjölnir*'s trigger as the thermal image revealed the half head of the master illusionist behind the curtain in the inn at the end of the street.

Old Mandelf swore like an overripe hippie suddenly jerked up by the collar by the man, his voice a ragged screech, and he fell backward as the wall he'd been covering beyond just exploded from the incoming Raufoss round. The old illusionist was scrambling fast now given his venerable age, and he barely missed having his head blown off by the roaring Barrett that thundered across the open scape of the street once again.

The illusion of the fires of hell suddenly erupting through the broken rocks and sands of the track through the village persisted, but the Ranger knew it was all an illusion, for he'd done his intel on this wizard and had focused himself to confirm by any means possible, sight, smell, listening, and even touching, that what he faced was not real.

It was a trick. That was all.

He stood and advanced, once more closing on the inn. Closing on his target.

It was at that moment that Seac and his archer sprang their trap. The first of the archer's fast-fired arrows landed with a heavy thud in the Ranger's assault pack, knocking the hulking Thor forward from the immense pull of the bow, then the second arrow, traveling at almost the same speed and timing as the first, slashed the Ranger's thigh and slammed into the ground vibrating like a tuning fork.

Thor twisted and fell, sucking dirt despite the burning sudden pain. He assessed the situation lightning-fast and spotted the swiftly moving archer moving across the rooftop on the other side of the street, pulling two more huge arrows from his large quiver, getting ready to nock them and fire again.

At the same time, the downed Ranger saw the savage and wild Mourne Elf in light black armor surge from the alley across the twisting way, massive broadsword raised high and ready to cleave the Ranger in half with one final downstroke.

Thor raised *Mjölnir* at the last second, ignored the searing pain in his leg, and sent a round right through the moving archer on the rooftops.

*Bull's-eye.*

It blew out the high archer's spine, the fast-moving

explosive round going straight through his back, the inky ruin-spray of blood and bone matter silhouetted against the moon that had peeked for a moment through the heaving angry boil of the dark fire clouds in the night.

The archer neither screamed nor cursed as he fell forward off the low roof, letting go of his arrows and great bow of renown and plummeting down onto the chipped rock and sands below.

He was already dead when he struck head-first and snapped his neck with a savage bone-rending *crunch.*

Thor pivoted, again ignoring the screaming hot pain in his leg at the action, and raised *Mjölnir* quickly with both hands to block the impending downswing of the dark elf's shining blade in the night.

The elf's face was pure blackest rage, his mouth set in grim determination as he came on, surging at the last second, his leather armor soft and worn, barely creaking in the night as his boots thumped across the sand and ruined rock to strike the Ranger before Sergeant Thor could defend himself.

*Mjölnir,* raised like some two-handed staff, caught the savage blow of the dark elf's blade at the last second.

And Seac the Raven's ancestral blade just shattered right there in a sudden spray of bright sparks.

The mercenary captain backed away in stunned disbelief

at all the bad that had befallen him, badness now embodied in his noble family's blade being sundered when it should not have.

If he thought that bought him something, some bit of unexpected mercy, some grace at the loss of such an ancient blade, he was wrong.

The Ranger was without mercy, for such is the way of Rangers.

Quick as a striking rattlesnake the angered Thor turned on one knee, the good knee, and blasted the dark elf point-blank right in the guts with the M105 anti-materiel rifle, practically blowing Seac in half with a sudden thunderstrike of wrath and flame.

The dark elf fell backward, dying, and cast his beautiful blue eyes at the moon, and was dead by the time his skull fractured against the remains of some badly flawed grave marker that hadn't been good enough for even the meanest of graves beyond the edge of the wall out there in the wilds of the unquiet dead.

# CHAPTER FIFTY-FIVE

MANDELF WAS FLUSTERED, AND THAT WAS PUTTING IT mildly. He'd cast his best defensive and offensive spells, and the Ranger had dealt with them and continued the relentless march up the street.

Now he was dry on phantasmal bolts. He'd hurled them at the Ranger and they'd seemed to stick for a moment, hissing and whispering dark fears, but then the immense brute had shrugged them off and slogged forward under their ghostly fear-crawling weight, closing on the inn Mandelf had thought would be a fortress, yet was feeling now more like a cage.

Next had been the *Mirror Images* the powerful wizard had cast. A powerful spell that was simply ignored. Thor pointed his powerful fire wand at the illusionist's real image, himself exposed, and fired. Mandelf Tallhat barely escaped getting turned to nothing but fast-moving blood spray and bone matter at the last second by burning a blink spell that suddenly hurled him off into another direction as a vortex of wind and noise opened up and spirited him off behind the bar with a great sucking noise.

The Smoke Wizard actually thought about running for his life at that point, but the only direction he could make for was the walls and the Fields of the Dead beyond. He feared not those buried and unquiet fiends, but it would be an open field for that cursed-powerful Wand of Fire this mysterious warrior... this *Ranger*... had kept after him with.

The renowned illusionist was running out of tricks fast and reality was starting to intrude on the narcotic dreams he surrounded himself with always.

In other words, the powerful blasts of *Mjölnir* were killing his vibe.

"And... I need my... magical *chi*..." whined the wizard as he tried to calm himself with another hit from the magical long-stemmed pipe he was so known for.

"Curse it all!" he hissed as *Mjölnir* thundered again and disintegrated more of the tavern.

So Mandelf relented and cast his powerful *Major Image of Terror* spell, summoning a mighty image of the gnoll God of the Hunt. The snarling three-headed terror suddenly came galloping across the wide space of cast-aside grave markers that lay beyond here and the walls Mandelf might escape into if this illusion was successful...

The Ranger ignored this spell once more, merely raising his thunderous fire wand and dispelling the image Mandelf had cast with the thermal sight without even launching one of his near-invisible fireballs that roared with power and thunder.

Mandelf swore bitterly, took a powerful hit of lotus, and threw *Phantasmal Horde* into the chaos for something to do as opposed to waiting for the fire wand to roar and Mandelf to be no more.

Phantasmal orc raiders, riding on nightmare snarling wolves of immense size with red flames in their eyes, came loping through the cracks in the walls, the horrid orcs of immense size ululating savagely and raising their cracking whips and flaming spears.

It was a fearsome image indeed, and Mandelf had seen major armies turn and run at its very casting...

But this time it failed as the other spells had failed.

Again the focused Ranger, kneeling and tying a tight bandage about the wound done to his leg, ignored these bloodthirsty imaginary orcish savages, the worst of most folks' fears, as they raced toward him and turned to nothing more than mere drifting smoke and disintegrating charcoal on the wind like the sketches of some great artist creating fearsome horrors on the fly with nothing but charcoal and papyrus.

Bandage secured, the warrior that had become almost grim death itself in the Smoke Wizard's mind, moved on the inn for the final attack.

Mandelf threw *misleading* and *seeming* spells, *hey-over-here*, and *this-is-not-that*, all intended to misdirect, while at the same time activating defensive wards and guardians against direct damage from the Ranger and his fearsome magical weapon.

Of things Mandelf had wanted to know, and make no mistake, Mandelf knew much given his long age and deep researches, he had wanted, before this battle, to know exactly how this northern savage had lifted the prizes and treasure inside the chest.

But no longer.

Now...

He wanted to know where this savage had gotten that terrific weapon of great power and might. All the things he could do with such a weapon as the Ranger's Wand of Fire.

Spell-cast black ravens formed like shifting shadows and raced around the bedraggled washed-out wizard as he sought the protection of the inn and prepared his last trap with which to enslave and destroy the grim and relentless warrior that came for him like unbargainable death itself.

The powerful fire wand roared and rained thunder and fire directly into the walls of the inn. Violent sprays of debris and shrapnel destroyed the flimsy heat-rotted walls and the has-been interior as rounds meant for the master illusionist were claimed by the protective shadow ravens the wizard had summoned as a final desperate defense.

And then the door disintegrated in an explosion of fire and debris.

Mandelf, cowering behind the bar, ancient addict's hands trembling like a lotus junkie's shaking for a fix, cast his last and most terrible spells as a final chance to change the game, damn the consequences that came with such strange and cursed spells.

Two spells, in fact.

Thor, inside the bar, stalking forward and following the Barrett's front sight, gripping the bipod, ready to rock the first man-sized target that appeared, scanned *Mjölnir* across the dark interior and devastated chaos of what remained of the shattered inn. He could not hear the wizard's frantic spell-murmurings because of the impromptu ear pro he had in to protect himself from the thunderous blasts of *Mjölnir*.

His cans had long ago given up the ghost.

*Mjölnir.*

*The Grinder.*

He pulled out of one ear a piece of waxed cloth with a deft flick, and heard the repetitive fear-mumbling of the target coming from behind what remained of the old weathered bar that had once served the lost and wrecked here.

And then... something strange happened.

Then... reality went away as the master illusionist cast *Wyrding* and *Prison of the Mind* at almost the same time.

This was a feat few illusionists or sorcerers could manage. But Mandelf had spent many years practicing his craft, and this trick had saved him from both dragons and armies a few times over.

And... it had consumed them in the process, for it was a dangerous spell on the order of a *Wish*. As dangerous to the caster as it was to the target.

And yes... even dragons have fears. Even regrets.

Everyone does.

The *Wyrding* combined with *Prison of the Mind* spells offered a game to the target. A game of a chance to change some past wrong, some horrible tragedy, into *what might have been*, instead of what was. The spell caused a shifting of the target into that *otherwhen*, blending reality and fiction and memory and regret, and loss, of course always loss... so powerful, so seductive... and offering a chance. A hope. Like some sweet murmuring lie... another drink for the drunk to think that perhaps this time... it will be different... a chance to do it all over again.

To get it right this time.

To cheat death.

And in the space of that horrible and dreamed-for dream, the caster has a chance to kill the target as the target tries once more... to save the lost person, right the wrong, or say what needed to be said.

If the caster succeeds, the spell disappears and the target is dead. If he fails...

... then he is lost forever in that unreal *otherwhen*, locked in a loop of madness ever-repeating forever, imprisoned within the regret, fear, and shame, a kind of loop in a hell that never ends.

The *Prison of the Mind* spell probed Thor's mind and found what it needed...

... and the *Wyrding* shifted the Ranger to that illusion of what was real, and what never was.

The world turned upside down, or felt like it did for a second, and then the inn disappeared.

Now the Smoke Wizard's challenge began.

The Ranger was standing at the edges of a movie set. Standing in the dark, the shadows, beyond the light. Watching her act.

The dead girl he'd once loved enough to possibly stay, and not leave.

*Mjölnir* was gone because it wasn't there.

He was just himself. On leave.

A long time and another life ago.

In a life not this one at all.

He watched Katie Malone, alive and not dead now as she was and had been, doing what she loved.

And Thor could not tear his eyes away from her.

Somewhere above it all, in the shadows high above the set, up in the lights and ropes where the riggers play and work, within the prison of Thor's mind, and the *Wyrding*... Mandelf Tallhat laughed, low and evil.

# CHAPTER FIFTY-SIX

KATIE MALONE WAS ON THE SET OF *FATAL STRIKE*. AT the moment this blockbuster movie is being filmed she is alive. In two weeks, after the Ranger who came out to the coast on leave to train her in weapons handling and moving under fire, or as his former scout team leader who now works as a stuntman put it to Thor, "teach her to be an operator," she will be dead in an accident.

And then both Rangers laughed over the phone about operators operating, and Sergeant Thor agreed to come out to the coast and see what he could do.

Plus, they could hang and talk about old times.

Thor, who had some time between pumps, came out to help and train, and along the way he fell for the dark-eyed beauty that had been the love interest in the latest Batman epic after almost getting an Oscar in a film about a dress store clerk who sells her soul to the Devil in order to get fame and along the way falls in love with a dorky but handsome blind pianist or some such yawnfest important-movie dreck.

In *Fatal Strike*, Katie Malone is a CIA analyst downrange in a third world hellhole gone hot with "incoming and intrigue," literally the awful tagline as the film will gross big because people want to see her latest movie and who cares how awful the tagline written by some chungo screenwriter is. In other words, Katie as the "CIA hero" is trying to save the lives of someone or someones in danger, *or* and possibly *and* prevent some terrorist plot from destroying the world this week.

Thor didn't care. It sounded cool.

She needed to know how to fire a sidearm and not do stupid things like hold it sideways or action-pose with it pointing at her head, or rack a round every time she had some cool dialogue to say, how to wear her chest rig properly, throw a punch or two, and of course drop targets with a tricked-out and very ridiculous M4 she gets from a "special weapons package drop" before she advances up a collapsing bridge getting hit by Russian or German or right-wing terrorists' missiles launched from a hijacked sub.

The script was currently being rewritten on the fly to be current with Deep State targeting.

Thor didn't care, but he had strong feelings about her prop guns.

Naturally.

Honestly, the prop department had a drum mag on the tricked-out M4 until Thor said there was no way anyone, absolutely *no way in hell* anyone with any kind of real world SOCOM experience, which Cinder Sloan, her character, was supposed to have, would use.

He disconnected the drum mag and flung it into a canal filled with prop scum.

"Hey!" shouted the prop master and then thought better of it when the Ranger growled and flexed his twenty-inch biceps as he made a fist.

So the producer and the director agreed that "this is the way," their words, and said they had no idea what they were doing and were grateful for the direction on how to, again their words, "keep it real" for the audience with a real live hero, "Thank you for your service," on set.

Thor said nothing to this. He was still simmering from the drum mag.

They were not men, and often he had few words for such loathsome creatures. The best he could do was treat them with respect as members of the same species and not waste any more of his time on them.

He had two weeks to get Miss Malone up to speed, and they went out to a range in the San Bernadino desert and along the way... they got to know each other. Real well in fact.

Hey, Ranger gonna Ranger, amirite?

He spent some days with her on set.

They spent some nights in Hollywood at her place.

They took a drive up the coast, Malibu, ate seafood at Gladstones. Saw a movie star, besides her. Made it as far as Santa Barbara in the evening.

Sylvester Stallone.

Thor actually thought that was pretty cool.

The sky was beautiful. The world out there was endless.

"You could take me out there," she murmured. "All the places you've been. All the places you want to go. We could go there. Together."

Thor nodded.

They were sitting on the hood of her high-end Land Rover. He was holding her.

She'd told him about being a prisoner, a very pretty one, in a gilded cage. She'd climbed the mountain of Hollywood.

There was nothing there.

She wanted to live. She wanted to love.

"This," she whispered as the sun fell into the wide Pacific Ocean. "This is real. You could take me. We could... go there."

The long story short is that Thor was this close to walking away from the Rangers. He was into her. Big time. And not the "star" her. But the real her. Even though he'd gone to a movie premiere and when the photographers appeared he turned away so they couldn't capture the face of this "New Handsome Mystery Man in Megastar Katie Malone's Life!"

"Why?" she asked. "Doesn't everyone want to be famous?"

She asked this honestly.

He shook his head and didn't tell her about all the bad guys out there in the world running scans to get at Rangers and special operations folk. If they couldn't get at them, then perhaps they could get at the ones... they loved.

Yeah. *Love.*

He could almost hear the other Rangers call him "gay."

It was that close for the Ranger.

Then he got the call. *Be back. Right now. World's on fire somewhere and Rangers got to go.*

That last afternoon at her beach house after they said goodbye, she looked at him, tears in her eyes. She didn't understand.

She was beautiful.

So beautiful she was almost alien. So beautiful it hurt.

"You could stay... we could go. You could just... walk away. *I'll* walk away... right now. We'll go and get on any jet going anywhere and it'll be just us now. Okay?"

But he left. Clock was burning. World was on fire. C-

130s on the tarmac, engines running.

And then two weeks later she was dead in a stunt car accident on set.

The world mourned.

But the Rangers were in it deep out there beyond the world and Sergeant Thor, scout team leader, wouldn't find out until he called her cell just to see how she was, and her assistant answered.

The news of her death had captured the world.

But by the time he got back from the pump it was old news and it had taken a call to find out.

"Oh... you haven't heard... what... happened to Katie..." said the girl who had been her faithful assistant. And then she began to weep into the phone.

*You could stay... and we could go. You could just... walk away.*

From the darkness beyond the lights on the set, Thor watched Katie Malone... acting. Alive again.

And he was frozen.

Even dragons have regrets.

We all do.

# CHAPTER FIFTY-SEVEN

A MOVIE IS A KIND OF MAGIC TOO. ISN'T IT?

Watch an old movie from when you were a kid, from your time, from long ago when the world was different and not the way it is now. Stars who were once young.

All those things are gone now. They're gone. You can never find them as they were, ever again.

Even the you who sat there spellbound in the dark of the movie theater on a Saturday watching Jack Flak *who always escapes*, and learning in the end that the boy's real hero all along... *was his dad.*

Or the girl in the movie you had a crush on and now she's as old, older, than you are when you look in the mirror and see a stranger and your old ruck-hump back hurts a little more than it did the day before.

A movie is a kind of... *unexplainable...* magic.

The scene Thor watches as he waits in the shadows beyond the set is green screen. But in the movie, it's that bridge scene. Under fire and pinned down without weapons due to just escaping an interrogation and torture deep in the jungle at a rebel camp, she has just seconds to evade her way up the bridge to the half-destroyed unmarked cargo van where the special weapons package is located.

The van is on fire.

But Thor is thinking... can I walk onto that set and say...

What?

Something.

*I'll stay. Live.* Tell her.

*Don't get in the vehicle in that stunt? And live.*

Come with me. And live.

The magic of the movie and Mandelf Tallhat's spell is so powerful, it feels that right at that very strange moment of *Wyrding*, fate intertwined, to the Ranger who is under its influence right now, and there is no saving throw for this as Ranger Wizard PFC Kennedy would have termed in his little game of pens and paper and funny-shaped dice, that for the Ranger many things are possible at this moment... So perhaps...

And because he is a hero.

A Ranger.

Always has been.

Always will be to the last, he crosses from the indeterminate darkness beyond the lighting of the set, the world where nothing happens in the movie, where existence is up for debate, and into the lights of the world within the movie where she still lives.

The world shutter clicks and flashes like an old-time photographer's camera capturing beautiful people called stars doing on screen what people do off screen.

And instantly Thor is on the special operations Little Bird in the movie, a strap hanger with three other chungo actors, who in the movie come in to get her up to the special weapons package after the veteran black actor with the great deep voice of a prophet, the admiral in charge of operations, says he can't risk the insertion. After the good old boy general who's played everything from a US senator to a cowboy and everyone knows him, says, "Scramble the fighters and flush the bombers. Get the ADA up over Iceland. We've got bears inbound on release trajectories. If your agent doesn't get across that bridge, Admiral, it'll be World War Three in about forty-five minutes. Bring your sunblock SPF one thousand boys, 'cause we got us a real old-fashioned gunfight at the moment going down on that bridge."

You remember that moment.

It was pretty tense.

Maybe someone squeezed your hand in the dark. Someone you loved. Someone who knew you wouldn't quit.

We were all scared.

We were all caught up in the action.

Meanwhile on the AH-6 Little Bird flying nap of the earth up the waters of the river, that actor who played the biker gang leader in the zombie movie and various other military hardcases shouts over the comm in standard movie operator word salad.

"Thirty seconds to insertion, boys. Watch your six and check targets. Kill everything not our girl on the ground."

At least he doesn't say, *"Listen up, people."*

Thor hates that one.

Every soldier does.

The Little Bird comes in fast and there's heavy tracer fire coming from the tangos on the bridge.

For Thor, who's been in it, strap hanger and all, going into a bad situation where everyone's already shooting at each other, this is pretty real.

Then he looks down at his gear and spots the drum mag on the SCAR.

And he swears.

The bird comes in and the LZ is pure white-hot fever.

He spots her down the bridge. Under fire. She's just down the bridge from where the Little Bird is going to put down.

If he can get to her and tell her...

The Little Bird pilot behind aviator shades looks back at the strap hangers and gives everyone a thumbs-up, saying, "Here goes nothin'!"

Movie line.

RPGs sidewinder up through the air like they do in movies.

The pilot goes in fast, flares hard, and pops smoke over the LZ while two other Little Birds let go on their miniguns and destroy vehicles on the unmarked LZs. And bad guys. They are cut to real shreds with blood spray and flying bone matter. It's horrific.

Like it is in real life.

It may be a movie...

It may not be...

Magic is live and loose in the air, and Mandelf, for all his faults... has woven a powerful spell to save his skinny bacon.

The danger is real. Real tangos get cut to shreds by the barking miniguns as hot brass flies away from both AH-6s like trailing bright death flotsam.

Vehicles on the bridge "movie explode" as bad guys go into the water.

Thor gets ready to unclip and checks his rifle.

The SCAR. With the damn drum mag.

The four-man team is off the bird, and it's away as more RPGs chase the pilot off into the air and down the river.

But those aren't his problems.

Incoming is hot and heavy all over the bridge and Zombie Show Biker Gang Leader now turned Special Operations Indeterminate Team Leader orders them forward to link up with "our girl."

She's, by this time in the movie, acquired a sidearm and is looking to get a rifle.

That's how it goes and it's not bad advice.

Despite the drum mag, Thor is opening up in short batches and embracing the fantasy. Tangos get cut to shreds and the special operations indeterminate team using movement and fire performs a flawless bounding overwatch down the bridge to the pinned-down star.

Cinder something-or-other.

Katie Malone.

Get to her and tell her not to do the stunt, Thor roars at himself as he drops a tango who just pushes firing wildly.

Thor tried to watch the movie. After she was gone. He couldn't.

The memories were too thick. He sat there in the darkness and just didn't think.

He moves, engages, and continues the push down the bridge, explosives from grenades to RPGs causing much havoc. He moves toward her and there is a part of him that knows this is not real.

Can't be real.

But... it feels real. And perhaps there's a chance...

The chungo actors special operations indeterminates who appeared at this point in the movie were all stunt performers and they all got killed except Zombie Biker Gang Leader.

He'll get killed on the van. He tells Cinder Cool Last Name to, "Keep it real," or some stupid thing before he stands up and mag-dumps to give her time to get the "special weapons package" open.

There's a part of Thor that knows... this is not real.

But there's magic. And maybe the magic is strong enough to bend time and change things.

Then there's the part of Sergeant Thor's mind that hears the incoming cutting air right past his bucket or slapping pavement skipping off into vehicles. One car explodes and Thor sees one of the operators in the team, just forward of his cover, take a round and get the side of his head blown off.

For real.

He knows this is real, and that dark magic is in the air...

And that part of him says if he can just reach her... tell her... then, maybe, he can save her.

He fights forward and it's just him and Zombie Biker Gang Leader character actor shouting "Move move move!" and "On me!" and "Last mag!"

They're just ten feet away from her and she's behind a car she's using for cover, bad idea, and Katie Malone the girl that would have gone on all his adventures, is popping over the shot-to-hell hood and bravely returning fire against... movie odds here... forty heavily armed South American special operators that in real life are no joke and can put out an immense volume of overwhelming fire and overrun targets quickly and effectively.

But she's returning fire.

*Good for her*, thinks the Ranger. Always a solid answer in most situations.

Sergeant Thor unloads another burst from the SCAR with the drum mag on a group getting ready to flank her.

"Hold position here, Sergeant!" shouts Zombie Biker Gang Leader Special Operations Indeterminate NCO. "I'll get her... then we push for the special weapons package. It's our only chance now!"

Thor copies the order and starts killing South American guerrilla killers on the bridge like it's a bodily function.

The SCAR is dry, and he ditches it for one of the other pickups. More guys die. Another pickup... this time a squad designated marksman rifle. He's engaging and Zombie Biker Actor NCO has her and he's pulling her up the bridge through the cars under a heavy volume of fire.

Thor clears a path so they can make it to the burning

van. He's just moving and shooting as fast as he can. His mind and eyes are wide open, and he reacts on guerrilla killers before they can shoot.

There's no time, or room, to cover.

The push is on hard.

At this point in the movie the Russian attack helicopter shows up and starts firing on the bridge.

And in this spell reality of *otherwhen* it happens too. Except Mandelf Tallhat is behind the controls of the Hind-D and whatever pickups Thor has aren't gonna do jack against the armored canopy of a warbird like that.

Rockets streak away from the wing pods and smash into the bridge. Cars explode and all three of them are knocked to the pavement amid flying dust and exploding flame.

"On your feet now, soldier!" screams the bloody Biker Gang Zombie NCO. "Come on! Move now! We gotta go for it or he's gonna cash the whole bridge out with a strike!" shouts the actor.

Thor engages three more bad guys, working the SDM rifle methodically like he's in real-time, pinning them down, making them suck dirt and putting rounds in them for their efforts.

He's buying time for the actor and Katie to make it to the special weapons package where she'll get her rifle and turn the whole show around.

In the movie.

Mandelf's spell reality might have other plans though...

The Russian attack helicopter pivots over the muddy waters of the river downstream, heaves her engines into high gear bleeding black smoke and exhaust, lowers her predator's nose, and starts back for its gun run on the bridge.

Thor clocks the pilot.

It's the Smoke Wizard, and some weird moment of worlds colliding crashes through his consciousness.

Ahead he sees the actor and Katie scrambling for the van. They're gonna get blown to pieces before they can get the case open.

The Ranger runs, leaps across the hood of a ruined bullet-riddled car, and makes it just in time to tackle Katie as the Russian attack helicopter doesn't go to rockets and instead uses the full dosage on the gun pods.

The world around the two of them, her in his protective embrace, him covering her as best he can, explodes violently all around them in a bright line of fire as the thundering thumping flying Russian war machine passes overhead raining brass and hovering farther up the river, its engines howling madness and promising death soon.

And in the background, later, when Thor AARs the whole bizarre episode... he will remember the evil sub-aural chuckle in the beat of the staccato blades of the Russian attack helicopter.

Thor gets to his boots because Mandelf is a question that needs answering right now. And the answer is...

Ground-to-air violence.

Biker Gang Zombie Actor is dead on the pavement of the bridge. A lot.

Thor pulls open the back door of the burning van and yanks hard at the "special weapons package" as the distant engines of the chopper begin to beat harder.

The "special weapons package" is large.

There's lots of stuff in it. And just like in the script and the movie, she's doing her bit getting the tricked M4 online and ready to do her thing to save the world.

Very businesslike.

Pro.

It's on now.

The Ranger on the other hand reaches into the foam core, the case is huge, and lifts out the rapid-deploy Stinger missile.

It was there in the movie.

Spells and fiction collide.

Thor moves away from her as she starts to engage bad guys pushing on their position. He has one choice here and this is it. There's no time to tell her not to do that stunt. Or to come with him, or he with her... is that even possible?

There's no time.

To do that will allow the Russian attack helicopter to rocket the bridge. They will die in the movie and the bridge will collapse into alligator-infested waters.

Movies.

Thor deploys the stinger, gets the lock-on tone almost instantly, and depresses the trigger for the firing solution.

An ear-splitting *whooooosh* and the sudden heat of the rocket washes over him as it ignites once it's flung itself safely away from the launcher, and it's a short flight track to the wizard behind the armored canopy of the attack helicopter.

Mandelf Tallhat explodes all over that river, and the rear half of the bird, all that's left of the desert-camouflaged Hind-D, goes into the muddy brown waters of the jungle.

The bad guys are pulling back now.

She has just enough time, in the movie and as the script reads, to send the coded data that will prevent the bombers from launching on Iceland.

But that's another scene. Another setup for the crew.

She turns to Sergeant Thor and before she can say, "Gotta get the SATCOM uplink initiated," her line, she stares at him for a long moment as though seeing something she had not expected. Some memory intruding on fantasy reality.

Something... very important.

As though she is just on the edge of recognizing him.

The one she loved before she died.

But she is not Katie Malone right now.

She is Cinder Sloan. CIA operative who saves the world.

She will not die in an accident.

Cinder Sloan will save the world, and for a moment, everything will be okay. And we will walk away from the dark of the theater and into the sunlight, talking fast and excited about the things in the movie.

What was cool.

Remember that part?

Thor drops the launcher and crosses the bloody pavement on the bridge, taking a big breath and getting ready to tell her to... just live. A message, in a bottle of a kind, that will save her. Maybe.

Is the magic strong enough?

Where is Ranger Wizard PFC Kennedy when he needs him most.

But she speaks first before he can say anything.

"You look... very familiar, Sergeant. D-did... I know you?"

As if in a dream. Worlds collide.

Happy endings... are sometimes possible. In movies.

And in life.

Magic in effect. Of a kind.

"A long time ago," he tells her. Terse, for there is no time and some unseen window, or a curtain, is coming down. He can feel it. "Listen... don't do the armored vehicle stunt that's coming up. Whatever you do... don't do it!" he practically shouts at her.

She nods, mumbling, "O-okay. I didn't really want... to. Seemed dangerous. I don't know why... but I've... I've always... trusted you. Haven't I? You were... very important to me. You've always..."

And the director yells, "Cut!" and the scene stops.

Darkness.

And the spell is broken.

\*\*\*

Thor in the shadows of what remains of the blown-out tavern at the grimiest edge of the City of Thieves looks around for her.

She's gone.

It's quiet and dark. The purple mist is gone, and he knows that Mandelf Tallhat too... is gone now.

Out of the picture. Pardon the pun.

Gone from here.

And no longer a concern in this tale.

And for a moment, like a terrible, or beautiful, dream

upon waking, fading at morning's light, he remembers everything that has just happened in the spell of *otherwhen*.

He remembers her.

Target down.

And Katie.

*You look... familiar. Did I know you?"*

He wipes away a tear.

She's alive.

Safe now.

And the clock is burning. He has to get to the Tower of Osirex soon to kick it off. If Sato goes before he gets there... could be bad if they think the Smoke Wizard got him.

The Ranger feels like not enough butter spread over too much toast.

Standard for Rangers.

"Maybe..." he mutters to the darkness one last time and tries to remember everything from the spell even though it's fading. He doesn't know enough of Kennedy's strange game of other worlds and magic.

But he's willing to believe in miracles. If at least this once.

We all have regrets.

Even dragons.

Even Rangers.

# CHAPTER FIFTY-EIGHT

THE WIZARD OSIREX TOSSED AND TURNED IN A HOT fever dream within the secure secret and silent vault in his high tower that was his bedroom.

His inner sanctum of inner sanctums.

The Palace of Nightmares, he often called it, thinking himself sly and arch.

Obsidian walls, black silk sheets, two alabaster buxom and dark-haired whores of the highest caliber lying drugged and mindless alongside him as the wizard suffered the images within his nightmare.

The Dreaming Sorcerer, that powerful entity himself, whispered to him of his utter failures and his total worthlessness now.

"This..." whispered the mysterious entity from across vast distances, that voice like some titan at the bottom of the sea where there is no light, and no love, "... is on you... Osirex. You have failed me."

"No, no, no..." murmured the wizard, throwing his obscenely tattooed pale arm across his tight-shut eyes. One whore whimpered like a child and tried to curl away from him. She was the weaker whore who was the talk of the town and just new enough to the flesh trade, or the horror that had become her life. The other, the stronger one, the beautiful panther, sighed as all the weight of that loveless sea of nightmares, and the deepest of its deeps, lay atop her just as it always had.

She would endure.

Just as she always had.

But... when would it end?

When?

Night terrors. Tossing and turning. Out there the big, blond, blue-eyed northern savage was coming for him. And Osirex knew there was no way out of it this time.

Baalubrozz had failed.

Mandelf was dead. And if not yet... that one soon would be. Osirex had sent the smoke-addled illusionist off to the edge of the city to draw out the enemy, and hopefully kill him there, saving Osirex's skin.

Now the Dreaming Sorcerer murmured, placidly within the terrible nightmare of horrors that encompassed Osirex all about, that the one called the Smoke Wizard was indeed... dead now.

And the one called... *Sergeant Thor*... was coming for Osirex as the hour grew late. Later by the burning sands.

Thieves were in the streets all about.

The Ape Men were on high alert and stalked the obsidian blood-marble halls, growling and snarling, waiting for the secret assault they could smell out there and coming on the night wind, for they were animals and had a sense for such things.

Torches suddenly guttered as though some unseen spirit had passed by the Ape Men guardians growling and snarling, wide nostrils flaring, angry eyes flashing. Red cloaks swirling.

The wizard had seen just one of his apes rip a dozen armed men to shreds.

And the whores... they too tossed, or whimpered, and would suffer the fate of the wizard this terrible night.

It was an ill-omen night within the Tower of Osirex and the air hung heavy and still.

"You have failed me... Osirex. For the last time... time... time... time..." The words of the Dreaming Sorcerer seemed to echo off into some vast dark promise of an eternity.

"No, no, no," whimpered Osirex and pled his case knowing he had no case to plead. The big Northman had vexed him, eluded him, and defeated his best. Now the terrible savage was coming for him, and of all the things running through the fevered brain of the wizard... it was how the heist was done that vexed him, and would not let him go.

Would not let him plot and have peace. Or a settled mind about the murder he would do, the revenge he would exact, the suffering he would cause.

The evil... still to do.

Like some Celtic knot in a dream that could not be answered.

How had this... *Thor*... done it, whimpered Osirex. If he could just know that, then perhaps... perhaps there was still some way out of this.

Perhaps the Dreaming Sorcerer... would relent? Save him?

How? How was it done? Osirex's tormented mind ran it all again and again on a loop without end.

Perhaps the Ranger had access to a powerful and unknown wizard who liked to craft potions or scrolls or even small curious artifacts. Yes! Perhaps it was that, and just that. Maybe? Or perhaps there were special secret spells involved. Spells created for deception and showing something other than what was wanted to be seen, distracting all from what was really going on.

The warrior was the bait? Perhaps? The spells and the item, or fantastical magical items, were the work. Yes! Osirex's mind screamed and scrambled. It was all misdirection. While the brawn distracts, the spells and potions, and maybe some secret item... something like a Bag of Holding or a Vortex Hole were secretly delivered into the Prize Chest. All eyes on this *Thor...* and that was the distraction. Yes! Perhaps? Maybe?

Who wouldn't be seething with envy and covetousness, noble traits as far as the wizard was concerned, as all eyes were on the winner of the contest in the Pit, and angry about that. Definitely!

Osirex would be.

Meanwhile that was the illusion. *Thor* was the illusion! The spells, the fantastic item, whatever it was... that was what spirited away the goods without detection.

Perhaps...

No.

Then the gray corpse of slaughtered little Baalubrozz, a tormented soul now, surfaced in the nightmare and reminded Osirex that all spells of magical detection had been run by himself.

No magic, no spells, no fantastic artifacts... involved.

So how was it done?

Baalubrozz moaned in torment and drowned within the black waters of the nightmare as Osirex screamed, "No, no, *no...*" once again.

His voice became lost on the vast and empty midnight storm-tossed sea as the Dreaming Sorcerer glared down upon him without care or consideration and nothing but cold contempt if anything.

"How did he do it?" screamed Osirex, the madness beginning to creep into the frustration of not knowing. "How..."

The whores shifted. The one who sighed turned away from feverish, sleeping Osirex, dark kohled eyes open, and considered the silver ceremonial dagger whose hilt was carved like a lecherous imp, and lay on the table near the black silk bed.

And once again, inside Osirex's fever nightmare, the question that could not be answered... spun and turned on itself again. Repeating once more...

"Lots of ways to do this," murmured Mandelf from the depths of the hell he roasted in. "Perhaps there was the fine use of a Dimension Door spell, Oss... Then... oh yes, yes... this is clever... reach into the chest and take all you want."

The flames melted the flesh of the illusionist's face and still the Smoke Wizard kept talking as his hat turned to black ash. Mandelf was more intent on providing answers that could not possibly be correct, than the flames that consumed him.

For now...

"Why, even a Wish spell might have done it if the stupid oaf who bested me, Oss, that... *Ranger*... had someone of decent caliber to write the proper words for him to phrase it properly!" Then the flames turned the wizard char-black and for a moment Mandelf began to scream in utter pain and unending torment as he gave the next solution to the riddle of how the Prize Chest had been looted.

A riddle that seemingly could not be solved.

"Ah!" screamed burning Mandelf as he tried to feebly bat out the flames that consumed him. His fabled long-stemmed pipe on fire and yet still it wisped its hallucinogenic purple necrotic smoke. The wizard stopped his sudden screaming and inhaled deeply, his eyes fluttered, and he continued once more. "They made an exact duplicate of the room! Haha! Now *that's* how he did it, Oss! Yes! I am absolutely convinced that's what the rake did! Everyone thought they were somewhere where they were actually not, and meanwhile his unseen and low allies looted the chest in peace and quiet! AHAHAHAAAAAAAAA it burns it burns it burns!"

The tormented soul of Mandelf Tallhat burned and burned and was not consumed in the unending conflagration.

And yet Mandelf continued with some whining pain and effort. The whole scene was insane, and Osirex felt his grip on reality slipping away completely as he witnessed what he was unable to stop. Unable to answer. He wanted out of this dream, now. Out of this forever nightmare loop, worse than anything he'd ever wanted...

No.

He did want something... else.

He wanted... to know.

He wanted to know how a mere *warrior*, imagine that... this *Ranger* of all people... had bested him. That should never have been possible! He was *Osirex*. A named wizard of the Thirteenth Rank. Heir apparent to the High Table. Someday... even one of the Five.

To be bested by something... something called a *Ranger*... a mere *man*...

A thousand times impossible. A thousand times never happened.

And yet... it had.

Mandelf spoke on and burned, consumed and not consumed by the writhing flames at the same time, sucking at his pipe and screaming in sudden bouts of pain between his gasping pauses. "They made a huge sacrifice... to some god... Oss... some god of... the thieves and got that one... got that one to do... the dirty work, *or*... they bribed... the priests... let them do it! Or, or, or..." Now the roasting illusionist began to giggle madly, insanely, like an animal that had lost its mind totally and completely and even utterly... "They replaced everything in the chest... with exact... copies and it's all there... it's all still there and this... and nothing was stolen and all of this... all of this... even the torment and the hell I suffer in now... it's just... it's a joke on us, Oss... a bad, bad and terribly horrible, good joke on us that will never... never... never... end..."

Mandelf's horrible screaming laugh echoed and seemed to never stop as it hammered at Osirex's fever-drenched brain in the nightmare, and suddenly the wizard surged up from the black silk pillows and the nightmare sleep and shouted in thundering rage that he *could—not—breathe*!

Panting and dripping with sweat he looked around.

The whores were startled out of their drugged states and one, the curling one, whimpered and tried to soothe him with that false candy-sweet baby doll voice he hated her for.

Even if it was contrived... he hated its *faux concern* and he shoved her from the bed onto the cold obsidian floor and shoved the other one there for good measure too.

Then he stalked from the bed to the lone silver mirror, dragging the black silk sheets as he did so. Then... he shouted at the smoky image barely seen of the Dreaming Sorcerer within the cold mirror's world.

Osirex screamed wordless rage. And continued to scream as the Dreaming Sorcerer reminded Osirex, murmuring pleasantly as though in a sweet dream, that he, the Dreaming Sorcerer, had no use for those who had failed him. And

Osirex had failed and there would be a price to pay for such failure.

Yes, there would indeed.

"No! No! NO! *NO!*" shouted Osirex, spitting and frothing at the mouth in babbling rage, lost completely in his anger and fear.

Osirex was so gone in his fury, he was unable to see the whore who'd felt the weight of the sea on her chest in her sleep.

The purchased beauty whose flesh was so curving and perfect and pale she was like some statue carved by a master. Her black hair shifted as she came toward him like a panther in the jungle approaching its unaware prey.

Osirex didn't, couldn't, see her, he was so gone with fury and fear.

He didn't see the flashing silver dagger she plunged suddenly into his back, driving it straight down, and into, his black thundering heart.

Not because she was trained to do so.

Or even paid to do so.

Neither of those things were so.

But because she was just... so tired of it all. Tired of the abuse. Tired of the arrogance. Tired of the wizard and his kind.

Tired of the way things were.

She'd had enough.

She drove the silver-sharp dagger into Osirex's back and watched as the wizard went to his knees, his silent mouth working like a fish out of water. His face apoplectic and purple with rage. His hands now claws, wild and akimbo as he tried to reach around behind his back and remove the blade that had killed him.

Then he fell over, dead.

She laughed a little. Half-heartedly.

Then she went back to the black silk bed and lay down. She would sleep now. Finally.

The fool was finally dead.

# CHAPTER FIFTY-NINE

"HEY THERE, TROUBLEMAKER..."

The voice was deep and dark and husky. But it was also seductive and had a slight teasing lilt underneath it all. It was definitely from what the Ruin called the South. The Red Desert and the great unexplored lands beyond the Kingdom of the Saur in the Lands of Black Sleep.

In the Before it would have been mistaken for a thick Jamaican voodoo accent.

It was the voice of a woman.

The final voice Baalubrozz had heard when he'd been led, person to person, to the Temple of Poesidius.

"What's the hurry? The one you seek... he real dead now. Stabbed by his whore."

Thor was hustling down the street under his heavy assault pack, getting close to the district where the Tower of Osirex lay.

The final target.

The last objective.

Then... the fade.

He was tired. Spread too thin. But he had to get there in time. If he didn't show, then Sato was under orders to make the hit anyway. The spell the Smoke Wizard had cast had rung his bell and for much of the run across the city, the Ranger had alternated his constant steps between a ruck-hump shuffle-run, and walking.

Just like road march standards for the Expert Infantry Badge. Twelve miles in three hours.

But he was fading.

And there was still much to do.

And... something strange had happened. After the dream, the vision, or the shift into some possible *other*... time... where the woman he loved was still alive... he'd brought something back... without intending to.

The last pickup he'd used.

He'd taken it off one of the dead South Am guerrilla killers. A slick Glock with three mags pulled fast from the dead man's rig. A G34. Threaded barrel and a targeting laser mounted in the grip. Port cut slide. The guerrilla killer, or the prop master, had spent some serious coin on the gun. Fast trigger and some other little adds.

It was slick.

Thor had picked it up, drilling bad guys as he closed on

the van after the SDM ran dry.

In kill mode he'd automatically taken it, shoved some mags into his cargo pocket, then kept working the problem of killing his way to the objective.

The burning van.

And somehow... it had come back with him from wherever he'd gone. Crossed over. Gone... *other*.

The guerrilla had even had *Ven y Llévatelas* laser-etched in a rather flourishing and gaudy script along the slide under the port cuts.

*Ven y Llévatelas.*

*Come and Take Them.*

As he'd moved off the wrecked tavern, the purple mist dissipating, the surreal memory of what had just happened faded as though it were attempting to erase traces of itself...

But how could he ever forget her?

He may have been a killing machine. But there are some women you never forget. Never.

He stuck *Come and Take Them* in his waistband and moved on and it wasn't until he was alternating his run-walk to the next battle that his mind cleared up enough and he finally pulled the pickup sidearm from where he'd stuck it and then stared at it in... disbelief.

*Curiouser and curiouser*, the little girl gone down the rabbit hole had said.

And maybe... just for a moment...

Perhaps it was a sign from her that, wherever she was now... she was all right. *Don't worry about me, Thor. I'm good now. Take this. There are monsters out.*

And...

*I loved you. Always.*

He stuck it back where it had been and kept moving on the objective because there was no time to spare, smiling at the strange *bigness* of a universe he hadn't thought enough about.

And then there was the voice from the shadows. Husky and dark. The smell of a fragrant cigar on the night's wind.

The owner of the voice stepped from the shadows as he stopped. She was a dusky jewel. Tight and compact. A taut belly and chocolate skin. Bright eyes almost yellow in the night like a cat. Long curly hair. High cheekbones. Gypsy clothing and many gold earrings, piercings, looping bangles, and large hoops in her ears. And also... one sparkling mega-ruby on a silver ring that seemed to light her face with a strange trickster light from her long and painted-nailed hands. Maybe she was from the southern deserts. Maybe from the east as far as Kungaloor, or maybe whatever Indonesia was now. And maybe... maybe even beyond the end of the world.

Her stubby cigar glowed red in the night as she inhaled

deeply on it and spilled smoke all over the street she'd just entered to confront him on his way to his business that still needed settling.

Behind her was an alley and a deep *other* darkness.

There were... eyes... back there.

"Hey there, troublemaker... where you goin'?"

And this was Lady Hudu.

# CHAPTER SIXTY

"YEAH... 'IM DEAD NOW, OSIREX IS, BUT DAT'S OKAY, WE got uses for dat one," purred Lady Hudu and watched Thor's face in the night seeking some sign that she'd left a mark on him with her news of the turn of events.

Her face was impassive, but clearly, she was holding all the cards.

She was young. Not more than twenty-five. Pretty. Seductive. And very dangerous.

"Enough about dat... I got an offer for ya, ya big thug. I'm gonna say it now to ya, and if I was you... I'd listen real good 'cause we in control now, Ran-ger. Ya hear dat... we in control now."

The Ranger said nothing.

"I know everyting, Ran-ger. Know how ya done it. Know what you gon' do next, and where ya goin' after it's all said and done. I even know where dat treasure is right now. And if I wanted it... I could go get it. Easily."

Her voice was sly. Thor said nothing and continued to listen.

"Don't believe me... okay, my big man... here's how it was done. There wasn't never no heist. Da priests took it off to where they went off to. A new city to run their tricksy games... and you and your little guild... you made it happen for dem. And you... Ran-ger... you took da blame for it all so everyone got hot and angry about what you had and how they could get their hands on it... 'steada lookin' where it went like Lady Hudu saw it go. I know. Lady Hudu sees all. Sees more than you think she do. Take that to the temples, sugar man."

Silence. Sergeant Thor remained still as a statue. She was feeding him intel whether she liked it or not, and now, if what she said was true, the game had changed. A new player was involved. And probably had been involved the whole time. And like some jackal... she was coming in to take everything at the last.

It was a solid plan. Thor respected it.

She continued.

"You saw it all, Ran-ger Man. Saw what was comin' was comin'. Saw dat dem greedy eunuchs and dem ever-shifty wiz... dey were gonna get 'round to doin' same soon enough 'cause both sides were tired of da way tings were. 'Specially dem eunuchs. Dey were gonna steal dat chest soon enough and dem priests were gonna get theyselves murdered straight-up cold. You saw dat and showed dem it was coming at 'em like a haboob outta deep deserts. Den, and dis was clever... you made a plan, and we knew it 'cause we had ears all up in your guild until dat one called Well Well sewed 'em up nice as you please. But we already knew da plan, Ran-ger. Madame Spider... she gots servants everywhere. So, we know you made da plan where everyone tinks it's you and chases you 'round dis old city, while meanwhile that treasure is on a galley tanks to da guild and headed out south into da mystery seas along da Red Desert. All you needed was little more'n a week and it'd be beyond da eyes of dey wizards and dem eunuchs. And everyone would tink it was you and den you were gonna get on your way anyway... weren't ya, Sergeant?"

She had it right. Mostly.

Thor had seen the way things would play once the power blocks of the city were explained to him after arriving here with Sato and meeting some of the guild. He'd planned the whole op and then taken it to Sato. A meeting was arranged with the priests and they were on board because they'd seen it coming too.

The Little Guild got some magic items from the chest and ten percent of the gold inside to make it happen.

Thor played the goat and led everyone in the city on a merry chase.

"But Lady Hudu don't care 'bout no treasure. Dat's nothin' to us. We takin' the city. We takin' the power. Already got it, really. Lady Spider's followers are everywhere and now... tonight, da lady herself comin' out from the deep where she got that weirdy aboleth in da underfortress down by the Lake o' the Dark all under her control. She gonna climb that tower wit her big ol' spider self and take dat body of da dead wizard and make him... *seem*... alive. Just like da watcher in da deep she got under her sway now. Zombie now. Serves da Lady."

Madame Hudu smiled, and her teeth flashed bright in the night dark of the quiet street.

"Den she gonna take over da wizards with da body o' dat wizard. So you gotta back off now, Ran-ger Man. We takin' da city now dat everyone's gut-stuck. Stay away from dat tower and take yo'self off ta de wilds where you tink you gonna be happy now dat you sick o' da city. All right. She sent me out here to tell you ta leave now. But lookin' at you, sugar man, Lady Hudu... she like what she sees, sugar man. You join me now, Thor. Come and take what you want. Be my champion... and we rule dis city for the Lady. She got big plans. Real big plans, sugar man."

Thor pulled the long-slide Glock from his waistband and mag-dumped on Lady Hudu right then and there.

As fast as lightning itself, suddenly the street was filled

with the roaring thunder of the gun.

But she was already gone, turned to smoke and mist, her laughter filling the street. Filling the City of Thieves as he ran to join Sato and the other thieves getting ready to go hot on the Tower of Osirex where the target was already dead, and a giant spider god was about to show up and take its prize in order to control the last powerful faction in the City of Thieves.

And then... then the city would have a new tyrant to make their lives miserable once more.

Same as it ever was.

# CHAPTER SIXTY-ONE

THOR REACHED THE RAPPLY POINT AND FOUND THE other thieves there in the shadows of an alley near the front gates of Osirex's tower.

Sato.

Well Well.

And Alluria with a large bow. A thin quiver on her pack. Their gear was set up for night work and they looked like dark striped wraiths in the night with their broken outlines made by black grease and soft gray chalk.

Thor gave Alluria a look, taking in the bow.

"Thought you were just a serving girl?"

The shapely Alluria merely shrugged girlishly, whispering, "I grew up on a farm with it."

"Plan's changed," said Thor, shrugging quickly out of his pack and watching the shadows all about. The city was still on fire. Roving bands of armed mercenaries were everywhere.

Anything could happen to ruin everything.

Which was how Rangers operated at all times, remaining vigilant and ready to adapt to changing situations, and in the end, ready and willing to use extreme violence at a moment's notice.

*"For Rangers... it's always get-it-on-thirty,"* as Sergeant Joe often liked to say. *"Always. Don't forget that, and make damn sure* they *never do."*

"Osirex is dead," began Thor. "Dark Cultists are on the move for this location, and they want that dead wizard's body tonight and probably right now. They're going to use it to take control of the wizards' guild."

Sato thought about this for a moment, questioned nothing, and nodded.

It was just Tuesday for Sato.

*"Hai,* Warrior. This is indeed their way, and this is not good. If they gain the dark sorcerer's body, then all will be lost. The city will become a madhouse... and soon enough, a charnel house. They are a death cult. It is only a matter of time before they begin their nonsense in order to save the world by killing everyone. So it has always been with their kind. I suspect even back to your times in the Before. We must make sure they cannot use his body."

"Agree," said Thor. "We've got to move fast..."

Thor was now applying the dark grease like the rest of

the team of thieves had donned, in order to break up their patterns in the night as thieves do.

"We've got to get to the top of the tower fast in order to be able to defend against..."

Thor paused and took a deep breath for this next bit. What he was about to say was crazy. Sure. But this was the Ruin and they were probably more used to dark terrors and ancient gods come to collect than he was.

He heard PFC Kennedy whisper, *"Embrace the fantasy, Sar'nt."* Then push his Coke-bottle RPGs, or BCGs if your prefer, Army issue "Birth Control" Glasses, up his freckled nose as his wan and watery eyes stared Thor right in the eyes, confirming the truth of the advice he'd given long ago.

Thor nodded to himself. Accepting it once again.

"Apparently their giant spider god is going to do the dirty work herself tonight. We gotta shut that down PDQ before this thing reaches the tower and breaks in. But... we need to get past all those Ape Men along the stairs and halls and there are probably traps... and that was never going to be easy."

Sato smiled.

"Warrior... we are thieves. We do not need to fight. We climb. As thieves do. Twenty counts of the sands and we shall reach the top of the tower, and from there we can use your great weapon against the spider god when she comes for her prize."

It was a sound plan.

"Unless..." continued Sato, "we are hindered from within the tower, Warrior. The apes have excellent senses, and they may detect us. The climb could become quite dangerous at that point."

Thor listened to the night out there. There was no sign of a giant spider coming. But... what would be the sign?

"We break into two teams now. You and Alluria will climb the tower and take my rifle. Myself and Well Well will clean the tower top to bottom and keep the monkeys busy while you climb. We take the top of the tower and defend against the spider god's attack when it comes. If we fail, you have the rifle, Sato. You understand its usage. Point it at the thing, right at it, and pull the trigger. The round in there will kill an elephant. If that doesn't do it, then we have nothing that will."

"*Hai*, Warrior. It will be so."

Then Sato and Alluria were heading toward the gate to stack, Sato slinging *Mjölnir* as he ran silently. Thor pulled the Glock, *Come and Take Them*, and laid it on his pack.

"Well, well," began Well Well. "Here we are. All dressed up and ready to kill. Let me handle the men beyond the gate, Thor. It's knife work and that's my favorite. Got a gift and all. Quick at that. It's my specialty and I like to work silent-quick. Apes will be another thing. I..."

Thor smiled and pulled the silencer from his assault pack for the issued Glock he'd cast away in the street days ago. Gently he threaded it onto *Come and Take Them*.

"That's what this is for. And this..."

Thor unsecured his tomahawk from his assault pack, laid it on the ground, then checked the mags for the silenced sidearm he'd secured from the assault pack along with the newly acquired ones. Camouflaged for night work as a thief, the Ranger shrugged into the pack and looked like a specter in the night as he placed the razor-sharp tomahawk over his left shoulder, resting it where he could simply swing it down and lay it right into any enemy who made the mistake of too-close-quarters combat with him.

Then he grabbed the silenced Glock.

"Last hit, Waste Man," grunted Thor. "Let's do it clean and quick."

"Well, well..." crooned Well Well softly. "That's how I like to do it. The Devil will drag them under... now. Let's work, brother thief."

# CHAPTER SIXTY-TWO

WELL WELL WAS A PRO.

Thor gave credit where credit was due and the man was poetry in motion, that is if poetry were an endless supply of specialty knives that seemed to appear at just the right given circumstances to eliminate the next sentry in the gardens of Osirex.

Gone was the summer parkland of pleasures and lights among the mad statuary that verged on the obscene and even the diabolical in some dark groves.

It was all clutching shadow and cold candle here just after the team of thieves violated the heavy locks at the front gate and Sato slipped a flat iron bar through the space they'd made to push the bar up just enough for Well Well to insert three quick spikes that negated the effects of the barrier. But before all this was done, a low whistle had summoned the guild's expert on magical traps and warded doors. Mingo, bag of tools in hand, scurried from the shadows of an alley

599

just down the way and did his work on the gate. Curses were negated, wards bypassed, and traps of the magical nature disarmed. The tall gate was slid open a crack, and Sato and Alluria diverted off through the undergrowth to the face of the tower they'd selected for their climb.

Sato had made sure there was climbing equipment ready, ropes and claws to get it done, all pre-positioned in the alley.

Just in case.

Again, the sergeant in Thor had to admire their preparation and teamwork and the quiet way in which the thieves spoke entire plans, updated, adjusted, and reacted to threats with their steady, near sub-aural murmuring cant.

Rangers definitely would have had a Thieves Guild Course right next to Ranger Sniper School, Combat Swim, EOD, and Combat Climb.

And only because it would have upped their game by magnitudes of order.

Rangers pursue perfection, wherever it takes them.

He smiled grimly at that, thinking of other Rangers he knew who'd totally be down for this.

As he watched Sato, laden with coils of rope and followed by the silently padding Alluria, her great bow at the ready, he was glad this turn of events after the Sea of Riddles had led him here. To them.

"Totally worth it," he muttered as Well Well began to

leave a trail of bodies while he swiftly moved up the main path toward the high black walls of the dark tower rising high into the late night.

There were guards in the garden. Rough-hewn mercenaries this Osirex had paid handsomely to guard his skin.

Even though the Ranger knew Osirex was dead now. Or he was if what Madame Hudu had said was to be believed. But who knew. Still, Thor had a feeling it was true.

And that the game had changed

He listened to the night and felt some... disturbance... some sudden shake in the ground come and go so fast it was hard to say it had ever happened the moment after it had.

The mercs were in teams of one or two, often too far apart for Thor's management, if they were his, to do any good for each other if mutual assistance was needed.

And the veteran thief and guild Waste Man took immediate advantage of this, moving among them swiftly like some concise undertaker who knew his business and knew how to get the ghastly parts done quickly.

Well Well was remarkably dressed in that his clothes were fine but not ornate. Well-kept and almost business-like as though he were some high street merchant who prided himself on his appearance as much as he did the expert goods in his shop.

He even wore a kind of hat that was rare among those of the City of Thieves. Almost like a leaning, smushed top hat, that was a matte-black.

There was very much the appearance of an Old West undertaker about Well Well, but it wasn't in the look, though it vaguely was, it was something else the Ranger could not put his finger on about the thief as Thor followed the front sight of the Glock and covered Well Well, ready to engage with a hushed shot in case the slightest mistake was made and an alarm at the last second could be given.

No such support was needed.

The first merc, a hard-bitten swordsman with slick gear and high hard boots, that drooping mustache they all liked to sport, along with the scars they wore proudly, got it reverse-grip style as Well Well appeared from the side and the shadows there. Icepick stick right to the stomach, Well Well murmuring his ancient song of the Devil dragging a man under, as the Waste Man placed his strong black-gloved hand over the merc's mouth while adding a second icepick thrust to the neck.

Gently, and quickly, something not done easily without much practice, the Waste Man laid the dying man to the ground and broke his neck with a final almost effortless push from the hand across the mouth.

Well Well clocked Thor and they proceeded right at the

next guy who was not more than ten feet away and staring up at the stars, his night vision spoiled by the torches the guards had insisted be lit for the night near the tower to keep their long watch.

This one got it with the reverse grip too, because he turned at the last moment and probably didn't even know why he did as Well Well made his approach from the man's blind spot. Instantly the Waste Man reversed his grip and sent a sudden slash across the unfortunate merc's face, and as the man reacted in horror, trying to pull his blade as his own blood ran into his eyes, then Well Well went all sewing machine of death and delivered easily six separate strikes to the man's armpit where the brachial artery lay waiting in horror of such overwhelming catastrophic damage.

Which was done fast and without the ability to negate.

The man actually whimpered and Well Well, still softly, almost sweetly, his voice a calm baritenor, helped the man down to his knees so he could rest as he died in a few seconds.

The two thieves clocked each other, Well Well indicating in a quick ghost whisper of thieves' cant where he intended to kill next, and they moved on quickly.

The next guard was large, a big brute with a giant axe he kept over his shoulder as he waddled along because of his immense size. This one whistled to himself and he was not a good whistler, and the tune he kept at he only knew a little bit of.

So, the whole thing was disconcerting and... unfortunately for this one also, it let Well Well and Thor know exactly where the bloke was the whole time as they approached him.

Just up the path and off to the left.

Well Well appeared like a wraith out of the dark, his black cloak covering his form until just at the last, as he literally went at the bruiser from the front, which was smart because this one had a habit of looking off and scanning too much and not really keeping track of what was in front of him.

Many years of being the biggest one in the deck had weakened the bruiser to ever expecting a frontal attack. Well Well had intuitively read this and made his attack swiftly right against the big man's weakest point, going directly at the axe man. Again, the reverse grip leading. Well Well struck the front of the man's knee, the bruiser staggered, and Well Well pushed suddenly and surprisingly forward, dropping his blade right into the space between the big axe man's thick bull neck and the shoulder. If this weren't enough, then Well Well grabbed the top of the man's head with that other black-gloved hand and twisted the blade toward the bruiser's throat before ripping it straight out the front.

It was brutal.

And the man had no time to scream. Well Well caught the huge bulk of the warrior easily, still murmuring his little song as he did so, and let the dead body down easily so it did not crash into the underbrush and give alert.

That one down, there were now only two more mercenaries further up the path before the two thieves reached the front door and dealt with the sentries guarding the entrance to the Tower of Osirex.

Well Well shifted almost invisibly across himself, and suddenly he was carrying a longer knife; the one he'd been using for the reverse grip was gone. Using this grip and knife, he slashed at his target to move the guarding hand of the weapon of the first merc they approached silently, just feet from his friend. These two were close together, and the Ranger thought he'd need to splash the other with the silenced Glock, but Well Well moved fast, slashing back, cutting the top of the first guard's knee, followed by an economical thrust deep into that one's femoral artery, then continuing his movement even as the other guard turned and made ready to shout the alarm. For his troubles the second guard got the saber-grip slash into his neck, followed by a suddenly savage downstroke right into the breastbone. If this were not bad enough, and the speed at which Well Well worked made it somehow both horrible, and calm, to witness, this was followed by the knife tip of the long blade expertly finding the man's xiphoid process.

Then Well Well, like some businesslike butcher working a tough cut on a thick tendon for the fine lady who wanted a roast for her family this next holiday, felt the end of the bone and suddenly surged, quietly, murmuring his little song as he did so, putting all his weight against that guard's hip, right against the handle, driving the long knife up, and cutting the diaphragm so that alarm was now impossible.

"And the Devil will drag you under..."

Thor splashed the last two at the door to the tower. Well Well had nodded as they studied the sentries, breathing only slightly heavily, and cant-whispered that the targets were clear for the Ranger, his brother thief, to deal with.

Thor put the first round in the guard on the left's skull.

The man was already drooling down the door, painting it with his own blood and bone matter, when the one on the right took two in the chest and Thor closed immediately, coming out of the darkness, walking fast and landing the last shot right in that one's skull as well as he looked on in horror at what his fate was and who, exactly, was coming to deliver it.

Mingo, the guild expert in the disarming of magical traps, appeared once more from the shadows as if he'd been there all along, and shortly the door to the Tower of Osirex was teased open safely. This done, the magical traps virtuoso slipped away into the night, departing with a thieves' blessing for Thor and Well Well, for combat, and there was sure to be that, was not his specialty.

The Ranger and the Waste Man entered the dark beyond the tower's violated barrier.

*"And the Devil will drag you under..."*

# CHAPTER SIXTY-THREE

OUT THERE IN THE DARK OF THE CITY, THE HUGE behemoth of a black spider hauled herself up from the deep tunnel that her followers, dead-eyed and worked to the point of near death, had carved from the under-city.

She was tarantula-like, but not one of those. She could spin webs of great powers beyond just physical ensnarement. She was also the size of a jumbo jet. Her fangs dripped poison, and she was hungry for not just flesh, which she'd had more than her fill of down there in the ruins of the lost forest near the deep lake in the dark, but for power.

The vampire had lured her here. The vampire had promised... much... power.

And now Ungwë the Enslaver would have all the City of Thieves for her own. She was ancient. She was Eld. And she was a terrible thing that even the demons who called themselves gods feared.

She known by many other, darker names than just the

Lady of Spiders.

As her eight hairy legs began to articulate across the city, crushing buildings she crawled over, and clambering across streets, ruining them as people ran screaming before her— she loved their sudden terror—the ground strikes of her legs were like the rumblings of a powerful earthquake shifting and destroying the foundations of the city.

She was coming for her prize within the tower of the wizard.

And then soon... all of it. Everything. It would be hers.

# CHAPTER SIXTY-FOUR

THE HALLS OF THE TOWER OF THE DEAD OSIREX WERE A howling, gibbering madness as the apes and the imps went mad at the scents of blood and prey.

But their offense was badly coordinated, or not even coordinated at all, and the Ranger and the lethal Well Well took complete advantage of this as they stalked and destroyed their way up the tower to distract those within and allow Sato and Alluria to reach the top with *Mjölnir*.

The last remaining human guards attacked the two thieves as Thor and Well Well made the stair, and the Ranger laid into them with the tomahawk, chopping and slashing, shooting those who hung back and waited to take advantage of any opening in the fray.

Meanwhile Well Well advanced on his next opponent, a spear man with huge brawny arms and good armor. Well Well ducked the first and only jab attack, going low and to the side as he wove around the blade, and suddenly he had another knife in his other glove. The trailing knife drove into the man's belly, and instantly the Waste Man wrapped around low and behind the jacked spear-carrier, delivered a heel trip, and inserted the knife like a handle. Then he turned the target onto his belly with total control, and with the other knife in his other hand he thrust the blade right into the cerebellum at the back of the spear-carrier's skull, beneath his conical helmet.

And that one was out of the fight as Thor hammered the last merc with three shots to the chest, punching armor. That guy sat down promptly to die and gasp about it.

Meanwhile, the halls all up through the tower turned to screeching mad howls as the apes came for their attacks.

They came down from terrible corridors higher up, black walls inked in cursed runes, blood symbols on the gleaming obsidian walls as the two killers fought their way forward and up, Thor putting rounds into the raging Ape Men, red cloaks swirling, fangs gnashing, crushing their skulls with the tomahawk as the shot apes were too enraged and stupid to realize they were dead already from multiple gunshot wounds.

An imp, demonic and leering, flung itself on scabby bat wings down from the upper corners of a rose marble vault that had been Osirex's trophy room of terrors as Thor and Well Well reached the landing that lay before that dark and horrific chamber. The imp had a tiny flaming short sword that threw shadows and hell-light across the hall of terrors, mythical monsters posed in death that Osirex had frozen still through some magical means. Perhaps they were still alive they were so life-like, frozen in mid-roar and charge, motionlessly waiting for some magical phrase to suddenly spring them back into life once more.

A magical phrase that would never happen now that the wizard lay in a pool of his own dried blood higher above.

The imp slashed at Well Well with the flaming short sword as it came for him. The Waste Man gave ground, knives out, one saber grip, the other reversed, luring the imp to make the mistake Well Well was waiting for as the homunculus gnashed its tiny needle teeth and growled like a lunatic. The imp finally made a lunge too far and paid for it quite quickly. Well Well stabbed low to cause the imp to bend for the pain the Waste Man had just delivered with the sharp gleaming shaving razor he was wielding now. Then, still murmuring his little song, Well Well threw a hook punch with the reverse-gripped blade.

And then...

He did this a lot. Over and over. Repeating the strike several times until the howling imp was cut to pieces and terrified, pitifully begging for its life and promising all kinds of "gifts" with which it could buy its way out of what was coming for it.

The Waste Man ignored all this.

Well Well turned placidly. "Run along now, my little poppit."

The imp hissed and sneered and turned to make off.

"Well, well... I love it when they run..."

The bleeding imp took off, got four steps, and was shanked by a long chunk of steel Well Well suddenly had in his hand. Expertly, right through the back of the imp's throat. Well Well ran the blade out through the front of its neck and ripped it away with a half-hearted shrug.

The gagging imp looked back at the Waste Man in horror and surprise. And hatred, as it surrendered to the deep black pit that would take it in just seconds.

"Tell him... *hi*."

Then the imp fell over in a gruesome pile of bloody and grotesque flesh, the bat wings wide and transparent as it began to smoke and hiss. The flaming black short sword lying discarded on the fine marble of the floor strewn with its black blood and foul-smelling guts.

Thor swapped to his last mag and made ready to push on the last levels of the tower.

# CHAPTER SIXTY-FIVE

"I FEAR WE WILL NEED TO BECOME WARRIORS NOW," muttered Sato as he watched from the top of the great tower of Osirex. The huge black behemoth of the titan that was a spider crawled over the rooftops and through the streets of the City of Thieves, and surely of all the dooms the city had faced, tyrants and terrors, there were none so great, and terrible, as what came for them all now.

It was beyond the end of the world.

The coming of the great spider was the beginning of some new horror. Some age of darkness that would never end.

Soon the beast would begin its ascent of the tower, and Sato could see no sign of the warrior.

People ran in the streets below.

Women screamed, hauling wailing children out of its path, grabbing quickly all they could carry away from the hideous bulk of the giant black thing as it ambled rapidly across the city like some terrible giant of nightmares and horrors that had become all too real. Brave men formed bands to stand against it. Not to defeat it, but to save their families by purchasing time to do so with their lives.

They grasped rakes, and picks, and shovels, and made fire.

But Ungwë was too terrible for this.

"Then we shall become warriors now, Sato."

The thief turned to face the beautiful young girl some called Alluria.

She smiled at him, holding her bow. "What...? Did you want to live forever, old man?"

And Sato made ready to defend against Ungwë the Enslaver.

Ungwë the Terrible.

# CHAPTER SIXTY-SIX

THE TOWER SHOOK AS THE GREAT SPIDER GRASPED ITS fastness and hauled itself upward, even as the very structure shook at its immense weight.

At that very same moment the Ranger heaved with all his might, muscles, and strength to prevent a giant ape-man, snarling and snapping its fangs right in his face, from ripping him to shreds as it was trying to.

Sergeant Thor had dusted the first of the last two apes as they made the final upper reaches of the tower. At the top of the rising stairs within the last chamber, curving around the wall of the shadowy vault, lay the bronze trapdoor to the roof where Osirex had performed his dark and obscene rites on nights of fullest darkness.

In the chamber below they had found the body of the dead Osirex and the two bleary-eyed whores.

The first ape had gone down howling and thrashing as the last of the rounds in the last mag of the Glock tore it to shreds with accurate and effective fire from the Ranger. The other maddened ape had bounded for Thor, claws out and reaching to strangle and tear at him.

Thor ditched the sidearm, roared for battle, and charged right at the beast, suddenly swinging his tomahawk downward and landing it right in the thing's hairy and muscle-swollen limb instead of the bullet-shaped skull he'd intended it for.

Claws raked.

The thing howled ferally and tried to bite the fast Ranger.

Then the powerful thing lunged and drove Sergeant Thor onto his back as it howled in anger and tried to tear Thor's throat out now that it had him on his back.

Meanwhile a trio of festering imps materialized out of the nether and went after Well Well, who became a whirl of flashing bright knives and a spinning black cloak as he went to work on them promptly.

The ape-man continued to try to rend Sergeant Thor into two separate pieces as it pulled powerfully at his arms and howled like the wild beast it was.

There was only one thing Thor could do now as he forced the foul-smelling snarling ape away from him with his body and every last bit of strength he had, pushing away the gnashing fanged thing as the savage beast barked and raged in his face, and at the same time lowering his right hand to pull the shank from off his thigh where Thor had it strapped.

The tomahawk had been jerked away with ape ferocity and twisting rage at being struck by it.

Now, fighting with all the strength he could bring, sweat and blood running down into his eyes, Thor slowly drew the shank out, arms trembling as he fought for every inch, and then, just as the ape tried to pull the Ranger's arms from his sockets with a vicious jerk, Thor twisted, letting the ape have free rein of his left side, and drove the chunk of steel that was the Ranger shank, crafted by a Ranger long ago, right into the ape's hairy ribs.

Thor followed this up like a twisting python and rolled with the knife, curled, and drove the heavy blade with his knee further up and into the howling wild beast, pushing right into the animal's heart as it thrashed and howled in pain beneath him now.

It went still seconds later, its fangs working open and closed as saliva and blood hung from their razor-sharpness. Finally its eyes glazed over in death as Thor stood up from it, retrieved the Glock and tomahawk, and once more, like some relentless thing that could not be stopped, made for the stair and the final battle waiting at the top of it.

The imps here were dead but there were further gibbering howls coming from not too far below, and these were not the howls of apes but the giggling wild insanity of yet more demonic imps coming through the various gateways and unholy portals the wizard had secreted throughout the tower as some kind of final defense.

"Well, well," said Well Well, panting and wiping the blood from his blades. "I'll hold them here at the stair. Don't know how much murder I can do against a giant spider, Brother. Go now... finish this and let's be gone soon enough."

Thor, covered in ape blood, nodded and stumbled for the stairs. Then he began to climb, and at the top he pushed open the bronze trapdoor and saw something he would never forget.

Ungwë the Terrible had reached the top of the tower.

# CHAPTER SIXTY-SEVEN

THE IMMENSE TITAN, TO THOR, LOOKED LIKE A GIANT yet strange and hairy tarantula. The hideous thing loomed impossibly over the top of the tower, using four of its legs to stabilize itself while the other grotesque limbs hovered over Alluria and Sato as they desperately dodged and fought back against its assault.

From its distorted belly, its rear really, great gobs of sticky webs rained down on Sato, encasing him, drowning him under the revoltingly sticky mass.

There were other masses of foul-smelling secretions all over the height of the dark tower, and it was clear the thief and the serving girl had been busy evading the webby casts from the giant thing well before Sato had finally been nailed by a direct strike.

Now the thief was being buried alive, and the Ranger guessed his friend wouldn't have long until he suffocated under the stinking wet pile being sprayed at him.

Alluria was shifting from position to position, firing arrows into the great black unholy mass of the leering eight-legged titan. These attacks seemed to do little against the hissing beast as it glared down with two red eyes malevolently upon its next victims.

Thor surged across the top of the tower, arms pumping, legs working.

He'd heard *Mjölnir* fire twice, and as he ran he could see the strange beast was dripping green blood that hissed and sizzled along the rooftop.

It had been wounded twice, but that hadn't stopped it.

The immense Eld spider stabbed one of its hairy tree-trunk-sized legs at him, and the Ranger had to throw himself to the side of his track just to avoid being pulverized by it at the last second.

Alluria shouted something at him, but he couldn't hear.

The Ranger worked the problem as he approached his weapon. Most likely there were three rounds left with which to use against the terrible creature. Powerful Raufoss shots, yes. But that was all that was left in the magazine if Sato had fired two. His assault pack on his back had the other magazines. Those would take a hot second to rock into the magazine feed.

Two shots hadn't gotten it done.

What would three do?

Thor reached Sato and slashed at the webbing to get his friend free as the spider scrambled away from Thor, hissing and rattling, working its way around the edges of the tower to strike at them from some new direction.

The impossible sight of this defied reason and logic.

But there it was.

Sato gagged, trying to say something as he drowned within the mass of webs.

The Ranger knew what his friend was saying, even though Sato was gagging on the horrible webbing.

*"Kill it... now... with your mighty weapon... Warrior. Or... we are all done... for."*

Three shots.

Sato gasped and sputtered. He was turning purple.

Thor grasped the webbed *Mjölnir* and wondered if it would even pull free with all the unholy mass of foul-smelling webs that clung to it.

He would use everything he had...

He took hold of it, his own hands now stinging with pain from the webbing. Some effect of the titan's powers.

The webs burned and froze those it encased in them.

Thor heaved at his weapon with all he had left, and it tore free as though it had wanted to. As though it too had lent some final effort, some power it possessed, to be in his hands once more.

Alluria closed across the roof, working the bow as fast as she could.

One arrow landed in one of Ungwë the Enslaver's unholy murderous eyes. One of many.

An ancient eye.

A thing that had seen the deepest darknesses not meant to ever be seen.

The eye pulped and the hideous thing reared and screamed in epic rage and pain, hauling itself up and overhead and away from them all like some massive tidal wave that would collapse in the next instant, crush them all, and collapse the tower.

Thor raised *Mjölnir*.

He didn't need three rounds.

"Just the one," he rumbled to himself.

Alluria arrived at Thor's side, cast down her bow and hauled at the webbing around Sato's face, desperately tearing away what she could so the thief could breathe.

"Now..." gagged Sato. "Aim... true..." he coughed. "Warrior. Aim true."

Thor landed the mighty weapon where he guessed the brain of the horrible thing must be. Steadying it against his powerful shoulder, grasping the front bipod, Thor pulled the trigger.

*Mjölnir* didn't just speak...

It thundered.

Lightning flashed.

The Grinder roared.

The black and hideous mind of Ungwë the Terrible was suddenly no more as the Raufoss round, a fifty-caliber BMG, Browning Machine Gun, multi-purpose anti-materiel high-explosive incendiary and armor-piercing munition, simply and devastatingly savaged the brain of the hideous Eld titan as it ripped straight through it, then shotgunned the fast-moving contents out the back of the spider's carapace along with much blood and many vital organs.

Raufoss means *Red Waterfall* in Norwegian.

Ungwë the Terrible fell from the tower, raining its blood and guts as it smashed into the gardens and streets below.

It was over.

# EPILOGUE

DAYS LATER.

It was a bright golden morning, and the wind was up on the high plateau beyond the City of Thieves. Not much. But some. The days would be hot for a little while longer, but shorter now.

Fall was coming.

Summer was over.

The three had left the city at dawn. Best to be beyond the Fields of the Dead before night. The Ranger. The thief. And the girl.

It was time for the final fade. Just as they had planned all along. The treasure of the Prize Chest was gone, and so were the priests. Best for all to believe the strange warrior called *Sergeant Thor* had taken it all and gone off to either spend it somewhere, or die in some cave with it piled all around him like some lost Delta warrior-king of ancient Ruin history.

Along a steep cliff with a last view of the city in the

distance, they stopped to drink water from their bags.

They had horses.

Armor.

Gear.

A mule with many supplies.

Thor had decided to head into the mysterious Eastern Wastes to see what edges he could find there.

Sato would go because he was Thor's friend and for now their paths lay together. And, as the thief never tired of saying, "I owe you my life, Warrior. So of course, I must go where you may perhaps lose yours so that I may buy mine back again."

And...

"Danger is where all the fun is, Warrior. Someone once asked me if I wanted to live forever. We shall see. All that matters now is this wind in the morning. It is pleasant and reminds us we are alive today. And that is a good thing to know before the battles we will surely find, for that seems to be the way of the road you seek. What more could a humble thief like myself desire than the wind in my hair at dawn?"

Thor said nothing and accepted this.

Alluria would go, for the Queen of Thieves had decreed it be so. The three were agents of hers, and the girl would bear needed messages should it be so required.

At that last series of cliffs where the City of Thieves

could still be seen, the Ranger turned back and looked one last time upon the beautiful jewel that was the city lying between the desert and the deep blue sea.

The golden domes, the towering minarets, the vast sprawl, and all the curious and mysterious alleys and ways within it were still mostly unknown to him. He thought of the Rangers, his brothers, probably on the march to Umnoth. He thought of those he'd known within the city. He decided he did not like wizards at all. They were dangerous and loved nothing but themselves and their hunger for power. The eunuchs had always been there in some form. Government. He hated it. What did it do but steal.

Then he looked south toward the little village by the sea.

He could not see it from here. But it was there. Omir and his family. They were there, and... they lived.

The owlish boy and his books and honest questions.

The little girl who wanted to do everything, but mostly to catch a butterfly before it moved.

The one thing he had failed at.

"Sato," said Thor over his shoulder before he rode on. The thief knew many wise things. Perhaps he knew. "How do you catch a butterfly?"

Sato laughed.

"Why, Warrior, would I want to catch a free thing? Even

if it is stupid like a drunk. It is free. And that is best, Warrior. Like us. We are free."

Thor turned to look at his friend, and as he did so, Alluria, astride her dapple-gray horse, cloaked from the sun and still pretty and ravishing, held out one finger, for there were many skirting butterflies dancing through the region as the weather began to change, wobbling and drunkenly dancing their way to where they would go next.

And just like that... one landed on her finger.

She laughed.

"Like this, Thor. They come to you."

Then the Ranger kicked his horse and rode off, traveling farther up the high plateau that led into the deeps of the Eastern Wastes and all the mystery and adventure that awaited them there.

Sato rode up next to Alluria.

"We follow him into a region few return from," he said to her, confidentially and low. "Are you sure of this matter we pursue?"

She nodded, and the beautiful little butterfly wobbled away on the morning wind. As they do.

It would be hot soon.

And they had far to go.

"Yes, Sato. The Pearl is everything. We must go with him until it is ours."

Sato said nothing for a long moment and watched the warrior ride on toward his destiny.

Then...

"*Hai*, my queen. I hear and obey."

The End

Sergeant Thor
will return in
*SGT Thor the Damned*

To our **Kickstarter Backers**! Your support for SGT Thor and Wargate Books helped to make this story possible!

## TO OUR GALAXY's EDGE INSIDERS

You've been there from the Land of the Black Sleep to Galaxy's Edge and beyond. Thank you.

Made in the USA
Coppell, TX
27 November 2023

24850813R00371